CREATED TO BE FREE

A HISTORICAL NOVEL ABOUT ONE AMERICAN FAMILY

JUANITA PATIENCE MOSS

Willow Bend Books
Westminster, Maryland
2001

Willow Bend Books

65 East Main Street
Westminster, Maryland 21157-5026
1-800-876-6103

WB0400

Source books, early maps, CDs -- Worldwide

For our listing of thousands of titles offered
by hundreds of publishers, see our website
at
www.WillowBendBooks.com

Visit our retail store

Copyright ©2001 Juanita Patience Moss

Cover illustration by Valaida Fullwood

International Standard Book Number: 1-58549-704-5

Printed in the United States of America

This book is dedicated to the fourth child of Crowder and Elsie Veden Patience

Lillian Mariah Patience Cuff
1883-1986

To Brenda + Margaret,

I hope you will enjoy my book.

Jessica 90:31

In African Tradition

I am Juanita Patience Moss, teacher /writer;

Daughter of Charles Edgar Patience, anthracite coal sculptor;

Granddaughter of Harry Brazier Patience, anthracite coal carver;

Great Grandaughter of Crowder Patience, slave/ soldier/ farmer.

TABLE OF CONTENTS

✦PART A

SECTION I   *TOBY THE SLAVE*

SECTION II   *CROWDER THE SOLDIER*

SECTION III   *CROWDER THE FREE MAN & ELSIE THE BOUND GIRL*

✦PART B

SECTION IV   *CROWDER AND ELSIE'S NEW HOME*

SECTION V   *CROWDER AND ELSIE'S FAMILY*

KNOWN FACTS

YEAR	MONTH	DESCRIPTION
1846		The slave boy Toby was born in Chowan County, N.C., actual birth date unknown. So his birthday was always celebrated on December 25th.
1858	August 1	The "bound girl" Elsie Veden was born either in Va. or Washington, D.C. (Conflicting records: census of 1870 records Va., while her Bible records D.C.)
1863		Seeking the Union Army, Toby, a 17-year old slave, ran away from a Chowan County, N.C. plantation.
1864	January 1	Toby enlisted in the Union Army. The roll call of the 103rd Pa. Volunteers garrisoned at Plymouth, N.C. reported him, then Crowder Pacien, as being present.
	April 4	Crowder Pacien was mustered into Company C of the 103rd Pa. Volunteers.
	April 17-20	The "Battle of Plymouth" occurred and was lost by the Union forces.
1865	June 25	Crowder Pacien was mustered out of the Union Army at New Bern, N.C.
	July 13	He received his last pay at Harrisburg, Pa.
1870		The census listed "Croder" Patience in Mt. Joy Borough, Lancaster County, Pa. and house servants Elsie Veden (12) and Dollie____(9) as living in Dillsburg, Pa.
1874	August 4	Crowder Patient (27) and Elsie Vedan (16) were married at the parsonage of the Evangelical Lutheran Church in Mechanicsburg, Pa. (See Veden spelled as Vedan on the marriage certificate.)

YEAR	*MONTH*	*DESCRIPTION*
1876	January 29	Florence was born.
1877	August 9	Harry was born.
1880	March 16	Rosa was born.
		The census listed Crowder, Elsie, Florence, Harry and Rosa Patience as well as Mariah Veden as living in Centermoreland, Pa.
1881		Crowder Patience was in the employ of the Schooley family of West Pittston, Pa.
1883	July 12	Lillian was born.
1886	June 4	Jessie was born.
		During the fall Crowder began working for Jesse and Isaac Carpenter of Exeter Township. This is the first year Crowder Patience was listed in the West Pittston directory.
1888	October 8	Mariah Veden Gould (Elsie's sister) died during childbirth, leaving behind a daughter named Hazel.
1892	February 11	Chester was born.
1895	January 14	Nyles was born.
1896	January 15	"Report of the Inspectors of Coal Mines of Pennsylvania" recorded that Harry Patience, laborer, age 17, single, at the Exeter Breaker had his arm painfully squeezed by having been caught in a conveyor.
1898	February 13	An infant son was born and died.
1906	July 4	Lillian Mariah Patience eloped to Binghamton, N.Y. with Charles Edward Cuff, originally from Mercersburg, Pa.

YEAR	MONTH	DESCRIPTION
1907	December 11	St. Mark's AME Church was formally dedicated in West Pittston, Pa.
1910		The census designated Elsie as M (Mulatto) and the rest of the family as B (Black).
	June 10	Rosa Veden Patience and Simon Peter Lee were finally married after a long courtship.
	June	Chester graduated from West Pittston High School and delivered an oration at Bethel AME church in Wilkes-Barre, Pa.
1912	June 6	Crowder's army pension was increased to $16.00 per month.
1913		Elsie Miller Patience, Harry's wife, died at the age of 35 from pneumonia.
1914	May	Chester graduated from Howard University in Washington, D.C.
1916	October 7	Harry purchased 34 Washington Street, West Pittston, Pa. from the estate of Jesse Carpenter. Here the second shop for carving coal art was located.
1918	December 25	Crowder's army pension increased to $24.00 per month.
1920		The census designated Elsie as B (Black). The M (Mulatto) category of the census became obsolete.
		Crowder was listed as residing at 828 Luzerne Avenue with his wife and all of his children. This is inaccurate because all but Jessie had left the homestead.
1921		Nyles Patience died at the age of 27 from the ravages of tuberculosis.
1926		Harry Patience died suddenly at the age of 48 from suffering a stroke.

YEAR	*MONTH*	*DESCRIPTION*
1928		An article appeared in the Pittston Gazette concerning Crowder Patience's interesting life.
1930	January 30	Crowder Patience died at the age of 83 years at 828 Luzerne Avenue and was buried in the West Pittston Cemetery.
1938		Jessie Patience Garrett had a diseased eye removed.
1940	October	Elsie Veden Patience died at the age of 82 at 828 Luzerne Avenue and was buried next to her husband in the West Pittston Cemetery.

CIVIL WAR VETERAN OF UNUSUAL CAREER IS VALLEY RESIDENT

Crowder Pacient Lived In Slavery Before The Emancipation Proclamation Of President Lincoln And When Opportunity Permitted He Joined Forces With His Deliverer.

KEEN IN RECOLLECTIONS

Few days of the year carry more meaning with them than Memorial Day. Once in each twelve months it is observed and throughout the land the disappearing ranks of the Blue and Gray form in line for the parade of honor to their departed comrades. Sixty-three years have passed since the last shots of the great Civil War were fired and few of the heroes remain.

As the lines are formed this year and the veterans grouped in the cars which will carry them along the line of march, to no one present will such a stream of memories return as to one wearer of the Blue from Exeter. To no other man in Wyoming Valley has such a great wealth and variety of experiences been vouchsafed.

An old and respected colored man is the one in mind. Now eighty-two years of age, a slave in the South before the war, a soldier in the Union Army, a farmer of old Wyoming Valley and a man who has held only two positions-- both of trust--for the past sixty years, who else could hold such a position in life here? Crowder Pacient is the name of this respected resident.

Crowder Pacient lives now with his wife and daughter on Susquehanna (sic Tunkhannock) Avenue, Exeter, just across the road from the golf course of the Fox Hill Country Club on the road which cuts from Exeter to the Susquehanna Trail above West Pittston. There he lives in a house provided after the smaller place in which he had spent many years had outlived it's usefulness. From there he has sent the rest of his family--four boys and a girl (sic three girls)-- out into the world.

Up until two years ago Pacient worked steadily for the Carpenter family, one of the original settlers of that part of the Valley. He came to the family, to the partnership of Jesse

and Isaac Carpenter, in the Fall of 1883. Work with horses is connected with his entire life. Two years ago, after going back to work too soon after a siege of pneumonia his need of a rest became apparent, his team of horses was shot and he, in his forty-fifth year with the Carpenter family is an honored retainer whose loyal services are respected.

Enlisted in War

When the great war between the North and the South first broke out, Crowder Pacient was one of the thousands of young Negro slaves in South (sic North) Carolina. With the coming of the war to free him and his race, naturally his sympathies turned to that cause which was for his betterment. At first too young to take active part, there finally came his chance. On April 4, 1864, at the age of eighteen, he took advantage of the opportunity offered and enlisted with the 103rd Infantry from Pennsylvania, then in South (sic North) Carolina. He joined Company C. of that regiment, most of which was enlisted in the western part of the state and in the Pittsburg district.

He was with this outfit through the rest of the war and came north with it. The last pay was given the men at Harrisburg and here Pacient left the 103rd. He was honorably discharged on June 25, 1865. Shortly afterward he located in Mechanicsville (sic -burg) and remained there about a year. "Long enough to be married," he says.

It was here that the horse began to become the force which directed his life activities. From his memory which is most remarkably keen, he recalls that a man named Green was shipping some horses to Pittston and he went with them. After delivering the horses he stayed in this section, first becoming employed on a farm along the Sullivan trail.

Work on the farm was scarse in the Winter and he turned to find other employment. His skill with horses again stood him in good stead and he was taken on by J.B. Schooley, a member of another pioneer family. With the Schooley retinue he was a coachman and he remained with that family for seventeen years (sic questionable) until 1883.

Then , forty-five years ago, he was put in charge of the horses of Jesse Carpenter and his association with that family still exists. It is such an example of loyalty on the part of the toiler and appreciation by the employer that would be most difficult to duplicate. It is fine and inspiring.

The Day of Big Farms

As is to be expected, most of Crowder Pacient's work with the Carpenters was with horses. For many years he was a teamster. Back in those days the farm on which he worked extended from the mountain to the river--as did all the old farms--and even included the island in the Susquehanna. That was also worked, says Pacient, and he remembers when a good crew of fifteen hoemen were needed there.

His memory needs no special effort to bring back the past and he tells of the long drives with the horses, necessary trips then: the regular drives to Wilkes-Barre, Scranton, and beyond; back of the mountain, too. "And at times," he ways, "I'd be so tired I could just drop down back of the horses and sleep."

But now Crowder Pacient's work with horses is over. He has seen the auto and the tractor slowly crowd them off the roads and fields and now his last team has been shot, so that his labors might end. But Pacient keeps busy. A neat lawn about his home and his tidy little garden show the results of his work. The only effect of his illness is "a bit of stiffness in my knee and leg," he says. He is really a remarkably well preserved and able man for his years.

He has kept up his active membership in the G.A.R., attends the meetings whenever able to do so, meets his old comrades of the war regularly and hopes to be able to take part in the Memorial Day parade this year. He wasn't sure he could but he was going to try hard. His place would be hard to fill and he will be sorely missed if not there.

The natural romance and interest which surrounds this old man from the South produce many ˉlegends concerning him, through the section in which he lives. The most popular is that Jesse Carpenter found him on the battlefield. It claims he ran up to Carpenter in the midst of battle, seeking assistance and remained with him to be brought home.

Crowder Pacient went into the Union Army of his own accord and was honorably discharged. Then following the trail of the hoof print, he came into Wyoming Valley and he still is here. Always with horses, he remained at his post until his last team was shot and laid to rest so that he, too, might also have peace and quiet.

Pittston Gazette 1928

PREFACE

This story is *uniquely American*. It is a story about a black boy expected to be someone's property for life, daring to dream of freedom. It is the life story of a tenacious young runaway from North Carolina who during the Civil War enlisted in an all white volunteer regiment originating in western Pennsylvania in 1861 and garrisoned at Plymouth, North Carolina in 1863.

I only recently learned that his presence in a white regiment, the 103rd Pennsylvania Volunteers, was so unique. Until that time of discovery I had not been aware that blacks who enlisted in the Union Army during the Civil War were expected to be segregated into the United States Colored Troops (USCT). I do not recall having read about them in any of the history books *I* read during the course of my education since at that time little had been recorded about them. This is the reason, also, why even well read Civil War buffs may have missed the fact that there had been 166 all black regiments. Many others who do know about the USCT are unaware that there had been additional black soldiers, as well, who served in *white* regiments, not in the *segregated* units. Difficult information to unearth because these facts are not recorded in history books. However, the names of those men are listed on regimental rosters in the National Archives in Washington, D.C. and easily can be found by a person like me, a descendant of one, who knows they were there.

There are only a few concrete facts actually known about the runaway slave, Toby, who became Crowder Pacien, surname later changed permanently to Patience. Children in "the olden days" did not ask parents to discuss their pasts. For at that time in history no one was searching for his or her "roots" and the dark pasts from which many of the adults had emerged were considered best forgotten. Certainly this was so among blacks wanting to forget *what* and *who* they had been. Many were concerned that their children would think less of them if they knew of their parents' struggle, having been forced to use whatever means it took just to survive, and then finally to pull themselves out of the degradation of slavery.

You see, to the adults those slavery days were in the far distant past. Tragic days filled with shame, hopelessness, and bitterness. Days from another lifetime. Past days not discussed. Certainly not with their children growing up free in northeastern Pennsylvania. Therefore, the sparse facts I have learned over the years are from relatives who actually knew this man whose genes I share, a man whom I intensely admire for having dared to dream, and for having the tenacity to follow his dreams. I did not have the pleasure of knowing him myself, but I do remember his wife, my great grandmother, Elsie Veden Patience, who died when I was eight years of age.

Using photographs and documents belonging to my great aunt, Lillian Patience Cuff (1883-1986), as the basis of my narrative, I have taken the liberty of embellishing known facts with my own imaginings as to what *might* have occurred during that period of history in which Crowder and Elsie Patience lived. The conversations are strictly from my own imagination and are *not to be taken as gospel*. The persons I specifically have called by name were actual people. However, I do not choose to reveal the names of some of the other actual persons, while others such as the corporal and his family, the young private, the lawyer and his wife are strictly fictitious characters.

What I have written concerning the Battle of Plymouth is factual and can be verified in history books. Dates and statistics mentioned throughout the book are accurate and deal with real events. Even though the corporal who wrote the war letters to his wife is fictitious, the events he describes are true.

I have searched the National Archives and other places such as Chowan County, North Carolina for evidence of just where Crowder Pacien actually lived before his enlistment, but I have come up empty handed. Neither do I know from which plantation he escaped nor do I know the name of his owner. Perhaps some interested person in the future will be able to find this last piece of the puzzle. Therefore, the description of where he was enslaved at the time of his escape is purely fictitious, a compilation of what I have researched and read in slave narratives concerning North Carolina plantations.

The story I have woven to explain how he got his name is strictly *folklore*. Why did he have a surname for a first name? *Crowder*. Names like George, William, as well as Biblical ones were quite common. And why was his last name one found nowhere else? *Pacien*. A word not found in any language?

The questions still remain unanswered. Therefore, I have chosen to include the information one of his grandsons, Robert Patience, gave me over thirty years ago when he handed to me the 1928 Pittston Gazette article concerning his grandfather. Other members of my family relate differing stories. However, until someone is able to verify the origins of Crowder Pacien, this story is as good as any. I am willing to accept it for what it is. *Folklore, not fact*.

Also in this book you will find the controversial terms "colored," "Negro," and "black" used interchangeably. The derogatory appellations of "darkey" and "nigger" have been used, also, because they, too, are part of our history. I have attempted to use what I thought was best for each time period, even though many of us have never felt comfortable with the labels bestowed upon us by the majority population. Since this book covers earlier periods in history, the latest hyphenated identification "African-American" is not used.

The narrative deliberately has been written in the present tense so readers might view the scenes as they would when watching a television show or a movie. Also the use of various dialects is to reflect differences in speech patterns among persons speaking the same language, but varying because of region and/or circumstances. Part B is not in chronological order for that would have made it impossible for me to tell the stories of the individual family members. The chapters are arranged in the order of the eight children's births.

My intent is to relay as much truth as possible as I tell my story. I find the period of history in which Crowder and Elsie Patience lived indeed fascinating because it spanned the days of the horse and buggy to the era of airplanes. Crowder and Elsie Patience lived in a period of time which fewer and fewer people remember today. Therefore, I wanted to record what I personally remember since I serve as a bridge between my great-grandparents who could not possibly have imagined our world of electricity and my grandchildren who cannot possibly imagine life without it.

My search for truth began in the summer of 1998 at a symposium where the USCT was being discussed and where I was told that there had been no black soldiers serving in white regiments during the Civil War when I knew there had been at least one. My great grandfather, Private Crowder Pacien of the 103rd Pennsylvania Volunteers. I determined at that moment if there had been one, there might have been more, and there were.

That discovery led me to decide to write a historical novel about my great grandfather, a forgotten Civil War veteran. From that time I have been led down divers trails of discovery, allowing me to interact with old friends as well as with new ones. Like Hansel and Gretel, I kept following clues, which then led me to others. For three years I have been obsessed with the lives of Crowder and Elsie Patience, trying to "get into their heads" as they have gotten into my soul. Asking questions like "Who were you really?" Becoming more and more aware of what had determined the course of their lives and how it has impacted on me, their great-granddaughter.

I wish to express gratitude to each person who has offered information and encouragement. If I happen to miss someone, I apologize profusely. Initially I must acknowledge my husband, Edward Moss, who willingly chauffeured "Miss Daisy" throughout North Carolina as I embarked on my quest.

My thanks go to certain persons without whom this book never would have been written. First my son, Eric Moss, who in 1998 provided me with a computer and was on the telephone constantly as I asked questions about my new "genie in the box." Because the phone bills were astronomical I was forced to rely on my church friend, Virgil Lewis, and my patient and long-suffering neighbor, Kenneth Breckinridge, for local help. During the winters in St. Petersburg, Florida, Sharon Johnson Swan and her daughter Simone were my computer consultants. My latest helper has been Darryl Vance who recently helped me solve some last minute computer glitches.

My actual journey began at the West Pittston Public Library where Charlene Bertie, librarian, as well as her able assistants, Beverly Williams and Lillian Matthews opened long-forgotten dusty tomes for me. They contained the history of Wyoming Valley and West Pittston, Pennsylvania as well as life in coal company patches and stories of the breaker boys. From the Anthracite Museum in Scranton I have Chester Kulesa to thank for unearthing the mining inspector's report describing my grandfather Harry's accident at the Exeter Colliery. He also provided me with valuable information concerning the breaker boys, as well as contributing two photographs for this book, particularly valuable to readers knowing nothing about the coal mining industry, now almost completely disappeared from Wyoming Valley.

From the Wilkes University Library I gathered information concerning the Civil War with the advice of Dr. Harold Cox. Thanks to John S. Joy, archivist at the Pottsville Historical Society for information concerning the black man, Nicholas Biddle. I met with Ruth Fulton at the National Archives in Washington, D.C. Historian for the 103rd Pennsylvania Volunteers, she directed me to the Library of Congress where I was able to find several books concerning the 103rd Pennsylvania Volunteers.

Searching for my great grandmother, Elsie Veden, took me first to Dillsburg, Pennsylvania where she had lived until she was married. There Larry and Joanne Klase, members of the Dillsburg Historical Society aided me considerably. In Mechanicsburg I was helped at the Public Library where I discovered facts concerning Civil War events which had taken place there. I also went into the Evangelical Lutheran Church to see where my great grandparents had been married in 1874, although the wedding had taken place in a parsonage no longer standing. My final stop in Mechanicsburg was the Historical Museum.

Without the invaluable information provided by Dorothy Spruill Redford, executive director of Somerset Place, Creswell, North Carolina, I would not have had an inkling about how North Carolina plantations differed so considerably from the sprawling ones of Virginia, Georgia, and Mississippi. She also put me on the trail of trying to find out from which plantation Crowder had come. At the Shephard-Prowden Memorial Library of Edenton I met with Rosalie Boyd who very graciously toured Ed and me around the lovely old town, basically unscathed by the Civil War. Here also I met with the owner of the Creekside Restaurant, Delbert White, who shared information completely new to me, the Jonkonnu festivities held on some North Carolina plantations at Christmastime.

At Plymouth, North Carolina I met with Harry L. Thompson, curator of the Port O' Plymouth Museum. There many artifacts are displayed concerning the battle on April 17-20, 1864, lost by the Union. He put me in touch with

Gerald Thomas, co-author of "Massacre at Plymouth" who spent some telephone time with me discussing his work with me.

On Roanoke Island I met with Wynne Dow, curator of the Roanoke Island Museum. He provided me with an overview of the island where the 103rd Pennsylvania Volunteers had been reconstituted after the battle. From there I learned about The Freedmen's Colony's annual celebration which fortuitously was being held that Saturday, October 16, 1999. It was there that I first heard about that colony which was active on Roanoke Island during the Civil War.

More research took me to the State Library, Raleigh, North Carolina where I received considerable help from Pam Toms of Genealogical Services as I was looking for the name Patience in North Carolina censuses. There, also, I discovered books of Union soldiers with the names of many black soldiers listed as having served in white regiments, not in the United States Colored Troops (USCT). Gratitude goes to Tom Broadfoot, owner of the Broadfoot Publishing Co. of Wilmington, North Carolina for his information and encouragement.

Just recently I had the pleasure of meeting A'Lelia Bundles, the great great granddaughter of Madame C. J. Walker, millionaire entrepreneur and philanthropist. I asked Ms. Bundles to read what I had written concerning hair care and her ancestor's work. I thank her for so graciously correcting it for me.

Special thanks go to my relatives who allowed me to "pick their brains" about our ancestors, Crowder and Elsie Patience. These include my father's 1st cousins, Florence Glover Smith and Bernice Lee Patience, two of the four surviving grandchildren; my 1st cousins, Betty Patience Claiborne, Katherine Patience Kennedy, Jane Patience Green as well as 3rd cousin, Rita Glover. I also have received much encouragement from others who were not born early enough to know our ancestors. They include my sister, Etta Patience Brown; and 1st cousins, Marian Patience Henry, Harold Patience who today lives in his grandfather Harry's house, Robert Patience, Warren Patience, and Lloyd Patience who led me to the Pennsylvania author, historian, and curator Charles Blockson for advice. Also thanks to 3rd cousin, Leroy Patience, for the knowledge he has shared with me about the GAR (Grand Army of the Republic). To all other cousins, nieces, and nephews, I thank you for your encouragement as I undertook this daunting task of trying to preserve our interesting family's history for all of you.

My gratitude extends to all my supportive friends who willingly offered their expertise in various areas: Dr. June Bohannon, Lois Marks, Rosemary Murphy, Dr. Kenneth Chambers and wife Grace, Kathryn Maguire, Ruth Harvey, and John Ward.

I thank those friends and relatives who were willing to spend time pouring through selected parts of my manuscript to express their feelings and to make corrections. They include the very first readers, my god-daughter, Gina

Simms and my daughter, Brenda Moss Green. Followed by sister-in-law, Constance Wynn; my stepmother, Alice Patterson Patience; god-daughter, Alvah Beander. Then friends: Dr. Christopher Brieseth, President Emeritus of Wilkes University; Dr. Georgetta Merritt Campbell; Dr. Byerte Wilson Johnson; Dr. Dianne Cherry; Pattie Barnes and her daughter, Dr. Beth Barnes; and Janet Kavanaugh. My heartfelt thanks for Reba and Lemonne Barnes, publicists; Vanessa Robinson, typist; Damita Green, editor; and Valaida Fullwood, cover artist for helping me in the last stages of getting this book published.

I had the pleasure of gathering facts for my book by talking with various persons in Wilkes-Barre such as Doris Wright Garrett, Judge Gifford Cappellini, and his wife Dorothy who shared their stories with me. Helpful West Pittston residents included Ronald and Marilyn Dietrich; Ronald and Marilyn Rogers; Betty Carpenter, daughter-in-law of Isaac Carpenter; Mayor William Goldsworthy; William Hastie, historian for the borough; old neighbors, Caroline Bertie Morgantini, Justine Gai Bonfanti, Louise Manganello, and Louise Vignali Coss.

A surprise from the past came from a long ago playmate, Jean Manganello Colurusso of San Diego who telephoned me one summer afternoon in the year 2000. Her aunt, also a former neighbor, Julia Manganello Cherba, tracked me down and so because of her I was able to converse with several old neighbors who had known my great grandparents.

Persons from other areas to whom I am grateful for information are Dr. Frank Smith, Council member for Washington, D.C.; John T. Zwierzyna, senior curator at The State Museum of Pennsylvania; and Shirl Spicer, curator at the Albemarle Museum, North Carolina. Thanks to Dr. Paul Creary and Roxanne Earnest for their hospitality in Harrisburg. They directed me to Carlisle and took me to the new Civil War Museum so I could find the brick I had purchased with the name of Private Crowder Patience, 103rd Pa Vols.

At the Library of Congress in Washington, D.C. I met with Albert Smith, reference librarian of military history and during the winter of 2001 in St. Petersburg, I had the privilege of conversing briefly with the renowned back historian, Dr. John Hope Franklin, who most graciously listened to this novice, encouraging me to pursue my research. I thank Bernie McCain of WOL, a Washington, D.C. radio station, for contact with the public and for his welcome words of encouragement. Thanks to Craig Scott, publisher, a Godsend in this world of trying to get one's book published.

My sincerest wish is for my readers to be enlightened, enriched, and entertained by this historical novel which is based upon true experiences of one American family. Most of all, I thank The Creator, whom I trust and serve, for directing me along the path.

INTRODUCTION

I see this incident as clearly as if it were happening to me today. The year is 1963 and this is the first week of a new school year. I am one of three teachers in charge of a study being held in the New Jersey high school auditorium where I have been employed for the past five years. After taking the attendance and settling her students, one of the other teacher-monitors quietly sidles over to my station. Since this is a "quiet study" she whispers to me discreetly.

"Winnie, may I ask you a question?" This is the only place in the world where I am known as "Winnie." Only because people mispronounce my name as "Win-nita," rather than the Spanish "Hua-nita."

"Of course," I whisper back, fully expecting to hear something pertinent to our study hall duties.

"I really need to know something. Tell me, just *what* was that march down there in Washington all about, anyway?" She is talking about the March on Washington occurring the month before.

Needless to say, since she has taken me quite by surprise I am just staring at her as I attempt to compose my thoughts. Taking advantage of my indecisiveness she continues, asking me with all seriousness, "Just what is it that *you people* want?"

I continue to stare at her, truly without feeling any malice towards her because I do believe this woman really bears *me* none. I realize that she simply has no understanding, having lived in a world unlike mine. Hers, an insulated privileged Caucasian world. Most likely I am the first black acquaintance she has ever had. Certainly I am the first black with whom she has worked on an equal footing.

"We want just what *you* want." I finally have the words. "A good job, a nice home in a safe neighborhood, education for our children, freedom from discrimination and segregation. Whatever *you* have, we just want the *same*. No less. We believe that's only fair."

Puzzled now, she looks directly into my eyes and with all earnestness asks, "But don't you think *you people* have to *earn* it?"

"*Earn it?*" By now I am losing my cool. Certainly getting slightly agitated at the "you people" bit which raises the antennae of black people every time. So I find myself responding rather forcefully, even though still whispering.

"*My* ancestors were earning it *here* while *yours* were still over *there* in Europe. For instance, *my* ancestors built the South. And with their *bare hands*. The economy of this whole country at one time rested on *their* shoulders. How do you suppose George Washington and Thomas Jefferson and all those other southern 'founding fathers' got so rich? It was by slave labor.

"And besides that, let me tell you this, too. One of my great grandfathers was a Union soldier during the Civil War. That was a hundred years ago. More recently my father's brother, Harold, was wounded during World War II during the battle at Anzio Beachhead in Italy. Lost a finger and carries shrapnel permanently in his arm. He saw many of his friends killed there.

"His first cousin, Nyles Glover, brought back malaria, from which he is going to suffer for the rest of his life. And that's just *my family. Earning it* is what my people have done for generations. And in spite of it, our rights systematically have been denied us through disenfranchisement, 'Black Codes,' Jim Crow laws, and all other forms of discrimination, existing even to this day. And so *that's* what that march was all about."

I know she really needs to understand that my people have been here *unwillingly* since as early as 1619. Even before the Pilgrims were to land at Plymouth, Massachusetts a year later. To planters at Jamestown, Virginia, Dutchmen sold twenty Africans they had kidnapped from a Spanish ship. This woman needs to be aware that without the forced labor of millions of Africans stolen from their homeland and spirited to this "new world" under the most inhumane conditions, this country may not have survived, let alone *thrived*.

She also needs to know that institutional racism in these United States was born out of the need for a consistent supply of labor for the ambitious and greedy. And she needs to understand that in order to *justify* the rule of "enslavement for life" Africans had to be deemed and treated as an *inferior species*. But *she* does not know any of this and *I* understand this is the reason for her asinine questions.

Thirty-eight years may have passed since that encounter, but I know even today there are many people still of the same mind as my colleague was back then. Therefore, I charge those who dare to peer down the annals of history. Begin with the year 1619 and if the cost of the stolen Africans' and their enslaved descendants' pain for 382 wretched years, their spilt blood, their rivers of shed tears are to be reckoned, then indeed we *have* paid. And the bill must be stamped *PAID IN FULL*.

PART A

PROLOGUE

August 1922

It is a lovely summer Sunday afternoon and as usual the Patience family has gathered at the old homestead. In the kitchen the "girls" are preparing the dinner while their spouses relax with Ma and Pa on the wide porch cooled by the shade of a thick veil of wandering English ivy vines. Today daughter Rosa's husband, Simon Peter Lee, has brought along his new Brownie camera.

"Look right at the camera now, Pa. Don't move none!"

Click!

"One more then. Jest ta be sure!"

"Hold still now, Pa. That's it. Good!" This directive coming from daughter Florence's husband, Walter Glover.

Click!

Crowder Pacien (Patience) stands soldier-erect and proud in front of his home in Pennsylvania, far from the North Carolina plantation where he had been born three-fourths of a century ago. The bright intelligent brown eyes of the grizzled septuagenarian gaze across future generations to his many descendants scattered far and wide from this small town.

Today the family is having a celebration for Elsie's 63rd birthday. All of her children are home, even the last living baby, the "apple of his mother's eye," the boy after him having been stillborn in 1898. Nyles, only twenty-seven years of age and knowing that soon he is to die from the ravages of tuberculosis, has traveled from Rochester, New York. Come back home to his mother.

Crowder is standing on the little boardwalk just in front of the shaded porch with its several comfortable white wicker rocking chairs. In late afternoons he enjoys rocking out here, watching the sun as it sets. Such a beautiful wide panorama of the western horizon there is from this porch. Always he looks for the first brilliant light in the sky. The "evening star" is what he calls it, not realizing it is the planet *Venus*. Seeing it always puts him to remembering about when he was a boy in North Carolina.

"Ma, come on now! Let's get a picture of you and Nyles," Peter Lee prods his mother-in-law.

Elsie takes some persuading, though, because recently having had the last of her teeth pulled and refusing even to try wearing dentures, she really does not want to pose for the camera, but she realizes how treasured this photograph will be. For everyone knows, but no one will voice, that the youngest brother, Nyles, will not be here to celebrate Ma's next birthday.

So Elsie perches on the top porch step with her sick boy sitting just below her. Sadly she looks at the camera as Nyles attempts a wan smile.

Click!

Now the Brownie camera has captured for all time a glimpse of the essence of two people, Crowder and Elsie Veden Patience, who sought and found contentment in a small Pennsylvania borough, West Pittston, the home of the Patience clan.

__Elsie Veden Patience__ with youngest son, __Nyles__ on
porch of 828 Luzerne Avenue, West Pittston, Pa.,
(circa 1922)

SECTION I

TOBY THE SLAVE

THE PATRIARCH
*Crowder Patience standing soldier erect in front
of the porch at 828 Luzerne Avenue, West
Pittston, Pa., (circa 1922)*

Chapter 1

The North Carolina Plantation

*T*he year 1863 is going to be very different from any other the young North Carolinian slave has ever experienced. Each of his prior years, months, weeks, and days have been much the same to his recollection, but in this his 17th year there looms hope. Hope for a change. In the fields the slaves are whispering, "Hey! Heerd de Yankees gittin' closer." This message passes furtively up and down the rows, reaching the ears of the young slave, Toby, steadily heaving his hoe to turn over the sweet potato crop.

He muses, *Yankees gittin' closer? Good! Means freedom be gittin' closer den.* This message is sweet to the boy's ears.

A flock of majestic Canadian geese noisily honks overhead. Glancing up at the "V" formation, he thinks, *Flyin' from duh no'th.* He knows well that direction—north. For to him north equates with *freedom.* And freedom is what Toby thinks about all day, and dreams about all night.

He gets back to his work quickly, just in case *Marse be near by checkin'.* Young Marse periodically canters his gray steed out into the fields where his "people" had better be working hard enough to suit him. Interrupting his daydreams Toby might hear, "Keep goin', Tobe! Keep goin'! Faster, now, Tobe! No dawdlin,' there. Bend yore back, Tobe! Chop them pokeweeds! Dig them 'taters, Tobe!"

At all of the times when he is in the fields the young slave perceives the berating voices of master as well as overseer, even when they are nowhere in sight. Therefore, Toby is a diligent worker, having no desire to feel the burning sting of that hickory stick those white men always have in their possession—to be flicked across a back when they think a slave is being lazy or even worse-- *impudent.*

Toby knows well what is considered impudent. Certainly no slave wants to be accused of that. Just for rolling his eyes he might receive a few licks, but for looking Young Marse or any other white person straight in the eye, neglecting to take off his hat in their presence, or failing to move out the way respectfully when they are passing? Now this certainly is *impudence* and definitely grounds for a good whipping! He also knows this is but a mild punishment compared to the fate of a slave daring to *steal* from Young Marse. Especially stealing one of his hogs running wild in the woods, fattening on nuts, acorns, and roots. Thirty lashes laid on the slave's bare back for the *first* offense, two hours at the pillory, and his ears cut off for the *second*, lashed to death for the *third!*

Not that there is any conformity among masters, though. "Don't need no outsiders tellin' me what Ah can or cannot do on ma own land!" So has Young Marse stated to other slave owners who are in ready agreement. Besides, who can possibly know what transpires out there on those distant and remote properties, where each plantation is a closed system? A fiefdom unto itself, its owner lord and master of all he surveys?

Toby already has known the smart of a twisted cowhide whip. The thick rope-like scars on his back are proof enough. Not many slaves he knows reach adulthood without having "deserved" a whipping of some degree. "Why, it's jest part of their 'seasonin'," some masters will justify. "Necessary tuh break their spirit. Teaches them tuh know their place real quick."

Young Marse's horses are broken in with much more compassion. No disfiguring marks ever will be found on their backs. However, a criss-crossed keloided back has become the *norm* for many of the slaves, making escape from the cruel lash the main incentive for running.

So when Young Marse appears in the fields, his slaves quickly step up the pace. More so even when they spy the overseer, a non-slave owning poor white man envious of the planter's wealth and position. Despising the blacks treated as valued animals not his own, he is not at all reticent about using his horsehide whip whenever he suspects slothfulness.

Indeed, when they are being overworked some do purposely feign illness, conjuring up stomachaches, headaches, or any other kind of aches they can get away with just to stay out of the hot fields. Productivity naturally slows down and so then Young Marse orders one of his "boys" to hitch up the wagon for going off to a slave auction. Perhaps one conducted on the waterfront of the lovely small town of Edenton where he has built a comfortable abode for himself. Not far from where the determined attractive young slave girl Harriet Jacobs (alias Linda Brent) had hidden for seven years, cramped in a cubbyhole in her grandmother's attic to avoid the unwelcome advances of her master, a very prominent citizen of Edenton.

Since Marse often may be away from his plantation for several days at a time, he needs to maintain a house in town for when he is there purchasing even *more* slaves to do the *same amount of labor* in his fields. Certainly not very economical, but most necessary for maintaining his social order.

This is because of his high expectations. He figures that if his life is to be even better than his father's had been (which certainly is the goal), then he has to maintain productivity. The work in his fields, he is aware, demands a consistent number of adult workers--close to seventy-five. Above average, considering that in 1860 of the total 385,000 slave owners only 2,000 had more than 100 slaves each with the majority of the remainder owning less than twenty, some even possessing as few as five. Young Marse's modest sized North Carolinia farm certainly is not at all like the sprawling Virginia plantations of the Washingtons at Mt. Vernon, the Lees at Stratford Hall, the Harrisons at Berkeley, George Mason's at Gunston Hall, or Thomas Jefferson's at Monticello.

Therefore, for his smaller plantation such a low number has been quite easy to maintain. He has no difficulty at all in replenishing his "stock" since he has close contacts with the slave dealers Price, Birch & Co. whose slavepens, coffles and auction blocks are well known up in Alexandria, Virginia. Famous for its production of slaves, Old Dominion's exportation of some 6000 annually sends hundreds of strong young "bucks" to North Carolinian auctions where on a good day Young Marse might be able to purchase a healthy one for only $1000, even though in 1863 the going rate is $1200.

"Can always tell its worth by its teeth," Young Marse explains as he enthusiastically volunteers a demonstration for prospective buyers standing nearby. After quickly mounting the auction block he forcefully pries open the reluctant mouth of one of the male slaves and then after distainfully slapping it shut, concludes, "Same like a horse." Fastidiously then he wipes his hands on a clean white handkerchief while barking, "Ah'll take this one! Throw him up on ma wagon!" The slave, even though strong and agile, cannot possibly get onto the wagon without assistance, his legs, arms, and neck being fettered by heavy iron chains.

At the very same time of this particular transaction, Young Marse might be selling off several of his youngest slaves, plucked that very morning from the arms of their broken-hearted mothers. The moment a robust black baby is born it becomes worth the sum of $200. "Evens out, more or less," Young Marse reasons.

In North Carolina the seasons have their distinctive sounds with the wind's rising and falling, birds' chirping, cicadas' humming, frogs' and toads' croaking, and slaves' singing a "call and response" in the fields, a leader sounding forth and the others replying. Keeps up the work pace and so the master has no reason to object. With the arrival of snow all sounds will get muffled and then silence will prevail.

As do the sounds, the sights of the seasons also vary. For after their initial vernal appearance in delicate chartreuse, leaves throughout summer deepen green, changing in the fall to gold, rust or brown, ultimately floating downward to leave naked branches filigreed against the fading light of the late afternoon sky.

Like puffs of cotton bursting from split capsules in the fields, cumulus clouds gently glide across summer skies azure as morning glories. Amber-tasseled corn and wheat wave in the soft breezes and fruits wait to be kissed ripe by the sun's hot rays. Annually white tundra swans and noisy Canadian geese arrive and depart while stately long-necked, long-legged blue herons instinctively remain in residence. In the fall, frost tenderizes and sweetens the large-leafed collard greens growing in the slaves' small truck-patches.

These seasonal rhythms are what determine the labor essential for maintaining Marse's plantation as a self-sufficient organism where everything and everybody has its niche. Even in winter, the work will continue with field hands metamorphosing into masons, carpenters, coopers, and blacksmiths. Young Toby becomes a cobbler.

With the arrival of fall any remaining crops must be harvested and at this time *all* of the slaves are required to work out in the fields, even the house slaves. Many of them are overjoyed to be out of the "big house" where they are required to be on call twenty-four hours every day. For Missie just might be requiring a glass of water or Marse just might want the windows closed (or opened) during the middle of the night. Or one of their children awakening from a frightening dream just might be in need of comforting. However, during the harvesting time when house slaves stay out in the cabins, too, they are happy to be following the same schedule as the field slaves with their work ceasing at the welcome sounds of clang, clang, clang, clang.

Harvestin' time comin' soon. Toby knows just what this entails. Sweet potatoes and peanuts dug, hay scythed, squashes and pumpkins separated from their vines, and the last of the coarse yellow corn plucked, having been left on their stalks to manufacture rich starch. For over the winter this is the sustenance for the cattle and poultry.

That supply of corn expressly grown for the folk in the "big house" is long gone, having been depleted months ago. Back in early summer sweet and tender ears of mixed white and yellow kernels favored by Young Marse were always picked just before each dinner meal. Everyone is aware that the *freshest* corn is the sweetest. Even Toby knows this because Aunt Cassie in whose cabin he lives has stalks growing in her small garden patch.

"Nothin's better tastin' than fresh picked corn." This he will reiterate all through his life each time he will slather an ear of corn with sweet butter, followed, of course, by several flicks of a salt shaker.

Toby knows that very soon the husking, peeling, shelling, and preserving of the harvested fruits and vegetables will begin. Each year he especially looks forward to the corn shucking time when other male slaves get hired from neighboring plantations, alternating farms in order to get the job done quickly. It is a time of unbridled boisterousness with each man vying to be the fastest shucker. Young Marse encourages them by offering prizes and by providing "spirits," while the slave women encourage with overloaded plates of sumptuous food.

The women's jobs mostly take place in the bustling kitchen, preservation of the harvested food being the main concern here. Cucumbers and green tomatoes get pickled in brine. Chopped red tomatoes, cabbage and celery mixed with seasoning spices are converted into chow-chow. Concord grapes get juiced for jelly and jam while the juice of the thick skinned white scuppernongs is converted into table wine. Some peaches are preserved with sugar while others get stuck with whole cloves and then brandied. Thin apple slices are dried for winter pies while the crispest spotless apples are barreled and scrutinized periodically for rot. For everybody knows what happens when there is even just *one* rotten apple in the barrel.

To prevent their early sprouting freshly dug carrot roots, sweet potato rhizomes, white potato tubers, and onion bulbs are covered with sand in *root* cellars. Full heads of cabbages get covered with soil and stored in *dirt* cellars. Salted beef and fish are stored in wooden boxes contrived from hollowed out tree trunks. However, the fattened hogs will not be butchered until January. The outside temperature has to be sufficiently low in order to prevent the pork's turning rancid during its hickory smoke curing. Afterwards hams and slabs of bacon will hang from the rafters of the smokehouse.

All of these activities must take place so the "big house" will be well stocked for winter. And also, most importantly, so that when Young Missie goes visiting she can carry with her one of "her" famous hams and some of "her" special preserves.

Every day up before the light of dawn, laboring in the hot fields until the curtain of dusk descends---now and forever---is what Young Marse intends for his slaves. But this is not going to be the fate of *one* of them. This is not going to be the fate of seventeen-year old Toby. No, for he has determined that he will be *free*.

Clang, clang, clang, clang. Hanging high from a post near the cabins, the large brass bell stridently summons the weary hands from the fields. Their long day's work at last is done. Ready now to plod with the others exiting the fields, Toby flings the hoe over his right shoulder.

The red-orange sun having just set, the dark silhouettes of tall stately longleaf pines are etched against the fast fading horizon. In the southwest corner of the sky the planet Venus beams brilliantly, catching the attention of the young slave. The first light in the night sky. The brilliant "evening star" induces the boy to do an "about face." His eyes automatically gravitate to the spot where he knows the North Star is always located, even though it has yet to put in its appearance tonight. *No'th. Goin' no'th. Some day soon.*

Bowed with fatigue, treading slowly, the field hands (males and females, young and aged) wearily drag themselves to the slave quarters, that pitiful collection of several square buildings located directly behind the "big house," situated so they are completely out of view from the front. In two rows facing each other the cabins are approximately 16 by 14 feet. Some may be a mite larger, but all are but a single room fashioned from rough hewn logs, equipped with sand floor, soot-laden ceiling, stick and dirt chimney, and two small windows opened and closed by wooden shutters.

Certainly because of the fireplace necessary for cooking and warmth, each cabin is a potential firetrap. Perhaps the chimney ignites. Perhaps flying sparks land on the sleeping pallets of rags or piles of stacked wood. Toby can recall when this very thing happened. The temperature had dropped suddenly one evening and like cattle, the slaves in an attempt to keep warm in their cabins had huddled together. As always, before the last adult lay down to sleep the fire had been extinguished. However, on that particular night an undetected spark was smoldering in the woodpile.

Too late the fire was discovered. Too late for the several unsuspecting families suffocated as they slept.

On his plantation Young Marse encourages his slaves to produce plenty of children for they are all his property. Just like his sheep, cattle, hogs, and chickens. Just like his bloodhounds and thoroughbred horses. All are his chattel. His belongings to do with whatever he wishes. Once he had made a pact with his slave women. "Give yuh a cabin of yore very own when yuh give me ten healthy pickaninnies." Ten babies or more should make a reasonable incentive he had figured. And when the girls reach puberty, they, too, will add to his collective worth, either by being sold or by breeding.

Since the soil on his plantation has been depleted of its vital nutrients, neither cotton nor tobacco any longer is profitable for Young Marse to produce. Therefore, too many of his fields are lying fallow, his knowing nothing at all about crop rotation. He knows nothing about planting legumes such as soybeans, alfalfa, or peanuts to put nitrogen into the soil. Even if he had, at this time in history there is no market for "goobers." And there will not be until a former slave, George Washington Carver, born circa 1860, will discover over three hundred uses for the peanut. Unsuccessfully, Young Marse even has tried planting Chinese mulberry trees, the food for silk worms, in the hopes that he might be able to get a raw silk crop.

What Young Marse does know, however, is that quick cash can be had by selling his slaves. He has been heard bragging, "Would yuh know, ma slaves been sold off tuh the best plantations in the South. Some way down there in Georgia, Alabama, and Mississippi. Why, even as far as Texas and Louisiana, would yuh believe?" Such knowledge fills him with a great deal of pride. Slave trading indeed has proven profitable for him since substantial numbers of slaves are needed to keep the wealthy planters and their families living "in the lap of luxury." Needed to cater to the every whim of the pampered upper echelons of southern society. Needed to produce the cash crops of cotton, tobacco, rice, and indigo for blue dye. Needed to toil until their bodies wear out.

Purposely, some planters travel to distant slave auctions just to be on the lookout for more young "breeders." Toby has heard about a certain master on a nearby plantation giving five women to one of his "studs," anticipating that each is going to produce several children, thus providing a new supply of laborers, and at minimal cost. Young Marse's speculation is, "Well then. There's profit tuh be made here, if'n when Ah choose sellin' them. 'Black gold,' that's what Ah call them. Pure gold, it is, fer ma coffers." Slave buying, slave breeding, and slave trading. This is the South's "peculiar institution."

Toby has heard that on some plantations a woman can earn her own freedom by producing a large number of children. He speculates, *Might be true. Don' know 'bout dat. Don' think on dis plantation, dough. Not by dis Marse.*

Young Toby has always lived in Aunt Cassie's cabin, it seems to him. He cannot remember ever living anywhere else.

"No, Ah ain' yuh mama," the woman had informed the boy many years before. "Don' know who yuh mama be. Don' know who yuh daddy be, needer. Don' know nothin' 'bout yuh 'cept Marse done put yuh in me arms when yuh jest a bitty boy an' here yuh be eber since."

Cassie, born into slavery some forty years ago and expecting to die in slavery, has lived, too, in this same dilapidated log cabin for as long as she can remember. Always this has been her home. She brags to her friends from other plantations, "Ain' neber been sold. Neber been beat, needer. Got duh bes' Marse'n Missie in de county." And this she sincerely believes, vowing to take care of them "'til duh 'chariot' come fer tuh carry me home."

Little does she and similar thinking slaves realize that sooner than they can imagine they will be given this choice. To *stay* or to *leave* their masters and mistresses. Some, generally house slaves, indeed will stay, out of loyalty to a kindly owner and his family. Others stay out of sheer necessity, possessing absolutely no skills whatsoever for entering the Promised Land called "Freedom."

Young Marse has known Cassie all of his life, being born in the same year. Her parents had belonged to his parents. Her home, the humble log cabin in the quarters. His, the opulent white "big house" built with the bare hands of his father's slaves--skilled carpenters and masons.

Many years ago Cassie and Young Marse had been playmates. As small children blacks and whites play together, but it does not take long for young masters and mistresses to realize the difference in their "places." When this happens no longer is there such a thing as *play* for the slave children. For the blacks their "place" becomes that of serving and obeying, while for whites it is of demanding and expecting always to be obeyed.

After her only child suddenly died during a summer whooping cough epidemic, Cassie conferred all of her maternal feelings to several orphans whose mothers had been taken ill, subsequently dying. Young Marse's orders had been then, "Now Cassie, yuh jest take care of these children. Put them in yore cabin tuh raise."

So this was how it came to be that Cassie lives alone in her cabin with her charges. With the passing of the years others have come and gone. Seems always there are some orphans who need her. "Only boy childs, dough," she insists. "Fer decency's sake."

Once some years ago she had not been alone. She had a mate whom she loved. Cassie had been just fourteen when Old Marse had ordered her, "Girl, time yuh have a man. Next Sunday ya gonna 'jump the broom,' yuh hear?"

This is what slaves do when they "marry." Just jump backwards together over a broom laid on the floor to signify that the man and woman will live together just as they would if they were truly husband and wife. And also to determine who is going to be "boss." The one whose feet do not touch the broom-handle. So slave men and women unable to marry *legally* and knowing they may be separated at any time the master deems, cohabit with his precarious blessing.

Cassie had been content back then, as content as a slave was allowed to be. In a short time she had learned to love the mate Old Marse had picked for her. The man had been purchased from a nearby plantation when a number of slaves were put on the auction block in Edenton in order to pay the owner's gambling debts. In such situations slaves are usually the first to go, even before the family's valuable silver and precious heirlooms. Ready cash. Black gold, *the slaves.*

Being very young, Cassie had not learned yet how dangerous it is for a slave to love. She had not learned yet that love could be gone as quickly as a bolt of lightning streaking across the sky. The busy "grapevine" slave telegraph ob dat place." The South's "peculiar institution" is so *peculiar* that fathers sell their own sons and daughters!

And so the man Old Marse bought did "jump the broom" with Cassie and then moved into the cabin where she herself had been born. The very same cabin in which her parents had completed their duty to Old Marse. "Mama dead tryin' tuh birth a already dead babe. Papa dead from duh chill he got in duh fields. An' affer dat Ole Marse done sold off all ma brothers an' sistahs. Never 'spect tuh see none ob dem agin in dis life." How she had screamed when the last one, "Baby Sis," was snatched out of her bed early one Sunday morning. The morning after Old Marse had a number of his cronies up at the "big house" where they had been drinking scuppernong wine and playing cards all throughout the night.

Cassie shared with other slaves that she has no idea why Old Marse had not sold her, too. She speculated, "Might be 'cause Old Missie like duh way Ah serbe duh table. Might be 'cause Ah neber slop duh gravy. Neber spill duh water an' neber drap soup on duh white tablecloth."

Or perhaps, Cassie thought, it could have been because she had always smiled, answering obediently, "Yes, ma'am" whenever summoned, which was quite frequently. Old Missie always seemed to be able to find something for young Cassie to do around "the big house." "Cassie, yuh help me with this now, yuh hear?" Or "Cassie, come here tuh me now, girl!" Old Missie's steady demands kept Cassie from ever having to go out to those unbearably hot fields and she was very grateful especially during harvesting when all of the slaves, even the house slaves, were expected to toil out-of-doors.

She detested going out into the blistering sunshine. Being the lightest complexioned of her mother's children, considerably lighter than any of her younger brothers and sisters, her face and arms burned easily. Small freckles dotted her face, shoulders, and arms. *Must be duh reason Old Missie want me 'round so much*, Cassie had supposed. *Old Missie lak her "high-yaller" girls workin' in duh "big house."*

No, it was because of something totally unimaginable to Cassie. It was because her quick smile, the distinctive shape of her nose, the way she tilted her head when she spoke all reminded Old Missie of her beloved younger brother, that reckless spoiled boy who had been heir to this plantation until his untimely death. It had happened early one morning while he was out racing his favorite stallion. "Fell off an' done clean broked he neck," was the story circulated over the grapevine.

And this had occurred only a few months before Cassie, her young mother's green-eyed light complexioned first child, had been born, the lightest of all of her subsequent children.

Old Marse had informed all his friends, "Never did trust that darkey Ah bought fer Cassie. No, suh! Didn't trust him from the first git-go. Wish Ah hadn't done it, but, yuh know, thought he'd make a good 'stud.' Looked mighty sturdy tuh me. Broad'n muscular'n all, yuh know. Good fer the fields. So then, Ah checked his teeth. Always got tuh look at their teeth, mind yuh. Yessuh, good teeth that boy had. Whiter'n ivory. Ah was so sure him'n Cassie would'a made good lookin' strong pickaninnies."

He continued, "Yessuh. Jest knew Ah didn't trust him ever since Ah first laid ma eyes on him. Hah! And would yuh know that darkey had the gall tuh look impudent when ma overseer put the chains on him and then pushed him on the wagon! Can yuh beat that, now? And would yuh know what else besides? Why, every time Ah seen him out in the fields he had an impudent look about him. And so Ah jest said tuh maself, Got tuh watch that darkey."

A sane slave knows better than to look impudent at his master. So Cassie had wondered to her friends, "What Old Marse be talkin' 'bout? Me man knowed better den look straight at Old Marse. Jest know dat me man got whipped cause Old Marse plain didn' lak him. Jest can' figure on dat."

What Cassie did not know was that her man previously had only one master and that master was his father, so he had been told. Not by his mother, though. Under the threat of death, slave women do not reveal the paternity of their children, especially when everyone can tell by looking at them that the father is white. Perhaps the master, or even one of his sons.

Denied, ignored, and then *sold* by his own father! The knowledge was just too much for Cassie's man to bear. Throughout his young life he had been conditioned by hatred, that of his master's and of the overseer's. So, eventually that hatred had engulfed him, consumed him, and finally controlled him. That hatred was directed toward the white man who owned him and, most of all, toward the system allowing it. And so when the hatred transferred to his new master Old Marse had no trouble at all in detecting it. Therefore, he had felt no compunction at all about selling the man, hoping that he would be taken as far away as perhaps New Orleans.

"He's definitely a dangerous one, that darkey!" Old Marse had determined.

By that time every white as well as every black had heard about slaves' becoming murderers. One in particular. That infamous "preacher" Nat Turner. Back in 1831 on a murderous rampage in Virginia he had killed his owners first. Then after a large contingency of slaves joined him, fifty-seven more white people were murdered in the duration of a single day. Nat Turner, too, had been conditioned, consumed, and controlled by hatred. Old Marse simply was not going to take any chances. Cassie's man just had to go!

"Jest gib me man time tuh fetch he jacket an' kiss me 'bye. Big belly an' all." Cassie had repeated her sorrowful tale many times over. "Lubed him an' den he be gone. Jest lak dat. Be gone fer eber," she had mourned.

Barely out of childhood Cassie was expected in her childbearing years to produce for Old Marse perhaps as many as ten healthy babies, each being worth at least $200. Later when older, their value would escalate. For instance, five year old boys large for their age have been known to bring upwards to $500. Cassie is aware of this fact only too well. For one morning before the roosters even had crowed, the overseer suddenly burst into her cabin. "Get up! Yuh get up now, boy!" he shouted, grabbing Cassie's five year old husky brother lying asleep on a pile of rags and then jerking him to his feet.

"Cassie! Cassie!" The little boy had pleaded frantically.

His sister had to stand by helplessly. She could do nothing for him except say, "Gwine be all right now, Lit'le Brotha. Yuh jest go on now wif Mr. Oberseer." Uncontrollable tears streamed down the faces of both slaves as the terrified youngster was being pushed out the cabin doorway and out of Cassie's life forever. After being left then with no children to hold, to rock, or to love she had her moments of sadness. On the other hand, however, she no longer need fear witnessing another child's being sold away from her at the whim of the master.

Now Old Marse was expecting Cassie to produce a reasonable number of babies for him to sell. After all, this was the only reason he was keeping her when he had sold all of her siblings. She was young, she was comely, she was healthy, and she had some "meat on her bones." Her teeth were strong and white. With all of those requisite characteristics she certainly appeared to him to be a "breeder."

However, he could not have sold her even if he had thought to because Old Missie explicitly had directed him, "Under no circumstances are yuh ever tuh sell Cassie." Even though after her brother's death *she* was the one who had inherited this plantation with its slaves, according to the law all became her husband's. Therefore, Old Missie never interfered with his dealings with the slaves, but on the issue of Cassie she was adamant. Old Marse did not know why, but since he readily admitted that he had no understanding of the ways of women, he did not question, knowing it would be futile to do so anyway.

And so another "marriage" had taken place, but no more babies were conceived. Cassie was glad. Then suddenly within days of each other both Old Marse and Old Missie died from influenza, passing ownership of the plantation to their only son. After that time things began to change in Cassie's life. For one thing her man fled the plantation. It happened on a moonless Saturday night when there was less chance of his being missed. Not until Monday morning at roll call. He had pleaded with her to go with him, but she was much too afraid. Never in her entire life had she been off this Chowan County plantation.

"Come on, girl. Go Sadaday night. No moon be out."

"No, jest cain't. Marse send out duh hounds. Ah's sceered ob dem. Dey kin tare a body apart. Anyways, Ah jest be slowin' yuh down."

Because he really wanted her to go with him, he had to state the ultimatum. "Den Ah gots tuh go ba maself. Fuhst, dough, Cassie, git me some onions tuh carry in me pockets fer tuh fool dem hounds wif. Den Ah be gone. Jest cain't stay 'round here no mo."

After that, even though she was sharing her cabin with another family, Cassie was left alone in the world—no parents, no siblings, no mate, and no child. That was when Young Marse entrusted the orphan boys to her care. He realized that she could have run off, too, but because she had not, he knew he could trust her.

And so her primary responsibility has been to create the kind of trustworthy, submissive, obedient slaves described in the "Good Book." This is what Young Marse is demanding. He is very adept at spouting Scripture when it serves his purpose and he likes to misquote a particular verse which has become "Servants, obey your masters," according to *the gospel of Young Marse*. And this is what Cassie does. She obeys and this is what she has taught her boys to do, also. That is, until lately.

Cassie's main job is to keep her boys fed well enough to be the kind of non-feeling, non-thinking, non-reasoning healthy human machines Marse requires to efficiently toil in his fields. "From day clean to first dark," week after week, month after month, year after year, even if it wears them out finally. She is to make them like Marse's fine thoroughbred bays hitched to his fancy landau. A blinder on each eye. Looking straight ahead. Not seeing what is on the left. Not seeing what is on the right. Just looking straight ahead.

"Jest do yer work now, slaves! Don't think! Don't hope! Don't dream! And certainly don't plan! Jest work, work, work fer yer master til the day yuh die!"

Yes, Cassie has been successful in keeping her boys' bodies healthy enough to efficiently work long hours in the fields. This fact is quite evident. But neither Cassie nor Marse have any idea of what her boys' minds are capable, albeit fettered with illiteracy. Shackled bodies, true, but not shackled minds! No, she has not been successful at all in producing the non-feeling, non-thinking, non-reasoning machines Marse wants.

At that task surely she has failed. Indeed they do feel, they do think, they do reason, and one in particular also *plots and plans*.

Now with the clinging soil from the fields washed from their hands and faces, Cassie's hungry boys are anxious to eat their long awaited supper. They have plopped themselves down on the rickety benches on both sides of a long wobbly wooden table. Covering its surface is a clean white remnant of a linen tablecloth Cassie surreptitiously rescued from the ragbag up at the "big house."

Throughout the cabin wafts the delectable odor of sweet potatoes' baking in the fireplace. They are for tomorrow's midday meal. Although the heat may be welcome on this chilly October evening, during the summer it can be intense in this hovel. Even with shutters opened wide, the small windows provide little cross ventilation. Often at night the boys will go out-of-doors to sleep under the deep blue-black North Carolina sky speckled with a myriad of brilliant lights. There to the basso serenading of courting male toads the exhausted boys quickly fall asleep. First though, Toby's eyes always gravitate to the "drinking gourd," its brightest orb, the North Star, fixed in the same spot always, pointing towards freedom. *No'th. Some day that's whar Ah'm a goin'. No'th.*

In this humble cabin not a morsel of food ever is eaten before giving thanks to the Almighty. The white folk in the "big house" always wait for the blessing of the table. Marse sometimes goes on too long doing the thanking, Missie and his children think. Cassie, too, believes a shorter version will do just as well and so that is what she has taught her boys. Her thoughts are that maybe if the food on her table were as ample as that on Marse's, her prayer might be longer because then she would certainly have plenty more for which to be thankful.

Many slaves imitate the ways of the white folk in the attempt at propelling themselves out of the degradation in which they have been forced to live. The reasoning being, "Why not? What dey say an' do be right. After all, ain' dey what bosses?"

So this is the reason Cassie insists upon having her table blessed. It is done that way up at the "big house." Since Marse always has the honor of blessing the table, she supposes that since he is a man, he must have more clout with the Almighty than Missie. Therefore, in her humble cabin in the quarters the task is always relegated to the oldest boy in Cassie's charge. In October of 1863 it falls to seventeen-year old Toby.

And so now he orders the waiting boys at the table, "Bow yuh heads." Then he intones, "Thank yuh, Lord, fer what we 'bout tuh recebe. Nourish we bodies an' souls. Please bless duh hands ob Aunt Cassie who made dese vittles fer us. Pardon we many sins. In Jesus' name'n fer He sake, Amen."

Having no fork, possessing only the wooden spoon he has whittled for possum stew and such, Toby uses his fingers for picking the tender collard greens out of a bowl he created from a hollowed out gourd. Seasoned with salt pork the collards had boiled for hours in the iron kettle hung over the fire Cassie built out in the yard. There, while tending to the boiling and bleaching of the laundry from the "big house," she also had kept her eyes on the boiling pot of greens.

Into his bowl the boy dunks a chunk of the yellow corn bread Cassie baked in her heavy iron skillet. Still hungry even after he has consumed his portion of what has been prepared for him, he tilts the gourd to his lips. As he swallows the salty greasy "pot likker," his thoughts are not on what he is eating or drinking, however good it may be. No, his thoughts are on freedom. His freedom!

"Mighty quiet tuhnight, Toby," one of the younger boys comments.

"Jest thinkin'. Jest thinkin'."

"Thinkin'? Hmmm." The younger boy smiles in a knowing way. "Thinkin' 'bout whut, Toby? Some gal yuh seed tuhday? Bet it whar dat new gal Marse jest buyed. Ah be thinkin' 'bout her, too, if'n Ah be yuh."

The other boys snicker. They know Toby soon will be old enough to take a wife. When his male slaves reach eighteen years of age Marse will let them choose a fourteen or fifteen year old girl to "jump the broom" with because he wants them to produce healthy babies for his profits.

"Naw. Don' habe no time be thinkin' 'bout no gal," Toby answers. "Ah got plans."

"Plans? Plans, yuh say? What kine'a plans?"

"Well, heerd tuhday de Yankees be gettin' closer."

"So?"

"So? Dat be meanin' freedom comin' at last. Ain' Marse Abraham Linkum up 'dere in de No'th be sayin' we be free? Yuh 'member we heerd dat when we be *plantin'* duh sweet 'tatas. An' now we be *diggin'* dem. Dey don' believe in no slavery up No'th, doncha know? And Marse shor ain' be tellin' we be free an' Ah don' 'spect he eber be gonna, needer."

"Yuh crazy, Toby. Yuh tink *yuh* kin eber be free? Ha! Marse be free. Missie be free. Dey chil'rens be free. All white peoples be free. Now how yuh tink yuh eber gonna be free? Humpt! Jest stick yuh big black toe outside dat front gate. An' den yuh see how free yuh kin be."

"Dat may be so, but Ah jest got tuh git tuh de Yankees," Toby is attempting to explain. "Den Ah be free. Jest know it."

Now Cassie interjects, "Toby, boy. Heerd Marse be tellin' Missie las' time Ah be up dere. Be passin' duh candied sweet 'tatas. Umm. Dey be so good with dat 'lasses an' all. Got a little bit on ma finger, doncha know?" The woman smiles impishly. She is quite ingenious in finding out how the white folks' food tastes, being verboten to the slaves. A spill here, a lick there, a dropped piece retrieved, a leftover from a plate.

"Go on, Aunt Cassie," Toby implores impatiently, knowing it is not fitting to interrupt when an elder is speaking. But he is anxious to hear more about what Marse had to say.

"Marse, he say duh...yuh know what kind ob Yankees he call dem. Well, Marse say dey be ober dere on Roanoke Island, where eber that be. Ah don' know. Any way, Marse say all duh brave soldiers ob duh South's gonna chase dem...Ah jest cain't mouth duh word he say. Dem...yuh know what kine ob dem Yankees. Gonna chase dem back up no'th whar dey be comin' from, if'n dey don't be killin''em all fust."

Toby listening carefully thinks, *Roanoke Island?* "Shor he be sayin' Roanoke Island, Aunt Cassie?"

"Shor as Ah be standin' here."

"Well den, Ah be lebin' fust chance Ah be gittin'. Goin' ober dere tuh Roanoke Island. Den Ah be free fer sho'!"

One of the boys is voicing his astonishment. "Fixin' tuh lebe here? Yuh real crazy, Toby! Be lebin' dis here place wid no papers? Be ketched an' be right dead, yuh is. Dem ole patti-rollers an' dey dogs be killin' yuh soon's dey be sniffin' yuh!"

With the utmost confidence Toby replies, "Nah! Dey ain' gonna be seein' me. Dey ain' gonna be ketchin' me an' shor nuff dey ain' gonna be killin' me!"

"Mebbe so. Mebbe so. Sho' hope yuh kin do it, Toby." All the boys nod their heads in agreement.

Tears quickly well in the eyes of the woman fondly gazing at the boy she has reared as her own son. She knows that Toby always can be counted on to do what he says. So not wanting him to see her tears, quickly she turns her head while promising, "Ah be prayin' fer yuh, boy, long as Ah be in duh land ob duh libin.' An' yuh kin be countin' on dat."

Chapter 2

Surviving the Ways of the White Folk

Now with the meager meal completed, the boys quickly turn to their nightly chores. With the arrival of fall darkness is descending much sooner. Upon returning to their cabins earlier each evening the boys now have more time to plug old rags in the chinks of the cabin walls to keep out chills and leaks, to sharpen axes and hoes, and to search for brushwood and dried animal manure--fuel for the cabin. Debris will be swept from the dirt floor. Periodically the walls get cleaned and whitewashed inside and out to discourage the habitation of pesky vermin, which Cassie detests. She uses this time to mend the latest rips and tears in her boys' paltry clothing.

During the special dinners Young Marse and his wife host when Cassie gets summoned to serve the dining room at the "big house," she learns much of the ways of the white folk. After years of having served Old Missie, Casssie is experienced enough to oversee the younger girls. Following her marriage the new Missie quickly had realized just how valuable Cassie was and also took notice to how well she was treated by Old Missie. And so after Young Missie became mistress of the plantation following the death of her in-laws, she knew she could count on Cassie.

For these very special occasions formal invitations are hand delivered to relatives and friends living nearby. These situations provide much welcomed opportunities for folk to visit, traveling in their carriages from miles away and remaining for several days, oftentimes bringing with them their own personal slaves (always referred to as "servants"). These times also provide the opportunity for the very prosperous Young Marse and his wife to show off their many possessions, including the large retinue of well-trained house "servants." When dinner is being served at three o'clock, long before the candles necessarily must be lit, Young Missie assigns a girl to stand directly behind the chair of each guest, just to do his or her bidding. The epitome of hospitality, this is, according to the gospel of Young Missie.

Since she prefers using her lighter complexioned girls to serve the table as had her predecessor, Young Missie once found herself in a very embarrassing situation. Before the War Between the States had begun, a visiting young Yankee relative remarked in astonishment as she observed the green eyes of the light skinned freckled slave standing behind Young Missie's chair. "Why, Cousin, I do believe that one of your servant girls is almost as white as I am!" And she had made that correct assessment without even seeing the slave's long light brown, almost straight hair hidden under her concealing head wrap, a requirement for all slave women.

Abruptly the animated dining room conversation punctuated with polite laughter ceased. Everyone stared uncomfortably down at the food on the blue willow pattern china dinner plates. No eye dared look up in the direction of the hostess whose alabaster face had turned crimson. When Missie adroitly switched the subject to what were the latest fashions in chapeaux her neighbors sighed deep breaths of relief, commencing once again with their eating and conversing.

A similar embarrassing moment had occurred when another Yankee visitor unwittingly commented, "My Dear, I do believe every time I come visiting I notice that your darkies are getting lighter. Why do you suppose that is? Seems to me they'd be getting darker, exposed like that to your hot North Carolina sun all the time."

After receiving no response to her quite accurate assessment she plunged on recklessly, not realizing into what deep water she was treading. In naivete she further commented, "You certainly do make sure to remind me to carry my parasol whenever *I* go outside in the sun." Since the possession of a skin white as alabaster is so important to the privileged women of the South they even place decorative upright fans near their fireplaces for fear heat from the fire just might put a bit of color in their faces.

Looking directly at the speaker while inwardly seething, Missie had replied saccharinely, "Do yuh believe so? Well, really, ma dear, Ah haven't noticed such a thing." Then deliberately turning away, with a forced smile she addressed the rest of her company. "By the by, our youngest daughter's doin' so well on the pianoforte that she desires nothin' more than for yuh tuh hear her play on next Sunday. Now Ah'm expectin' yuh all tuh come. Yuh hear me now. No excuses will be accepted."

Those nosy Yankees, she thought with disdain as graciously she directed the ladies' retiring from the dining room. They would be taking their tea in the drawing room while their gentlemen remained behind to smoke their cigars, drink their brandy, and discuss business, or politics, or any other topics not considered suitable for their ladies' genteel ears. Perhaps even the green-eyed slave girl whom Marse would declare "off limits" to his disappointed guests.

Always noticin' things refined folks don't discuss, Missie continued to ruminate while forcing herself to smile graciously at her guests. Things not spoken about, perhaps, but certainly not going unnoticed by the mistresses of those plantations where some of the light skinned; redheaded or blonde; wavy or straight haired; blue, gray, hazel or green eyed slave children bear a striking resemblance to their own children.

At these special times when Cassie gets summoned to the "big house," she first will go to the kitchen, deliberately separated from the main house in case an uncontrollable fire starts. Behind a folding screen in the scullery she cleanses her body with a sweet smelling soap before donning a freshly starched calico dress, white cotton petticoat, and pantaloons, all provided by Young Missie. Cassie ties in place a freshly starched checked gingham apron and wraps a clean white turban to conceal her light-brown hair. Now to her way of thinking she is looking just like all of the other serving girls.

Cassie always looks forward to going up to the "big house" because afterwards she will have plenty of "talk" to share in the quarters, besides acquiring some of the special food Marse and Missie favor which is forbidden the slaves. Foods such as potted salmon, baked ham glazed with honey and scored with dark heads of whole cloves, moist corn bread stuffing with tasty bits of sage sausage, beaten biscuits slathered with freshly churned sweet butter, and white cake covered with coconut icing.

The boys never know what Aunt Cassie will surprise them with after having been up to the "big house." How she manages to get her little stock back to the cabin is her own secret since all food is locked up in the larder and everybody knows the only keys to it hang from the chatelaine tied around Missie's ample waist. Missie who always has Cassie poised to do her bidding. And so it is from behind Missie's chair Cassie watches and listens, *learning the ways of the white people.*

Slaves are forever watching. Slaves are forever listening and learning. And slaves are forever remembering much of what they have seen and heard. Strange thing, though, the white folk just go on saying what they please about *anything* and *everything,* just as if the slaves were invisible. The white folk must think the slaves are blind and deaf, as well as *stupid.* Then again, some owners are beginning to doubt the latter. Otherwise, why pass laws stating that it is a legal offense to teach blacks to read, write, or cipher?

No slave on this plantation is able to do any of those things. Marse is in total agreement with those laws intended to prevent the teaching of slaves anything except how to perform manual labor. Even so, there always have existed well-meaning whites in disagreement with these laws and deliberately breaking them. For instance, on a Chesapeake Bay farm in Maryland a young slave boy was taught by his mistress to read and to write. *Dangerous skills,* contributing to exactly what the slave owners are afraid of. A successful *escape* from slavery. And now in 1863 that former slave signs in beautiful script the name he chose for himself as a free man. *Frederick Douglass.*

Toby has never so much as touched a book. He knows what a book is, for certain, because when returning to the plantation after delivering produce to the Edenton marketplace, he might be read to from what Marse calls the "Good

Book." *Be dere a "bad book," too?* Toby has wondered, but, of course, there is no one to whom he can ask such a question.

Whenever Marse reads aloud from the handsome gilt-edged goat skin morocco leather covered book, the passage is usually something about servants' obeying their masters. To Toby's way of thinking any book telling some people to be the owners of other people can be only so *good.* He wonders if it says in that book that masters have the right to beat their slaves, even to the point of death? Does it say that masters have the right to lash their slaves with the whip or to cut off their ears, fingers, or even their feet, or to brand their faces with "R" as punishments for running away? Does it say in that book that white men have the right to rape black women and then to send their own flesh and blood to the auction block?

Toby has no idea what that book says to slave owners. Those who call themselves God-fearing men. Pompously sitting with their families in reserved church pews each and every Sunday morning, some of those very same men having visited the slave quarters only the night before.

The little Toby knows about "The Good Book" he has gotten from the Sabbath meetings Marse allows the slaves to hold. During the summertime, religious services are conducted in a nearby cool shady grove. By law an overseer or another white male must be present or no gathering can take place. At least, no gathering *known* to Marse!

The "preacher" on this particular plantation is the coachman who listens intently while he waits outside the white folks' church. Then with his own interpretation he relays to his "congregation" the message he has heard. Some basic theology may get lost in the translating, but the slaves are unaware of this. All that matters to them are the underlying messages of hope they hear.

On one particular Sunday evening when returning to their cabin, Toby shares his thoughts with another boy, "Lak whut Preacher say 'bout dat man Moses. 'Bout how he done took dem Hebrew chil'rn an' carried dem tuh dey freedom. Dat's ma favrite story. How 'bout yuh?"

"Got's tuh 'gree wif yuh, Toby, on dat. 'Bout crossing duh Red Sea an' all. Tink duh Good Lawd's gonna be freein' us lak dat?" the boy asks hopefully. Such a question Toby can not answer. All he knows is that *he* is going to find a way himself to be free.

By way of the "grapevine" he has heard about a black woman the slaves call "Moses," Harriet Tubman her *true* name. The "grapevine" has carried the message that after her own initial escape this remarkable woman sneaked back into Maryland many times, spiriting away hundreds of slaves all the way to

Canada, including her own parents and siblings. Marse's slaves wish the woman they call "Moses" would come by their way.

"*Go down, Moses. Way down in Egypt land. Tell ole Pharoah, let ma people go,*" longingly they sing under the whispering pines of North Carolina, far from free Canada. The white folk listening to the singing hear only the familiar religious message, the Old Testament story of Hebrew slaves and their Egyptian captors. The black slaves, however, hear something else entirely. They are listening for the messages hidden "between the lines." The codes for escaping.

"Steal away, steal away, steal away tuh Jesus." *We be lebin' soon.* "Swing low, sweet chariot, comin' fer tuh carry me home." *Waitin' fer duh wagon.* "Ah'm bound fer Caanan land." *An' we ain' goin' tuh stop 'til we gits tuh Canada.*

Only a small number of slaves faithfully attend the religious meetings, mostly women and children. Cassie insists upon all of her charges' attending until they leave her cabin permanently, either to be sold or to "marry." After they "jump the broom" they will have to move to another cabin with room enough for a young couple and their future children. Cassie will not have any females around her cabin stirring up trouble among her boys.

Toby always enjoys the fervent music at the religious gatherings. For decades now having traveled over thousands of miles, channeled through a myriad of voices, the music of Africa has been improvised, harmonized, synchronized, and spiritualized. Miraculously surviving, even during these bitter years of enslavement, because even though the physical bodies may belong to Marse, their souls belong to the Creator.

And so unbeknownst to the singers, most having no knowledge whatsoever of that distant continent, Mother Africa's music now in 1863 is being lifted up to the Almighty in the piney woods of the North American South. A cappella. No instruments, drums especially forbidden because of their potential for stirring up trouble.

So there is only the exquisite harmony of plaintive voices crying, "*Nobody knows duh trouble Ah've seen.*" Hoping, "*Swing low, sweet chariot, Comin' fer tuh carry me home.*" Petitioning, "*Come ba here, ma Lord. Come ba here.*" Lamenting, "*Sometimes Ah feels lak a motherless chile.*" Signaling, "*Steal away, steal away, steal away tuh Jesus.*" Sustaining, "*An' when Ah gets tuh heaven, Ah'm gonna put on ma shoes, ma robe, ma crown, an' jest walk around heben all day.*"

Toby enjoys the singing, his pure tenor soaring like eagles on wing. The loneliness, *for surely he is a motherless child*; the hopelessness, *for certainly, every day is always the same*; the longing to be free, *for definitely that is his intent* all momentarily disappear. And for the remainder of his life Toby will remember the purity in the voices of the enslaved singing even "in a strange land." Singing of freedom, but unwilling to wait any longer just for the *heavenly* kind. Yearning now for the kind of freedom the Yankees have to offer *here on earth*.

Oh, freedom, oh, freedom. Toby hums a new song to himself as he swings his hoe. *An' before Ah'll be a slave, Ah'll be buried in ma grave, an' go home tuh ma Lord an' be free.*

So Toby does not mind attending Sabbath meetings with Aunt Cassie. However, some of the other boys mumble and grumble. One boy expresses the views of all the others when he declares, "Don' believe in no god lak dat. Don' believe in no white man's god. Nosuh!" Understandably, the boys doubt the existence of such a god who allows some men to be slaves and others to be their masters. Privy to only what Marse wants them to know, the boys do not have anyone teaching them the truths found in the Bible. So, no, they *cannot*. No, it is that they *will not* believe in such a god who favors white people over black people.

Besides, they really do prefer seeing what the older males are up to on Sunday evenings. The boys believe that much more fun can be had from observing *them* than from sitting in boring religious meetings. Some of those men love to gamble, drink their home-brewed alcoholic concoctions, and oftentimes get into a fight, usually over some woman. Men who play the banjo, guitar, harmonica, or fiddle oftentimes get summoned up to the front yard of the "big house" for the purpose of entertaining Marse, his family, and friends. White folk certainly do take delight in seeing "their darkies" jovially acting like buffoons, grinning widely to show their pearly whites, singing loudly, and "juba" dancing—that high stepping frenzied dance form indigenous to the plantations.

"Yuh see how happy'n content they are? Why, they're jest like children needin' tuh be taken care of. And yuh certainly can see that we take mighty good care of our 'family,'" so the paternalistic Marse and Missie are fond of telling their company, especially visitors from the North who openly may be critical of the master/slave relationship. Toby questions, *Family?* That may be how Marse thinks of his slaves, but Toby does not feel as though he is any part of *Marse's family*.

Cassie is aware that her boys will try any old excuse not to go to the meetings, but by now from experience she knows all about pretenses of boys. "Jest wipe dat look right off yuh face now! No sullen boy be libbin' in ma cabin." Repeatedly she admonishes, "Come on! Smile, now! Doncha know no sullen slave las' long on dis place. Marse don' tolerate no sullen. Smile! Always be smilin' lak Ah tells yuh!"

Smile! A vital rule to be followed by all of the slaves, no matter what their age. *Smile!* Always flashing your strong glowing white ivories. Goes a long way with a master forever on the lookout for impudence. *Smile!* Even after the quick-tempered ornery overseer lays his ten-foot rawhide whip on your bare back because you could not finish your rows before nightfall.

Smile! When your precious child or loving spouse or sibling or friend is sold away, never to be seen again. *Smile!* When Marse or his son or the overseer or any other white man looks a certain way at your precious daughter who is approaching puberty.

Smile! When your stomach is empty, when the torrid sun dehydrates your body and your lips are parched from thirst. *Smile!* When bloodthirsty mosquitoes inject giant itchy welts on your skin, when sneaky mice steal your meager ration of corn and voracious weevils get into the rest. *Smile!* On days when the rain never ceases and even though you do not have to go to the fields you are confined to your flooded hovel.

Smile! When dampness invades your lungs and all throughout the night you hear a cacophony of hacking coughs. *Smile!* When the floor of your cabin is miry as a pigsty and your pile of sleeping rags is wet. All your clothing, too. And you have not slept all night.

Smile! And even before the sun takes a peek over the eastern horizon, you hear the clang, clang, clang, clang of the morning's wake-up call. All the time *smile* while inwardly you are crying your bitter tears.

And so Toby, having followed Aunt Cassie's sage advice, has smiled all the way to his 17th year, *all the while plotting and planning.*

Chapter 3

Surviving in the Fields

During any season dawn always arrives much too soon for the bone-weary slaves. Now with the reluctant sun appearing later on these autumn mornings, Cassie finds it even harder awakening. She must be the first one rising, though, assuring her boys' getting out to the fields on time so as not to suffer from the overseer's wrath. First, striking a small rock against a piece of steel she bends to light the morning fire. A spark then ignites the scrap of cotton fabric she throws on the brush laid last night in the fireplace. When her boys awaken bowls full of hot water will be ready to warm their empty bellies. This is all the breakfast they will have before heading out to the fields.

Because Toby is a such a sound sleeper Cassie has to shake his shoulder several times in order to rouse him from his dreams, especially now that she realizes those dreams are of freedom. *Mus' be all duh harder fer dat boy be comin' back tuh dis here place now dat freedom be on he mind,* she muses.

Groggily awakening, all the boys quickly follow their brief morning rituals. Hastily relieving themselves out back, they pause afterwards to dip their hands in a bucket of water to wash the sleep from their faces. Before returning to the cabin they clean their teeth with short twigs pulled from the cypress tree behind the cabin.

After tying a chunk of corn bread and two still warm sweet potatoes in a clean scrap of tow-cloth, Toby pulls on his last year's too small jacket of cheap "shoddy" (wool recycled from old rags). The last few mornings have been quite chilly. Around his neck he knots the ragged bandanna needed for controlling the sweat which oftentimes pours down his face when he is laboring in the hot fields. On his feet he wears a pair of holey brogans several sizes too large with "room enough to grow," according to Marse. Lastly Toby slaps on his head his soft three-year-old sweat stained felt slouch hat. He should have received a new hat last year, but when Marse had looked at it he concluded, "Nothin's wrong with that hat, boy. Maybe yuh'll get a new one next year."

The planters certainly know they have to provide sufficient food for their human animals if they are expected to work to capacity, but concern about what they are to wear while they are doing it is an unnecessary expenditure. So the parsimonious masters mete out as little clothing as they must. Early on when Old Marse was alive, the slave women who worked in the fields had woven a homespun itchy material to be fashioned into a crude dress for summer wear. There would be a hole for pulling over the head and a length of rope was tied around the waist to keep the dress in place. However, nothing at all was worn underneath.

The slave women had wished, 'Sho' lak somethin' tuh keep away duh scratchin'." The more fortunate Cassie had shown them the cotton pantaloons she wore. They had belonged to Old Missie who had become quite corpulent in her later years. The other women then became desirous of possessing undergarments like Cassie's, but articles of underwear were not *necessary* items, the stingy Old Marse had maintained as he pinched his pennies. Again he had justified his actions by asking, "What do darkies know about decency?" That is what he called his "people." "Darkies." Antebellum "gentlemen" like Old Marse usually refrained from using the coarse appellation of "nigger."

Now Young Marse makes a bargain with the women living in the cabins after taking notice of the plump healthy looking hens noisily cackling and roosting so freely all around the slave quarters. Many of the women are raising the chickens for their own supply of eggs and meat. So Young Marse approaches the women with, "Make a trade with me. Yuh give me some of those hens. Then Ah'll give yuh some cloth." On large looms located in one of the outbuildings several slave women weave a functional cloth for the basic needs of the plantation.

Cassie definitely is interested in such a deal. She is sure that with the sharp wooden needles Toby has whittled for her she can stitch up a fairly decent looking dress. Perhaps even one with long sleeves for protection against the sun's rays when she has to be out-of-doors boiling the laundry or tending to her small vegetable patch. Up for the bargain she and some other women have begun to coop up those elusive chickens whose ultimate fate is to be fried crispy golden brown in hot lard and then served on blue willow china to the occupants of the "big house."

Yesterday morning upon seeing that the water in the wash bucket had a thin surface glaze of ice, Toby had decided to pull on his raggedy last year's cold-weather clothes. Marse is not going to dole out the new supply until Christmas day when annually each of his male slaves is allotted a new blanket, a single pair of woolen trousers, a short woolen shoddy jacket, and two long sleeved itchy osnaburg flax shirts. Shoes and hats generally are replaced every two years. To Toby his shoes seem worn and holey enough to warrant a new pair this year, so he is hoping.

His tow-cloth summer pantaloons are ready now to join his pile of sleeping rags. Frayed as they are they are scarcely decent, but that should not matter to slaves, according to Marse's rationalization. They have been patched so often the patches are now in need of patching. Besides, the mornings are much too chilly for wearing only those lightweight cotton trousers and an old flax shirt from last year's supply because immediately when Toby swings open the cabin door, cold air rushes in to nip his face. He is glad to be wearing warmer attire on this crisp October morning as he pauses to bid farewell to the woman leaning against the doorframe of the cabin. "See yuh tuhnight, Aunt Cassie," he promises as always before hurrying to catch up with the other hands heading out to the fields. She gives him a small nod and slight wave.

Mebbe, an' then agin, mebbe not, she is thinking now that she knows what is foremost in the boy's mind.

As the sun is rising, so also is the temperature, but, fortunately, not too high today. Toby prefers this pleasant Indian summer weather. The days are not as hot, or as humid, or as long as in summertime when the Dixie sun bears down unmercifully. Even to a son of Africa the humidity can be oppressive.

On this particular morning the wind is whispering through the glade of longleaf pines at the edge of the fields, but, thankfully, there is no sign of rain. *Don' know what's duh worser. Too hot, too cold, or too wet? No need fer worryin', dough. Dis be a good day,* Toby concludes. The sun just above his head now, the boy's shadow has almost disappeared beneath his lean body. *Rest time comin' up soon,* he eagerly anticipates.

Clang, clang, clang, clang. The voice of the brass bell stridently reverberates across the distance to the fields. The hour for the midday meal has at last arrived. Other than the bowl of hot water Cassie had plied him with in the morning, this will be the first nourishment Toby has had this day, Marse's slaves being allowed to eat only twice a day except during the harvesting time. Then they are allowed time for a quick breakfast of corn meal mush sweetened with sorghum molasses.

After removing the battered felt hat from his head to wipe his sweating brow with his bandanna and then rubbing his hands together to rid the loose soil, Toby sits down by himself in his sweet potato row, preferring his own company so he can think, dream, and *plot.* Carefully he unties the scrap of tow cloth wrapped around the crumbling corn bread and baked sweet potatoes. Peeling back the thin brown covering to expose the bright orange flesh of the rhizomes, first he sniffs their sweetness, causing his empty stomach to grumble loudly in anticipation.

Sweet potatoes will keep his body going most of the day, Toby is well aware. These rhizomes are packed full of energy, but he does not know the why's and the how's. He does not know that when slavers had needed a cheap abundant food source for their human animals they found it in sweet potatoes. Indigenous to South America, they do very well in North Carolinia soil. So now they serve as an important food staple for the slaves rather than the more expensive wheat flour. White flour is used on this plantation solely for baking loaves of bread, biscuits, fruit pies, cakes, dumplings, and pastries for the "big house." Sometimes on Sundays if she is feeling particularly magnanimous, Young Missie will treat the youngest slave children to snow white beaten biscuits slathered with sweet sticky sorghum molasses.

In the fields young black boys under age twelve, doing their best not to slosh, lug heavy leather buckets of fresh cool water. Not old enough or strapping enough yet for work in the fields, they are at their first job. All throughout the day, these boys trek back and forth to the creek, toting water to the hot and very thirsty slaves.

"Watah boy! Watah boy!" Calls from all directions come from the fields.

Carrying that life-saving liquid to be drunk and/or poured by the ladleful on overheated heads, the boys scurry up and down the rows. "If'n duh creek be low, Mr. Oberseer better not be ketchin' yuh wastin' no watah," the slaves caution each other.

While hastily gulping down their food, young mothers nurse their babies under the sheltering shade of nearby shrubs or trees. The infants are tended there by children not yet old enough to work in the fields or to tote water, girls remaining the longest in the job. All of them, also, are in need of some of the precious water being toted by the boys.

"Ober heah, watah boy! Ober heah!" Mothers call and beckon from under the shady trees. Those nursing are allowed a little more time for rest. One very young mother, however, seems to be dawdling, playing with the small baby she holds in the crook of her arm. The other women warn, "Girl, don' yuh be takin' too long now, case Marse or Mr. Oberseer be comin' close by!"

Sighing as a tear trickles down her cheek, the young mother reluctantly places her infant back in the shade, even though aware her baby is not getting enough nourishment. Likewise are the other women aware, muttering among themselves, "Babe jest be birthed four weeks past. Need she Momma. But dat girl best git back in duh fields fer duh whip git laid on she back. Dat pore girl be needin' restin', too, but Marse be needin' he fields worked mo'." These older women have seen too many slave babies die from neglect because their mothers have to be in the fields. They know also that many slave mothers die from overworking and over breeding. As they return to the fields all they can do is to shake their heads in pity for both the baby and its young mother.

A water boy is passing down Toby's row. "Hey, Toby!" he calls out. He is one of the younger boys in Aunt Cassie's cabin. "Hey!" Toby responds, remembering his water boy days. Now gratefully he reaches out to accept the long handled wooden ladle which will touch the parched lips of all the men and women in the fields today. Not knowing anything about "germs," this communal partaking of water is truly one of the tests for the "survival of the fittest." However, many slaves just "up and die" and no one knows why they develop "the runs." Marse calls the sickness by another name. He calls it "the flux." Toby only knows that regardless of what it is called, a large number of slaves suddenly can be stricken and no one has any idea why.

Clang, clang, clang, clang! Seems like no sooner than he swallows his last bite of corn bread, Toby is being summoned back to his labor. Back to his digging and his sweating. In the summertime he wears just his lighter weight tow-cloth pantaloons, sans shirt, but now the weather has become too cool for wearing just those trousers, even with a shirt. On chilly mornings, then, he must start out in his warmer clothing.

However, by early afternoon his body is being irritated all over. Last year's winter clothing sticks to his skin. His back itches unmercifully from the refuse flax out of which his shirt was woven. His head is soaking wet under the hat he needs to shade his eyes from the sun's direct rays. Even though, regardless of these human discomforts, the sweet potato rows loom ahead, going on as if forever.

Late afternoon. Close to four o'clock. Toby's shadow has lengthened once again. The day has become quite warm by now. He already has removed his woolen jacket, tying its two arms around his waist. Since the sun is at his back now he no longer needs his hat for shade. So he removes it, stuffing it behind him under his jacket.

From the daily exposure to the sun his skin, naturally a ginger brown, has turned a burnished copper. The sun does not affect Toby adversely, but unlike him, there are those who cannot tolerate the intense rays of the sun. He has seen slaves' collapsing in the fields, dying there from sunstroke and dehydration. So young Toby is one of the more fortunate ones because he can work all the day long, subsisting on his sweet potatoes and drinking the fresh cool water toted by the water boys.

Chapter 4

Heard it on the Grapevine

Already Toby has been able to see his own breath in the early morning chill as cooler temperatures accompany the shorter days and the longer nights of the fall. He knows that the ideal times for escaping are late fall and early winter when it is not too cold yet and when the sun rises later and sets earlier. Toby has set his mind on what appears to be the impossible, having no doubt at all that if he attempts to get off this Chowan County plantation without proper identification papers from Marse and gets caught by the hateful patrols, he might be killed on the spot.

He has heard that since the beginning of the War of the Rebellion, droves of poor young gun-toting white men accompanied by their trained bloodhounds are just itching to catch run-away slaves. Patrols called patterollers have formed, bent on routing out black fugitives to return to their masters, for certain compensation it is understood, of course. Sometimes the itching to catch a black man gets so uncontrollable the patterollers take things too far. Over the "grapevine" news recently reached the plantation about a runaway who had been beaten to death after his capture.

"Didn't mean tuh kill him, suh, but that d____d niggah jest up'n died." This is what was reported to the man's owner.

"Aaah! Pay it no mind! He jest one'a them impudent niggahs. No count, no way," stated the master disparagingly when he learned of his slave's death, even though several years ago he begrudgingly had paid $1500 for the man. Surely, though, he would rather have had the runaway returned so he could have done the beating himself in front of all of his other slaves. "Teach 'em a lesson. Show 'em what happens when niggahs run."

Then to punish the slave even further, his owner might have sold him to someone down in Georgia or even farther south where, according to the "grapevine," slaves are forced to work nineteen hours a day. "And if'n he tries tuh run agin he'll have a lot farther tuh go if'n he thinks he'll get all the way tuh Canada. Those people up there ought'a be horse whipped. Hung, too. That's what we do tuh thieves down here in Chowan County. Mize well say they're *stealin'* our property." Others are in total agreement. And some owners, the "grapevine" has warned, even have been known to chop off a runaway's foot while reasoning, "No chance of that niggah ever runnin' off agin."

Now in 1863 as the invading Federals are penetrating farther and farther into the South, as more and more slaves are stealing away under the cover of darkness, the number of patrols accompanied by their baying bloodhounds is increasing. In a state of shock the owners are watching their lucrative profits steadily dwindling, resulting in fading fortunes. And so they are demanding that their property, their *black gold*, be returned immediately!

Toby is not about to do anything stupid, not with his freedom's being guaranteed by President Abraham Lincoln and not with that freedom only a short distance away, that is, wherever the Yankee soldiers are. Therefore, not having the same sense of urgency as had all of those before him in years past, he is not "fixin' tuh jest up'n go."

Not like slaves who had owned the same dream of freedom, responded to the same magnetic pull of the "drinking gourd," and fled by way of the Underground Railroad, that railroad having no tracks. Many escapees upon reaching safe-havens like Stroudsburg, Montrose, and Erie in Pennsylvania; Rochester in New York; Toledo in Ohio; or Detroit in Michigan chose to remain there. Others, however, continued on until they reached the safe borders of Canada where they were sure no one could come after them.

Like other railroads this Railroad has its conductors, too. Such as the "Black Moses" (Harriet Tubman) who in the 1850's led on foot over 300 escapees to their freedom. Such as those conductors who carried slaves to safety in covered wagons and carriages, one such daring conductor being James Fulton of Clarion County, Pennsylvania who had successfully hidden runaways in farmhouse attics, root cellars, tool-sheds, smokehouses, dairy houses, and barns. His younger brother William is a soldier now in the 103rd Pennsylvania Volunteers presently garrisoned at Plymouth, North Carolina, just across the Albemarle Sound from Edenton.

As a member of the Associated Seceder Church, a branch of Presbyterians, James Fulton was a staunch abolitionist. Even though being quite aware that the penalty for helping escapees was the astronomical fee of $1000 and six months in jail, from 1847 to 1855 he had taken the risk with other ministers of his denomination. They would pass two to seven men at a time along the Railroad from Virginia, north to Lake Erie where they could cross the border into Canada where a safe haven was guaranteed.

The Underground Railroad also has *courageous* conductors like William Camp Gildersleeve of Wilkes-Barre, Pennsylvania who hides runaways in a special compartment built into his hay wagon. It has the *bold* black conductors William Still, a successful coal merchant in Philadelphia; David Ruggles in New York City; John Mason in Kentucky who eventually will deliver approximately 1300 slaves to Canada; as well as conductor Elijah Anderson in Ohio. The Railroad has *dedicated* conductors like Levi Coffin who oversees all the stations in Cincinnati, Ohio.

There are *daring* conductors such as Native American Daniel Hughes, married to a black woman, who with his canal barge transports north hidden runaways from Havre de Grace, Maryland. There are *dauntless* conductors like John Fairfield, the enlightened son of a Virginia slave owner, who poses as a slave trader. Also in other disguises he returns many times to the South. One time while pretending they are part of a funeral procession, with Fairfield's aid twenty-eight slaves are able to escape.

Now in this year of 1863 Toby is aware that slaves have escaped from even this very plantation in Chowan County. Aunt Cassie's man was one of them, leaving on a Saturday night, knowing he would not be missed until Monday morning's roll call. Toby also has heard about slaves from neighboring plantations waiting until the moon waned before stealthily sneaking away.

However, he has no knowledge of the ingeniousness runaways like Henry "Box" Brown who spent twenty-six hours as boxed cargo shipped to Philadelphia. Or of stowaways covered with stacks of wood or piles of coal on boats heading north. Or of males posing as females and *visa versa*, as well as lighter-skinned slaves pretending to be their own masters or mistresses. For instance, the almost white Ellen Craft posed as the *master* of the darker skinned William who was in reality her own husband! Some runaways carry forged papers written oftentimes by their own hand, maintaining that they are intending to meet owners awaiting their expected arrival. Still others leave after borrowing precious papers of manumission from friends or family already set free.

What Toby *never* hears being relayed by the continuously busy "grapevine" is that many blacks are met with much hostility and bigotry in those northern cities, frigid not just in temperature. For instance, he has no idea that in July 1863 an explosion of anti-black sentiment resulted in bloody New York City race riots, leaving many blacks dead. He has no idea that fear and resentment have been building from the coal fields of Pennsylvania to the slums of Boston and Philadelphia, especially among the immigrants who had fled Ireland during the devastating 1845 famine when a blight rotted their fields of potatoes. To their way of thinking the liberation of the slaves will result in their overflowing the North, competing for jobs. The European immigrants do not realize that American blacks are *agrarian* people. Coal mines factories, foundries, and mills do not beckon these children of Africa, much preferring to remain in the warmer South. That is, *if only they could be free.*

Even if Toby were aware of all of this he still might feel that those who have successfully escaped at least now are free from the South's "peculiar institution," especially if they have reached Canada or Nova Scotia where freedom is guaranteed to them. So, no, this is not the right time for Toby to be leaving. He will know when it is. He just has to be *patient.*

By way of the "grapevine" slaves are hearing, "Yankee soljers don' be wantin' no colored joinin' up wif dem, eben dough Ole Marse Linkum say dey kin." Some hear, "Oh, shor, dey takes yuh, but yuh jest be a slave agin doin' all dey dirty jobs." Still others hear, "No, dey gib out soljer clothes an' a gun an' make yuh a Yankee, too." While many others respond with, "What eber dey do be better dan here." So relays the "grapevine." Always busy, passing even inaccurate bits of information such as, "All black folks in duh No'th be habin' good payin' jobs an' be libin' in fine houses jest lak duh white peoples."

Another dubious message Toby hears is that if slaves remain with their masters throughout the conflict, they will be manumitted. Freed, that is, once the *South* has won the war. Of course history will preclude the fruition of such a promise. If indeed, there ever was such a possibility, about which Toby certainly has his doubts. It makes him wonder if all the slaves were to be set free who then would do all the digging, planting, tending, harvesting, cooking, cleaning, laundering, mending, serving, nursing, grooming, mucking, and of the other tasks the slaves have to perform daily.

He knows with certainly it would not be the dainty, delicate, genteel, magnolia blossom-complexioned Missie who has never done a lick of work in her entire life. "Don' know one end ob duh broom from duh udder. Sho' do sew purty, dough," Cassie has conceded. For all throughout the well-appointed rooms of the "big house" are found chairs and foot rests covered with Missie's intricate needlepoint created on her loom set up in the drawing room. Toby also knows without a doubt neither would it ever be the courtly Marse. Not that patrician and southern "gentleman farmer."

Marse goin' tuh set all ob us free after duh war? Don' b'lieve it, Toby concludes. And he has no intentions of staying around to find out, either.

No, soon this bitter life of slavery is going be over for him. He has determined that his children will be born into freedom. Being aware that children born to a slave woman are always the property of her master is the main reason he shies away from getting involved with any of the eligible young girls he soon might choose for a mate. He does not intend ever to see his children torn from their weeping mother's arms to be sold at the whim of Marse because he may be in need of some quick money to cover his gambling debts or perhaps to purchase an additional plot of land. To be sold if Marse's crops fail one year or if one of his friends desires a slave companion for his child. Or if a relative craves a handsome decorative "pet" boy clad in black velvet and white lace to adorn his carriage. Or if a male neighbor fancies a nubile young female bed-warmer for cold winter nights.

No, he has determined that soon this wretched life of slavery will soon be over for him. He will become a free man, able to own his own land and to have a dog, *if he chooses*. He will be able to hire out and to buy and sell goods, *if he so chooses*. This is what freedom means to Toby. To be able to do just what he *chooses*.

Chapter 5

Run, Toby, Run

Suddenly Toby stands. He listens intently, perceiving something different in the air today. As usual, insects are sending out their staccato notes. As usual, ebony crows are emitting their raucous territorial caws. As usual, slaves in the fields are singing a "call and response." As usual, these sounds are reaching Toby's ears, but something is very different on *this* day. Could it simply be that he is not hearing the sounds of Marse's stallion's noisily clopping through the fields? Or is it that he is not hearing the bellowing voice of the latest overseer?

Dis last one be lazy, Toby has thought after noticing that the man does not seem to be overseeing as much as his predecessors had. Instead, after making sure all hands are present the stone-faced man may canter his steed out of the fields, showing up again whenever he pleases. Many slave owners utilize black drivers, but this master has never done that. So there is not even a "head" black in charge of the fields on this day.

Cassie has shared with Toby something she had overheard up at the "big house." "Marse done took Missie an' dey chil'ren tuh stay wif she kin way down tuh 'Lanta, Georgia whar she done come from, now dat dem, yuh know whut kind-a Yankees Marse call dem, be gittin' so close by." It is quite noticeable to Toby that the slaves are working much more slowly now with Marse *in absentia*, with a less frequently seen overseer in the fields, and with freedom just on the horizon.

Toby goes back to his work, soon pausing again to listen. Definitely there is something different in the air today. An unusual quiet, making Toby determine, *Tuhday be duh day.* Leaving behind his hoe and stealthily moving toward the cover of drying cornstalks, Toby takes off in his search for freedom. Heading east to Roanoke Island in order to find the Yankees!

One of Cassie's younger boys has paused briefly to remove his slouch hat. Just about to wipe his wet brow with the raggedy bandanna he has pulled from around his neck, looking up he observes Toby's flight. He thinks, *Dere he go! Run, Toby! Run! God bress yuh, Toby. Sho' hope yuh kin make it.* Then slapping his hat back on his head, the boy resumes his work, knowing that he will be the one informing Aunt Cassie that, hopefully, Toby will not be coming back to her cabin tonight or any other night.

✦

As the boy speeds through the dark primal woods he knows full well in which direction he is running, having been off this plantation innumerable times before when produce was being transported to the marketplace in Edenton. On such trips sometimes Marse himself accompanies the wagons, but more often he sends trusted "servants," always carrying the necessary permits, of course. When Marse does go along young Toby gets taken to tote. And these are the times the boy is happiest because Marse allows him to hold the reins, guiding the team of horses down the dusty country roads. Toby seems to have a way with horses. He respects them and they in turn obey him.

Being very particular about his animals, Marse makes certain his prize horses are carefully groomed, properly shod, well fed with fresh oats, crushed beans and bran, and carefully protected from the elements in their individual clean well built, well ventilated 12x12 foot stalls. There they are provided with only the freshest sweet smelling hay. Only the best of care for Marse's horses! This certainly is not what he accords the human animals he owns, forced to subsist cramped together in stifling 16x14 foot cabins placed out of sight behind the "big house."

One summer day while returning from the marketplace, pleased by the manner the boy was handling the team, Marse offered, "Jest might let yuh handle ma carriage team one of these days, Tobe." When the boy had replied obediently, "Yessuh!" Marse suspected Toby's widening grin was his jubilant response to the possibility of being granted such an honor from his master.

Not so! Toby simply was *amused,* knowing full-well Marse's future plans were not at all *his.*

Now tearing through the woods Toby knows something about where he is heading. He knows that Roanoke Island is located directly across the wide body of water. Over where the sun comes up. He knows this because he has always been listening and remembering what he has heard. *Don' know jest when Ah might be needin' tuh know 'bout dat,* he would think while tucking away some interesting bit of information.

For instance back in 1861 soon after he had learned from the "grapevine" about the firing on Fort Sumter by the Confederates in South Carolina, Toby had overheard Marse and his friends in discussion about a particular war effort. One of the men was asking, "Did yuh'all hear the latest? Every one of the church bells in Edenton's gonna be sent up tuh Richmond, they say. Then they're all gonna be melted down and turned in tuh cannons fer our boys."

Another man replied, "Yessir, did hear that. But Ah know they won't be sendin' the Baptist bells. No way tuh ever get them out of the tower."

"Yessir, that's so. Heard, too, that they want a lot of other metal objects tuh be donated as well," Marse continued. "Well, Ah'm goin' back tuhday tuh see jest what Ah can muster up. Ah'm shor there's some extra kettles hangin' in the kitchen. And we can certainly do without so many candlestick holders. Our dinner bell, too, Ah imagine. Jest have tuh get ma wife newer and better directly after we win this here war."

Sho' wish Marse'd git rid ob dat big bell, too. Toby was thinking about the brass bell hanging on the pole near the cabins, regulating the comings and goings of the field slaves with its strident clang, clang, clang, clang.

Another time Toby had been listening when Marse and his friends were expressing their concern over Edenton's proximity to Roanoke Island now in the hands of the Yankees. Before the Union Navy took possession of the island on February 8th just two days prior, no one in Edenton had been taking the possibility of a Yankee threat seriously.

"Yuh know," one of the men was warning. "We're in a very vulnerable position here in Edenton. What if those d____d Yankees decide tuh come on over here?"

Another was speculating, "Yuh certainly are right about that. And with us out there at our places we won't be of any help tuh the town. Ah'm thinkin' we got a problem here what with all our boys gone off tuh fight. Those d____d Yankees can jest come right in any time'n totally destroy the place."

Then Marse concluded, "Well suh, what the town needs are some strong fortifications. But Ah guess it's too late fer that, jest like what happened at Elizabeth City. The d____d Yankees jest took it over. We'll jest have tuh pray that they don't decide tuh come on over here. Now Ah best be gettin' back tuh ma wife and children. Ah may have tuh be takin' them down to Atlanta where Ah know they'll be safe."

He felt he needed to explain his own situation to the others, all standing in a huddle on the waterfront. "Left my people tuh the new overseer, yuh see. He's not nearly as good as them Ah've had in the past. All the good boys gone off tuh fight. Don't know why this one's around here still."

Marse then beckoned to Toby who was standing at a respectful distance, but close enough to overhear what had transpired. "Tobe!" His master was ready to go and needed Toby's assistance in getting up onto his wagon. "Now don't ya'all expect tuh see me back in town fer some time. Ah jest hope'n pray there won't be no trouble here 'cause then all the women'n children's gonna be at the mercy of them blue devils."

Marse would like to go off to war, too, but an unfortunate fall from a horse many years ago had broken one of his legs. Not having been set correctly by the local veterinarian, it had left him with a decided limp and nowadays he cannot walk without the assistance of a cane. Following Marse's departure all of the remaining men promptly took their leave, each going his separate way, with life's continuing as always in the quiet lovely little town of Edenton, North Carolina.

That is, until early on the morning of February 12th, Abraham Lincoln's 52nd birthday. Certainly not many people south of the Mason-Dixon Line were even thinking about it. In Edenton homes the residents were "breaking their fast." Downtown businesses already had opened their doors. Produce laden carts having arrived from nearby farms were stationed on Main Street. Approaching them were brightly turbaned slave women carrying large woven reed baskets for toting home fresh eggs and winter vegetables as well as the apples they were about to purchase for their mistresses.

It was, as usual, just an uneventful morning in Edenton. That is, until a frantic shout was heard coming from the direction of the wharves. "Yankees comin'! Yankees comin'!"

Indeed, rounding Cherry's Point was the frightening sight of three Union gunboats. *Hull, Perry* and *Lockwood*. The terrifying message quickly reverberated throughout the town. "Yankees comin'." The produce-wagons promptly left Main Street. The owners of businesses swiftly closed and locked their doors. And with empty baskets slave women scurried away to relay the dismaying news to their mistresses, many with husbands gone off to the war.

"Missie! Missie!" the slave women screamed frantically as they flew through doorways. "Yankees be comin'." Some were as frightened of the bluecoats as were their mistresses. However, others knew exactly what the presence of the Yankees could mean for them, but, of course, they certainly were not going to let on to their mistresses.

All of the inhabitants of Edenton promptly went into hiding as best they could with shutters tightly closed and doors securely locked. Some folk anxiously hurried down into root cellars. Others scurried up into attics, aware, however, that regardless of what they did, if the Yankee sailors were to turn their guns on the town, all would be lost. For there were no Confederate defenders here. Only old men, women, children, and slaves. All were praying fervently, the slaves even.

Their prayers seemingly were answered when the dreaded Union officers peacefully disembarked, allowing the worried citizens to breathe deep sighs of relief. Unlike the small town of Plymouth just across the water, Edenton was to remain intact due to the influence of the many unionists in residence there.

Toby knows well the directions in which the wheel-rutted dusty country-roads traverse and the swift rivers flow. For years now he has been observing *and remembering.* He is very familiar with the dense woods capable of hiding him and with the treacherous miry swamps capable of drowning him. Familiar, too, with the flat terrain in this part of northeastern North Carolina. Certainly familiar with the direction of north because he has been planning to escape ever since he was old enough to know anything about freedom.

And just when was it Toby first began thinking about freedom? Could it have been on that day when Marse sold a handcuffed passel of slaves, including several young boys from Aunt Cassie's cabin? Or was it on that terrible day when all the slaves had been forced to witness 100 lashes being laid on the back of a slave who unsuccessfully tried to run away? Or was it when it had dawned on Toby that every person was *created to be free,* whether black or white. Whenever it was, freedom then became the sole focus of his life.

Toby is wondering now, *Jest when Ah be missed?* Certainly not until the morning roll call, he is certain, but not necessarily then, either, due to Marse's absence and then with the lazy overseer's sometimes not showing up at all to take a roll call. *Wid him bein' new an' all, he might not eben know if'n a boy be missin' 'til he look real good. By dat time Ah be long gone.*

With the sun's tucking itself behind the western horizon, darkness commences its spread from the east like spilled black paint rushing to engulf the sunset's streaks of mauve, saffron, burnt orange, indigo blue, and magenta. Vivid colors, the portent of another beautiful day tomorrow. At any other time Toby would have paused, lingering to gaze with awed appreciation. At any other time he would have been welcoming the arrival of nightfall, signaling the end of his labors for the day.

But not this evening. In fact, darkness is descending much too quickly since Toby thus far has been determining his direction by the sun's position. As long as there is some degree of light he can be cognizant of his direction. After nightfall, however, he will have to depend upon the position of the "drinking gourd" or the feel of the soft green growth on the north side of trees. He has to be careful, though, not to scrape up against those thick vines roping their way up the sides of their host trees. Once when he was widening fields replete with those shiny green "leaves of three" Toby had experienced what havoc poison ivy can wreck on his skin.

Glancing overhead through the canopy of tall pines he sees a dense cloudbank's forming. Toby realizes that this is going to be a long, moonless, starless, and lonely night.

He detects the sound of rushing water up ahead and as it steadily becomes louder he knows very soon he is going to be at the bank of the Albemarle Sound. At times driving along the river road with Marse, Toby had observed on the banks men who were "taking pains" to conceal their boats in thick brush. If only he can find one of them now! Moving furtively along the bank, he carefully feels his way through the darkness, hoping to bump into one. He does not have to go very far before he locates a dugout, lying upside down, fortuitously equipped with two paddles.

Toby never in his life has been in a boat. Never before has he had a paddle in his hands. However, he knows here is a way to get over to Roanoke Island and he will do whatever it takes to get there. First righting the dugout, he pushes it into the water to test for leaking. *Dry as a bone*, he determines after rubbing his hands over the bottom. He realizes, though, that he must wait for the first light before attempting to cross the water. So he pulls the dugout back onto the bank and then "beds down" in the dry bottom for the duration of the night.

After fitful dozing, at last he spies a sliver of light beginning its spread along the eastern horizon. He knows that is the direction of Roanoke Island then. He knows that is where he must go. *Where the sun comes up,* he is thinking. Pushing the dugout into the water he attempts to ease himself into it, but immediately it starts to take him in the wrong direction.

No, straight across. Dat's whar Ah got tuh go fer tuh git tuh duh Yankees. Don' know how long it's gonna take. Got tuh git dese sticks movin'. Steady now, boat. Dis ain' nothin' lak no horse. Jest got tuh move dese sticks. Jest got tuh keep control. Don' want tuh go in no udder direction. Jest straight across. Got tuh git across fore dark come agin.

As the light increases he is able to spy large boats on the choppy pewter colored Sound. Yankee gunboats on patrol. They are quite a distance away from him as he hugs the shore, not close enough to be shot, but not too far out, either. He does not know if he will be able to swim, never having had the opportunity before, but if the dugout capsizes, he certainly will find out soon enough. *Row, Toby, row!* The sun steadily is ascending, leaving the eastern horizon behind. *Row, Toby, row!* Now he sees one of the gunboats purposely coming toward him! *Row, Toby, Row!*

As the gunboat gets closer to the dugout with the hard paddling boy in it, a loud voice yells out over the water. "Hold on there! We're comin' ta get ya." So Toby gets picked up by a gunboat fortuitously on its way to the very same destination as his. Roanoke Island. His arms ache unmercifully from the unaccustomed paddling and so he is overjoyed to be relieved from completing the remainder of his journey in the precarious dugout. The sun has already set when the gunboat unloads its cargo, including Toby, onto the shore. "Walk straight ahead," is the only direction he is given.

After disembarking he travels some distance through the dark piney woods before discovering a clearing in the underbrush. Through it Toby can see numerous campfires' blazing in front of canvas tents. He hears the familiar snorting and whinnying of horses, loud talking and laughing of men, as well as an unfamiliar musical instrument's laboriously wheezing a melancholy tune.

As he observes the men's preparing their evening meal he realizes that he has had little food today. On the gunboat a colored sailor had given him a bowl of soup and a chunk of bread. So now he is ravenous, but there is nothing at hand for him to eat. Back in the cabin at this time of the evening he would have been partaking of Aunt Cassie's filling hot food. Perhaps some fish the boys might have caught. Perhaps a raccoon or 'possum they might have trapped. Certainly greens and "pot likker." And always corn bread made out of her supply of corn meal Marse allots.

Toby has no idea what those soldiers are preparing for their evening meal. They just might be using their government rations of salt pork and dried beans. Or perhaps some pickled beef with which they could be concocting a stew by using wild onions and any other fresh vegetables they may have found nearby. And if they could not find any fresh ones that day then, they might be using the dehydrated vegetables provided by the government. "Sure don't taste nothin' a'tall like Ma's good stew," the homesick younger soldiers complain in frustration while stirring their unappetizing concoctions.

Always accompanying the soldiers' meals is that army staple, hardtack. Made of flour and water it is a white cracker about three inches square and one-half inch thick. Nearly unbreakable and labeled by the men as "sheet iron," or better yet, "worm castle" because invariably the cracker hosts maggots and/or weevils. The only way to make it edible is by soaking it in hot water or coffee.

"Best look in your cup first and be sure ta skim off them dead bugs," is the soldiers' admonishment to one another.

"Well, guess it beats starvin' ta death," the men try to rationalize as they carefully go fishing in their coffee mugs.

At sunset the bugle had sounded retreat and the flag had been lowered. Now through the darkness words of a melancholy tune are drifting toward the spot where Toby is hiding. A song the boy has never heard before. A favorite of both Johnny Reb and Billy Yank, the lilting melody of "Lorena."

The whine of the accordion is an unfamiliar sound to him. Toby is familiar with fiddle, guitar, harmonica, and banjo, but this sound is quite different. He wonders what it is he is hearing. More importantly, though, he is wondering just how he will be able to reach freedom without getting shot first.

Real dark now an' ma face an' dese clothes be real dark. Sho' don' wanna be taken fer no wild bear tuhnight.

He has come this far. Now with freedom directly in front of him he will just have to wait patiently until dawn, even though his empty belly is groaning. Even though his feet in the oversized holey brogans are blistered and bleeding; even though every muscle in his body is screaming with pain. He knows he is not going to die from these temporary discomforts and so he continues assuring himself, *In duh mornin' den, Ah be free.*

A bugle is sounding now. Before tonight Toby had never heard the sound of a bugle, either. At ten o'clock the staccato notes of "Taps" are calling the weary soldiers to extinguish lights and take their well-deserved rest. Now on Roanoke Island, North Carolina the camp of Union soldiers is quiet, the night pitch-black. The only movement is that of pickets (guards) on duty.

Toby gathers up a pile of dry tulip, hickory, and oak leaves. Then he lowers his aching body onto the rustling pallet. His old woolen clothes so irritating earlier feel good to him now. *Leas' it be a dry night,* he contemplates. *An' it ain' dat cold.*

No, he is aware that he has been much colder than this in his Aunt Cassie's cabin during winter months when night winds blew their frigid breath through unstuffed chinks in the cabin walls. Also, this is not so very different from the way he always has slept. On a pile. In Aunt Cassie's cabin he had slept on piles of old clothes much too tattered for repairing, falling apart from their many washings. It will be quite a few years hence before he is going to know the comfort of a soft mattress covered with smooth clean sweet smelling white cotton sheets.

Now before dropping off to sleep he is thinking of Aunt Cassie's belief that "cleanliness is next to godliness." "Ain gwine be no little critters libin in dis cabin." She was determined about that. Therefore, ritually every Saturday in her large iron kettles she boils, scrubs, rinses, and wrings for drying in the hot sun all those filthy raggedy stinking clothes her boys must wear all week. When functional enough only for bedding the rags again get boiled, scrubbed, rinsed, wrung, and dried in an effort to destroy the ever present vermin lurking in the dirt of the cabin floor. Inadvertently she is keeping her boys in reasonably sound health by destroying disease causing germs.

Sunday, the day of rest for the slaves, is anything but that around Aunt Cassie's place. This is the day when she performs the same ministrations on her reluctant boys that she does on her rags. Starting very early in the morning she builds a fire out in the yard for heating the water her boys draw from the well. Then she pours the water into her favorite cast iron caboose kettle, the very same one she uses for boiling laundry, manufacturing lye soap from oak ashes, rendering hog fat after the slaughtering, and making beef tallow candles for the "big house."

Aunt Cassie orders her boys, "Shuck off dem clothes now an' scrub yuh body all ober! Den take dis warm water an' rise off!" Not rinsing well enough can cause the boys to itch and squirm all through the Sabbath meeting, something Aunt Cassie simply will not tolerate.

All of the smelly grimy clothes the boys have been wearing all week get tossed into the kettle of boiling water. Later with a long forked tree branch Aunt Cassie hoists steaming pants and shirts up and out of the pot, heaving them onto a tree stump where she pounds them with a short heavy branch. Afterwards she flings them into another kettle of hot water for rinsing. Then finally after a good wringing they are laid flat on the grass to dry in the sunshine.

"Close dose eyes real tight now!" she commands her grumbling charges. "An dunk dose heads down in dat bucket!" For Aunt Cassie has prepared a bucket of warm soapy water for drowning any resident head lice. First, though, she takes a rag to scrub larkspur behind each boy's ears. "Dat's whar dose little critters be puttin' dey nits, yuh know."

Her next order is for the boys to shine their brown skin until it glows by using some of the beef tallow she uses to make candles. "No *ashy* boys be goin' tuh meetin' wif me." The very last directive she issues is for them to put on their least raggedy clothes. The ones saved just for Sundays. Since Aunt Cassie has taken great pains to mend every tear, these are designated their "Sunday-go-tuh-meetin'" clothes, just a tad better than the rags they wear every day to the fields. "No *raggedy* boy be goin' tuh meetin' wif me, needer."

Now while drifting off to sleep, Toby thinks fondly of his Aunt Cassie, realizing he will never see her again. He takes comfort in remembering her promise. "Always be prayin' fer yuh." He hopes that she knows he will never forget her. The boy falls into a deep slumber, too weary tonight even to dream of freedom.

SECTION II

CROWDER THE SOLDIER

Chapter 6

The 1862 Letters of a Corporal of the 103rd Pennsylvania Volunteers

*T*oby finally has located the Yankee soldiers he has been seeking. Those soldiers guaranteeing his freedom. Several regiments of the Army of the Potomac are on Roanoke Island while at the same time others have been garrisoned across the Albemarle Sound at the little town of Plymouth on the south bank of the Roanoke River. One such regiment is the 103rd Pennsylvania Volunteers of which nine of the ten companies are always at Plymouth with one always being garrisoned on Roanoke Island. In August 1861 to February 24, 1862 the 103rd had been organized in western Pennsylvania at Camp Orr, Kittanning which had been situated on the Armstrong County Fair Grounds.

Several years prior to the war a young farmer from Cumberland County with his wife and son had migrated to Pittsburgh, seeking employment in the iron furnaces. He was one of the many ambitious young men leaving their parents' farms for good paying jobs in cities of the industrial North. As a resident of Allegheny County when the War Between the States had erupted, he joined the 103rd Pennsylvania Volunteers, being mustered in on February 15, 1862.

Before starting off, all of the recruits had been granted a ten-day furlough to get their affairs in order. So the man had delivered his wife and young son back to the security of his parents' farm in Cumberland County, there to remain for the duration of the war. Now he frequently composes letters to his wife, even though he had been forced years before to leave the schoolroom after having completed only the fourth grade. His father had been in need of his son's labor on the farm and after that time the young man no longer had any reason to write down much of anything. Now twenty years later as he corresponds with his wife, it is quite apparent he has forgotten the spelling of some words.

Washington City
March 6th, 1862

My dear wife,
You can see that I'm in Washington City now. After we left Camp Orr on Feb. 24th we had to bord a frate train on the Allegheny Valley Railway. It went to Pittsburgh first. Then it went to Camp Curtin in Harrisburg. We marched to the capital bilding where we

got are regimental flag on the 26th. Governr Curtin hisself give it to us. After that we borded the train & went on to Baltamore. People were watching us when we got off the train there. They didn't look friendly at all. There's a lot of rebs there who own slaves. So nobody knows if Maryland's gonna leave the Union or not.

After that we had to march across Baltamore to get to another train to take us south to Washington City. Arrived at the Baltamore & Ohio stashun on March 3rd. After that we had to march up Penna. Avenew. Hard to believe here we was Penna. soldiers marching up a avenew named for are very own state. We think maybe that's a good sign. Then we marched up 16th street to a hill they call Meridian. Heard that it's on a exact longitood line. The 77th they say. Remembered that word from school. Don't know if I spelled it rite. That's why they call it meridian I guess same as longitood. Have to wait til I get home to look it up on a map. Never expected to see this city in my lifetime. But here we are camped in the capital of are country.

This city is layed out like this. The streets are named with letters and numbers & the very wide avenews are named for the states. We're camped just north of W street which goes east & west & between 14th & 16th. They travel north & south down threw the city.

Guess who I run into today. You remember my cousin from Adams County who was at are wedding. He had a grand time dancing with every pretty girl. Well he come here with the 101st. We was both glad to see each another I can tell you.

Don't have much riting paper. Please send some with stamps cause I don't know where I can get some more if the sutler wagons don't come by soon. Remember me on the Sabbath when you go to the throne of grace. Love,

Meridian Hill
Washington City
March 15th 1862

My dear wife,

I take my pencil in hand with the hope that it finds you & the boy in the best of helth. Today I met up with my cousin again. We plan to do some sightseeing soon as we can. Want to walk down the 14th Street hill to get a good look at the capital building. Could see it when we got off the train but not real good. We can see it from here on this hill. Its a good walk away. There putting a tall dome on top of it. I hear that a statue's going to stand on top of the dome. That's really going to be up in the air. Wonder how high. Maybe someday I'll see a pikchure of it done. I know I won't see it for real cause once I get back home I'm staying rite there.

Heard about the monument that's going up to honor Pres. George Washington. Like to see that too. They stopped bilding it cause of the war. Supposed to be very tall when its finished. One of the men in my company told us that. Seems to know alot about everything. Got some books in his tent. Reads every chance he gets.

Anyway he says that the monument's going to look like some kind of a needle from Egypt. Don't know what he means by that & neither does anyone else. What needles we want to know. Says to look in a book about Egypt. But he don't have any books about Egypt in his tent. Tells us that those needles are tall pillars with a little pyramid sitting on top of them. Can't imagine what that looks like cause pyramids are big that I know. Saw a pikchur of one once. He says there's one needle in Egypt they call Cleapatra's needle. Remember her from history. Had something to do with some Roman king. Julius Ceeser I think. When I come home I'll have to get some books from the schoolmaster. I'm sure he'll have what I need.

Don't know how much longer we'll be here. The boys're getting restless. Want to teach those johnny rebs a lesson & then get on back home. Please rite soon.

Love,

Alexandria, Virginia
March 30th 1862

My dear wife,

I take this pencil in hand with the hope that this letter finds you & the boy well. Thank you for sending the paper & stamps. Was very happy to hear from you & to know that everything's going good & Paps has enuff help. Hope to be back home in time for the harvest.

Looks like we might be moving out of here soon cause we had to fix enuff food to carry with us for 3 days. Got plenty of that hardtack. Won't starve but I mite brake my teeth. Then I won't be the handsome fella you married. Ha ha. I'm riting this letter to you now cause I might be bording a ship on the morrow. Expect we'll meet up with some johnny rebs before long. Not a one here now but this here Alexandria's a secesh town even though the Yankees have taken over. Moved in last May & the people left behind in the town are not too happy about that.

Yesterday afternoon about 4:00 we left Washington City for here. I have to say that we looked good when we marched down the 14th Street hill. Lots of people lined both sides of the street to see the parade. They was waving flags & cheering u on. Made us feel like we're doing something worth while. We had to cross the Long Bridge over the Potomac River. Over on the other side's Virginia. Could see a lot of ships docked there.

This town of Alexandria's very old. Might have been pretty at one time. They say that George Washington did alot of business here. Never seen so much red brick. Brick's everywhere. The bildings & the sidewalks too. They got some brick pattern called herringbone I never seen before. Some of the streets they paved with rocks from the ballast of ships from way back. That's rocks they used to put in empty ships for weight. Now it keeps the dust down in front of houses of rich people. One of them streets is called Prince Street. The streets here are very dusty & get real muddy when it rains.

No shouts here like we heard before. Not many people were in the streets anyway. No body came outside to see us. They closed there shutters tight. The bildings all looked empty but we knew there was lights behind the shutters. The only people who seemed glad to see us was the colored ones. We got some waves & smiles from them.

It was pitch black when we finally got to the field where we was to sleep. We unrolled our blankets & slept on the bare ground. I was bone tired as you can imagine. You know how I need my sleep. Didn't get much though. I was too cold. Was chilled to the marrow.

Today snow's falling just when we're about to leave. Any other time I'd think it was pretty. Makes me long for a sled ride with you sitting behind me holding on hard.

Instead I'm here getting this letter off to you before I have to go. Riting it in a tavern. Some of us wanted a warm breakfast & so me, my cousin & two friends William Fulton and Franklin Mohney from over in Clarion County got permishun & ended up here at Gadsby's its called. Man who served us haint a secech so he says. Promised that he'll send this letter on to you. Hope so. Just have to trust him I guess.

On the way back had to stop by the apothecary's to get some Dr. Caldwell's syrup for one of the fellows who keeps getting stomakakes. He was feeling too poorly to come with us today. Man at the tavern told me to go to Stabler-Leadbeater's. Its so old too. This is one old town I think.

Walked past the Marshall House. That's where Col. Ellsworth got shot to death last year when he pulled down the rebel flag flying there on the roof. The innkeeper shot him & he got killed too for his effort. Passed the church where Pres. George Washington went. Its called Christ Church. Its made of brick too. There's a graveyard next to it with lots of famous people buried there. I hear not Washington & his wife though. Hear there buried on their own place called Mount Vernon. That's about nine miles south of here on the river.

They say that Gen. Robert E. Lee used to go to that church too. The two families are related I hear tell. That's the Lees and the Washingtons but I don't know how. Heard that Lee used to live right here in Alexandria when he was a boy. They say he's a great soldier because he went to West Point. Too bad he didn't stay up north then. When we win this war I expect he's going to be sorry he picked the wrong side.

Don't know when I'll have a chance to rite again. Will keep you in my prayers & I know your doing the same for me.

Love,

Harrison's Bar Landing
Virginia
Sunday, July 13th 1862

My dear wife,

A very exciting thing happened on the 8th. Pres. Abraham Lincoln visited the Army of the Potomac for a review. Just seeing him raised are morale. He's real tall & with that stove pipe hat of his he looks like a giant. Towers over the tallest man in the regiment. He's 6 feet & 4 inches so they say. We was very proud that he came to review us & we did are best to make are officers proud. We hope Gen. Casey was proud. He's such a fine man & a good leader too.

We was in a serious battle a few days ago. I'm alright as you can see. Wouldn't be riting this letter if I got shot. Got so close to the rebs though that we had to whisper so they wouldn't hear us. Several of are men got killed in the battle I'm sorry to say. We was surprised that a bugler sounded for them when they got buried. We was used to hearing three shots.

Today some of the men are sick with bad stomackakes. Some think its got to do with the water. Has a foul smell to it. I've taken to boiling any water I drink like Ma used to do after a flood muddied up the creek. Maybe that'll help some. So far my stomack has been feeling just fine

The place where we are now has a very old house on the bank. Belonged to Gen. Benjamin Harrison they say. So this place they call Harrison's Bar after him. Today I stood watching the water in the James River. Never seen the tide come in & out before. Read about tides in my school books too. The water comes up the banks just so far. I thought for sure it was going to overflow. But then it backs up. Just like that. Its an amazing thing to see.

Please I can use some supplies for sewing on buttons. They keep falling off my jacket. I'm sure if you put them on they would stay put. Should've let you teach me but I didn't know I'd ever have to know how to use a needle. Please send me a book of needles, scissors, a thimble & some spools of black & white thread. No sutlers been by us lately. Don't know why. They usually are following the army everywhere in their wagons. They have all kinds of things to sell us.

Went to church services this morning with my cousin. Felt real good afterward cause I knew you and the boy was praying for me.

Love,

New Berne, North Carol.
December 23rd 1862

My dear wife,

Once again I take my pencil in hand hoping that this letter will find everyone well. This is the time of the year when there's a lot of sickness I know. Take good care of yourself & the boy.

Had a pretty bad thing happen to us when we was on our way to Norfolk, Virg. All of are extra clothes like my heavy coat was put on a ship to take them there. The ship sunk just like that. Nobody knows why. Wasn't even no rebs around. All of the 103rd's important records was packed in boxes & put on that ship too. Now there all lost. I'm going to have to replace my clothes. Got enuff money for that. Sorry that I'll just have to take it out of what I was planning to send home. So you won't be getting as much as usual.

Arrived back here 2 days ago. Camping to the east of what they call the Trent River. I'm feeling pretty good. Some of the boys have come down with bad coughs. There hacking all over the place. Need some of your good remedy of onions, sugar & molasses. That would make them better right fast. We're in swampy areas & are feet are wet all the time. They itch something awful. Sometimes I think its going to drive me crazy. Try to dry my feet good but then I have to put my damp shoes back on again.

Got to chop down thickets of vines to get over to the rebs though. Chased them clean all the way back to where they come from we hope. Are job now is to cut them off from their capital. That's Richmond, Virginia you know. That's where they get there food & other supplies from. Had to burn some bridges & tear up some rails near the town of Goldsboro. We just got to stop them.

Here we're all looking forward to Christmas. Know the boy is too. He's too old for toys now but I'm sure you'll be able to give him a nice day. How I wish I was going to be there with you. Next year for sure. Won't be much like Christmas here. Maybe I'll be able to find a little tree to chop down. Don't know what I'll decorate it with but I'll think of something. We'll have the day off to do what we want. Not that there's much to do in the way of fun. But after morning worship we're free to relax. Wonder what we're going to have for Christmas dinner. Maybe the cooks'll fix us something special. Won't be a beef roast like Mam makes I'm sure.

When you go to the throne of grace on Christmas pray that I'll be home soon at least to see the dogwoods in bloom. I'll open my presents then & I hope I'll have a few to bring back to you & the boy. I promise to get something real pretty for you from the sutlers when I see them next.

Love,

Chapter 7

Yankees Garrisoned at Plymouth

The sounds of the earliest birds' hunting for their first meal of the day awaken the boy who is lying on his pallet of dry leaves. The sun has not yet made its appearance and the woods are dark still. Soon afterwards Toby is able to spy a thin sliver of light slowly beginning to illuminate the eastern horizon.

And once again he is hearing the sound of a bugle. At five o'clock sharp the crisp morning air resounds with reveille's announcing another long day for the Federals garrisoned here on Roanoke Island. Another day for hoisting the 21 starred and 13 striped flag of the Union. Another day for enduring the hours of detested drilling. Another day for consuming food fit only for a hog's slop trough, as homesick farm boys are quick to point out. Another day for being away from home and family. Another day for simply trying to remain alive.

To the steady beat of snare drums, the Union flag makes its ascent to the top of its pole, declaring its authority for all to see. As he peers intently through the small gap in the tangle of underbrush, Toby can see that those men rousing the others without a doubt are wearing the uniform of the Yankees. Light blue trousers with a dark blue blouse. All of these sounds and sights stir the blood of the young black runaway.

Groggily poking his uncombed head through the open flaps of his canvas tent, the corporal from Cumberland County feels his face being nipped by the crisp October air. Wearing whatever he can throw on quickly, he joins the other Union soldiers, also in motley attire, lining up for the first of three daily roll calls. Later after tidying up he will consume the breakfast of flapjacks he bakes in the bottom of his round sheet-iron mess pan.

Then after attiring himself in his proper uniform, the corporal will be ready for the first of this day's tiring, tedious drills, lasting perhaps up to two hours at a time. Necessary backbreaking battalion drills with each soldier's wearing certain of his accoutrements. For the double time *light marching* orders or for skirmishing drills (simulated battles) he is loaded with only a lightweight Haversack and a canteen flung over his left shoulder. A heavy leather knapsack is carried on his back, belt and cartridge box around his waist, and a long heavy rifle securely held against his right shoulder. However, for the *heavy duty marching* drills each man is expected to carry close to fifty-eight pounds after adding his heavy woolen great coat, the "pup tent" (one half a shelter), a warm blanket, and a clean change of clothing.

Back in 1862 on blustery February 8th soon after the Union forces captured Forts Hatteras and Clark on the Outer Banks of North Carolina, Maj. Gen. Ambrose Burnside had arrived here on Roanoke Island with his 10,000 troops. The general, recognized easily by his distinctive huge mutton chop whiskers, seems to have initiated a new style for men, "sideburns," the anagram of his name Burnside.

With him came a motley flotilla of all types of boats. Sailboats, passenger steamboats, coal scows, ferryboats, tugboats, converted barges as well as makeshift gunboats. Labeled "Burnside's Expedition," with considerable ease they were able to overtake Roanoke Island protected only by some 3000 Rebels and seven gunboats.

A most strategic spot situated at the mouth of the Albemarle Sound, this swampy island of Sir Walter Raleigh and the "lost colony" history, only ten miles long and two miles wide, has prompted the Yankees into believing they must always be ready for a surprise attack from the Confederates. Unbeknownst to them, however, the opposite has been true. For up to the present time, the defense of their capitol at Richmond has been far more important. Now in late 1863 the main goal of the Federals here on Roanoke Island is to choke off rebel maritime supplies. Particularly, to keep the South's vital exports of cotton and tobacco from being exchanged for English imports of efficient Enfield rifles and ammunition.

From his hiding place Toby is studying the soldiers while musing, *Sho' want tuh be lak dem. Will duh Yankees let me be a soljer fer real? Did Marse Linkum really say dat a colored boy lak me kin be one?* To the slave Toby what these disgruntled freeborn white soldiers are begrudgingly enduring would be an honor and a privilege. He longs to be able to fight for his own freedom and for the freedom of those he has left behind. With utmost confidence he contemplates, *Ebery colored person be free when duh Yankees win.* Toby gives no thought whatsoever to the possibility that the Confederates might be the victors in this bitter War Between the States.

Now determining that there is enough light to safely approach the camp, with hat stuffed under one arm he ventures to the edge of the clearing, standing motionless for a moment while checking his bearings. Finally after inhaling a deep breath, Toby steps forward to where he easily can be seen and yet far enough away not to be shot. Cupping his hands then, he bravely cries, "Hallo! Hallo!"

At first no one hears him, the Yankees busily tending to their numerous morning tasks. With log huts being erected for winter quarters the sounds of noisy hammers and saws as well as the loud voices of yelling men cover the boy's shouts. So he hallos again, much louder this time. Several soldiers looking up now instinctively grab their Austrian muskets kept in immediate reach at all times. With weapon extended one young soldier slowly walks towards Toby.

"Freedom!" Toby bravely yells. "Lookin' fer freedom!"

At that the soldier waves the boy forward. Hat in hand, Toby cautiously moves closer to the Yankee camp. With musket still pointed the soldier not much older than Toby warily is watching the sinewy, medium sized Negro teenager slowly approaching in his worn out oversized brogans. The young soldier immediately takes in the dull brown woolen trousers being held up by a length of rope, the short brown shoddy woolen jacket, and the light colored flax shirt which probably had itched the boy's skin unmercifully until it had been worn enough to be "broken in."

Concluding that here is just another harmless colored refugee, the soldier lowers his musket and responds to the plea, "Ya want freedom? Well, ya come ta the right place."

"Yessuh. Thank yuh kindly, suh."

The colored boy needs no instruction as how to address a member of the Union army. "Sir." That is what he has been conditioned to call *any* white male and so for Toby, enlisted man or commissioned officer, each always will be addressed as, "Sir." Such respect is not found among many of the white soldiers, some of whom curse, threaten, and even physically fight their officers. The majority, volunteers signed on for a short three month stint, do not feel as though they have to take any orders they do not like. Especially after the realization that most of their officers are as inexperienced as they, many having been elected by popular vote rather than on their merit.

"So? What'a we gotta lose?" they question. After all, they will be back home just as soon as their brief adventure at playing soldier is over, so they expect. After their ninety-day stint they all will be going back to their farms or back to work in factories or mines. *So what could possibly be the consequences?* These had been their thoughts at the *beginning* of the war. However, those three short months have stretched to three long years, necessitating an "about face" change in attitude. The volunteers have learned that indeed there are dire consequences for deliberate disobedience.

As Toby enters the camp most of the troops do not give him even a second glance. Once rendered harmless he quickly is dismissed from their minds as they go about attending to their more important activities. *What's one more contraband?* This is their attitude since already there is a large contingency of escaped blacks here on Roanoke Island. Like Toby the cryptic message from the "grapevine" has informed them if they just can reach the Yankees they will be free. And so in droves they have been fleeing nearby plantations.

However, because of the large number of contrabands now here on the island, a serious problem is developing. Vital questions must be answered. *How are they all to be fed?* Heretofore, they ate whatever their masters had provided. *What will they wear?* The clothing on their backs is all they possess and when they arrive oftentimes it is in tatters. *Where will they be sheltered?* Certainly not in army tents. *What are the Yankees to do with these refugees, following them as the children of Hamlin did the Pied Piper?* The answer is to be found nowhere in the soldiers' realm of understanding. All they know is that they did not come here to take care of colored refugees. They have been given no directives to follow. And still the runaways come! By January 1864 more than 2500 of them are here on the small island.

Solutions must be found. And soon.

The young Union soldier escorts Toby to the brown field tent of the recruiting officer. "Sir, this man sez he's come lookin' fer freedom."

Seated at a small rectangular wooden table placed in front of his tent, the officer ceases his writing, blowing the ink dry before peering up at the young colored boy standing so still, head deliberately lowered so as to have no eye contact. Then with his chamois cloth pen wiper the officer cleans the excess ink from the tip of his quill pen before asking, "Well now. What's your name, young fella?"

Young fella? Toby wonders if that is what they call free black men up North. Heretofore, he has only been addressed by white folk as, "boy."

"Toby, suh. Marse call me 'Tobe' when he want me fer somethin'." His head is lowered still because never in his life has he looked a white man directly in the eyes.

The recruiter is well aware of why the boy is not looking at him. "First off, Toby," he directs. "Lift your head up and look at me! It's all right." The boy still hesitant, the officer speaks again, "Look at me, Toby! Lift your head up now and *look straight at me!*"

As the boy is making a feeble attempt with complying, the officer continues, "Now let me tell you this, Toby. I'm going to give you your first lesson as a free man. You always look at a man *straight in the* eye!"

The boy tries again, this time raising his head somewhat higher. "All right, now," the officer says with approval in his voice. "That's much better."

Smiling, he continues. "Now I assure you that you'll be safe here, Toby. I guarantee nobody's going to come looking for you in this place," he promises. "By the way, which direction did you come from, anyway?"

"Come from ober dat way, suh," the boy replies, pointing in the direction of the Sound. He still is having difficulty looking directly into the eyes of the white man, though.

"So, Toby, know the lay of the land around here?"

"Some parts, Ah does, suh. Neber been on dis side ob duh watah b'fore, dough." His head is lifted even higher now, but his eyes still do not quite meet those of the white recruiter.

"That's all right. Perhaps you can be of some help to us sometime in the future." His thoughts are that Toby might be used some day as a spy or as a guide.

Then he adds, "By the way, Toby, did you run away because your master was mean to you?" This career soldier from the North has heard many a horror story relayed by contrabands, the majority telling of the cruelty of masters, overseers, and even mistresses. Also having read Harriet Beecher Stowe's very popular *Uncle Tom's Cabin*, he is familiar with the character of the sadistic overseer, Simon Legree. Naturally then, he is curious about Toby's motives.

"Nosuh!" Toby emphatically states. "He ain' so mean if'n Ah jest be doin' me work. Jest don' want tuh be nobody's boy no more. Nosuh, Ah jest wants tuh be free."

"That's commendable. Most commendable. Well, let me say this first off. I think you're a real brave fellow, Toby. Now then, I can give you a job here in the camp. Assisting our cooks. How's that sound? Can you cook?"

"Oh nosuh! Cookin's women's work!" the boy replies, surprised eyes looking directly at the recruiter now. "Ah always be workin' in duh fields."

"Sorry, Toby. That may be so. And we do have a few women cooking for us, but they don't *live* in the camp. So it's like this. You want to stay here in the camp?"

"Yessuh!"

"All right then. If you want to stay, then you're going to have to work hard. And this is the job that I need done. I'm in need of cooks. You see, many of my men are down with the ague." Seeing that Toby has no idea what he is talking about he clarifies, "You know, 'the shakes.'"

Toby nods. "Yessuh." He knows about "the shakes."

"So, you see, Toby, I can use you to help the cooks out."

Toby is remembering what he had heard on the black "grapevine." "Sho', dey takes yuh, awright, but den dey be makin' yuh be dey slave." So he feels he had better be explaining his intentions *right now.* "Beggin' yuh pardon, suh, but Ah want tuh be a soljer. *Not a cook.*"

The seated recruiter gazes up intently at this brave colored boy standing so still in front of the table, now finally having enough nerve to look him straight in the eye. Not so very long ago the recruiter's answer would have been, "That's impossible." But not now. President Lincoln finally gave his approval for Negro men to join the Union army and they are enlisting *en masse* in the United States Colored Troops (USCT).

"Oh, so you want to be a soldier, do you, Toby? Well, I've got to tell you now. That depends on your age. You've got to be eighteen to be a soldier. Did you know that?"

"Nosuh."

"Well, you do. So just how old are you, Toby, anyway?"

"Well suh. Christmas las' Marse say Ah hab seventeen years. Don' know dat fer sho'. None ob duh boys in duh cabin whar Ah libed knowed 'xactly when dey been birthed. So we jest say it be duh same lak Jesus. Yuh know, suh, duh 25th day ob December. Don' hab tuh be doin' no work on Jesus' birthday, yuh know, suh."

"All right then. Christmas is only a few months from now, Toby. You'll be eighteen then, we'll just say. And when the men reenlist on January 1st, you can join up at that time. Then you can be a real soldier, uniform, and all. How's that sound to you now?"

"Fine, suh. Sounds jest fine."

"All right then. Think I'll send you over to Plymouth. No colored recruiters are here right now looking for men like you. I'll just send you over to the 103rd Pennsylvania then. They've lost quite a few men to sickness. Too many." He ceases his words for a moment to shake his head in sorrow and disbelief.

"Hard to believe now. We got more men dying from *sickness* than from getting *shot in battle!*" The officer pauses once again as he sadly reflects upon the truth he has just stated.

Now looking up again at the young colored boy standing so patiently, he continues, "Meanwhile then, Toby, you've got to wait 'til you're eighteen. Up until that time we'll feed you, give you warm clothes, and some money to boot. Ten dollars a month. Now how does that sound to you? Better?"

Sounds mighty good to this ex-slave who never so much has felt the weight of a coin in his palm. "Money ob ma own? 'Magine dat. Yessuh! Thank yuh, suh!"

The recruiter is aware of the heroic exploits this past July of the 54th Massachusetts (Colored) Infantry. He is aware of the valor shown by those proud enlisted men daring to face certain death on the parapets of Battery Wagner, South Carolina. He very much is aware of the dauntless courage and determination demonstrated by those 600 inexperienced colored soldiers.

And so the recruiter decides to take a chance with this young black man who is standing before him. A man yearning for freedom so much he is willing to risk his life for it. However, the recruiter is wondering, *Is he going to have the necessary fortitude to deal with whatever discrimination he may have to face in this camp of white Pennsylvanians? Many of them hadn't so much as even seen a colored person before this war. Now here's this Toby who wants to be soldier. Well, I'm going to let him sign up with the 103rd then. They need cooks. Enlist him just like any other man. Don't have any idea how he's gonna get treated, though. I guess we'll just have to wait and see.*

So Toby boards the *Massasoit* to be carried west across the choppy Albemarle Sound from Roanoke Island to the mainland. To the small town of Plymouth on the south bank of the Roanoke River. There like many of the other contrabands, he is placed under contract to work for the army. His job is to assist the cooks. And this is quite agreeable to him because he has been given the promise that on January 1, 1864 he can enlist in the Union Army to become a real soldier.

A year ago on the first of January 1863 with his Emancipation Proclamation President Abraham Lincoln had declared freedom to all slaves in the eleven states in rebellion against the Union. However, contrary to popular belief, this piece of paper holds only a *promise*, not an *assurance* of freedom for the slaves. Lincoln has no jurisdiction whatsoever over the states in rebellion. They have left the Union. How then can he set their slaves free? And, besides, it seems the proclamation holds the promise of freedom only *if the slaves are successful in escaping* or *if they volunteer to enlist in the Union Army,* exactly what Toby is about to do.

However, the President does have jurisdiction over the slave owning border-states of Maryland, Delaware, Missouri, and Kansas as well as certain Union occupied sections of Virginia, Louisiana, and Tennessee. The question, therefore, has been posed, "So why does he not free these particular slaves?" Some people answer by saying that perhaps the 16th president has no intention of letting loose upon the United States 200,000 mostly illiterate and unskilled blacks, all victims of the South's "peculiar institution." Not having been in favor of slavery prior to the war, President Lincoln had been of the mind-set that the slaves indeed should be freed. However, emancipated *gradually and with compensation given to their owners*. And also prior to the war he had been in favor of colonizing those blacks in places such as Liberia, Haiti, and Latin America.

Therefore, with his proclamation Abraham Lincoln in reality had emancipated *not one* slave. Not until December 18, 1865 when Congress ratifies the 13th Amendment to the Constitution will the colored people of the United States be free. That date will be the true "Day of Jubilee" for the descendants of kidnapped Africans. The South's "peculiar institution" at last will be declared dead, albeit not laid to rest.

In May of 1863 when President Abraham Lincoln had stood at the head of a long rectangular table to address the members of his cabinet, he stated that the army was being severely depleted by disease, death, and desertion, and that the draft had been an utter failure. His deep-set gray eyes looked down intently at the serious upturned faces of the seated men nodding in total agreement. They all were well aware that Lincoln's words were quite accurate.

Especially concerned because the number of desertions was on the rise after the useless slaughter at Fredericksburg with approximately 13,000 casualties, the cabinet was listening intently. The President continued by saying that the North, however, had yet another source of manpower left.

The members of the cabinet were quite surprised, wondering just where Lincoln was expecting to find more men. From foreign countries as George Washington had? Mercenaries from France, Germany, Austria, or Poland? Or was President Lincoln perhaps proposing to lower the enlistment age? *Most of the cabinet members would not agree to that,* each man was thinking to himself. And so they had not the slightest inkling of what their President was about to say next, for they absolutely had no idea what source of manpower was left yet untapped in the North.

President Lincoln steeled himself for the volatile reaction he expected to erupt when the cabinet heard his next words. On that day the long lines etched so deeply into his gaunt face seemed to be even more prominent. His surprise announcement was that *he had decided to allow colored men to serve in the ranks.*

And as Lincoln had expected some members of his cabinet reacted in shock and outrage with one's leaping to his feet to flatly state, "Our boys'll never fight along side them!" With one's pounding his fist on the table to predict, "They'll all be cowards! You just mark my word!" And with one's flailing his arm in the air to allude, "They won't know how to fight! At the first battle they'll all turn tail and run!" However, the President was adamant, firmly standing his ground.

Lincoln's decision had come even *after* the First Louisiana Native Guards composed of *gens libres de couleur* had been formed in 1862 soon after the fall of New Orleans. Originally a Confederate regiment, it was composed of well-off free men of color, some of whom even owned plantations and slaves. This already organized unit had the distinction of being the first colored regiment to receive official recognition in the Union Army. Lincoln's decision came even *after* the First South Carolina Volunteers and the First Kansas "Colored" Volunteers had been organized, albeit *without* the government's official recognition.

Against the sage advice of many a Washington politician and while continuing to buck the tide of popular opinion, the President had established the Bureau of Colored Troops on May 22, 1863. Black men at last were being given *permission* to fight for their own freedom. Black men now were being given the *opportunity* to disprove those unfounded theories that they would be cowards in the face of battle.

President Lincoln finally had "reached out his strong sable arm," as the fiery black orator and abolitionist Frederick Douglass called the President's allowing blacks to join the military, albeit at a lower pay. Insultingly at a laborers' wage. Each man being given the paltry monthly sum of $10 of which $3 is to be *deducted* for clothing in contrast to the white soldier who is receiving $13 as well as an *additional* $3.50 allotment for his clothing.

Now at the end of 1863 Frederick Douglass's sons, Louis and Charles, are in the famed 54th Massachusetts Infantry. That regiment from its beginning has fought without receiving any pay whatsoever, flatly refusing to accept the demeaning lower amount. Eighteen months have to pass before the government is willing to grant equity in pay for colored and white. However, some totally unsympathetic Northerners are of the mind the Negroes should be content simply with the privilege of just being soldiers, regardless of the pay they may receive.

Frederick Douglass's two sons, like most other black recruits, have been segregated into the United States Colored Troops (USCT). Swiftly laws are passed, guaranteeing that those black regiments are to be led only by *white* officers. However, in spite of this mandate, a small number of colored men do manage to become commissioned, including a physician, Major Martin Delany of the 104th USCI (Infantry).

Very quickly colored regiments fill with men anxious to fight for the freedom of their race. Inexperienced as they are, oftentimes they get sent much too speedily into action. However, the word is out! Black men fight *gallantly*. They are not *cowards,* proving themselves at the ill-fated battles of Port Hudson and Milliken's Bend, both near Vicksburg, Mississippi. Here large numbers of black soldiers sacrifice their lives, as well as at Battery Wagner, Charleston, South Carolina where the men of the 54th Massachusetts demonstrate their valor.

Now at the end of 1863 up the Roanoke River seventy miles from Plymouth a division of the Rebel army has been posted at Tarboro, a most strategic town for the Confederacy because of its railroad depot. A rumor prevails that nearby at the small town of Hamilton an ironclad ram is being constructed in preparation for a Confederate attack on the Union fleet protecting Plymouth. If successful, this tactic will enable a Rebel land force to defeat the Union's army regiments garrisoned there.

While assisting the cooks, Toby, patiently waiting to be eighteen so he, too, can become a *bona fide* soldier, overhears the soldiers' conversations when they gather for their meals. Usually they are jesting and laughing, but today they must be concerned about something quite serious, not attacking their food with the usual amount of gusto.

"A Confederate ironclad? A ram, did'ya say?" one is questioning. "Up river? Well, if that's the truth, it could be a real threat ta us down here at Plymouth. A real threat, ta my way of thinkin'."

"Su'pose it can get down river this far? Comin' from Hamilton'n all?" another queries.

A third soldier adds his opinion to the speculations. "Naw! Don't believe it can. River's much too narrow down around these parts. And besides, ya know that Fort Gray can take care of it before it even gets down river this far. So yuz can jest put that crazy ironclad notion outta yer heads!" His confidence restoring that of the others, they begin to consume their meal with much more enthusiasm. "Say, Toby, got some more of that good coffee of yers?"

"Yessuh. Comin' right up." While pouring the strong black coffee into the soldiers' tin cups, Toby contemplates, *An ironclad? What's dis ironclad?* Toby has never heard of such a thing before today. Whom can he ask? *Maybe one ob duh udder colored men jest might be knowin',* he is thinking.

At this particular time on the mainland at Plymouth there are about twenty Negro recruits. Runaways like Toby, as well as several freed men. There is one in particular who seems to possess a wealth of valuable information. As a free man he has traveled around North Carolina, relating how he has seen the majestic snowy mountains rising in the western part of the state and how he has dipped his feet in the Atlantic Ocean in the east. So Toby decides to seek him out to ask him about the rumored ironclad.

"Boy, yuh be dis old an' don' be knowin' whut a ironclad be? Whar yuh been all yuh born days?" The older man laughingly signifies. Black folk love to signify. It is bantering, a friendly "one-uppance" kind of teasing.

"Nosuh. Don' know what it be. Neber heerd ob one."

"Dat's all right. Yuh mus' be from ober dere pas' dose piney woods, den. Far away from duh riber."

"Not 'xactly. From cross duh water. Chowan County. Past Edenton."

"Oh, well den. Eber seed duh steamboats on duh riber? All a huffin' an' a puffin' an' a blowin' smoke up in duh air out tru dey chimney. Be snortin' lak a mean ole bull, doncha know?" He laughs heartily. "Could hardly b'lieve ma eyes when Ah fust seed one."

He continues, "Whut a ironclad be? Well suh, den let me tell yuh all about it. Would yuh b'lieve dey takes one ob dose steamboats an' nails iron pieces tuh cover all ober de outsides? So den it looks jest lak a snake's skin. Den dey gots dem a ironclad fuh tuh ram duh enemy wif. Ah seed duh one duh Rebs call duh *Virginny*. Ain' nothin' tuh be scared 'bout, dough. Dose steamboats jest too big. Won' neber be gittin' dis far down riber."

The boy has seen boats steaming up and down the Chowan River near Edenton. In fact once when they were on a return trip home from the marketplace to the plantation Marse had pointed out one of them to Toby. "See that boat there, boy? Well, Ah'm expectin' tuh take me a ride on one of those some day real soon now."

Toby has difficulty conjuring up such a boat being covered all over with metal, but he figures it must be so, if that is what the Yankees are saying. It makes him ponder, though, over the thought of such a Confederate tactic. An ironclad to retake Plymouth? Could such a thing really be possible?

Back in 1860 antebellum Plymouth had been a lovely thriving small North Carolina town of tree canopied streets, red brick sidewalks, and stately white wooden houses surrounded by manicured lawns and neat beds of colorful flowers. An important port on a waterway, at that time the only viable means of transporting the South's important cash crops of cotton and tobacco from inland. A vital flourishing center for the sale of lumber, pitch, tar, and turpentine. A growing community, population 409 whites, 401 slaves, and 62 freedmen. A very peaceful place indeed.

However, since early 1862 the Federals had occupied this small town on the south bank of the fast flowing Roanoke River, eight miles from its mouth. And now a victim of the War Between the States, Plymouth is not the peaceful prestigious pretty place it once had been.

The Confederates had tried retaking it on December 10, 1862, their intentions being the removal of the "safety net" provided here at Plymouth for runaway slaves, conscription dodgers, unionists, and white refugees now so disillusioned with the South's cause. So the rebels launched an early morning surprise attack, having been lying in wait for just the right time. A time when the town might be the most vulnerable. Finally the opportune time had come. The day after Lieut. Commander Charles W. Flusser sailed the *USS Commodore Perry* up into the Chowan River.

In his absence the town got rampaged by the rebels. Many businesses were burned deliberately, as well as residences from which frightened inhabitants attired in only their bed clothing were forced to flee into the frigid early morning air. Even though considerable damage was done to the town, it still was to remain in the hands of the Federals.

By the end of 1863 about 2800 men from four infantry and artillery units are garrisoned here. This number includes nine companies of the 103rd Pennsylvania Volunteer Infantry with the tenth, Co. F, having been on Roanoke Island since June.

The soldiers from the North now are reassuring each other by surmising, "We got enough men here ta hold this place, fer sure. With our four forts and two redoubts the Rebs can't get ta us easy like. And besides that, ya know, we got all the gunboats ta protect us from anything comin' down the river. Ironclad ram or no."

Continuing with their reassurances, the Yankees recount that farther up the Roanoke River, Fort Gray will cut off any land communication, regardless from which direction the Rebels choose to approach the town. Fort Wessells will protect approaches from the southwest via Washington Road and then there is Fort Williams, the largest and located right in the center of town. It will command Acre Road, entering the town from the south in its direct center. So to the Yankees' way of thinking, all entrances to Plymouth are very well covered.

Toby, like all the other blacks, is familiar with the local terrain. He knows of the nearly impassable *woody* swamps, several of which lay south of town. Then there is that murky *morass* around the southwest corner of town and the *miry* swamp beginning south of it, extending north to the river. He knows of the tangling of vines, shrubs, and trees, forming thick impenetrable woods. So he, too, has been confident that Plymouth would remain safely in the hands of the Federals. However, now with this rumor of an ironclad ram on the river, he is becoming somewhat apprehensive.

Since Federal occupation, the town of Plymouth has become a Mecca for slaves escaping from nearby plantations, the number of contrabands having grown considerably in the past two years. News being spread rapidly by the "grapevine" divulges that "Old Pap," as the fifty-three year old West Pointer Gen. Henry Walton Wessells is affectionately called, will provide security for the refugees and their families. True, he does not turn them away, but this is not at all what the officer from the North was expecting to do: look after colored refugees.

Slave owners are stupefied by their "people's" sudden determination to leave the only kind of life they have ever known, even though totally unequipped for "crossing over Jordan." Totally unequipped for entering into the "Promised Land," that unknown realm called "Freedom." Owners actually are feeling *betrayed* by "their family," always having served so faithfully while smiling and appearing to be perfectly satisfied with their lot, except, of course, those *ingrates* attempting escape. Shocked and dismayed, some owners have come to realize that they may never have really known their slaves at all! *Two-faced like Janus.* The owners are wondering what *really* had been going on in the minds behind the *grinning masks*, now asking in astonishment, "Could it possibly have been freedom *all of the time?*"

A shantytown has emerged on the edge of the Great Dismal Swamp, a most dangerous place characterized by its deep tannin-tinted black water. Where a forest of cypress trees stands with upward protruding knobbed "knees." Where the water abounds with venomous water moccasins called cottonmouths by some folk.

Possessing few amenities of civilization, this medley of dilapidated shacks constructed of staves split from pitch pine logs houses black escapees who are living just as they always have. Except that now they are living with *hope.* With makeshift latrines having been dug, cleanliness and sanitation are being attempted. Three zealous white missionary ladies, Mrs. Freeman and her daughter Kate along with Mrs. Coombs from Ohio, have organized a school attended by persons of all ages anxious to learn how to read, write and cipher, knowing that these skills are necessary tools in "Freedomland." And the Sunday evening religious services now have "real" preaching delivered by a "real" preacher from the North.

Equipped with only their *faith*, these runaways have leaped blindly from bondage to freedom. Blindly since the state of bondage is what they know only too well, while the state of freedom is completely unknown to them. However, they do know which is the preferred one, especially for their children. And so in large numbers they flee the plantations to be under the protection of President Lincoln's army, albeit totally ignorant of the Yankees' reason for fighting.

To preserve the Union. The runaways do not know that this is the true reason why the white men of the North have left the safety of their homes to come down here to fight. The refugees are under the mistaken assumption that it is to *free them*, which is what the "grapevine" erroneously has relayed. In the meantime, however, many of the Yankees finally are figuring out that the key to the South's economy is in *its slaves.* So although not starting out to emancipate them, this is exactly what the soldiers are doing now, some even riding from farm to farm, informing the slaves that they are free to leave.

And so the slaves continue arriving at Plymouth from nearby plantations such as Somerset, Sahara, and Pea Ridge owned by Josiah Collins, Ebenezer Pettigrew, and John Newberry respectively. The slaves are being classified by the Federals as "contraband." Spoils of war just like any of the Confederates' other possessions. Just like their horses and cattle. Therefore, the Yankees feel justified in allowing them to stay. The first time in their lives being paid to do anything, many of the refugees are eagerly contracting with the army as cooks, teamsters, personal servants, laborers, and laundresses.

Not wanting to be thought of as mere "things," though, many blacks object to the term "contraband" being applied to *them*. Since they are free now, they want to be categorized as "citizens." Even though they may not be "things," they are not allowed to be citizens of this country. They are unaware that they are not even considered "whole" human beings according to the South's method of evaluating slaves. According to the Constitution of the United States, for purposes of congressional representation and taxation each slave is counted as *3/5 of a person*. And because of this, each master is very careful to account for each and every slave in his possession, albeit not by name. Only by gender and age.

So until this controversial problem can be solved, the ex-slaves simply are being called "colored refugees." And not until 1868 when Congress ratifies the 14th Amendment will the word "citizen" ever be used in reference to people of African descent.

The "shakes" from ague are quite common among people living near southern swamps, the white soldiers from the North not being exempt. During a single week alone two hundred and forty men of the 85th New York Regiment garrisoned at Plymouth report sick. Although some of them do survive their bouts of alternating chills and fever, others less fortunate get buried in the graveyard next to the unfinished new Grace Episcopal Church surrounded by twelve sycamore trees, each named for one of the disciples of Jesus. Many years later published in newspapers, "Ripley's Believe it or Not" will feature these same twelve trees. It seems that during a lightning storm one of the trees was struck and died. And, *believe it or not*, it was the one named *Judas!*

Once the weather turns chilly no new cases of "the shakes" ever appear. No one can figure out why. Not the doctors even. And strangely, the black refugees do not seem to have as much susceptibility to the illness as the whites. No one knows the reason for this, either. No one even knows the *cause* of "the shakes." Of all the theories proffered—miasma from the swamps, foul smelling drinking water, tainted food, or even thin blood—none are anywhere near the truth.

For it is not known at this time that the pesky biting female mosquitoes propagating in the swamps are the real culprits. Those insects being the hosts of a minuscule parasite—one causing in humans the dreaded disease known as *malaria*. And certainly not known is the relationship between malaria and a certain human blood condition, "sickle-cell anemia." For at this time in history no one even knows that humans have such things as blood *cells*, let alone that they might be sickle or crescent-shaped instead of the normal round. Certainly no one knows that a human carrier of the sickle-cell trait has a *guaranteed immunity* to that terrible disease transmitted by the bite of the female *Anopheles* mosquito. And now here in Plymouth, North Carolina no one knows that immune carriers are among the refugees with origins in the malarial infested continent of Africa.

Whenever they can find the free time, Toby and his closest friend, twenty-one year-old Private Richard West, a runaway from nearby Bertie County, enjoy visiting with some of the folk in the shantytown. Although not considering himself especially frivolous, Toby does take great delight in listening to the melodious singing and syncopated clapping as well as the harmonicas, banjos, guitars, and tambours. He enjoys watching the energetic dancers performing their intricate shuffles and high stepping jigs as they engage, so it seems, every muscle in their agile bodies. However, he is not drawn to gambling, drinking, womanizing, and fighting as some of the men are. If he has to fight he figures it will be for something worthwhile. And so when the other black soldiers signify about his seriousness he "pays them no mind." Toby has plans.

Now that he knows considerably more about that "Promised Land" up North he intends seeing it one day for himself. Fast current rivers called by strange sounding Indian names—Monongahela, Susquehanna, Lackawanna, Juniata, Allegheny, Youghiogheny, and Delaware. Towering mountains whose deep valleys are dotted with verdant emerald farms. Cities, towns, and boroughs where a colored man might earn a living. Where he can be married legally by a "real" preacher who will include "til death do us part" in the ceremony. Where he will have the assurance that his freeborn children will learn to read, write, and cipher.

Chapter 8

The 1863 Letters of the Corporal

Fort Williams
Plymouth, North Carol.
Friday, May 9th 1863

My dear wife,

I take this pencil in hand hoping that this letter will find you & the boy in the best of helth. I know how much you love the spring so I know you are feeling good except that I'm not home yet.

Some of the men here are suffering from sickness but I got no complaints. Many of them have the shakes. There sick for a couple of days & then there alright for a while. Then they get a fever & chills & there sick all over again. So far I don't have the shakes. Don't know where they come from. Some say the night fumes from the swamps. Could be. There sure are a lot of swamps here all foggy & smelly. If its true I don't know how to stop breathing it in then.

We was ordered Saturday morning to pack are napsacks & fall in & we marched to the New Berne wharf. There we got on bord the ship they call the Thomas Collyer. At night we sailed out. In the morning of the 6th we sailed into the Albamarlee Sound past a pretty little town called Edenton. Could see it from the deck. The ship stopped there for a short while when the officers went ashore but we had to stay on bord. Then we crossed over to the mouth of the Ronoak River. We sailed to this here small town they call Plymouth. Thats just like where the Pilgrims landed in Massachusis. By the time we got here we was very hungry. It was about noon so we stopped & ate before we marched on to the field where we stayed overnight. Next day we went to a big fort in the middle of the town. They call it Fort Williams. Two of the companies went inside the fort but we was ordered to pitch are tents outside.

There are only a few towns people left around here. Most probably left after Plymouth fell into are hands last year. There's a lot of colored people around too. Guess they ran away from there owners. Don't know what they expect us to do for them. Maybe they just want to be safe. That could be enuff for them. Can't tell what there thinking.

Can't imagine what it would be like to be owned by somebody else like an animal. I know I couldn't stand it.

This here town might a been pretty once before it was burned down. Seems are gunboats caused some bildings to catch on fire when the town was first took in '62. Then I hear what was left the rebs burned down a few months later. It's too bad. Appears like it must have been an important place once upon a time. Its located right on the Ronoak River.

Sure would like to do some fishing when I get some spare time. Hear there's plenty of shad & trout. I can cook them over a fire in front of my tent. I'd certainly relish some fried shad roe. Won't taste nothing like your good cooking but its better than salt pork & hardtack. I'm sick of it.

When I come home I want some of your sauerbraten with potato dumplings. Then I want some corn pudding & coleslaw & apple pie & whatever else you want to fix. Haven't had any sauerkraut & mashed potatoes since I left home. My mouth is hankering for some of your fried oatmeal scrapple & a big piece of shoo fly pie covered with whipped cream, too. No need to worry about me complaining about your food ever again. Rite soon please. Love,

Fort Williams
Plymouth, North Carol.

My dear wife,
I take my pencil in hand with the hopes that this letter finds you & the boy in good helth. Got no complaints just that I wish I could go home. This last month has been very hot here. Thunderstorms come every few days. Then the lightning's so brite. Keeps up for hours.

Are uniforms are so hot but we got to drill in them each & every day & we have to carry are weapons too. Today we didn't do so much drilling. Never have to do much on the Sabbath. However we had to march for two whole hours. Captain said we was so sloppy & we'd shame him for sure at the review. Maybe its true. We was so hot & loaded down.

Had some excitement here on the 11th. A fire started at the fort. Two companies was target practicing & for some reason a busted shell started a fire. Lots of excitement when the boys was running around filling lots of buckets of water. They formed a human water line & then they got the fire out *at last. But what they really needed was a modern fire wagon just like ares in town.*

You know what I told you about putting sod all around the tents. That's so to keep the dust & mud down after it rains. Well we finished all that last week. Did a good job I think. Thanks to the rain the grass is taking good & the place looks nice & fresh.

Yesterday Company F sailed over to Ronoak Island on the Gen.'s dispatch boat. Carries the mail every day. Guess they'll be gone for a few months. My buddies William Fulton and Franklin Mohney from Clarion County are in that company. Wish I was going too. I'm sick & tired of this place. A change would be nice. Maybe when there company comes back in six months mine will get to go.

Couple of days ago I met some fine fellows from the 12th New York Cavalry. They come riding in with there flags waving. Made quite a sight. There uniforms were all trimmed with yellow where mine has blue. In case you don't know blue's the color for the infantry and yellow for the cavalry. Lieut. Alonzo Cooper showed his horses to us farm boys. Think I should be in the cavalry as good as I can ride but its too late now. The cavalry sure has got some fine horseflesh & the men are all good riders. They have to train every day too. Then when they get done some of the colored men have to go out & clean up the field before we can go out and drill. To my mind there not doing such a good job at it. Sometimes they miss some of the manoor the horses left behind. I just don't know how they can miss it unless there doing it on purpose. Its sitting right there just as big as day. You can imagine how disgusted we are if we step in it when we're marching.

Got to finish riting now cause I want to get this out for the 10 o'clock mail. Got your letter two days ago. Tell Mam I'm doing fine & not to worry none. Glad everybody's good.

    Love,

Fort Williams
Plymouth, North Carol.
Sunday, June 28th 1863

My dear wife,
I take my pencil in hand hoping that this letter will find you & the boy in the best of helth. The wether here is

very rainy but it is very warm. There puddles of water all around. The sun's not drying them up fast enuff cause every day it rains again. Many of the men have the shakes & are laid up in the hospital. Thank God I'm fine so far. Don't know why the shakes come to some men & not to others. Just am grateful they don't come to me.

An interesting thing happened last week. The 1st D.C Colored Regiment arrived on the 11th. They come from Washington City. Never thought I'd see so many colored men in are blue uniforms. Carried themselves well I must admit. Was impressed as I watched them marching in perfect precishun. Better than my company does I must say. We seem to straggle along so. Captain's always complaining about that. What impressed me the most was the seriousness on their faces. We had all heard that Pres. Lincoln was going to let the colored men join up what with all the trouble he had with the draft. Lots of us objected. Some said they wouldn't fight alongside of no colored men.

I guess Pres. Lincoln felt he had to do something fast. Its not fair the way some rich men can pay $300 for somebody to take their place either. Some are calling it a rich man's war but a poor man's fight. Heard all about those terrible riots up in New York City last month. I guess not everybody's so eager to teach those johnny rebs a lesson or two.

Just guess I had never expected to see any of those colored men the same place as me. This is the first time I've been up close to any. One thing about them that surprised me was all of the different shades there skin is. Saw some who are very dark & there are some white as me & you. I asked about that since I thought they all had to be together in units for just colored men. I was told that the men who looked white were colored too. Don't know how that's possible. They say that only the officers are real white men. Can't figure why anybody wants to call those men colored when they look white to everybody. One of them even has eyes the color of blue like yours. Even saw a red headed fellow. Just don't understand it at all how there colored. Wonder what those fellows are going to do after this war is over. Know what I'd do if I was them. Most of us don't think those colored soldiers will be very good in battle. Wonder if they ever had a rifle in their hands before. First trouble they'll probably all turn tail & run. That's what most of us figure.

Are regiment was happy to get new Springfield rifles on the 8th. We like them better than those old heavy Austrian muskets. They shoot better but I'm not going to get into that. You wouldn't understand. Just be happy that we got better arms. Glad we got them when we did cause soon after I had to go on picket duty. Wasn't supposed to but with so many men sick we have to do there jobs & are own too. Rather be on picket than be sick with the shakes or a stomackake. So I'm really not complaining.

You'll be happy to hear that an agent from the Christian Commission is here. He preached all this past week. I went to hear him when I wasn't on picket duty. Reminds me of are revrend. Preaches rite out of the Bible. My Testament's getting torn real bad. I carry it always right over my heart. If you can find one the size of this one you give me before I left then send it to me please.

Sorry I have not been able to get home for even a short visit. None of us got that furlow they promised us. Say they can't let us go home now that we're so close to pushing those rebs back where they come from. They say they need are experience. That may be so but we're all sick of war. Just want to sit on my front porch with you sitting beside me while I smoke my pipe in peace. Want to see the boy running & throwing a stick to his new pup. That's all I want. Be sure to pray for me on the Sabbath.
Love,

Fort Williams
Plymouth, North Carol.
Thursday, Nov. 26th 1863

My dear wife,
I take my pencil in hand on this National Thanksgiving day hoping that you & the boy are still in good helth as you was when last I heard from you. This is my second Thanksgiving away from home. Hope you both had a good day with your family & that you didn't get snowed in like last year.

Went this morning to worship service. Lt. Col. Taylor from the 101st gave the address. The 101st & the 103rd always seem to be together now. Saw my cousin afterwards. He's fine too. He sends his regards to you, Mam & Paps.

Last week when we formed for drill the captain asked us to shoulder arms if we was willing to reenlist as veterans on Jan. 1ˢᵗ. Guess how many did. Not a single one. I didn't. No one else moved either. We all want to go home. We only signed up for three months in the beginning. Now its almost three years & they want us to sign up again. I say no. Let some other men come. Maybe if I don't sign up then I'll be home by the end of January. Would walk all the way if I had to. Pray that I'll be home soon.

Are winter quarters will be warmer than the tents were. We're bilding log huts now to keep out the cold. Its surprising how this town's changed since we got here. It looked real awful before. Now it looks better. There's the forts & now the log huts. I imagine there was nice houses here too before the town was burned.

Its getting to be too crowded what with all the slaves running away to here. After the rebs put in a conscripshun act there's a lot of white men here too who don't want to go in the Reb army. If there between 18 & 45 there supposed to go in. But all they want is to stay home on there farms. There poor farmers who are being rounded up by the rebs & forced to fight. So many of them have come here instead and brought there families too for safety. Didn't dare leave them behind. There's a whole regiment of North Carolina men here now who have joined up with us. They tell us that the rebs call them Buffalos. Didn't say why though.

Last month the dispatch boat took a large number of colored people east over to Ronoak Island. They should be safer there just in case there's trouble here. There just waiting for this here war to get over so they can be on there way. Right now if the rebs catch hold of any of them they'll be sent back to being slaves. I know I'd do anything not to do that too.

Rite soon. I look forward to your letters always. Thanks for the flannel shirt & the wool socks you knitted for me. I really needed them,
Love,

Chapter 9
A New Name for Toby

The recruiter feels compelled to discuss with the Negroes something quite vital before their being mustered into the Union army. "Men, now before you get sworn in I need to tell you something very important. You see, many very determined Rebs have vowed to kill any of you colored men they find who've taken up arms against the South. That's even though their President, Jefferson Davis, says that he wants you returned to your owners." Standing proudly at attention in their blue uniforms the colored recruits listen intently to the officer's words.

"They say they'll shoot dead any colored man they find in blue. And they say they'll kill the white officers who trained them, too." The recruiter pauses to be sure his words are sinking in. "Men, do you understand what I'm telling you?"

Yes, of course, they understand. No recruit, however, is going to change his mind about joining the Union army. Each one considers it his personal responsibility to take up arms against those who have vowed to keep him and his race enslaved. Indeed the colored soldiers have a powerful reason for fighting fiercely when contemplating the fatal consequences awaiting them if the Union does not win this war. And they are very aware that not only are they fighting for their *own* freedom, they are fighting also for the freedom of those they left behind. Remembering their officer's dire warning, all of the colored men have good reason for apprehension upon hearing about the threat of the Confederate ironclad ram.

As the year 1863 is closing, the Federal forces garrisoned at Plymouth, North Carolina still do not believe the Rebels have any possible chance of retaking the town. Especially not with the protection of the fleet of Union gunboats, *Bombshell, Ceres, Miami, Southfield,* and *Whitehead* commanded by the efficient Lieut. Commander Charles Williamson Flusser. And so the Federal soldiers feel most confident that no boat, ironclad or not, possibly could be a real threat to the well-fortified Plymouth.

In this positive climate a young colored refugee named Toby, aged eighteen, will enlist in the Union army. *Tuhmorrow be de fust day ob January. Be a new year. Be a new man. Be a real soljer. No more "Tobe," what Marse call me. No more slave name fer me.* These are Toby's last thoughts as he drifts off to sleep on the final day of the year 1863.

Several days ago Toby had been summoned to the tent of the recruiter who had just completed concocting a new supply of ink by mixing a black powder with water. Toby had stood patiently, watching the officer sharpen a brand new quill with his penknife.

"Mornin', suh."

"Good morning, Toby. I just wanted to inform you that on the first day of January you'll officially become a member of the Union Army, just like you was promised. First, though, I need you to give me some information." He had placed a clean sheet of white paper on his table next to the bottle of ink and quill pen. Picking up the pen, he was ready to record the boy's responses.

"Now then, Toby. Know where you was born?"

"Yessuh, Ah do. Chowan County."

In his spidery handwriting the officer recorded what Toby said. "All right then. Age?"

"18 years, suh."

"Occupation?"

"Suh?" The young black man's forehead furrows. He does not understand just what the officer is asking.

The officer looks up at the boy. "Well Toby. You see, I need to put down what kind of work you were doing before now."

Now Toby understands and quickly responds by asking, "Oh! Does yuh got tuh put down on dat paper Ah be a slave, suh?"

"No, Toby. I most certainly do not. I'll just put down here that previously you were a laborer. That's what you've been since you came here."

Sounds better, Toby thinks. He realizes that what goes down on that paper can be forever. "Thank yuh, suh."

"Now for your name. 'Toby,' first?" The officer's pen is poised, ready again to dip into the jar of black ink.

He is surprised at Toby's quick response. "Suh, now if'n yuh don' mind, Ah don' want tuh be called 'Toby' no more. Cause dat's what Marse call me an' now Ah ain' belong tuh him no more."

"That's so. All right. So you won't be 'Toby' then. You can be whoever you want to be. By the way, you do realize that you'll need two names, don't you?"

"Nosuh. Hadn't thought none 'bout dat."

"Well, you're a free man now, Toby. Free men are required to have a first name *and a last name*. Just one's not going to do for you any more. So then? Want to use your master's name? Some folks do, you know."

"Oh! Nosuh! Don' want Marse's name!" the boy answers vehemently.

"All right then, just what do you want to be called?"

"Suh, Ah admire whut yuh be thinkin'. Take any name yuh be gibbin' me. A free man's name. That's all. Hab no particulars."

"All right then. Umm." The officer rears back in his chair, hands folded behind his head as he contemplates. "Now let me think about this." After a short time he rights his chair, saying, "Before this war I knew a fine gentleman by the last name of 'Crowder.' He was from Union County, though. Makes me wonder what's happened to him because of this war. Anyway, Crowder's not a common name like John is. Your name'll be unusual then. So how about being Crowder from Chowan County? Why not? What do you think?"

"'Crowder'? Hmmm." Toby took a moment to mull over the name. Then with a pleased smile he replied, "Yessuh. Never heard ob dat name before, but do b'lieve Ah kin lib wid it."

Picking up the quill, the officer dips into the ink to write "Crowder." Looking up again at the boy he continues, "Now then, what about your last name? Some free men take the name of 'Lincoln.' You know, after their emancipator. How's that? What do you think? 'Crowder Lincoln?' Think you'd like 'Lincoln' for your last name?"

"Nosuh. Mind yuh, Ah do admire Marse Linkum an' all, but his name jest don' suit *me*."

"A name to *suit you*, is it to be?" the officer chuckles. "Well, I'll really have to think hard about that one." Again placing his hands behind his head he tilts back his chair as he ponders a last name for the young colored recruit. One that will suit *him*.

After a few moments, he bolts up while declaring jubilantly, "Ah! Yes! I do believe I have just the name! Certainly does suit *you*! 'Patient.' Toby, you've been a most patient man since you arrived here last fall. I certainly do admire you for that. I expect there'll be many 'Lincolns.' And I suppose even 'Washingtons.' But I doubt that you'll ever run into another 'Patient.' No, I suspect it'll be a name of your very own."

Born on a plantation near Hale's Ford, Virginia, a reddish-haired gray-eyed mulatto slave boy named "Booker," aged seven in 1863, is going to think himself quite unique when he chooses "Washington" as his last name. He will say that not many other people have the privilege of choosing their own name. However, he is not quite as unique as he imagines.

"A name ob ma very own, suh?" Crowder chuckles softly "Yes, dat name'll suit me jest fine Ah think."

"So then, Crowder Patient. Congratulations. On the first day of January you'll be able to enlist in army of the United States of America."

"Yessuh. Thank yuh, suh."

"Dismissed."

The name of the new recruit is recorded with a strange spelling "Pacien," not a name or even a word found in any language. Due perhaps to the interpretation of the recorder's listening to Crowder as he speaks his name, variations of the spelling will be found on different documents. Perhaps the first recorder did not hear a "t" on the end of his name as Crowder pronounced it and the writer spelled phonecically what he was hearing. Whatever the reasons, the name is spelled *first as* "Pacien," to be followed by "Pacient," "Patient," and lastly the permanent "Patience."

The slave boy Toby now has metamorphosed into the army recruit Crowder Pacien. With three months of training ahead of him, will he be able to do what is expected of him? Will he learn how to be a soldier as he steels himself against bigoted slights and slurs? There is but one answer for eighteen-year old Crowder Pacien. *Yes, he must*.

He has already heard stories of prejudice such as the one about young white soldiers from the North, paradoxically fighting for the freedom of all persons, who think it great fun to throw bags of white flour into the faces of unsuspecting black refugees. He has heard of other mean-spirited tricks, like throwing live cartridges into the open fires of the blacks. Gleefully the white soldiers laugh as they watch refugees showered with soot and ashes suddenly leap to their feet. And so to be able to endure these stories and all the bigoted barbs he hears being leveled at the contrabands, Crowder remembers his Aunt Cassie's admonition about *smiling*. Therefore, he continues to smile, at least outwardly as patiently he waits. Waiting for the freedom *to do what he chooses*.

Finally the several long months of scrubbing, paring, peeling, and chopping have passed. On January 1, 1864 the boy Toby, enlists in the Union Army as Crowder Pacien, being assigned to Company C of the 103rd Pennsylvania Volunteers. Since he is not able to read the terms of his enlistment for himself, these have been read to him for his understanding.

P. | *103* | Pa.

Crandes Pacin

Appears with rank of _____ on

**Muster and Descriptive Roll of a Detach-
ment of U. S. Vols. forwarded**

for the *103* Reg't Pa. Infantry. Roll dated

Plymouth, N.C., April 4, 1864.

Where born *Chowan Co. N.C.*

Age *18* y'rs; occupation *Laborer*

When enlisted *Jan. 1*, 1864.

Where enlisted *Plymouth N.C.*

For what period enlisted *3* years.

Eyes *Black*; hair *Black*

Complexion *Black*; height *5* ft. *5* in.

When mustered in *April 4*, 1864.

Where mustered in *Plymouth N.C.*

Bounty paid $ *100*; due $ *100*

Where credited _____

Company to which assigned *C.*

Remarks: *Enlisted in accordance
with G.O. 73 Oct. 7, Sec. 10,
series 1863 from War Dept*

Book mark: _____

_____ *Green*
Copyist.

(839)

Enlistment record on January 1, 1864

Now the first roll of the day is being called. The young black recruit anxiously listens for the sound of his new name. The names are in alphabetical order, but Private Crowder Pacien does not know anything about this. He is just standing patiently. Following several successive roll calls he will know just when his name is about to be called.

"Pacien, Crowder." There it is! He hears his new name. A *free* man's name.

"Here, suh!"

The ex-slave boy for whom a last name had never been needed before is now a member of the Union Army, having been forced to wait until December 25, 1863 when he celebrated his 18th birthday. It was the best birthday he had ever experienced in his young life because at last he is *free*. Oh, yes, he knows he must labor still, but now without a whip's incentive.

Each year he always enjoyed his birthday because it coincides with the Jonkonnu (pronounced John Canoe) festivities. A week of revelry originating in West Africa, it is practiced on many plantations in North Carolina such as Somerset Place. Perhaps practiced ever since 1786 when eighty slaves had been imported there directly from Africa. On that particular plantation the celebration called "John Koonering" always takes place on Christmas Day, the one day of the year slaves are allowed on the *other* side of the white picket fence separating the "big house" from the rest of the plantation. The one day of the year the field slaves are allowed to cross that border which every other day separates blacks from whites. The one day of the year the master and his wife deem to shake the hands of "their people."

Perhaps it is from Somerset Place in Washington County the custom has spread across North Carolina to other places such as Edenton in Chowan County where the young slave girl Harriet Jacobs lived hidden in her grandmother's attic before her successful escape to the North. Here, too, the festivities are held on Christmas day where they are called Johnkannaus. Bands of performing slaves are allowed to come into town from nearby plantations and even though varying from place to place, the carnival atmosphere always is the same.

On Marse's place Jonkonnu has dancing masked male slaves lavishly costumed, heads decorated with cattle horns and rear-ends with cattle tails. The boisterous dancers run around beating their sheepskin gumba boxes, loudly striking jawbones and metal triangles, noisily blowing wind instruments, imbibing rum which at any other time would be verboten, and begging monetary gifts from Marse and Missie after having entertained them.

From other plantations Marse has heard disturbing news concerning escapes and thefts, even murders during this time of unbridled frivolity. However, in spite of his nervous concern he tolerates this lax period of Jonkonnu with the expectation that as soon as it is over his boisterous slaves are going to revert back to docile workers for yet another year. However, some of his cronies such as William Pettigrew warn Marse that he is being much too lenient. Because of the trouble it had caused in prior years, Jonkonnu is prohibited now at Pettigrew Place on Lake Phelps. Marse's reasoning, however, is that his "people" need this time for gaiety and enjoyment. Then they will have something to look forward to the next year.

Crowder Pacien is happy not just because he is finally a free man, but also because he now is a recruit in the Union army. Maybe he is eighteen years old and then again, maybe he is not. Age does not really matter when it comes to fighting, such as in the case of a tall husky sixteen-year old from York County, Pennsylvania. When he expressed the desire to join the Union Army his father had objected vehemently while his mother broke down in tears due to the fact that her older boy already had gone off to the war.

Intending to join the army, one of the hired men left the farm to return to his home in Indiana County. At the same time the sixteen-year old had sneaked away, too. Prior to standing in front of a recruiter for the 103rd Pennsylvania Volunteers, the boy first had placed a sliver of paper in his shoes with number 18 written on it. Then upon being asked if he were over eighteen he answered with straight face and crossed fingers, "Yes, sir! I'm over eighteen."

Seen hoisting Springfield rifles much too heavy for their frail immature bodies are cow-licked freckled-faced, smooth cheeked boys who, as anyone can see, are closer to having fifteen years than eighteen. Seeking adventure just like that young private from York County, they temporarily have escaped the tediousness of farms, factories, mills, iron furnaces, and coal mines of the North for what they had thought would be a short lived three month duration of soldiering. Sadly, though, many of these youngsters are never to see home and family again.

Surprisingly, the Federal army does not seem to have an age limit at the other end of the scale since the oldest soldier is said to have *eighty* years. Neither do they refuse on the grounds of height. The tallest recorded soldier is 6'11" while the shortest is only 3'4" from the tips of his boots to the blue kepi set jauntily atop his head.

On January 2, 1864, the very next day after Crowder Pacien's enlistment, his company, C of the 103rd Pennsylvania Volunteers, receives orders to replace Company F over on Roanoke Island where the Federals are concentrating on protecting the entrance into the Albemarle Sound. This is necessary in order to prevent the Confederates' importing and exporting with Europe as well as having access to salt supplies from the Atlantic Ocean. Then on the following day, January 3rd, Company F with the corporal's friends Privates William Fulton and Franklin Mohney will return to Plymouth, thereby assuring that nine companies of the 103rd always are present on the mainland.

Attired in his blue uniform, kepi on his head, Crowder Pacien gathers his possessions so as to be ready by five o'clock, joining others boarding Gen. Wessell's dispatch boat, the *Massasoit*. The new recruit is to receive his military training on Roanoke Island, not here at Plymouth. It does not really matter to him where he gets it. What matters to him only is that at last he is in the Union Army!

So once again he finds himself sailing across the gunmetal gray Albemarle Sound. As he leans against the railing the brisk breeze nips his face while his tongue detects a briny taste on his lips. Large white seagulls, ever on the alert for a tasty meal, caw and flap while tailing the ship. Crowder wonders if Marse ever did get to sail on a steamboat like he had wanted. *Yessuh! Wish Marse could see me now*, he chuckles to himself. *This sho' beats drivin' his team.* At that thought he emits a hearty laugh.

"So? What're ya laughin' about, Pacien? Don't see nothin' funny about goin' over there ta the island. Ya know, I was expectin' ta be goin' home by now," one of the young Pennsylvania soldiers grouses.

"That's so," Crowder replies, "an' Ah'm sho' sorry yuh ain'. Somethin' come tuh mind, an' Ah jest had tuh let it out. Hope it don't bother yuh none."

"Nah. Don't bother me none. Only wish *I* had something ta be glad about." The young soldier has no idea on this brisk January morning that he has plenty to be glad about, but not until three months hence will he know just what.

Crowder is indeed sorry to have to leave behind his newfound friends, especially the affable Richard West of Co. I. They have promised to look for each other after the war is over. However, fate is going to bring them together before that time!

The enlisted men of the 103rd choose to fix much of their own food in open fires outside their "A" frame tents, realizing that the inexperienced army cooks do not have the "know how" to prepare decent meals. On the other hand, the commissioned officers have no intentions of preparing their own meals. And so this is the job assigned to Private Crowder Pacien. A cook to serve the officers since he is already experienced. Not exactly what he wants to be doing, however, much better than the backbreaking fatigue duty assigned to many of the other black soldiers.

On spring days back on the plantation when torrential thunderstorms would prevent his going out to the fields, the boy had watched his Aunt Cassie's preparing meals. And so he had somewhat of a vague idea how things are done, even though he never had to do any cooking himself before last October. At that time he quickly learned how to brew a mean pot of coffee, so black and strong, so the soldiers said, it might "float an iron wedge." The officers he serves now customarily imbibe four to five cups a day, something not at all good for their stomachs. When they report to the doctor's tent to complain about gastric upset, he tells them to stop guzzling so much coffee, but stubbornly they refuse to heed his advice.

A certain officer has taken a liking to Crowder. Admiring his positive attitude, his never complaining about whatever, whichever, or whomever. The officer is learning a lot from the young black recruit. About surviving adversity, about making the best of whatever happens to be facing him, about tenacity. About how cheerfulness and laughter, even whistling can relieve stress. And Crowder, conditioned to see and hear and wait, is learning much, as well. Learning about how things are done by the men from the North. Learning about the diverse lifestyles and occupations found in the state of Pennsylvania. Learning how to improve his speech. All the while waiting patiently for the Yankees to become the victors of this War Between the States so he can continue on his journey north.

Meanwhile, the officer is learning to eat foods he has never heard of before. Such as "greens." Crowder had watched his Aunt Cassie use chunks of greasy salt pork for seasoning whatever vegetables she could grow in her little truck-patch right outside her cabin door. Collards being her very favorite greens, she would have them boiling in the iron kettle when her bone-weary boys came in from the fields. On chilly evenings especially, she would ply them with steaming bowls of "pot likker" to warm their bellies. Little did she know that the nourishment so needed for keeping her boys functioning efficiently out in the fields was right there in the bottom of those bowls.

The officer, also, is grateful to warm his belly with Crowder's "pot likker" from boiled collards, kale, mustard, or turnip greens found growing on nearby farms. And Crowder often bakes a skillet of corn bread, also something the man from the North had never tasted before. "Umm. As good as a piece of cake! Especially when you spread some honey or molasses on it," compliments the officer, washing down his last bite with a swallow of Crowder's strong black coffee.

The officer is learning to relish a plateful of boiled cabbage, carrots, turnips, rutabagas, or white potatoes, all seasoned with *bacon* when it can be found. Crowder, however, is used to eating his vegetables seasoned with less desirable hog parts—ears, snouts, tails, rind, feet, and even the head. He has his doubts, though, that the officers would appreciate eating, let alone even knowing about, any of these.

Chuckling to himself as he goes about his work, he considers just what might be the reaction of the white officers from the North if he were to serve them a plate of chopped *chit'lins*. He is certain the soldiers knowingly would not relish consuming *hog intestines*. However, for generations black folk have survived by eating the leftovers of white folk. Amazing how to future generations of blacks a "mess" of greens and heap of chitterlings dashed with hot sauce will become a delicacy. They will be high on their list of "soul" foods. Vivid *reminders of survival*.

Sometimes, a slab of bacon can be found on a nearby farm, but if not, Crowder then is forced to use the army rations of salt pork. "What? Salt pork again?" a disgruntled officer complains, examining his bowl to spy small chunks of fat glistening there among the white beans.

Wistfully the officer shakes his head from side to side as he remarks, "Will I be glad ta get home ta my wife's good cookin'," admitting that he really had not appreciated it much before.

The Federals have been issued orders to scour the countryside. First, routing out all Confederate sympathizers. Then confiscating equipment such as saddles and harnesses. Dismantling split rail fences to use as cooking fuel. Demolishing railroads and bridges. Foraging for food. Searching for anything of value, especially jewelry and silver. And if they have no use for what they find, destroying all of it, the fate of thousands of bales of cotton the rebels had hoped to export.

Often the Yankees come across smokehouses well stocked with cured hams and icehouses with brandy, all of which the soldiers confiscate. Sometimes farmers are found who have not sympathized with the secessionists or who now wish to placate the invaders. A certain farmer, upon seeing "the handwriting on the wall," willingly offers the invading Federals a substantial portion of his bounty. Reasoning with his wife, his premise is, "Maybe if we give them some food now, then they won't come snoopin' around later. Won't start diggin' an' lookin' fer what they think we hid." His concern is justified because indeed his wife has buried silver and valuable jewelry under her mother's gravestone in the small family cemetery fenced in by wrought iron, only a short distance from the farmhouse.

Many times, however, when fresh food cannot be found, Crowder must resort to preparing the dried white army beans and yellow cornmeal provided by the government. Importantly, he has had to learn how to skim off the weevil carcasses floating to the top of the kettles of soaking beans.

Scrutinizing his bowl, an officer had once asked, "Just what are these black specks in my soup?" When Crowder looked, he knew just what they were, but he was not particular about the officer knowing.

"Could be jest some ob dose spices Ah use tuh spark up de beans, suh.

"With legs and wings?"

Aware that the officer is ever on the lookout, Crowder knows he has to make sure black specks never again appear in the soup.

Chapter 10

The 1864 Letters of the Corporal

> Fort Williams
> Plymouth, North Carol.
> Jan. 5th 1864

My dear wife,
Glad to hear that your Ma's feeling better now. The croup's hard to get over what with that coffing & all. I had a bad cold a while back but some strong hot tea laced with a little turpentine & sugar chased it rite away. Know you thought I'd be back home by now. I did too but this war's not over yet. Wish the rebs would just give up & go back home but it don't seem like there going to. Pres. Lincoln says he needs old soldiers like us to win the war. There's too many new ones who don't know what there doing. I'm just glad are boy's not old enuff to be in this war. Only can pray that it'll be over before he is. There's some young boys here who should be back home in the schoolroom & here there shooting rifles.

We've been offered a $400 bonus & a 30 day furlow if we sign on again. Most of the men wasn't going to do it but when we got to thinking about what we could do with all that money & we all want to go home if only for a little while. So most of us signed up again. Made me a corporal too. Hope you don't take this too bad. Think of all we can do with that money. I'm supposed to be a veteran now with whatever that gives me when the war's over. Pray that it'll be soon. Just waiting for that furlow. For sure I'll be home by Easter. Maybe at the time I'm home the war'll be over & I won't have to go back.

Co. C left here three days ago to replace Co. F over on Roanoak Island. Don't know why it couldn't be my company. Sure could use a change of scenery. I'll have to ask William Fulton or Franklin Mohney in Co. F what it's like over there by the ocean. Told you about them before. There best friends from Clarion County. I never seen the ocean you know & that's something I always wanted to do.

Heard rumors about a rebel ironclad ram getting bilt somewhere up the river. Its supposed to be a big boat with metal nailed all over it to protect it. It'll get destroyed for sure if it trys to come down here. Are army & navy will see to that. It won't get past Fort Gray I know. That's about three miles from the town.

Thank you for the Christmas card. I'll cherish it forever. I keep it in my Testament with your lock of yellow hair. Had a nice church service on Christmas morning. Sang all the carols. One fellow played his cordion. Everybody was longing for home you could tell. Three years away from are familys is too much. Got a fairly good meal cause all of the cooks worked hard for us & we was pleased.

Some colored boys joined are regiment. Pres. Lincoln said they could join the army last year when he freed the slaves. These boys are called assistants to the cooks but I think they do all the work. Don't know what they plan to do after the war. Maybe they'll go back to Penna. with us. I'm sure they won't want to go back where they come from. When we get finished with those rebs there won't be nothing to go back to anyway I expect.

One of those colored boys had been waiting around for months so he could join up too. He wasn't 18 yet. On Jan.1st when we reinlisted as veterans he joined up. Before that I got to talk to him once when are cook took sick. Made some good coffee for us. Real black & strong. Never talked to a colored man before like my friend William Fulton has. He tells me that his brother James was a conductor on what they call a underground railroad. That's cause it don't have no tracks but it carries the slaves to safe places. Anyway Fulton's brother helped a lot of escaped slaves get through Armstrong and Clarion counties on there way to Canada. Hid them in his barn.

Guess I was just curious. Wondered what the colored boy was thinking. Don't talk nothing like us. Sometimes its hard to understand what he's saying. Asked him what his name was & he told me Crowder Pacien. Seems like a good sort. Has a friendly smile. I asked him if he had plans when this war's over. Said he wants to go up north. Told him that's what I want to do too. Go back home in the north. Told him that maybe we'll meet up again someday up there. He's in Co. C the one that went to Roanoak Island. I'm sure that's the last I'll see of him. Wish him well.

There's a little bit of snow on the ground today. Its not like at home where the snow stays for weeks. Wish I could go down the hill on the sled with the boy. Tell him to be sure to sharpen the blades good & steer clear of the trees. Please rite soon. Love,

Fort Williams
Plymouth, North Carol.
Jan. 16th 1864

My dear wife,

I take pencil in hand hoping you & the boy are both doing good. Got no complaints about the state of my helth. Thanks for the new flannel shirt & socks & gloves. Could use a scarf too when you get the time. Know you had to get new sweaters ready for the boy to stay warm over the winter. The barn gets real cold when he has to be out there doing the milking.

Saw my cousin yesterday in his new uniform. We all got new the first of the month & the 101st got a different kind of hat too. Its called a Hardee hat. Its black felt with real stiff rims. They fasten one side up with a brass eagle with wings all spread out like its flying. Told my cousin he looked right smart. Told me that all the men hate the hats. Feel like fools in them he said. They favor there blue ones. Kepis there called. Only have to wear them Hardees for dress though. Told him that the folks back home will be very impressed especially that girl he keeps telling me about. That made him smile a bit. Can just see him all spiffed up going calling. He's a right handsome fellow if you remember. Looks a lot like me don't you think. That should make you smile I hope.

I'm sending you some money. Its not so much as the last time cause I had to pay $9.50 for a great coat. Its heavy & we need it for this cold wether. Feels good when I'm on picket duty but its too heavy for drilling. Unless its bitter cold I just leave it behind. Also had to buy a new pair of shoes. Cost all of $2.05. Seems mighty dear to me. My fingers are stiff from the cold so I'm going to stop riting now. Please you rite soon.

Love,

Fort Williams
Plymouth, North Carol.
April 3rd 1864

My dear wife

I take my pencil in hand hoping this letter finds you & the boy in good helth. Am feeling pretty good myself. The *wether here is pleasant at this time of the year. Spring comes earlier you know. The dogwoods already bloomed. Leaves are out on the trees. Its very pretty here now. Think we're going to get an early spring. Wish I could be home to see are dogwoods up in the woods.*

How we're all hoping this war will be over soon. We're sick of it. It's been three years already. Each day I'm hoping to be told that I can at least come home for a while to see you. I really miss you & the boy. Miss Mam & Paps too.

We all had a little fun on April fool's day. Never heard the men laff so hard. All of us was eating supper together like we do from time to time even are officers. Somebody salted the apple pies for a joke. Was right funny when we got a taste of it but the funniest was when Captain did. He yelled out. Used some bad words but I'm not going to tell you what he said. He yelled Cook! What's wrong with this pie? Did you drop the salt box in it? The cook didn't know nothing about it & we all had a great laff.

Been playing that new game called baseball. Some of us are getting real good at it but that won't do us no good when we get back home. No money in playing baseball. Its just for sport. I know I'll have too much work to do on the farm anyway & the only free time we get is on the Sabbath afternoons & you know Paps don't hold with nothing frivlous on the Lord's day. So I guess I'll be leaving my baseball playing days behind me when I come back home. I'll teach the boy how to play though. Think him & his cousins are going to like it.

I'm sending you a good amount of money that I got from the paymaster. He was back with are pay. Got no place to spend much money here. Can't even get tobacco no more. Been smoking corn silk instead. Won't gamble my money away so don't you fear. Take what you need and buy yourself something pretty & then put the rest away for when I come home.

Today are regimental flag got sent back to Harrisburg. Going to get are battle honors added to it & then it'll get sent back to us. We're very proud to march behind it but we'll just have to do without it for a while. Maybe the war'll be over before it gets sent back. Pray that it's so.

Love,

Fort Williams
Plymouth, North Carol.
Friday, April 15th 1864

My dear wife,
The wether here has been rainy & miserable for the last few days. Can't stay dry no how. Feet are wet & itchy all of the time & my clothes stink from the damp. They never seem to get dry.
Got some very bad news last Saturday. Took this long to rite to you cause I feel so bad about it. You know how I long to be home with you. Been told that the threat of the rebel forces is too great so us experienced men can't go home on furlow. Can't believe the unfairness of it. We're all so miserable. Everybody feels mightly low.
Some of the boys are suffering bad from the shakes. The doctors call it the ague. They dose the boys with some medicine called Ayers ague cure but it don't cure nothing as far as I can see. Still the shakes come & nobody knows why. I just thank God that they haven't found me yet. Just heard one of the fellows from Allegheny County tell that there's some cases of the smallpox over there and they got sent to the pest house. Hope none of them are any of are friends. Please stay away from over there.
Heard again stories about an ironclad ram being bilt up river. Some carpenter who used to work on it come over to are side. Says its more than a story. He says its true. We're not worried tho. Are gunboats in the river will take care of it. Those rebs don't know what there up against. Lt. Flusser knows his business. He's the commander of are gunboats. Heard he was born in the South but stayed loyal to the Union. Sure do admire him for doing that. Hope he gets alot of recognition after this here war's been done with. He should.
Tomorrow night I'm looking forward to going over to the Methodist Church. There's going to be a band concert the Conn. boys are putting on. We can all do with some lively music. Remember to pray for me so I'll be home soon at least by are anniversary in August.
Love to you & the boy & Mam & Paps

Chapter 11

The Battle of Plymouth

At the beginning of March in the year 1864 the rumors had been escalating concerning a Confederate ram's being built up the Roanoke River. Now truth is supplanting rumor when a carpenter, formerly a worker on the ram, defects to the Union forces garrisoned at Plymouth. "Yessir. It's true. A brand new ram's bein' built up river," he reports to the Federals.

What is so unusual is that this boat is not being built in the customary manner in a shipyard. Instead its keel is being laid in a cornfield along the Roanoke River. Afterwards the ram will be completed at the Halifax Navy Yard and then armed at Hamilton, a mere thirty miles up the river from Plymouth. All ready then for attack.

"This ram's nothin' a'tall like the *Virginia* was," the carpenter warns. The fabled *CSS Virginia* originally had been the Federal frigate *USS Merrimac*. Unfortunately for the Union, the country's premier shipbuilding facility happened to be located in Portsmouth, Virginia. Even before Virginia had seceded from the Union, one of the very last to do so, an unsuccessful attempt had been made by the Union to scuttle the *Merrimac* so as to prevent her falling into the waiting hands of the enemy. So unsuccessful was the attempt that the Confederacy had been able to completely restore the *USS Merrimac*, converting her into the ironclad *CSS Virginia*.

"No, nothin' a'tall like the *Virginia*." The carpenter repeats and then goes on to further explain, "Yuh see, this particular ironclad's bein' built from 'scratch.' Now that's so it'll be jest the right size fer sailin' down the Roanoke. Clear down here tuh Plymouth is what they're intendin' tuh do."

Like wild fire the disheartening news spreads throughout the Union camp. Prior to this time Plymouth had been so very tranquil several officers felt secure enough to send for their wives and children. However, now with this new disclosure, the women are made to promise that at the very first sign of danger they immediately will take themselves and their children to the safety of Roanoke Island.

Upon hearing this latest disturbing report, Gen. Wessells requests from Department Headquarters a reinforcement of 5000 men to add to his nearly 3000. He has become quite concerned over the possibility of such a formidable attack by the enemy now so intent upon capturing the Roanoke, one of the several rivers patrolled by Union gunboats. At this time there are only about 10,000 soldiers in all of the District of North Carolina as it is, and Gen. Grant had already been making plans to consolidate, abandoning Plymouth, sending the men somewhere more strategic.

So, "Request denied," is the disappointing reply received from Gen. Wessell's superiors under the assumption the rebels are concentrating their efforts elsewhere. And because of this Gen. Wessells mistakenly is led to believe the Confederates are not planning an attack on Plymouth at all!

And so here at Plymouth, North Carolina life hums along exactly as it had been doing before. Everything is so peaceful and quiet that on the morning of April 16th when the gunboat *Tacomy* arrives to lend aid, Gen. Wessells promptly sends it to New Berne where he mistakenly believes it will be needed more. He is relying on a report he has received stating that the Rebs are concentrating not on Plymouth on the banks of the Roanoke River, but rather Little Washington on the banks of the Tar River.

In Fort Williams Crowder's friend Richard West, cook of Company I, overhears several soldiers discussing some daunting concerns. "Say? Heard the latest? Cavalry reports they seen Rebel scoutin' parties out on Washington Road. Out about four miles, they say," one soldier is stating.

A second responds, "That so? Well, I hain't worryin' none, though. Fort Wessells's protectin' that approach. The 85th New York shouldn't have no trouble a'tall holdin' it if some of them Rebs do decide ta show up. Probably hain't nothin' a'tall fer us ta be worried about." His meal completed, he takes a final swallow of coffee as he prepares to exit the small group. "Gotta get ready now fer the concert. All of yuz goin'?"

"Sure thing," the first soldier replies as he, too, pulls himself up from the ground. "That 16th Connecticut's got a real good band, ya know. Wouldn't miss it fer the world."

And so on the pleasant spring evening of April 16th the Yankee soldiers relax, enjoying a rousing concert of martial music. Soon after returning to their camp and retiring to their cots, they hear the melancholy notes of "Taps" reverberate through the air. The men drift off to sleep.

On the morning of Sunday, April 17th as the sun puts forth its appearance where the eastern sky touches the Albemarle Bay, brilliant rays first kiss Roanoke Island before slowly gliding westward across the Roanoke River to the four forts and two redoubts at the small town of Plymouth. Reveille is bugled. Drumbeats roll as the Stars and Stripes ascends the poles. Men groggily poke their uncombed heads out between the flaps of the canvas tents. Cooks and their assistants are all set to serve breakfast. However, as the bright new spring day begins, the cold long fingers of doom prepare to clutch the unsuspecting blue-coated soldiers garrisoned at Plymouth, North Carolina.

Sunday's being the soldiers' day of rest, there is not as much labor to perform, or drills to endure, or orders to obey. However, the cooks and their assistants still must toil hard even on this day since food has to be prepared and served. Even so, on this exceptionally lovely day there will be some time for relaxation for them, too.

Private Richard West of the 103rd's Co I, as well as several other colored soldiers, have been anticipating this evening because a wedding is going to be held in the shantytown and they have been given permission to attend as long as they are back in camp by 9:30 p.m. No "jumping the broom" for this happy couple. There is going to be a "real" wedding. A "real" preacher is going to perform the ceremony. And so the couple will be "real" husband and wife in God's sight, albeit the marriage will not be legal in the eyes of the government.

Sho' wish Pacien whar here, West thinks. Being aware that Crowder would really enjoy himself tonight, West misses the presence of his friend. There will be good eating, of that he is certain. West hopes there will be some of his favorite sweet potato pie to be swallowed with swigs of persimmon beer. No doubt there will be much laughing, singing, dancing, and signifying. *Colored folks sho' do know how tuh hab a good time,* he is happily anticipating. He does not realize this is what has sustained his people through these past two hundred and forty-five bitter years of enslavement. Their God-given humor, their ability to laugh, their joviality, their music, and most of all their spirituality. White folk have always been stymied over how a body so enslaved could find anything to laugh about.

After breakfast and regimental inspections, the men gather for the compulsory Protestant services being conducted today by Col. Taylor of the 101st Pennsylvania Volunteers. Just an ordinary Sabbath in the lives of the Federal soldiers stationed here at Plymouth, North Carolina where they are still waiting, although no longer patiently, for that promised thirty-day furlough.

Back on the 9th of January those who re-enlisted and were *veteranized* had been given the first installment of their $400 bounty as well as a large sum of back pay from the quartermaster. Many of the men, like the corporal from the 103rd already have sent their money home to their dependents, some of it deposited directly into banks for security purposes. But other men have not and so with new uniforms on their backs and money "burning a hole in their pockets," they are now more than anxious to go home for a visit. The orders are expected to come momentarily, perhaps on the very next boat from headquarters at New Berne.

Just yesterday, however, one company of the 16th Connecticut had experienced great disappointment. Instead of receiving the expected good news of their going home on furlough, the troops were informed that they were being reassigned to Roanoke Island. And so following the morning worship service the men listlessly gather up their belongings, grumbling while boarding the *Massasoit.*

Lined along the railing of the deck they watch Plymouth's becoming smaller and smaller as they are sailing east. One very disgruntled young soldier is not reticent about voicing his feelings. "Don't know why we gotta be the unlucky ones here. Everybody else'll be goin' home. And will ya jest look at us? Gonna be stuck over there on that God-forsaken island. And fer who knows how long!"

Another speculates, "Yeah, jest bad luck on our parts, I guess."

After the religious service soldiers not assigned to picket duty are free for a few hours to do whatever they please. Some polish their muskets. Others mend their clothing with holes in their socks seeming to be an epidemic. Or like 101st Pennsylvania Infantry Quartermaster Sergeant Edward Boots, they might pen letters home. Or like 85th New York Infantry Private Charles C. Mosher they may be keeping diaries. Or like 103rd Pennsylvania Infantry Corporal Luther Dickey of Co. C they might record in journals, all to prove invaluable in the future. Still others choose to be playing games of chance or participating in that new sport called baseball, using wooden poles for whacking cloth-covered walnuts to see how far they are going to fly.

This is how the Yankees generally occupy themselves prior to the main meal on Sundays. Customarily eating at midday around one o'clock, the men are left afterwards with a few free hours just for relaxing or finishing those games of cards or baseball begun in the morning. Dress drill is scheduled for five-thirty.

Now it is nearing four thirty. Shadows are lengthening. A short time earlier, Private Richard West, Co. I, 103rd Pennsylvania Volunteers, had completed his duties as cook and now finally has some free time. Standing in front of his tent he has finished spiffing his uniform in preparation for the wedding later this evening. Finished the examination of his dark blue blouse and light blue trousers for dirt and grease spots. Completed blackening and buffing his shoes. Brushed all specks of lint from his blue kepi. And now satisfied that he is going to make a decent appearance, he prepares to shave with the straight edged razor he first must sharpen on a thick leather strop.

He does not relish the ordeal of shaving, but his beard is sparse and he does feel much better groomed when clean-shaven. Plagued by unsightly razor bumps, he is in envy of another colored soldier whose ancestry includes

Cherokee. One day Richard West had come to the realization that he was never observing any facial hair whatsoever on the man.

"Say, how come yuh neber got no hair on yore face?" Richard West had inquired when it finally dawned on him that this man was indeed unique since all of the other colored men bore some semblance of a beard, having little time during the week for shaving.

"Eber seed a Cherokee wid a beard?" Richard West was asked in return.

"Can' say dat Ah hab." Now if the truth were to be known, he never had seen a Cherokee, but he was not going to lose face by admitting that fact.

Just before five o'clock, having heated enough water to make a mug of soapy lather, Richard West is about to shave. He lays aside the razor strop, having deemed his straight-edged razor sharp enough. Squinting at his reflection in a piece of broken mirror missing most of its silver backing, he proceeds to dip his shaving brush into the tin mug. At that very instant he hears several shots coming from the picket line! Realizing that picket shots in the daytime are not to be taken lightly, immediately he lays aside his shaving brush. Those shots could mean *serious* trouble!

Now looking up, he sees a member of the cavalry galloping down Washington Road. He is heading straight to Gen. Wessells' headquarters! Whatever it is that the general orders is enough to cause the 12th New York Cavalry to quickly mount up, riding out to investigate. But within only moments it is returning!

Private West can hear the frantic shouts. "The Rebs're coming! The Rebs're coming!" The galloping horses of the cavalry are being prodded to run as fast as possible. The equines fairly *fly* across the dusty surface, all four hooves simultaneously lifted off the ground as their riders yell desperately. One returning horse is carrying its mortally wounded rider.

Now Richard has no doubt at all that the shots he had heard *are* very serious. Very serious indeed! He hears the frenzied warning being relayed throughout the camp. "The Rebs're coming! The Rebs're coming!" Indeed Confederate Gen. Hoke's division of over 10,000 men is coming after having driven in the cavalry videttes and capturing nine infantry pickets on the Washington Road outpost.

A shrill whistle sounds, followed by the command, "Fall in! Fall in!"

Surprised Federals everywhere scramble quickly, donning their blue blouses and forage caps, grabbing their Springfields and ammunition boxes, then rushing to defend their assigned positions at the fortifications. The rebels, making their first appearance up river on the right, are shelling the Federals' earthwork Fort Gray, located on the bluff at Warren's Neck two long miles away up the Roanoke River and completely isolated from the other forts.

Private Richard West hears the deafening artillery barrage being rendered during this his first battle. Never before in his life has he heard such a loud cacophony. Cannons blasting, rifles firing, grenades detonating! The explosions, he surmises correctly, are coming from the direction of Fort Gray, causing him to consider that if Fort Gray is defeated, then perhaps very shortly Fort Williams may be, too. He wonders just how long the 103rd and the 2nd Massachusetts Heavy Artillery are going to be able to hold out here. For days? Or perhaps only for a matter of hours.

Of what he is certain, though, is that very serious trouble lies ahead for him and the other black soldiers, as well as for their white officers. Picking up his rifle, ready to join the fray, he thinks of that rebel vow about which the recruiter had warned. For a moment his thoughts stray to Private Crowder Pacien safe over on Roanoke Island with Co. C, and now he is glad his friend is not here, after all.

The specter of death looms in the faces of all the men at Plymouth—both Federals and Confederates, whether black or white. White soldiers on both sides are desirous of having some type of identification somewhere on their bodies in case they get killed in battle. So they have begun writing their names on handkerchiefs or scraps of paper, securely pinning them inside their uniforms. By use of these first "dog tags" they hope if they are killed their bodies will be identified and then sent back home to their families for a proper Christian burial. Not so for the black soldiers. There will be no one to claim those bodies.

If'n Ah'm killed Ah'll prob'ly jest be shoveled in a unmarked grave whar only de Lawd Hisself will know ma name, Richard West predicts as the din of battle accelerates.

The unrelenting noises of battle coming from cannons, rifles, and grenades continue until the blessedness of darkness finally descends. Weary soldiers on both sides are directed to sleep in all of their clothes and accoutrements, guns close by their sides. That is, if it is possible for anyone to sleep at all.

Near midnight amid the noise and confusion frightened officers' wives with their children hastily board the mail steamer. On this night two trips to Roanoke Island are required for transporting all of the sick, as well as other noncombatants, including families of the "Buffaloes." Even wives and children of black men who, although not soldiers, stay behind to fight--some doing so willingly, others coerced.

Now while standing on the deck prior to the *Massasoit*'s departure, the gallant Lieut. Commander Flusser makes an attempt to reassure the weeping officers' wives. Some unknowingly just have bidden a final farewell to their husbands. "This is what we've been waiting for these last several months. The rebels' ironclad ram!" Then to add a little levity to the situation he continues, "Ladies, I give you my word! I promise you that little *lamb* of theirs is going to be no trouble to us at all. You just mark my word! You'll be back with your husbands just as soon as we take care of it. Never you fear! Our forces *can* and *will* prevail! Of this I am surely certain!" And he means every word.

Near three o'clock on Monday morning Fort Gray once again gets bombarded. Skirmishing continues all throughout this day. Then at dusk from every direction the Rebs begin to open fire on the small town of Plymouth. Finally after having to charge Fort Wessells four times even though being repelled by grenades, the Confederates are able to capture the fort just before nightfall.

Illuminating the whole area, the bright full moon rises over Fort Williams where the 24th New York Independent Battery and the Massachusetts Heavy Artillery are still replying vigorously with three thirty-pounder cannons. Now having fulfilled their duties, some of the skirmishers run back into the fort where immediately they spot a company of colored recruits. Belonging to the 37th USCT, they are here at Plymouth awaiting orders, expecting to be sent to Virginia where they will be mustered into the army before joining their regiment. Prepared to fight and, if need be, die for their freedom, these men are standing eagerly, guns held ramrod straight with bayonets gleaming and readied.

This battle is not going well for the Federals. Neither on land nor on water. For shortly after having been disabled by a shot through her steam chest, the Federal army steamer *Bombshell* sinks, even as she reaches the safety of the Plymouth wharf. Just before 10:00 p.m. the Rebs are finally quiet.

But not for long!

Tuesday morning much before dawn, in order to create a diversion the Rebs once again open fire on Fort Gray upriver from Plymouth. Their strategy is to draw the Federals' attention from what now is happening *on the river*. For at 3:00 a. m under the bright moonlit sky, the brand new Confederate ironclad ram *Albemarle* with her formidable eighteen foot metal covered prow and with huge volumes of black pitch-pine smoke blowing out of her stack, stealthily slips by Fort Gray. So brand-new is the ram, she just had been commissioned on Sunday, April 17th at 2:00 p. m by her commander, James W. Cooke. So brand new, the last of the thick iron plates were being attached to her decks and deckhouse as she cast off to begin her purposeful voyage down the Roanoke River. Her destination? *Plymouth!*

Undeterred by the Federals' futile attempts at narrowing the river with pilings, sunken debris, and even torpedoes (mines) which have been placed far too deep to be at all effective, the ram safely sails past Battery Worth. For some unexplained reason the rifled Parrott gun there carrying a chilled end shot weighing two hundred pounds does not fire. That is, until it is much too late to be effective.

The prows of the Federals' *Miami* and *Southfield*, former ferryboats, have been lashed together by long spars with chains to form a "V." Lieut. Cdr. Charles Williamson Flusser, commander of the flagship *Miami*, has hoped that the two together might possibly immobilize the rumored rebel ironclad, if indeed it ever should materialize.

Then at approximately 3:45 a.m., powered by two 200-horsepower engines with stern propellers, the dreaded Confederate ram *Albemarle* indeed does materialize to deliberately steer her long metal prow directly into the *Southfield*, successfully sinking her. The remaining Union wooden gunboats, except for the *Miami*, are forced to retreat then to the safety of the Sound. And after its fatal blow to the *Southfield* the rebel ram arrogantly sits down river, thereby preventing any reinforcements from reaching the now isolated Federal troops garrisoned at Plymouth, North Carolina.

Several years prior when serving as an instructor at the Naval Academy, the Annapolis born Lieut. Cdr. Flusser had been well known and well liked by all. That is, until he chose to remain loyal to the Union. Consequently, he had lost all his old friends who chose the cause of the South, declaring that the war was being fought over *states' rights,* while the North was declaring that it was being fought over *preserving the Union.* Flusser, however, felt it was really being fought over *the odious issue of slavery's polarizing the nation,* pitting friend against friend.

At one time he had gone out of his way to befriend one of his students who had gotten himself into some trouble, a future navy lieutenant by the name of William B. Cushing. Ultimately, he had been expelled from the Academy. However, when the war broke out he stepped forward to offer his loyal services to the Union Navy, readily having been accepted. In the very near future this same Lieut. Cushing is going to play an important role in the drama now enfolding at Plymouth, North Carolina.

While standing on the quarterdeck of the *Miami,* Lieut. Cdr. Flusser makes a futile attempt at shooting from a bow gun a shell with a ten-second-fuse, intending to send it directly down the smokestack of the Confederate ram. Unfortunately though, instead of hitting its mark, the shell rebounds and explodes. Deadly parts ricocheting off the tough iron hide of the *Albemarle* tear mercilessly into the unprotected body of Lieut. Flusser. And with the lanyard of the gun still held tightly in his hand, he collapses to the deck. Tragically, just before daybreak Lieut. Cdr. Flusser is killed. The undamaged *Miami* then slowly sails downstream, joining the other wooden Union gunboats already there.

On Wednesday morning, April 20th much before dawn, the rebels open fire once again. Hissing minie balls are whizzing everywhere, even to penetrating one of Private Richard West's calf muscles. Although the Federals are concentrating on trying to save Fort Williams situated in the center of town, by now it is apparent the rebels are winning the Battle of Plymouth. So one by one Union companies are compelled to raise the white rag of surrender.

In his eagerness to obtain the victory, the audacious young twenty-seven year old Confederate, Brig. Gen. Robert H. Hoke, a North Carolinian, requests a personal meeting with the much older Union Brig. Gen. Henry Walton Wessells. Under a flag of truce Gen. Hoke delivers his ultimatum as courteously as is possible, considering the circumstances. Gen. Wessells refuses, though, returning to Fort Williams even under the threat of *"no quarter,"* that is, indiscriminate slaughter by the victors.

So with heavy heart he agonizes over the fact that two-thirds of the garrison have already been captured. And now manning the fort are only the 24th New York Independent Battery and two companies of Massachusetts Heavy Artillery. How he dreads the thought of having to capitulate to the enemy!

However, after deliberating with his officers during the next hour, Gen. Wessells finally acknowledges that rebel sharpshooters are killing the men at the guns. So he determines that a further holdout is useless. With sinking soul he feels that at least by surrendering now he is taking away that threat of "no quarter." True, that may be, except for the "Buffaloes" and the blacks.

Therefore, before eleven o'clock in the morning, the despairing Union general orders the lowering of the tattered Stars and Stripes and the raising of the white flag of surrender. Then an hour later with colors waving, the garrison marches out of Fort Williams to ground their arms. In mortification Gen. Wessells must surrender approximately 2000 men, the wounded Richard West among them. To the victors are relinquished 28 artillery pieces, approximately 500 horses, forage, wagons, sutlers' stock, over 5000 stands of small arms, a large supply of ammunition, and more than 300 tons of that northern fuel coal, so desperately needed to satisfy the voracious appetites of the Confederates' ironclads.

A clamorous chorus of the distinctive rebel yell accompanies the replacement of the Union's Stars and Stripes by the Beauregard Battle flag. Now it is the Confederate flag triumphantly flying over Fort Williams in the center of town. A bright square of red with a blue saltier (two diagonally crossed blue bars) spangled with 13 white stars representing the 11 seceded states plus one each for the divided states of Missouri and Kentucky.

All of the surviving Federals who had been garrisoned at Plymouth now henceforth are prisoners of the Confederacy. That is, except for those "Buffaloes" and perhaps some blacks escaping the night before, well aware of what might befall them if captured. The defeated Yankees now are prisoners of war and, as such, are expecting to receive civilized treatment from their captors. All of the surviving members of the 103rd Pennsylvania Volunteers who have been garrisoned at Plymouth are surrendered except for a lucky few. Those hospitalized, those away on detached duties, and those in Co. C, fortuitously garrisoned on Roanoke Island.

Gen. Wessells has two requests to make of the conquerors. First, that his men be allowed to retain their brand new clothing and second, that they not be robbed. Those requests are granted before he is separated permanently from his troops and taken with his staff and 850 other captured officers to be sent to various places such as Libby Prison in Richmond and Morris Island outside of Charleston, South Carolina. Eventually exchanged and returned to New York, the General is never to lead his men again.

After this final day of battle, April 20, 1864, from the 103rd Pennsylvania Infantry, 24 officers and 461 enlisted men will be reported killed, wounded, or missing. Although outnumbered five to one, the Union troops at Plymouth have fought gallantly. And they might have been victorious had it not been for Lieut. Comdr. C. W. Flusser's unfortunate death on the quarterdeck of the *Miami*, thereby eliminating protection from the gun ships.

On this fateful Wednesday morning two regiments consisting of 800 men finally are on their way to Plymouth. However, it is much much too late.

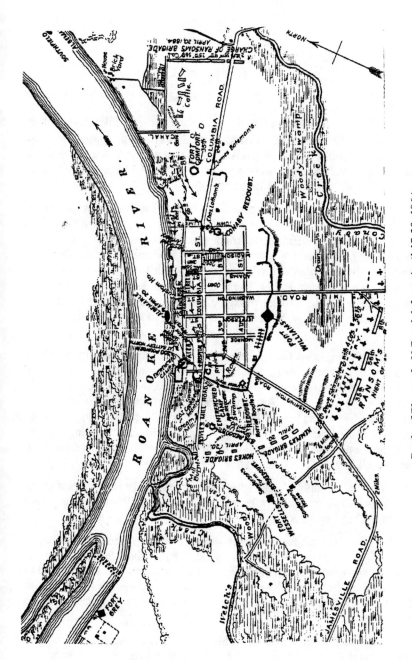

Battle of Plymouth, N.C and defense April 17-20, 1864 by Capt. R.D. Graham, 56th Reg. NC S.T. after original by Solon E. Ellis, 27th Mass. Vol. Militia, October 1863

Chapter 12

Yankees Surrender

Orders are being barked at the Federal prisoners. "File singly! Stack your weapons!" The mound of wood and metal is growing rapidly. Now the corporal who faithfully writes letters home, his cousin, and friends William Fulton and Franklin Mohney as well as the other captured Yanks somberly steps forward to add their precious rifle to the rest.

They are about to be marched off to the small town of Hamilton some thirty miles away, the place where the "Buffaloes" may get identified. That derogatory North Carolinian appellation has been given to anyone who exchanges his Rebel cadet-gray coat for a Yankee blue one. Some say the name originally may be attributed to a roisterous young Rebel deserter said to be "as hard to rope as a wild buffalo." He has organized a motley group of marauders who roam all over North Carolina, pillaging, burning, and wreaking havoc. And worst of all to the Confederates, they spread the news to the slaves that they are free.

After the firing on Fort Sumter, South Carolina in 1861 and following the secession of eleven southern states, two young brothers along with several neighboring boys from small farms near Greensboro, North Carolina eagerly had enlisted in the Confederate Army. Characterized by some as "the epitome of chivalry" and by others as gallant "gentlemen soldiers," the gray-coated Confederates at first were perceived as romantic, dashing, and daring figures. But after three long years of killing, the brothers have become disenchanted with the war, as well as with the Confederate's cause.

"What're *we* fightin' fer?" the younger brother finally is questioning "We don't own no slaves. Alls we hear nowadays is 'bout them niggahs. 'Bout keepin' them whar they belong."

"Don't matter tuh me none, one way or t'other whether they're free or not. Ah jest figured that this war was su'posed to be all about lettin' us live our lives like we want tuh. Not lak what Old Abe Lincoln up there in Washington sez," the older brother responds. By now both are suspecting the futility of the war and their only desire is for it to be over and done with so they can return to their parents' farm.

The older brother continues, "This here war's over fer the South. They jest don't know it yet. But Ah shor do." And his brother is in total agreement. So one night after "lights out" when they are certain everyone is sleeping, the two brothers covertly leave their Confederate regiment to seek out the 2nd Loyal North Carolina Volunteers garrisoned at Plymouth. And so when the battle erupts the two young brothers from Greensboro are here with 166 other "Buffaloes."

Knowing about the twenty-two captured "Buffaloes" who had been court-martialed, convicted of high treason, and executed in Kinston last February, an officer of the North Carolinians advises his men, "Men, it's my suggestion that in the event of yore capture yuh don't want tuh be usin' yore real names. So now while yuh still have the time, yuh should look over the list of dead Yankees. Best be pickin' out one of them names." After that he changes out of his officer's uniform to dress as a private and to assume a dead Yankee's name for himself.

The elder brother also has been meting out some advice. "Now yuh know that they'll kill us if we're caught. We're traitors. We're 'turncoats' 'cause we deserted." Indeed they had turned the color of their coats from gray to blue, something not taken lightly by the Rebs.

"Now yuh listen tuh me real good, Brother. If we're forced tuh give up, jest don' say nothin'. Nothin' a'tall! Jest pretend yuh a Yankee. Soon's we open our mouths they'll know that we ain't. So if Ah'm caught and they figure out who Ah am, don' even look at me. Brother, do yuh understand? Ma don't need no two dead boys. Promise me now?"

"If yuh promise tuh do the same." And so the pact between the two brothers was affirmed.

After the long hot march to Hamilton the fatigued Federal prisoners are being forced now to pass between a gauntlet of yelling Confederates who are bent on seeking retribution. Here the traitorous "Buffaloes" are to be identified. And here the pact between the two brothers is put to the test.

With heads bowed, eyes to the ground, the blue-clad soldiers pray that none of the "Buffaloes" are going to be identified. Slowly they trudge by the "eagle-eyed" Confederates. The two brothers from Greensboro have deliberately separated, not wanting to be anywhere near each other because they favor so, each praying if one is identified the other will not be.

"Hey now. Look'a there!" One of the homespun butternut garbed Confederates nudges the soldier standing beside him. He points to a particular bluecoat. "Hey! Look see! Ain't that a fella from over there by Greensboro?"

"Ah'm not so shor now. Let me take a look." The second Reb steps closer to take a better look before replying. "It does look a mighty lot lak him, though."

"Yeah. Well, Ah'm shor that's him. Seen him at a barn dance once. Should'a stayed where he b'longs." So while pointing, he yells out, "Hey! This here's one of them dirty 'Buffaloes.'" And immediately the younger brother is seized.

Don't make no sound, silently he implores his elder brother who in horror must stand by helplessly.

So it is the elder who must watch his brother being dragged away. He is one of the unlucky "Buffaloes" on April 24th unceremoniously hanged from trees lining the road. *Lord, please be with my brother.* Uncontrollable tears trail down the elder brother's face. And he is not the only "blue belly" shedding tears as five other "Buffaloes" get recognized. Fortunately, the majority are not.

After completion of the "Buffalo hunt" the 101st and 103rd Pennsylvania Volunteer Infantry, as well as the other Federals captured at Plymouth, line up to begin a wretched march. It is now Sunday, April 24th. "Wonder where they're takin' us?" This is the first question on the lips of all of the Federals as wearily they are being forced to march the last ten miles to Tarboro, located seventy long miles from Plymouth. The second question asked is, "Wonder when we're gonna get somethin' ta eat?" By now all of their rations have been exhausted.

On Monday the 25th after reaching the bank of the Tar River, they bivouac in sight of the Tarboro Bridge. There the Rebs provide a kettle and some water for each prisoner to cook his meager cup of corn meal and black-eyed peas with a miniscule cube of bacon for seasoning.

While consuming his unappetizing meal the corporal comments to his friends William Fulton and Franklin Mohney about how pretty he might have thought the town was had he not been a prisoner. However, with the sun's intense rays beating down on him for two whole days and with heavy rain drenching him on the third he has been too miserable to be appreciative of much of anything. Here in Tarboro while being exposed to all the elements, these prisoners of the Confederacy have been provided with no tents or barracks for shelter. *It's gotta be a lot better than this where they're takin' us*, the corporal optimistically presumes.

Early on the morning of Friday, April 29th the orders are snapped. "Fall in!" The Federal prisoners begin lining up for the short march to the Tarboro railroad depot. When the battle began last Sunday the soldiers had been preparing for a regimental dress parade. Subsequently, the 101st Pennsylvanians still are attired in their new uniforms as well as their detested "Hardee" hats, causing them to resemble the Massachusetts Mayflower Pilgrims of old. And so while marching in formation through Tarboro on their way to board a southbound train, the corporal's handsome cousin and his comrades get dubbed "Plymouth Pilgrims" by the curious townsfolk. In a circus-like atmosphere adults and children line the streets to get a good look at the defeated Yankees.

"Get in there now! Pile right in! Push! Yuh kin get more in there! Go on! Move back!" The Federal prisoners by 50's and 60's are being herded into stifling, fetid two-door boxcars. Passing first through the small North Carolina towns of Goldsboro and Wilmington they arrive in Charleston, South Carolina on Sunday, May 1st where they finally get to breathe fresh air once more. But after only several hours they are forced again to board a southbound train. This time, however, on open flatbeds. Even when the hot sun beats down on them unmercifully or when they are drenched by sudden downpours, the wretched Yankee prisoners much prefer these to the closed suffocating boxcars.

Now they are traveling through the Georgia cities of Savannah and Macon. The dejected Yankees have no inkling as to where they are going. They have no idea that they are on their way to the small little-known town of Andersonville, Georgia where at Camp Sumter the most infamous Confederate prison is located. Where close to 50,000 Yankee prisoners of war will get packed into that lamentable 26-acred log stockade. Where hopelessness reigns king.

On Tuesday, May 3rd about 400 totally exhausted whisker-faced members of the 103rd Pennsylvania Volunteers stagger single-file through the gates of the fifteen-foot tall stockade. The corporal's eyes previously so heavy with fatigue suddenly fly open in shock! A gasp! Utterances of disbelief spill from his mouth!

For what he is seeing is indeed shocking. There are no tents, log huts, or barracks! He sees nothing at all being provided for shelter. No protection whatsoever can be found anywhere for the Yankee prisoners except for their blankets or the ground sheets for each half of the two-man pup tent they carry on their backs. In addition they soon discover that no open sinks have been dug for sanitation. Neither are any medical supplies available. Instead, here at the Andersonville Prison in Georgia is found only an over-abundance of vermin, filth, disease, suffering, and death.

In its fourteen months of its existence 49,485 captured enlisted Federals will be brought here, a number close to 13,000 not surviving, including 181 of the 103rd Pennsylvania Volunteers. These unlucky men die not from having been shot on the battlefield, but from diarrhea and dehydration, dysentery and typhoid, malaria and yellow fever, measles and smallpox, tuberculosis and pneumonia, scurvy, bronchitis, gastrointestinal parasites, or simply from the ravages of starvation.

This crosshatched letter arrived in Cumberland County thirty-one days after it had been written. Because of the scarcity of paper the corporal from the 103rd first had turned his precious piece so he might write first on the longer side. Then he turned it to complete his message across the shorter side.

Andersonville, Georgia
May 6th 1864

My dear wife,

I know you have been wondering why you didn't get no letters from me lately. Not had much of a chance to rite before. This has been a very bad time. The rebs fooled us with that ironclad ram of theres & they took Plymouth back. We fought hard all the boys did but the rebs beat us bad & now we're there prisoners.

Ended up down here in Georgia & its very hot. Got here at Camp Sumter on the second day of May. Next day we went into the stockade right past the reb in charge. Name's Captain Henry Wirz. Sounds from his voice like he might a been born in Germany. Talks a lot like Grandpa. Hope he's not one of are folks from over there. Any Wirz in your family. Don't know of any in mine. Don't trust his looks. Has a mean look about him. His left arm is in a sling. Must a got wounded somewhere along the way I don't know. Cusses like nobody I ever heard before.

Well maybe we won't have to worry about him for long cause I expect to be getting exchanged for some rebs soon. That's the deal I hear. Two rebs for one Yank. They get the best deal I think. Don't know why its that way. Shouldn't be I don't think. After all, there the ones that started all this infernal mess.

I'm out of paper. Had to borrow this peace. If you send me some in a package maybe I'll get it. Just send it to Andersonvile Prison, Georgia. Don't know if I'll get it or not but please try. Also send me a few dollars from the money I sent you. I'm so glad I sent it to you when I did. Raiders in the camps took all the money the other fellas had from their bounty. There Yanks like us so its hard to believe they would do that. But there are things here to get if you got good Yankee dollars. Just hope I get it in your letter.

Not going to describe what its like here cause I don't want to worry you or Mam. Just want you to know that my cousin & our friends William Fulton and Franklin Mohney are here too & we're going to stick together & do all we can to make it home in one peace. Pray for us both at the throne of mercy. All my love,

Your devoted husband.

As the corporal with his cousin and his friends William Fulton and Franklin Mohney are entering the stockade at Andersonville Prison the possibility of their being exchanged is futile. For on the very day the Battle of Plymouth began, April 17, 1864, Union Gen. Ulysses S. Grant had determined that the exchange of prisoners decidedly had been in the Confederates' favor. It seemed to him that the Rebels being returned to their lines were in much better physical condition than the exchanged Yankees who are not able return to battle quickly due to lack of proper care when they were the unwilling guests of the Confederacy. And this, he felt, could be an issue when Gen. Sherman makes his destructive swath across Georgia from Chattanooga, Tennessee, eastward to the beautiful seaport of Savannah, Georgia.

Months later when the Federals do get closer to Andersonville, the Confederates become fearful that if Sherman should reach the prison he could add over 20,000 Yankees to his manpower. So the Rebs decide to move all of those prisoners capable of walking, the corporal's friend William Fulton among them, one of only nine of the original members of Company F of the 103rd Pennsylvania Volunteers to survive the war.

When he and the others arrive at their final destination of Charleston, South Carolina they get marched into an old racecourse to remain there until the new prison site at Florence, South Carolina is completed. Unfortunately, the deadly diseases of smallpox and yellow fever break out within the ranks. The former is a highly communicable disease caused by a virulent virus while the latter gets transmitted by a particular kind of mosquito, just as does malaria. This time, however, by the species *Aedes aegypti*.

On February 27, 1865 Private William Allison Fulton, suffering from the ravages of prison life (scurvy, rheumatism, and diarrhea), gets released from the Florence Prison. Going first to Annapolis with other parolees, he then is sent to a hospital in Baltimore, remaining there until his discharge in August of 1865. Finally he returns to his home in Clarion County, Pennsylvania where he marries the younger sister of Franklin Mohney, his best friend who had served with him in Company F.

The bride's brother, however, is not present at the wedding. Sadly, he is buried at Andersonville.

The 103rd has been reconstituted on Roanoke Island under the capable command of Captain Thomas Cochran of Co. C. One by one, the absent soldiers report for duty. Some had escaped during the Battle of Plymouth. Others were returning from sick leave. Still others were paroled from Confederate prisons.

Private Crowder Pacien prays that one of these days he is going to spot his good friends West, Garrett, Harding, and Grandville's arrival at the camp, too. He would certainly like to introduce them to the new friends he has made among the colored folk living here on Roanoke Island at the 600-acre Freedmen's Colony. Here they have found a safe haven due to the efforts of Rev. Horace James, a Massachusetts chaplain in charge of organizing a colony for the refugees.

Heaven on earth is what the people are feeling. *Heaven* because each family has been given enough land for building a small house and planting a vegetable garden. *Heaven* because both men and women are being hired by the army, paid the laborer's wage of $10 a month as well as being provided with rations and clothing for their children, missionary barrels stuffed with clothing already arriving from the North.

Heaven because men and women can be married with these words included, "Til death do us part." *Heaven* because schools and teachers are being provided for children no longer living under the threat of being sold away from their parents, one such teacher being Elizabeth James, the unmarried young niece of Rev. James. *Heaven* because the children are learning to read, to write, and cipher in preparation for productive lives in "Freedomland." *Heaven* because they are able to gather *openly* to lift their voices to God in praise and thanksgiving. *Heaven* because the adults may "let in the light" by learning to read the Bible for themselves, knowing now there is more in the Good Book besides what Marse loves to misquote as "Servants, obey your masters."

When Private Crowder Pacien first arrived on Roanoke Island with Co. C he had discovered a flourishing colony composed of runaways from nearby plantations. How surprised he had been to find refugees here living in conditions far superior to what he had seen in Plymouth. This due to the fact that in 1863 Rev. James had been given a directive from the Federal government to provide the refugees with tools and other essential implements conducive to their survival on the island. Therefore, here on Roanoke Island the Federal government is assisting colored families, especially those of men who have enlisted or who have been sent elsewhere to work under contract for the army.

The first winter was an extremely hard one due to unusually cold weather, as well as the burgeoning number of refugees. The unoccupied land on the northern end of the island had been surveyed and divided into lots, streets and avenues for the habitation of the refugees. But soon there were far too many. They just keep coming and coming. And although they try to help each other as best as they can, now there simply is not enough space, food, or clothing to go around.

To make matters even worse, in April 1864 during the Battle of Plymouth a large contingency of refugees arrives on the *Massasoit* and the numbers swell to well over 2500. Noncombatants including contrabands all have been brought east from the danger of Plymouth to the safety of Roanoke Island.

P | 103 | Pa.

Crowder Tacien

colord under Cook Co. C.

Pvt. , Co. C , 103 Reg't Pennsylvania Inf.

Appears on Returns as follows:

Feby 1864 (Colord Under Cook)
Gain. Enlisted
in the Regt Jan 1-64
Roanoke Isld
(Asst Cook)

Apl. 1864 to May 1865.
On duty Assisting
Colord under Cook
(Pvt Co. C)

Name appears also as
Crowder Cacien
Crowder Tacien

Book mark:

A. W. Elliott

(546) Copyist.

Muster record from Roanoke Island- April- May 1864

At last the war is nearing its end. All reports, official and unofficial, indicate that the Union is the victor and now, understandably, the soldiers are beginning to become quite restless. They want nothing more than to go home! And after this horrific war even the coal mines, factories, mills, and farms from which they had escaped are going to look mighty good to them.

Due to the reporting by former prisoners-of-war to their regiments, discipline here on Roanoke Island is not as tight as it is elsewhere. Because of the severe deprivations these war-weary soldiers have suffered they are granted much more freedom than they would have been accorded under any other circumstances. This laxity, however, gets some of them into a great deal of trouble.

For instance, since government food rations never have been anywhere near what might be considered as satisfactory, the soldiers are used to supplementing their meals by pillaging the surrounding areas for food. So under cover of darkness some of the ex-prisoners-of-war have begun skulking around, stealing chickens from the contrabands who then loudly protest to Colonel Lehmann. Even though the soldiers subsequently are given orders to remain in their quarters at night, they pay little attention, stubbornly continuing to go on with their poaching.

One night about twenty ex-prisoners-of-war decide to sneak out for a dance being held at a nearby home. When Col. Lehmann is made aware that his order to remain in quarters is being disobeyed so flagrantly he is furious, immediately sending a company to arrest the revelers and to securely padlock them in the log guardhouse until morning. Then one soldier is ordered to remain on duty all night, standing guard in front of the only door until Col. Lehmann can put in his appearance to mete out what he considers an appropriate punishment.

A highly disciplined soldier, the colonel expects his men to be likewise and when they are not, he is known to become very annoyed. So at dawn when he approaches the guardhouse he already is in a foul mood. He orders the guard to open the door. The soldier becomes so rattled he drops the keys. Finally the door of the guardhouse swings open.

Empty! All of the men are gone! Unbeknownst to the soldier guarding the door in the front, during the night the prisoners had dug themselves a tunnel, allowing them to crawl out the back of the guardhouse. If at all possible, the colonel is even more furious than he had been before!

So even before reveille is bugled he storms the quarters, demanding that the culprits step forth. Of course no man does. The Colonel then indicates that he knows who they are and that it will go much easier on them if they confess. The miscreants are well aware that he does not know their identities and so they all stand as one. Consequently, the enraged Colonel metes out a punishment to the *whole* detachment, to the innocent as well as to the guilty. He orders it into exile. All of the men. They are going to be sent to a bleak place called Coanjack located on the Dismal Swamp Canal, totally isolated from civilization since it seems that they cannot act civilized.

Fortunately for everybody, the war is at its finale. So instead of their going into isolation, the men are going *home*. Col. Lehmann will laugh with those same men at a future reunion because by that time he, too, will think it a funny war anecdote to recount.

No one possibly can imagine how short-lived the *almost* Utopian colony of blacks on the north end of Roanoke Island is to be. After the Confederacy's surrender, the victors no longer have any need for the black men who are returning here to their families. Therefore, government rations no longer will be given to the families. Teachers no longer will be provided for the children. And worst of all, the land on which homes painstakingly and lovingly have been built by the refugees is going to be returned to the former owners, thereby leaving the freed-men and women with absolutely *nothing* tangible of their own.

Everything gets taken from them—houses, gardens, church, and schools. That empty promise of "40 acres and a mule" is *never* to materialize here, either. However, the *intangible* education they have received during their brief sojourn at the Freedman's Colony on Roanoke Island, North Carolina never can be taken from them.

So beginning in May 1865 the freedmen pack their meager belongings to begin exiting the island by the hundreds in search of employment. Some to be scattered on the mainland. Some to settle in all black enclaves like Princeville, North Carolina, while still others head north and west. Friends and families are being separated again. And like with so many other black families, bonds are being severed without any expectation of their ever being forged again. That is, not until 110 years later when a writer by the name of Alex Haley inspires future generations to seek their roots, searching for their unknown ancestors by name.

There are those who choose to remain on the island, however, living in an area later designated as the town of Manteo, North Carolina. Many of the men get hired as farmers, working then for the owners of the island who have returned to reclaim their land. Other freedmen who also choose to remain are fishermen and oystermen. With great pride they are going to relay their stories to future generations, the descendants of the little known Freedman's Colony of Roanoke Island.

Not until six long months after the disastrous siege at Plymouth does the Union Navy miraculously take possession of the little town once again. It happens on November 1, 1864 with the Federals' remaining there for the duration of the war. When Private Crowder Pacien, along with the surviving members of his regiment over on Roanoke Island, hears the welcome news he shouts a loud Yankee "Hurrah," rejoicing as he, too, throws his blue kepi high into the air.

For circulating is a story about a twenty-one-year old navy lieutenant, William B. Cushing, a brash young officer with a reputation of being a prankster. Because his Spanish professor had not liked him, due, perhaps, to the fact that some teachers have a hard time dealing with pranksters in their classrooms, the nineteen year-old Cushing had been forced to resign from the United States Naval Academy. Now it seems that he has performed the gargantuan prank of his young life!

Lieut. Cushing had been incensed upon hearing of the unfortunate death of Lieut. Commander Flusser, his former instructor at the Academy, his mentor, and trusted friend. After pleading unsuccessfully to authorities about finding a way to destroy the threatening Confederate ram *Albemarle* sitting on the Roanoke, Cushing, being the daring, determined, and dauntless individual that he was, vowed to do something about the insufferable situation himself.

What can I do to effectively 'kill' that ram? He knew that as long as she was anchored near Plymouth she was a constant threat. Basically she was inactive at the time, but certainly could be reactivated at a moment's notice. She was just sitting there in the shallow river, collecting algae. *Oh, yes, that Albemarle's a "sitting duck." Just waiting for me,* Cushing had concluded.

During innumerable sleepless nights he had pondered, one idea after the other discarded as being unfeasible. Finally it came to him! *A torpedo! Yes, that's the answer! An effective torpedo armed with at least 200 pounds of gunpowder. A torpedo's my solution!* Then another concern suddenly invaded his thoughts. *But without a submarine, how can I possibly do it?*

Stymied for a time, he finally resolved, *I know just how. I've got to use a torpedo that can be delivered by a small steam launch. Yes! That's my solution!*

So on October 27, 1864 under a protective moonless sky, under the mantle of dense fog, Lieut. Cushing formulated his clandestine plan for reaching that vessel of abomination—*CSS Albemarle.* His intentions were to explode a charge under her metal protection at water level, thereby creating a hole large enough to drown the behemoth.

Along with several other men he had been able to sneak up to the *CSS Albemarle.* Close enough for a sailor aboard the ram to spy the small launch's making its approach. He laughed heartily at what he was beholding. "And jest whut kind'a ship is this su'posed tuh be?" ridiculing just as did the giant Goliath while watching young David wind up his slingshot.

The sailor never received an answer, for at that very moment the determined young Lieut. William B. Cushing avenged the death of his friend Lieut. Commander C. W. Flusser. With a spar torpedo he was able to sink the *CSS Albemarle*! Never again would the Confederate ram be seen floating arrogantly on the Roanoke River. Never again would she be a threat to the Federals. Instead she would scrape the river's bottom until her raising by Union forces following the recapture of Plymouth.

And what is to be her final fate? Is it not ironical that the *USS Ceres*, having been chased by the Confederate ironclad during the fateful Battle of Plymouth, would be the one designated to tow the enemy ship to the Norfolk Navy Yard? And following her eventual $2500 sale at a Navy auction in October of 1867, the once feared *CSS Albemarle* becomes a useless pile of junk, leaving behind only her battered smokestack for future generations to view at the North Carolina Hall of History in Raleigh, North Carolina.

Chapter 13

The Fate of the Black Soldiers

So what happened to the black soldiers who had been garrisoned at Plymouth, North Carolina prior to the battle? Those black men with the threat of execution hanging over them like the sword of Damocles?

When the 103rd Pennsylvania Volunteers' regimental roster indicates that colored soldiers are captured or that there is no further knowledge about them, then the worst is presumed. This is the kind of information recorded concerning Privates Samuel Grandville, Co. B and Dolphus Garrett, Co. K. Following his capture, Titus Hardy (alias McRae) of Co. K, however, was known to survive, reclaimed by his master.

Private Richard West of Co. I happened to have been cleaning his uniform when the battle began. Therefore, he was attired in his civilian work clothes when the garrison in Fort Williams finally was forced to surrender. So West, looking not at all like a soldier, was enslaved once again, too, but he knew what he *was* and it was not a *slave* any longer. No, he was *a private in the 103rd Pennsylvania Infantry*!

Put to work by his captors for nine months and eight days, repairing the breastworks at Rainbow Bluff located beyond Plymouth, he had bided his time, waiting for just the opportune time for escape. He, too, was familiar with the local terrain, having lived in the neighboring Bertie County and so with frostbitten feet he was able to make his way, taking five whole days to reach Plymouth again under Yankee occupation. Transported east by gunboat to Roanoke Island Pvt. Richard West rejoined his regiment there, meeting up once again with his good friend Pvt. Crowder Pacien.

Many stories circulate concerning the fate of the other black soldiers. Just which stories are to be believed? Can it be the testimony of Sgt. Samuel Johnson, Co. D, 2nd US Colored Cavalry? His documented story states that he had been assisting in the recruitment of contrabands for the cavalry when the Battle of Plymouth began. Learning about the imminent surrender and knowing that he should not be caught in his blue uniform, he changed quickly into civilian clothing. And so when Fort Williams fell, when the garrison marched out with their flags flying, Johnson was taken prisoner, not to be mercilessly shot, not to suffer in the Rebs' prison at Plymouth as had Private Nelson Sheppard of the 24th Independent Battery, New York Light Artillery. Instead he was returned to his former state of bondage.

After his escape Johnson will swear on July 11, 1864 in an affidavit that he had witnessed the lining up and massacring of black Union soldiers. He will swear that he saw many randomly shot, some hanged, and others bludgeoned to death with the butt end of muskets.

Can the story told by Lieut. Alonzo Cooper, 12th New York Cavalry be believed? He relates that after he had been taken prisoner he was held on the nearby Johnston farm. He will tell how he could hear the erratic fusillade of gunfire as Rebs on horses shot blacks attempting escape through the swamps. He will say also that he saw those who did surrender lined up and shot.

What about the story told by a third witness, Second Lieut. B. F. Blakeslee, Co. G, 16th Connecticut Volunteers? His is that he saw Confederates shoot three or four hundred Negroes and two companies of North Carolinians ("Buffaloes") who had joined the Federals. He calls it a "massacre," likening it to that at Fort Pillow which had occurred only eight days before the Battle of Plymouth. After the surrender of that Tennessee fort, Confederates heinously shot and killed all of the 292 black troops of the 11th USCT, the majority formerly freed slaves. Some had been burned to death while others were buried alive.

Or can one believe the diary of Private Charles C. Mosher, Co. B, 85th New York Infantry, brigaded with the 103rd throughout the duration of the conflict? He records that a massacre had occurred at Plymouth when vengeful Rebs chased and shot all black soldiers who were heading for the woods in an effort to escape.

Another story by an unnamed member of the 16th Connecticut Volunteers relates that during the afternoon of the 20th of April, the Rebel cavalry shot dead every black soldier found hiding in the woods. This witness put the number killed in the vicinity of one hundred.

These stories and others have been refuted by the Federals, labeled as exaggerations and contending that if these atrocities really had occurred, surely the surviving blacks would have complained. However, complaining is not what blacks do instinctively. For in their life experiences they have never had anyone to complain to, except their God. So to whom would they feel they could complain? And if they did, who did they feel would believe them? And then even if they were believed, who would care? This has been the *black experience*. Possibly, these survivors are just so grateful to be alive that all they desire is to close this horrific chapter of their lives and finally to be able to move on.

There is nothing mentioned in Gen. Wessell's report concerning a massacre of colored soldiers by the Confederates. He does state, however, that a number of Union North Carolinians left their companies without permission. Indeed they had, knowing what would befall them if captured. They had fled in canoes or swam across the Roanoke. Some held onto logs traveling downstream;

others hid in the swamps or among the cypress trees. The general does not state if any of those men were colored. However, having been aware of what awaited them at the hands of the Rebs the colored soldiers as well as the Confederate deserters certainly would have taken their chances in the swamps until Union gunboats might rescue them. However, concerning this number there are no statistics.

The Confederates likewise declare such stories of a massacre as blatant lies. However, there is no doubt that while attempting escape, many of the blacks as well as native North Carolinian "Buffaloes" deliberately were killed by Confederates' vowing "no quarter" for them. Again there are no numbers of those fulfilling Richard West's prediction of their being buried where only the Lord would know their names. Perhaps the very crux of this matter lies with the word "massacre," having different meanings to different interpreters.

Recorded in the Regimental Roster of the 103rd Pennsylvania Volunteers Infantry is the following information:

"Pacien, Crowder, Private, Company C. Mustered age 18, April 4, 1864-June 25, 1865. Cook, colored, apparently escaped capture following Battle of Plymouth, North Carolina, April 20, 1864."

The reason for his having escaped capture and/or death is because Company C misses the battle, fortuitously not being at Plymouth with the other nine companies of the 103rd. By a stroke of fate it is on Roanoke Island and so is Private Crowder Pacien.

He need not fulfill his commitment of three years because on April 4, 1865 victorious Gen. Ulysses S. Grant marches into Richmond, the capitol of President Jefferson Davis' Confederacy. Four long bitter years prior almost to the day on April 13, 1861 a flag representing the new rebellious South had been raised over the Capitol Building, replacing the then detested Union flag. Now once again the Union's Stars and Stripes triumphantly waves over Richmond, Virginia.

Five days later the brick McLean house in a small Virginia town called Appomattox Courthouse becomes the meeting place for two proud West Point graduates both having served in the Mexican War, but who had chosen opposite sides of the conflict. At four-thirty in the afternoon, stiffly seated on his faithful gray horse Traveler, Lieut. Gen. Robert Edward Lee, attired immaculately in his formal gray uniform, rides to meet his fate as well as that of the defeated Confederacy, not knowing what to expect from the victors. The stocky, bearded Union Gen. Ulysses Simpson Grant, not having had the time to change out of his dusty field uniform, has no desire for any further humiliation of his defeated enemy. Therefore, out of respect for the man who had fought so valiantly, Gen. Grant does not accept Gen. Lee's sword, the customary manner for surrendering.

Now the bitter War Between the States has ended. The war between the armies and navies of the North and the South is finally over. The war-weary men at last can go home. That is, except for Gen. Robert E. Lee who never again can return to his stately Arlington, Virginia mansion overlooking the Potomac River directly across from Washington, D.C. The property is the inheritance of his wife, Mary, daughter of Washington Parke Custis, grandson of Martha Parke Custis Washington.

Just two days following the announcement of his resignation from the Union Army all of the property had been confiscated. The house was occupied then by the Federal government and all the surrounding lands converted into a graveyard for Union soldiers and called Arlington Cemetery.

However, even though the war has come to its end, the following dilemmas remain like dregs in the bottom of a coffee cup. The lasting enmity between the two regions. The bitter legacies left by the institution of slavery, including future confrontations even in the year 2000 concerning the flying of the Confederate flag over South Carolina's Capitol Building in Columbia. Including the Mississippi vote in 2001 to retain the Confederate emblem on the state flag. Both incidents are to erupt in places where one segment of the population will view the flag as a symbol of *their cultural heritage* while another will view it as a symbol of *their ancestors' enslavement.*

Unanswered questions will continue to persist. Will it be possible for the psychological shackles carried for generations by descendants of slaves, the products of the South's *peculiar institution,* ever to disappear? Will it be possible in this nation described as "one under God" with liberty and justice to ever be for *all*? Will the the day ever arrive when skin color is secondary to one's character? Or better yet, *not even be an issue at all*? Even one hundred years after the Civil War ends this still will be only a *dream.* The dream of a young black preacher named Martin Luther King, Jr.

And finally, the most important question of all. Can his dream become a *reality* in the 21st century?

Military records verify 178,895 names of men who had been in the *segregated* United States Colored Troops (USCT) and approximately 18,000 in the *integrated* Navy. Still remaining unacknowledged is the number of colored men who had served in all white army regiments, albeit many were cooks, but all *bona fide* soldiers. Military rosters and pension records attest to this fact, such as in the case of Pvt. Crowder Pacien of the 103rd Pennsylvania Volunteers.

During the Civil War deaths of black troops were recorded as 32,369, a number more than 1/6 of all those serving and 40% higher than found among their white counterparts. *This pertinent question has been asked:* "Why was this so?" *The answer:* "Because of poorer over-all conditions."

Poorer quality of food. Less pay for months with which to purchase their necessary warm clothing. The overwhelming "fatigue duty" of digging, mucking, chopping, and building. *Poorer* quality of medical care because many white doctors refused to care for the black soldiers. *Poorer* preparation and training, as well as *poorer* equipment when being sent into battle.

Finally, the Confederates' "no quarter" (no mercy) policy towards blacks. Some Rebel regiments actually went into battle waving a black flag to indicate just that. And even if they did escape death, the captured blacks suffered more hardships than did their white counterparts. Imagine attempting to stay alive by gnawing on a leather shoe! That is what one surviving black prisoner-of-war described as having been his experience in the Confederate prison at Plymouth.

Even after the war ends in victory for the North, those blacks (men who had "to fight for the *right* to fight") are to receive no recognition for their invaluable contributions. For instance, Union veterans on May 23, 1865, 200,000 strong, members of The Grand Army of the Republic (the "terrible swift sword") victoriously parade for two consecutive days in an impressive review up Pennsylvania Avenue in the nation's capitol. They are the armies of Generals Meade and Sherman, each parading on a different day. However, not *one* of the USCT's 138 infantry, 13 hard artillery, 13 light artillery, or 7 cavalry is present. One explanation offered is that there had been no black regiments in the armies of Meade and Sherman. Certainly not in Sherman's because he had been most adamant about not having any blacks in his army.

Prior to the parade in D.C. the Army of the James on April 25th had paraded through Richmond. Black soldiers marched with white soldiers. However, not so in Washington. And that is the sight remembered by the American people. They will remember only victorious *white* soldiers marching in the two-day Washington parades with not one black unit present, just as if they had never served in the war at all. Not even the Fifth USCT Massachusetts Cavalry, which with two white regiments had been the *first* to enter Richmond following the capitulation of the Confederate capitol.

One member of that regiment was a twenty-year free colored man by the name of Samuel James Patterson, born on June 24, 1844 in Berwick, Pennsylvania. Since at first there had been no opportunities in his native state for a colored man to join the army, he had made his way to Massachusetts. After serving at the Battle of Petersburg and other campaigns, after being at the surrender of Richmond and after receiving his discharge at Clarksville, Texas on October 3, 1865, he will settle in Wilkes-Barre, Pennsylvania. Interestingly, in the future the families of the two Civil War veterans unite when two of Samuel's granddaughters marry Crowder's grandsons. Alice Morris to Kenneth Patience and later her younger first cousin Alice Patterson to his brother Edgar.

Sadly, the black soldiers who had made up 10% or more of the Union Army will be forgotten, accorded little recognition by the victors until interested persons begin to research and write books concerning the exploits of the USCT. However, it is going to take more than 130 years for those courageous "invisible" black men to finally become a *visible* remembrance in the history of this country. It will take the dedication of a bronze sculpture in Washington, D.C. during the summer of 1998. Originally the dream of Civil War veteran George Washington Williams, more than a century later it will become the dream of Council member Frank Smith of D.C.'s Ward 1. Finally the dream will become a reality.

Sculptor Ed Hamilton's impressive eleven feet high "The Spirit of Freedom" honors the USCT and their 7,000 white commanding officers. The semi-circular Civil War Monument, its wall displaying authenticated names etched on stainless steel plaques, fittingly is located in an area of the nation's capitol called "Shaw," named for the stalwart commander of the 54th Massachusetts Volunteer Infantry (USCT), Col. Robert Gould Shaw.

On the monument are found the following words:

CIVIL WAR TO CIVIL RIGHTS AND BEYOND

This memorial is dedicated to those who served in the African American units of the Union Army in the Civil War. The 209,145 names inscribed on these walls commemorate those fighters of freedom.

The seeming discrepancy between the two totals (178,895 and 209,145) of USCT is due to the fact that there were in numerous cases, more than one man with the same name. Also raising even higher the *total* number of black soldiers in the Civil War is an undetermined number of Negroes having served as enlisted men in several *all-white regiments*. Some of those men had been light skinned enough to "pass" as white, thereby making the retrieval of their names from military records impossible except by descendants who know without a doubt that their ancestors' records are there.

Still others, identifiably black men, had not been categorized by race on their regimental rosters. Titus Hardy and Richard West, cooks in the 103rd Pennsylvania Volunteers, were two such soldiers. These men as well as Dolphus Garrett, Samuel Grandville, and Crowder Pacien whose race had been documented on the regimental roster should be recognized as Union soldiers, also, albeit they had served in white regiments and not in the USCT. These men along with others whose names have yet to be retrieved from the National Archives still remain *invisible* simply because few know they even were there. <u>That is, until now!</u>

Following his discharge from the Union Army in 1864, Crowder Pacien becomes a proud life-long member of the GAR (Grand Army of the Republic), the fraternal organization providing social and political activities for veterans of the Union Army. Sixty-five years later his West Pittston, Pennsylvania grave will be marked by a Civil War veteran's head stone easily recognized by the characteristic shape of the marker. Flanking it are the GAR Stanchion and American flag replaced annually by a fresh one each Decoration Day (Memorial Day).

Gravestone of
Crowder Patience,
West Pittston Cemetery
West Pittston, Pa.

ACT OF MAY 11, 1912.

No. 1,140,513

Reissue

UNITED STATES OF AMERICA

DEPARTMENT — of the **INTERIOR**

BUREAU OF PENSIONS

It is hereby certified That, in conformity with the laws of the United States _____ Crowder Patient _____ who was a Private Co. C, 103rd Regiment Pennsylvania Infantry

_____ is entitled to a pension at the rate of _____ Sixteen _____ dollars per month, to commence June 6, 1912 and Twenty dollars per month from December 25, 1913 and Twenty-four dollars per month from December 25, 1915.

Given at the Department of the Interior this _____ twenty-sixth day of _____ March one thousand nine hundred and _____ thirteen and of the Independence of the United States of America, the one hundred and thirty-seventh

_____
Secretary of the Interior

Countersigned.

_____
Commissioner of Pensions

am

Pension record for Crowder
Patience

CERTIFICATE IN LIEU OF LOST OR DESTROYED
DISCHARGE CERTIFICATE.

To all Whom it May Concern:

Know ye, That *Crowder Pacien* , a *Private* of *Company C, One hundred & third Regiment of Pennsylvania Infantry* VOLUNTEERS, who was *enrolled* on the *first* day of *January*, one thousand eight hundred and *sixty-four*, to serve *three years*, was *Discharged* from the service of the United States on the *twenty-fifth* day of *June*, one thousand *eight* hundred and *sixty-five* by reason of *muster out of company.*

This Certificate is given under the provisions of the Act of Congress approved July 1, 1902, "to authorize the Secretary of War to furnish certificates in lieu of lost or destroyed discharges," to honorably discharged officers or enlisted men or their widows, upon evidence that the original discharge certificate has been lost or destroyed, and upon the condition imposed by said Act that this certificate "shall not be accepted as a voucher for the payment of any claim against the United States for pay, bounty, or other allowances, or as evidence in any other case."

Given at the War Department, Washington, D. C., this *fourth* day of *June*, one thousand nine hundred and *Twelve*.

By authority of the Secretary of War:

Adjutant General.

(A. G. O. 150)

010513

Discharge record for Crowder
Patience

SECTION III

CROWDER THE FREE MAN
AND ELSIE THE BOUND
GIRL

Chapter 14

Dillsburg, Pennsylvania

*T*his April morning in the year 1874 has dawned clear and crisp with the orange sun just commencing to peek from behind the dark Pennsylvania mountain range. Dew wets the leather shoes and jeans legs of the colored man starting out for work. In the distance he hears the discordant choir of several roosters welcoming the brand new day.

Crowder Pacient has always been up and out by the "crack of dawn." Accustomed now to the rhythms, sounds, and sights of the changing seasons just as he had been years ago before on the North Carolina plantation of his birth, he has discovered that here in Pennsylvania they are very much the same, except for the longer northern winters and shorter summers.

In 1865 as soon as he had received his last army-pay at Harrisburg, Pennsylvania, Crowder immediately set off *to do what he chooses.* First he headed east to Lancaster County where he had been told he might find work on the huge farms owned by the Pennsylvania Deutsch. Crowder did not intend to stay in one place for any length of time. He was getting used to coming and going, *as he would choose,* enjoying his life of freedom as he explored his new environs here in the North.

Especially amazing to him was how northern farms could be run so efficiently with only the labor of the owners themselves and perhaps a few hired men. Whereas Marse needed at least sixty-five slaves' laboring from "sun up to sun down." Of most interest to Crowder, though, was the horse auction. Arriving from their prosperous farms were long-haired Amish men conversing in German, wearing their distinctive clothing of broad brimmed straw hats, indigo blue shirts, and black trousers braced by suspenders. Sturdy and reliable horses were very much in demand for working the farmers' fields as well as for pulling their black buggies. Consequently, the bearded, sans mustache, men came from many miles away, arriving very early to bid on the best horseflesh.

Crowder stood by watching as they searched for the healthiest young horses. He observed how each animal's mouth got pried open so its teeth could be carefully scrutinized. The farmers were well aware that horses younger than four years of age still were in possession of their "milk" teeth, the temporary ones. The farmers were aware, too, that canines develop only in stallions and in one under five years of age, those "eye" teeth were not yet present. No one ever attempted to fool those astute men.

Always having been interested in horses, Crowder specifically looked for jobs on farms where he might be put in charge of the teams. As the years have passed his expertise with horses has grown while his reputation as a good worker has spread. According to the census of 1870, one farm where he had worked was in Mount Joy, Lancaster County. Prosperous as that farm was, when winter arrived there was not enough work for him, and so again he moved on.

Then something very dismaying for the Pennsylvania farmers occurred in 1872. The tragic horse epidemic "epizootic" swept mercilessly through the farms. At the place where Crowder had been able to find work that year every last one of the horses succumbed to the dreaded disease. Anxiously the question circulated, "Will the cattle get it, too? After all, they graze in the same pastures as the horses." Fortunately, the answer was, "No, because it is strictly a horse disease." But until it could be controlled, oxen were used for draft purposes, something Crowder found to be most difficult. He was used to the *obedience* of horses, soon arriving at the conclusion that oxen definitely have minds of their own!

Just last week he had begun working on a farm on the outskirts of a small community in York County. Dillsburg, 16 miles southwest of Harrisburg, Pennsylvania's state capitol. Here the times for plowing and planting arrive later than they do in the South. Except for his being in charge of a team of horses, these tasks are much the same as he had performed before the war. However, now there is jingling in his pockets. His horde of coins steadily is increasing, but certainly not at the rate he would wish.

He finds that boarding takes a big chunk out of his earnings. Decent clothing costs a sizable amount. Leather shoes to fit his feet properly cost more than he wants to spend, having to purchase several pairs each year since they wear out so fast. Becoming soaked in the fields causes the leather to harden, ultimately cracking. Once when the soles were wearing thin he had traced his feet on pieces of cardboard to fit in the bottom of his shoes, but when a hole finally broke through the sole he found the cardboard to be of little help.

Whistling a lively tune as he swings along the narrow lane running behind several neighboring Dillsburg residences, Crowder takes notice of a young female in a barnyard. From the basket she carries over one arm she throws handfuls of corn to the expectant brown hens clucking at her bare feet. "Here, chick, chick, chick! Here, chick, chick, chick!"

"She's short. Prob'ly jest a child," the man assumes, not being able to appraise the girl's features hidden under a wide brimmed bonnet. He can see only her straight black hair braided into a single plait falling down the middle of her back.

At the same instant he is scrutinizing her she turns, glancing up to see a colored man in the lane. This is not so unusual a sight. Carrying brown burlap sacks containing all their worldly goods, colored men often have come to the back door of the house to request a hot meal in exchange for chopping wood or mucking out the stable. There usually is some work to be found for them.

Afterwards they wait on the back porch for their meal. The housekeeper sometimes will serve them a heavy German fare before sending them on their way. Mashed white potatoes, sauerkraut seasoned with bratwurst, and apple butter slathered on white bread. Sometimes she mixes freshly made cottage cheese with apple butter, creating a concoction as tasty as a sweet dessert. And always there is a pitcher of cool milk for the thirsty transients.

This must be one of those men, the girl is thinking. Her eyes fix inquisitively on the colored man striding by. *No, he's not stopping here.* Upon seeing her gaze in his direction he politely tips his straw hat. She gives a small wave of her hand in return. *Friendly people in that house*, he surmises.

The girl is not just being friendly. She also is curious. Curious about colored folk. Following a devastating smallpox epidemic in Washington, D.C., a number of children belonging to free colored people living there were left orphaned. Several churches had become involved in their plight, making arrangements for their care. A certain prominent Dillsburg lawyer and his wife, upon learning of the situation through their son who had relocated in Washington, agreed to take into their Pennsylvania home two little orphaned colored sisters to be "bound" as servants until their sixteenth birthdays. And this girl Elsie was one of them.

As far back as she and her younger sister Dollie can remember they have lived in this small borough of Dillsburg, population less than 300 inhabitants. The girls have been reared to be house servants, assisting the housekeeper. Elsie remembers when she was too short even to reach the sink in the kitchen pantry, having to be lifted onto a wooden box so she could wash and dry the dishes.

In an attic room with a single unscreened window Elsie and Dollie share a creaking rope-stringed bed with a mattress of goose down. The window can be flung open in hopes of catching passing cool gusts of air, never enough, though, on sweltering summer nights. Intended to keep out insects, the thin piece of muslin at the window keeps out any cooling breezes as well. And during summer downpours when the window by necessity must be kept closed, the two girls become drenched with perspiration. Downstairs on the second floor the bedrooms all have screened windows for keeping flies out during the day and mosquitoes at night.

✦

Elsie knows that the lawyer and his wife are not her parents. For one thing, they are much too old, already grandparents. Secondly, when their grown children visit they address the man and woman as "Father and Mother," whereas Elsie and Dollie have been directed to address them as, "Sir and ma'am."

"Ma'am, where's *our* Pa'n Ma?" Elsie had asked one afternoon as she was carefully pouring a cup of tea for the lawyer's wife who was crocheting in her sunny upstairs sitting room.

"I think they must have died from the smallpox, Elsie."

"Smallpox? What's *that*, ma'am?"

"It's a terrible *terrible* disease. It kills a lot of people."

"Oh." The girl had looked crestfallen. Then she asked, "Did our Ma'n Pa live here, too? In Dillsburg?"

"No, Elsie, your folks lived in the capitol of this country. That's Washington, D.C. It's quite far away, you know."

"Oh." The girl paused before asking, "Well then, ma'am, how'd Dollie'n me get *here*?"

"Now, you see it was like this, Elsie. My husband and I wanted to bring you *here*. Out in the country where you can grow up healthy and strong. Otherwise, they would have just put you in an *orphanage* in Washington. I'm sure you wouldn't have liked that. No, you wouldn't have liked that one bit. There just would've been too many of you children all crowded together like that! Now I know that you realize when you're sixteen you can leave here, of course. That is, if you want to. You know, to get married or to learn a trade. Perhaps dress making. I've always considered that to be a respectable trade for a woman."

Elsie nodded and replied, "Yes, ma'am." The girl appeared to be mollified, but only for the time being.

As she grew older, Elsie became aware that in the summer months Dollie's arms would become several shades darker than usual. Her body under her clothing would be as light as ever, but her exposed face and arms tanned to a light golden brown. Elsie with black hair and dark brown eyes may have tanned slightly, but not nearly as much as Dollie with light brown hair and hazel eyes. Even the housekeeper's young son had begun to take notice. Holding his summer-tanned arm next to Dollie's for comparison, he would exclaim, "Dollie's arms are the brownest!" And that had upset the girl, making her wonder, *Why am I the different one?*

Why do Dollie's arms get so brown in the summer? Her sister wondering, also, mentioned it to the housekeeper one spring day when the two of them were out in the backyard at the clotheslines, beating the dusty woolen Oriental rugs being readied for their rolling, mothproofing, and storing, all requirements over the summer months.

Although the older woman's nose and mouth were protectively covered with a clean neckerchief so she would not convulse into sneezing and coughing and although the full expression on her face could not be seen, the pained look which quickly flickered in her eyes was not missed by Elsie. The woman hedged uncomfortably by saying, "Can't rightly tell ya that, Elsie," not wanting to deliberately lie, but knowing that *she* was not the one to enlighten the questioning girl.

Somebody needs ta explain a thing or two ta Elsie and Dollie, the concerned housekeeper was thinking.

"Ma'am." She broached the subject with the lawyer's wife. "Elsie's been askin' me all sorts'a questions."

"Yes? What kind of questions?" The wife momentarily ceased her knitting to look up at the housekeeper.

"Like why Dollie gets so brown in the sun. I didn't know what ta say ta her. It's not my place ta tell her anything."

"Yes, you're quite right. It's not your place. And I want to thank you for telling me, though. I'll have to see to it." She had known that the day eventually would come when she and her husband must tell the girls about themselves. First, though, she had to talk the situation over with him for this situation must be handled with much delicacy.

And so after agreeing that it probably would be best for them to talk to Elsie together, the lawyer and his wife summoned the girl to the upstairs sitting room. "Come, child," the wife invited. "Here, sit beside me." She patted a place for Elsie on the pink rose brocaded love seat as the lawyer lowered himself into a matching chair.

"Elsie, we think it's time for you to learn some important things about yourself and Dollie," began the lawyer reluctantly.

Now Elsie had been in and out of this room all of her young life, but this was the first time she ever had been invited to *sit*. Bound girls in general were not invited to *sit* in their employers' sitting rooms. And so trembling, she was fearful of what she was about to hear. She was wondering what important things they could possibly say about her and Dollie. She was worrying that they were about to send them away. She was concerned that they would have to go back to Washington to live in an orphanage like other orphans who have no Ma and Pa.

The lawyer was making an attempt at composing himself. He was agonizing, *Just how will I ever find the proper words for this child?* This child bound to him and his wife as a servant. This child they never had intended to *care* for, but they do. This child gazing at him with such trust.

After clearing his throat, he commenced, "Elsie, now you and Dollie are not Germans. You know, like the rest of us in this house." She was looking at him puzzled because she had never really thought about such a matter before.

He paused momentarily before continuing. Clearing his throat again, he went on to explain, "No, Elsie, you and Dollie are....ah...." He heaves a deep sigh. "You are...umm...*colored girls." There! Now I've said it!*

"Colored girls?" With incredulity in her voice Elsie repeated lawyer's words. "Colored girls? No! Why, that can't be true, sir. Our skin's *white!*" she exclaimed in astonishment while staring at her pale hands. Then she looked over at his for comparison before adding, "Just like *yours, sir.*"

Besides, Elsie knew that she and Dollie certainly did not look at all like the colored men stopping by from time to time begging for work. Or like the colored people she had seen on the streets of Mechanicsburg when she shopped there with the housekeeper. What she had observed about them was that they come in many different shades of brown. That she found to be quite interesting. Some she noticed were as dark as freshly brewed coffee, while others were the tone of a bright new penny, and some even the shade of a walnut.

The lawyer's revelation made her contemplate. *Maybe then some of them white men asking for a meal could be colored, too?* That sudden realization then forced Elsie to question, *How on earth can a body tell if they was or if they wasn't?*

The wife tried to proffer a conceivable explanation to the now thoroughly confused young girl. "Elsie, you see it seems that colored people can come in many different shades. Some they call mulattos and they can be just as white as us Germans. And others are really very dark brown. And then there are many shades in between."

"Why is that, ma'am?"

In discomfort the wife glanced over at her husband who was not coming to her aid at all in the awkward situation they have found themselves. He was not about to get into *that topic.* Miscegenation, as it was called. So with no intentions of truthfully answering Elsie's question the wife had responded, "Well, child, I guess that's just the way the good Lord decided colored people should be. Can't question that now, can we?" Wanly she smiled at Elsie, praying that such an explanation would be of some value to the confounded girl.

"No, ma'am, I guess not," the girl obediently answered, knowing full well that she was going to question.

"And now, you see, it just so happens that when Dollie's outside in the sun her skin gets a little browner than yours. I suppose it's because you and Dollie are *mulattos*."

First Elsie had been told that she was a *colored* girl. Then she was told that she was a *mulatto*. In utter confusion she had asked, "Mulattos? What does that mean, ma'am?"

The wife had no idea that the word originally had been derived from "mule," that hybrid cross between a donkey and a horse. Even if she had known she certainly would not have told the now thoroughly confused girl.

"Mulattos are people who have one white parent and one colored one, I believe." The nervous woman was making an attempt at an explanation, feeble as it was, having absolutely no idea of the complexities associated with the mixing of the two races over the past 150 years.

Living in a small northern town where there are no colored residents, she had no knowledge of the 1866 "miscegenation" law stating that any person having *one fourth* or more Negro "blood" was deemed "colored." She certainly could not foretell the 1910 law decreeing any person having *one sixteenth* or more Negro "blood" will be deemed "colored." Never has she heard quadroon, octoroon, mustee, or any of the other *invented* names intended for specifying the amount of colored "blood" a person may have. She has no idea that in the future those mixtures would become so confusing that the white population will simply adopt the "one drop" policy. In the 1920 census persons having *any* colored ancestry at all will be deemed "colored."

She certainly could not foresee that "one drop" policy's leading to the 1920 census's elimination of that third caste of people previously labeled Mulatto (M), changing them forever to the category of Black (B). By that time it will be impossible, anyway, to ascertain just what percentage of black or white most people are. And by the middle of the twentieth century the majority of colored people living in the United States are going to be mixtures of African, European, and Native American.

Also by then, countless numbers of unknowing American whites will be descendants of those mulattos who had passed forever into the white world. Interestingly, at the very last years of the 20th century there will be some whites willing to own their colored ancestry. These include several descendants of Eston Hemings, proven by DNA testing to be the mulatto son of the third president of the United States, "with liberty and justice for all" Thomas Jefferson.

Elsie, turning then to the uneasy lawyer, had asked, "Sir, you're saying that our mother or father was *colored*? That's what you're thinking? And that's why Dollie turns brown in the summertime?" And now she also was wondering to herself, *Is that why my hair's so black?*" No one she had ever seen had hair dark as hers.

"Yes, that's what we suspect, Elsie," he gently answered, in reality suspecting a colored *mother*, not the other way around. As one who had done some traveling, he was well aware of the South's "peculiar institution."

Dollie could *not* fathom it at all when Elsie attempted to explain what the lawyer and his wife had revealed. The younger girl just kept her long sleeves rolled down even on the hottest of summer days and wore her sunbonnet constantly. She just was determining not to be singled out as "the different one."

One morning while shopping with the housekeeper at a dry goods store in Mechanicsburg Elsie and Dollie overheard the unfamiliar melodic lilt of Ireland. Two young Irish girls employed on a nearby farm were busily conversing. Quizzically glancing in their direction Elsie and Dolly were amazed to see for the first time a head of hair the color of flames. The owner of the long fiery locks animatedly was giving her order to the clerk standing behind the counter.

"Why's she talking funny like that?" Dollie whispered to her sister.

"Shhh! She'll hear you. We'll just have to ask the housekeeper."

"Those girls come from some place way across the ocean. Ireland, it's called," the older woman explained to Elsie and Dollie. Then she added, "Some people think *we* talk funny, too, ya know."

That the girls could not discern because all of the people they knew talked in the same way. Elsie and Dollie spoke English in the manner of the Pennsylvania German lawyer, his wife, and their children. Both girls had the desire to be well spoken in preparation for that time in the future when they would leave their "bound" state, having no idea that the speech patterns of this community might differ from others.

Second generation Pennsylvania Deutsch (misnamed Dutch), the widowed housekeeper whose husband did not return from the war, may have spoken German with her friends and relatives, but, otherwise, she used English because she wanted her son to speak it well. However, sometimes around the house she would lapse into German if she were to become excessively agitated. Such as when the clothesline broke, tumbling all the clean laundry to the dirty ground. Or when a cake baking in the oven "fell" or when she discovered the milk was spoiled because the cow had gotten into some wild onion grass. Then out would spew the German!

One day Dollie asked, "Sister, why can't we go to school like the housekeeper's boy? I want to learn how to read and write, too." As she dried the supper dishes she was watching the little boy who was perched at the table. With a piece of white chalk he was practicing his penmanship on his black slate.

"Don't rightly know, Dollie. First chance I get I'll ask the Mrs. about it, though."

At this time in Pennsylvania certain expenses were involved with children's schooling even though the Free School Act had been passed in 1834. A building furnished with desks and other necessary equipment had to be provided. The teacher's salary needed to be paid, even though many times it was in "script." Perhaps free room and board with a family, or, if not, a supply of spuds to last over the winter, fresh hens for Sunday dinners, eggs and a slab of bacon for breakfasts, loaves of baked bread, bushels of apples or jars of jellies, and other preserves.

Stacks of wood were needed for feeding the voracious appetite of the pot-bellied cast iron stove set smack-dab in the middle of the schoolroom floor. Individual primers, writing slates, and chalk all had to be purchased from the general store. Warm clothing, heavy shoes, and galoshes were vital for the long treks through rain, sleet, and snow. And all of these were, of course, the responsibilities of the parents.

In the first place the lawyer and his wife were under no obligation to educate Elsie and Dollie, mere servants in the household. They were there to work "for their keep" and always there was plenty of work to do. In 1873 life certainly could have been much worse for two little orphaned mulatto girls. Secondly, the lawyer and his wife probably would not have been able to send them to the local school, anyway, because there may have been white parents not in favor of colored girls' (even if they did not look so) learning side by side with their children. There was a Colored School up in Mechanicsburg, but it was much too far away for Elsie and Dollie to attend.

One morning when she was carrying a lunch tray to the lawyer's wife who was reading in her comfortable upstairs sitting room, Elsie wistfully asked, "Ma'am? Why can't me'n Dollie go to school? To learn how to read, too?"

The answer the wife gave Elsie did not reveal the *entire* truth. "Elsie, you see, I really need you and Dollie here to help the housekeeper with the work. Perhaps after you leave here you'll get a chance to learn how to read and write," she suggested, purposely adding nothing about their having to go to a segregated colored school. "It takes a lot of time, you know, to learn to read and write."

"Yes, ma'am," Elsie replied. *Well, if not me, I'll make sure Dollie does.*

Chapter 15

The Suitor

Now in the spring of 1874 Elsie is almost sixteen years old. In just a few months she will be able to leave this family to which she has been bound for as far back as she can remember. She is wondering, though, *Leave? And to go where? Not to get married, that's for certain.* She knows that most of the girls she sees at church are usually spoken for by age sixteen, that is, unless they have something drastically wrong with them. And according to this small Pennsylvania farming community Elsie and Dollie Vedan do have something drastically wrong with *them.* They are *colored.*

Early marriages are encouraged here. A man settled down with a wife and family will not be apt to go off searching for greener pastures, so parents hope. Early on then, informal liaisons between neighboring families often get established. The young people are abetted by the adults through various social get-togethers such as taffy pulls, barn raisings, ice skating and quilting parties, spelling bees, dances, and any other such opportunities for young people to appraise each other. Even to encouraging "bundling," which is also called "bed-courting," a unique Pennsylvania Deutsch custom.

Elsie knows she can never be part of this local tradition. Boys in this tight-knit community all have been told that Elsie is not white, even though they have no idea why their parents have said such a crazy thing. She certainly looks white to them. These boys all have been warned by their parents, "If you dare marry a colored girl, even if she does look white, we'll disown you. There won't be no *colored* children in this family." Consequently, the boys keep their distance from Elsie.

This conclusion is due to a mistaken assumption by those having no knowledge of the mechanics of genetics. They do not know that children born to a colored parent and a *pure* Caucasian parent can never be any browner than the darker one. Therefore, if she were to marry a white man, Elsie with her pale skin could never produce a brown child. But since these pertinent facts are not known, Elsie is a pariah in this community. An embarrassing incident already has happened. Once when she was at the general store a bag had slipped from her hand. A young boy standing nearby quickly picked it up from the floor, handing it to Elsie. Before she even had a chance to utter a "thank you" she sighted the livid face of the boy's father as he not so discreetly summoned his flustered son.

So she knows very well there are no eligible men around here for her to marry. She will have to go somewhere else to find herself a colored husband. Perhaps back to Washington where the lawyer's wife said she and Dollie had been born. That is a long way from this Pennsylvania borough, so she has been told, and she has absolutely no idea how to get there. Besides she will not leave her sister behind. Elsie will just have to bide her time until Dollie reaches sixteen. Then they both can leave together.

To Elsie it seems perfectly natural to want to find a husband. Every woman wants one, she supposes, because how else could she ever have her own home and her own family? She has observed that the church membership consists mostly of married women, their husbands, and numerous offspring. Even if widowed at an early age most women will marry again in a short time. Likewise, if a man loses his wife he, too, will find a replacement very quickly, especially if he has children. It is not at all unusual for him even to marry his deceased wife's sister. So Elsie has come to the conclusion that in 1874 a husband is a *real necessity* for any woman, colored or white.

Therefore, on the second morning when Elsie spies the same colored man swinging up the narrow lane she decides to scrutinize him the more. What she observes is a sinewy, medium-tall brown-skinned man, face the color of burnished copper, a man decidedly having more than her fifteen years. *He must have a wife*, she speculates, as once again he politely tips his straw hat. Pleasantly he smiles as he continues on his way.

Well, now, maybe he does, Elsie. And then again, maybe he don't. Only one way to find out. Just gotta ask him. That is, if he comes by this way again tomorrow morning. And with these daring thoughts taking root in her mind, the usually shy girl returns to her many chores.

Early the next morning Elsie scoops extra grain into her basket and after feeding the hungry clucking hens she ventures closer to the narrow lane, even though she knows the hens never go down the yard this far. And so when she spies the same colored man ambling up the lane she pretends to be busy searching for runaway hens. "Here, chick, chick, chick! Here, chick, chick, chick!" the girl calls out to imaginary birds. As usual the man is whistling a merry tune. Drawing near the yard on the third day, once again he sees the barefooted dark-haired young girl. She is much closer to the lane today, however, and facing him. His discerning eyes tell him that the pretty girl most *definitely* is not a child.

He calls out, "Mornin', Miss," tipping his straw hat. *No reason not tuh be polite*, flashing his radiant smile.

"Morning," she replies softly, approaching the wooden fence at the edge of the yard. "Where do you work at?" she asks, speaking with that Pennsylvania accent to which he has become accustomed these past nine years.

He stops in the lane in order to answer her question. "Jest up yonder. At the place that's got the big pine out front. Know it?"

She recognizes in his speech the southern cadence she has heard before when colored men have stopped by requesting work. "Oh yes. I know that farm." She pauses for a moment before adding, "*I* work here."

"Oh! That right?" He had presumed her to be a daughter of the resident family, not someone working for them.

"Yes. I'm their...*colored girl*," she continues. *That should give him a start*, she thinks. And she is not disappointed.

Now he stares at her incredulously. *Colored? That can't be. She looks like a white girl tuh me.*

"How's that again?" he asks.

"I'm their 'colored girl.' Me'n my little sister Dollie, well, we have to work here 'til we're sixteen. She's only twelve now. And so when we leave here we gotta find jobs, you know, or maybe...." Now she deliberately takes a long pause before bravely continuing, "...or maybe to get married."

She waits for the last words to sink in. They sink!

Crowder has never taken the time to seriously contemplate marriage. He had thought he would like to have a family of his own *some day*, but the years have passed by much too quickly. Nine wonderful years of freedom to do just what he chooses. Nine years of moving from place to place, just enjoying his new life in the North.

Since the end of the war he has been saving his money. So it is not that he is penniless. Far from it, in fact. He has more money than a lot of men. It has occurred to him from time to time that he probably should settle down, but so far where he has been working he has not met any eligible colored girls. And now he is fast approaching his twenty-eighth birthday.

Still in shock from the girl's startling disclosure, he can do nothing but say, "Hope yuh have a fine day, Miss." Shaking his head incredulously, Crowder continues up the narrow lane to the farm with the tall white pine tree in its front yard.

Today his mind is not concentrating on his plowing and planting or even on his favorite horses. Neither is Elsie's on her cooking and cleaning. At dusk Crowder again passes by the house. From kerosene lamps yellow light streams through the window panes, but in the empty back yard there is no sight of a small girl with a long black braid falling down her back.

One of the more observant boarders comments during supper, "Mighty quiet tonight, Pacient."

"Thinkin'. Jest thinkin'."

"Thinkin'. Hmm. Must be about some woman."

Crowder just smiles.

The next morning Elsie is awake much before the light of dawn. She slips carefully out of her side of the creaking bed, trying not to disturb her still sleeping sister, unwilling to have to explain why she is getting up so early.

After splashing her face with the cold water she pours from the tin pitcher into the blue and white speckled porcelain lined basin, she quickly brushes and braids her silky long straight black hair. Throws on a petticoat over her shift, pulls up her bloomers, hooks her dress, ties on a clean cover-all apron, and stealthily climbs barefoot down the creaking attic steps. Tiptoes soundlessly down the back stairs to the kitchen to retrieve her egg basket from its peg on the pantry wall. Fills the basket with chicken feed, some extra today. Then carefully opens and closes the squeaking screen door to go outside to feed the hungry hens and the rooster, even before he has the chance to crow his raucous welcome to the new day.

Now on the fourth day when Elsie again sees the colored man making his way up the lane, she immediately goes to the fence. It now has become quite apparent to Crowder that the girl has been waiting for him these past *two* mornings. And the very thought quickens his pulse as well as his step.

Unlatching the gate she takes a bold step directly into the lane just as he reaches the edge of the property. Removing his straw hat politely he introduces himself. "Crowder Pacient, at yore service, ma'am." Through dark brown eyes the girl gazes up at the man's smiling face while replying in her soft Pennsylvania accent, "Elsie Vedan, sir."

"Well, Miss Elsie, gonna be a lovely day tuhday, don't yuh think?"

"Yes, Mr. Pacient. I certainly do."

Now with these formalities completed, Elsie has an important question to ask this colored man. And he has one to ask her, too, but neither one knows how to approach the other. This kind of *repartee* is new to both of them.

She sighs. *I simply got to know. That's all there is to it*, she determines, heart pounding with trepidation. "Mr. Pacient, do you mind if I ask you a question?"

She feels her face warming before she hears his reply. "And jest what is it yuh want tuh know, Miss Elsie?"

This is your chance, Elsie. Now or never! "Well, I was just wondering…if there might be a…." Then after taking a deep breath, she bravely continues, "…a *Mrs*. Pacient?"

Crowder finds it hard to believe this pretty young girl has been thinking about him at all and now to find out she is wondering if he is married or not! He wants to let out a hearty laugh, but afraid that might scare her off, he just smiles that expansive smile of his, replying, "No, ma'am! There izzen't no *Mrs.* Pacient."

He, too, has a question. "Now can Ah ask somethin', Miss Elsie?"

She nods affirmatively."Yes, of course, Mr. Pacient." So with great difficulty Crowder, who is never at a loss for words, continues, "Was wonderin'…um…jest…um…when it's that…yuh'll…um…be sixteen."

There. It's out, he thinks, heaving a deep sigh of relief.

Without any hesitation at all on her part, Elsie replies, "On the first day of August." She adds with emphasis, *"This year."*

Quickly in his head he is calculating. *It's now the middle of April. Then August's only three'n a half months from now.* He is also figuring she already may be making plans to leave this place. She already may have another fellow in mind and even if she does not, she may think Crowder much too old to come calling on her, young as she is.

Hat in hand, Crowder is fidgeting now, very uncomfortable, never having been in a situation like this before. Sweating profusely even though it is only early April, heart pounding faster and louder than usual, he wonders if he dare ask his next question.

Elsie, not quite five feet, looks up questioningly at this colored man with sparkling dark-brown eyes set perfectly in his burnished copper face. She is noticing that suddenly he appears to be quite uncomfortable. Perspiration is beading on his brow even though she does not perceive it to be especially warm today.

A blue and white checkered bandanna is tied around his neck. After unknotting it he begins to wipe his wet brow. *Didn't reckon it was gonna be this hot tuhday,* he muses to himself.

Elsie is standing there, wishing he would say something else to her in his soft southern drawl, the sound of which is very pleasant to her ears. His nerve somewhat restored by her remaining at the edge of yard instead of immediately returning to her chores, he finally regains his composure.

"Miss Elsie?" He is pausing to collect his thoughts. Clearing his suddenly husky voice, he asks, "Miss Elsie,…um…do yuh think…um…it would it be…um…fittin' fer me…ah…tuh call on yuh?" Now in 1874 a young man's "calling on" a young woman means only one thing. He wants to see if the two are suited well enough for marriage.

And without even pausing to think it over because she already has planned what her answer is going to be, just in case, Elsie answers, "Why, yes, Mr. Pacient. I would be honored."

Heaving a big sigh of relief Crowder now queries, "Will Sunday evenin' be all right? Some time around seven?"

"I think that'll be just fine."

It's already Friday, Elsie realizes. With the basket of the eggs she finally has collected for breakfast she flies back to the house. She has a lot to accomplish before a young man can come calling.

First thing, she has to ask permission of the lawyer and his wife. Perhaps they may not think it fitting for Crowder Pacient to call. After all, this colored man is a total stranger. When Elsie enters the kitchen after returning her basket to the pantry, she approaches the housekeeper who is kneading dough for the loaves of white bread she bakes each Friday.

"Check the oven for me, will ya, Elsie?"

"Yes, ma'am." Grabbing up a teatowel, Elsie carefully swings open the oven door, then sticking her hand in just far enough to feel the degrees of heat. "Feels hot enough to me."

"Good," the housekeeper responds. "These loaves'll be ready in jest a minute."

"Ma'am?" Elsie is in need of some sage advice.

"Yes, Pet?" The older woman turns to glance at the girl whose face seems a little flushed. *The oven is not all that hot*, the housekeeper thinks. So with concern she asks, "Feelin' all right there?"

"Yes, ma'am. I feel fine."

"What's the matter then?" The housekeeper can see that something certainly is very much amiss with the girl.

"Well, ma'am, I need to tell you something. You see, in the morning I been talking to a fella who works up the road at that place with the tall pine tree out front. He passed by and spoke to me the other day. Every day now we say a little. Today he asked if he could come calling. He's colored, *just like me*, you know," she clarifies.

When the girl had first started her explanation the housekeeper's concern was that a transient upon discovering Elsie was not white would reject her. The housekeeper does not want that kind of hurt ever to touch Elsie of whom she is very fond. So she is relieved when Elsie finishes.

She certainly is quite surprised when the usually diffident girl reveals that she has been in conversation with any man at all, let alone a colored stranger, but she knows Elsie is now approaching her 16th birthday and soon may be wanting to leave this place. And the housekeeper knows there are no young men nearby who will court this pretty mulatto girl. Elsie probably will have to go to York, or maybe to Harrisburg, or even as far away as Pittsburgh or Philadelphia to find a colored husband. Perhaps then, this young man will be just the answer to Elsie's dilemma.

"Oh! Why, I think that's mighty fine, Elsie. Ya just go on and explain yerself ta the Mr. I'm rest assured that he'll approve."

And so it is with the lawyer's approval, a *young* man, *colored like Elsie,* is going to come to call on Sunday evening at seven o'clock.

While attending to her usual Saturday chores, Elsie eagerly is anticipating Sunday evening. She has so many things to do beforehand such as sweeping the side porch and dusting the furniture where she is going to entertain her caller. Such as baking a batch of sugar cookies for serving him. After all of her chores are completed on Saturday evening, with the water she has collected in the rain-barrel she washes her long black hair. Afterwards, she checks her best dress for rips and spots, mends a hole in the heel of one of her stockings, and blackens her high top buttoned shoes.

In church on Sunday morning she cannot keep her mind on the sermon as she fidgets in the last pew where she always sits with Dollie, the housekeeper, and her son. *Is Pastor speaking longer today?* She wonders, having no idea of the passage of time. At the beginning of his sermon the pastor's custom is to place his timepiece on the pulpit so he will know just how long to preach. However, no one else keeps track of the time. That is, unless some bored man very discreetly pulls out his pocket watch.

With her mind not at all on the sermon, she is wishing, *Hope it don't rain. I'm not sure he'll come in the rain. Hope it's not too hot. He won't be very comfortable walking way out here in the heat. Hope the Mr. won't ask for two servings of dessert for supper. Hope I'll get the kitchen cleaned up in time to put my good dress back on and pin up my hair.* And all this for Elsie to do by seven.

✦

In the front hall the mahogany long-case grandfather clock's heavy brass pendulum steadily swings back and forth. Soon it will announce the hour of seven. Hair pinned up, dress neatly pressed, shoes blackened and cheeks pinched for blush, Elsie is ready to greet her gentleman caller. When she asks permission to go to the edge of the back yard to wait for him, the lawyer's wife answers, "Oh, no, Elsie. That just wouldn't be fitting. Wouldn't be fitting at all." She insists, "The young man must be introduced to *us*. If we're going to do things, we must do them *right*. That's what I always say."

The tall slender clock brought many years ago from Germany by the parents of the lawyer's wife strikes seven a short time before the colored man, felt hat in hand, knocks on the back door of the large russet brick Georgian house. The wife advises Elsie, "Now count to ten before you open the door. You wouldn't want to appear anxious, you know."

Elsie is attired in her best "Sunday-go-to-meeting" dress, light blue and trimmed with lace on the collar and cuffs of the long sleeves. With two black braids wrapped around her pert face, cheeks flushed and eyes sparkling with anticipation Elsie slowly opens the door.

All prepared to greet the caller who is *colored just like Elsie,* the lawyer and his wife standing just behind the girl, gasp as the open door reveals a very black (in their estimation), very old (by their standards) colored man. *Oh, no! He's much too old! And he's much too black for our Elsie,* are their very first thoughts.

However, they are realizing, *It's too late to do anything about it now. We'll be cordial to him. We'll welcome him into our home this one time. But we're going to speak to Elsie about this!* Even though these thoughts are not verbalized, both the husband and wife are certain each will be in total agreement with the other on this matter.

"Sir and ma'am." Elsie is making the necessary introductions. "I'd like you to meet Mr. Crowder Pacient."

"How do you do, Mr. Pacient?" asks the lawyer as he politely reaches his right hand out to Crowder.

"Jest fine. Thank yuh, suh. Ma'am," he replies, shaking the lawyer's hand and bowing his head respectfully in the wife's direction, all the while smiling his smile.

After completing the formalities, Elsie, completely oblivious of the disapproval of her employers, directs Crowder onto the side porch where she has set out a large plate of sugar cookies and a pitcher of cold milk. From Dollie's garden Elsie has gathered a large bunch of yellow trumpet daffodils arranged in a lovely cut-glass vase which the Mrs. has allowed the girl to use.

"Will you take a little refreshment, Mr. Pacient?"

He is quite overheated in the borrowed suit the boarder who had been so inquisitive lent him when Crowder mentioned he was "goin' courtin'." Crowder does not possess a suit of his own. No need to until now. So yes, some cool refreshment would be very much appreciated.

Elsie pours him a glass of cold milk and places several sugar cookies on a china plate. "I made these myself," she proudly informs him.

The hour passes quickly as they talk about their pasts. He tells her that before the war he had been a slave in far off North Carolina. He shares with her a few anecdotes about his experiences during the war, only those appropriate for a sheltered young girl's ears, however, like how he had to learn how to cook. She tells him about her life here as a servant, herself never having known anything at all about slavery.

Elsie knows something about the war, though, because she was almost five years old when early in late June 1863 Rebel cavalry came to town. Led by the flamboyant Gen. James Ewell Brown "Jeb" Stuart, so easily identified by the scarlet lined cape fastened around his waist by a gold sash. By the white buckskin gauntlets covering his hands and especially by the ostrich plumed hat perched on his proud head. With sabers straight as steeples on the town's churches, the Confederates had ridden through Dillsburg in search of supplies. Meat, bread, coffee, tobacco, and especially corn for their "johnnie cakes." When they offered the merchants worthless Confederate script they were refused. So the Rebs just confiscated anything and everything they wanted.

Most of the nearby farmers had their horses stolen because the Rebs were looking for suitable ones for their cavalry, stallions less than twelve years old. Their age is easily discerned simply by checking the shape of the horses' teeth, always flattening with age.

The older stallions and mares they just left behind. The lawyer had been very relieved when the Rebs had not visited his property in town. His two young stallions out in the stable most certainly would have been taken had the Rebs stayed a few days longer. Fortunately they had not.

For it seems no sooner had they made camp in a nearby field, an order came to quickly get themselves over to a particular town at a crossroads located about twenty-two miles away. Gen. Robert E. Lee had been waiting there in anticipation for Gen. J. E. B. Stuart's news of the Union army's whereabouts.

However, for days he had not heard anything from Stuart and his cavalry. Needless to say, Lee was quite disappointed and displeased with the man he had heretofore so openly favored.

Neither did the raggedy Rebel force commanded by Brig. Gen. J. B. Jenkins stay very long in nearby Mechanicsburg, the northernmost place the Rebs would reach. Using their worthless Confederate script they were there for only three days. Long enough, though, to purchase horse feed and rations for 1500 soldiers. Long enough to steal the Union flag from Burgess Hummel's residence. Long enough to insult the townspeople by forcing them to witness an irreverent Rebel's use of their sacred Union flag as a saddle. Long enough to engage in several skirmishes before they, too, on Wednesday, July 1st were fatefully summoned to the same small town at a crossroad. *Gettysburg* was its name!

Fortunately, neither Dillsburg nor Mechanicsburg went the way of the undefended small community of Chambersburg, approximately twenty-five miles east of Gettysburg. It lay squarely in the middle of the Shenandoah Valley through which Gen. Robert E. Lee in June 1863 had launched his second and last grand offensive. The town was occupied on July 30th by the Rebels with demands of a ransom of $500,000 in greenbacks or $100,000 in gold. Since the townsfolk were unable to raise such an astronomical sum, the business section of town was burned, leaving Chambersburg, Pennsylvania in ruins.

Elsie vaguely remembers overhearing the lawyer and his wife in discussion concerning those incidents. They had been worrying about their married daughter who was residing in Mechanicsburg. That was how they happened to be aware of the chain of events taking place there. And so this is the extent of Elsie's knowledge of the Civil War.

As the young couple continues to converse they discover many things they have in common, such having no idea who they really are because they never knew their parents. And they talk about their dreams for the future such as having a family of their own because they want the feeling of belonging, something neither one has ever had. They are both surprised at how comfortable they are with each other. Elsie has never talked so much to anyone before, except, of course, her sister Dollie.

When Crowder asks if Elsie might consider him as a suitor he warns her that he is a lot older than she is. "Be twenty-eight on Christmas day. That's when Ah celebrate ma birthday," he explains. "On Jesus' birthday. That's 'cause Ah don't rightly know jest when Ah been born."

She replies that he does not look old to her. But she does have a problem, though. She will never leave Dollie behind because her sister has no one else but Elsie. After Crowder assures her that she would never have to, she answers his question with, "Then I will consider you."

So as the conversation on the side porch is transpiring, in the parlor the lawyer and his wife are discussing Crowder's advanced age and especially his *color*. She says, "He's much *much* too old for her. Why, he's got gray hair already! He's got to be all of thirty!"

He says, "And just *look* at him, will you? He's too *too* black. Oh, just think of Elsie's *poor* children! Why, they'll all be black, too. What on earth will become of them? They'll have no chance in life. Absolutely no chance at all! No, we must do *everything* we can to discourage her." And on this opinion the lawyer and his wife are definitely of one accord.

Meanwhile, Elsie wants Crowder to meet her sister before he takes his leave. In the back yard Dollie has been trying to finish weeding her garden before complete darkness descends. Now that April has arrived this has been happening a little later each evening. Once Dollie had wondered about this. Why the sun sets later each evening.

"Sister?" she had asked. "Notice how the sun's going down later now? Not the same time like last night. Ever notice that?"

Elsie had noticed that during the winter months she washed the supper dishes by the light of a kerosene lamp, but in April she did not need it. She knew it was at the same time because the grandfather clock would have chimed *seven* times already. She had noticed that when the weather was hot in summer months the sun sank behind the mountains much later, sometimes even after the clock had chimed *eight* times. But she never had the urge to wonder just *why* until Dollie asked her.

Elsie's answer was what it always was, "Let's ask the housekeeper, Pet. Maybe she'll know." But when they had they still did not receive an answer to satisfy them because whenever the housekeeper did not know how to explain something she simply said, "Because God wants it that way is what I su'pose."

That time being unsatisfied with the housekeeper's explanation, Dollie chose to pursue the subject further by going to the lawyer's wife, approaching her with, "Ma'am, Elsie'n me, well, we was wondering about something." The woman had been arranging a spring bouquet of multi-colored tulips and bright yellow trumpet daffodils in a delicate Waterford vase to be placed in the sitting room where she does her reading, corresponding, crocheting, knitting, needlepoint, as well as afternoon snoozing.

"You have something you want to ask me, girls?"

"Yes, ma'am. Elsie'n me... Well, we was wondering something. We was wondering why the sun's going down later every night? Then we was wondering if it could keep on going down'n down'n down. And someday *never* come back up again!"

The woman smiled in amusement at Dollie's questions. "Oh, no, girls! You don't have to worry about that ever happening. The sun's not going to keep going down later and later. Why, there's a time when it stops doing *that* and then it'll start to go down *earlier* again. You'll see. And then after that winter will come again."

The two girls are looking at each other in wonderment as the lawyer's wife continues, "Girls, you notice how in the winter the sun goes down really *early?*"

They both nod affirmatively. "And in the summer it goes down really *late?*" Again they nod. "Yes, ma'am."

"Well, that's what happens *every* year. That's the way it's been since the time of Creation."

"But *why?*" the still wondering Dollie dares to ask.

The lawyer's wife is stumped over the question of "Why?" She herself had never wondered why and if she ever had learned the reason from her schoolmarms she does not remember it now. And if her own children had ever asked she does not remember that, either. Anyway, if they had wanted to know they probably would have gone straight to their father.

So her response to the girls is that she will have to get the answer from her husband, who as far as she is concerned, knows just about everything. When she finally gets around to broaching the subject with him and he realizes it is the question of the servant girls, he is amused.

He certainly has no intentions of educating his wife about the earth's rotating and revolving, or of solstices and equinoxes, or of latitude and longitude. He knows that as a *mere woman* she could not possibly grasp those scientific facts and certainly Elsie and Dollie, illiterate servants--colored at that-- would have no inkling whatsoever. Anyway, he has more important things on his mind. Like running a successful law practice. Therefore, his condescending answer to his wife is, "Dear, you told the girls right. That's the way the good Lord planned it at the Creation. And so that's the way it is."

He dismissively flaps open the morning edition of the local newspaper. "Now if you don't mind, *I'm* going to read my paper."

Dollie has an affinity for growing beautiful flowers and in her spare time can be found kneeling in the garden, hands buried in moist dark soil. Her hands are no lady's between using caustic lye on the laundry, washing dishes, scrubbing pots with harsh soap, and pulling weeds before planting her annuals.

Right now she painstakingly is picking out small stones and twigs from the soil, preparing it for her most favorite flowers, the colorful bright-faced pansies. She especially takes delight in arranging the deep purple variety with yellow.

Elsie directs Crowder around to the back of the house. "Dollie, this here's Mr. Crowder Pacient, I've been telling you about."

The younger girl quickly jumps to her feet as she pushes back her bonnet. She wants to get a real good look at this man who has caught her sister's fancy. Crowder is observing that Dollie already is the same height as Elsie even though three years younger. Elsie is a very petite girl.

"How-do, Mr. Pacient?" she asks politely.

"Jest fine, thank yuh, Miss Dollie. Doin' jest fine."

Darkness is fast approaching as the first night of courting ends and unbeknownst to the young couple, *the last*. Elsie walks with Crowder to the edge of the yard where he unlatches the gate in order to step out into the lane. Turning and reaching out to place the girl's small strong hands between his large calloused ones he speaks softly in his pleasant southern drawl, "Goin' tuh say good night tuh yuh now, Miss Elsie."

"Good night, Mr. Pacient."

"Be seein' yuh in the mornin' then." He then retreats down the lane, turning once to wave to the small figure still standing by the gate.

Yes, you certainly will, she is thinking with confidence.

When she no longer is able see him, with sprightly steps, a happy demeanor, and with lifted spirits now that her future is looking so bright Elsie returns to the house. This euphoria is to be very short-lived, though, because the lawyer tells her outright, "Elsie, what can you be thinking of? That man's much *too old* for you!"

The girl is taken aback by the degree of disapproval she is detecting in his tone of voice. Respectfully she responds, "Sir, he's only *twenty-seven*."

"*Only* twenty-seven!" Then turning to his wife, incredulously the lawyer repeats himself, "*Only twenty seven,* she says!" Then he turns back to the girl who by now is quite upset. "Must I remind you, Elsie? You're only *fifteen*!"

"Pardon me for saying so, sir, but I'll be *sixteen* in August."

He knows full well when Elsie will be sixteen and he knows that she will probably want to be leaving here soon, but he also knows that she will never leave her sister behind. So he had figured that she would be staying on for the time being, at least three more years. He just may have figured it all wrong.

The lawyer is continuing his assessment of the colored caller. "Besides, just *look* at him!"

Elsie has looked at Crowder Pacient and she very much likes what she sees. She likes his ready smile. She likes the way his dark brown eyes light up when he gazes down at her. Oh yes, she definitely has been *looking* at him.

"I *have* looked at him, sir."

"Now, Elsie, do you realize that if you marry *Crowder Pacient* your children will be *black*?"

"*Black*?" She pauses momentarily to mull this over before replying, "Well sir, begging your pardon, if that's what they are, they'll still be *my* children. And I'll love them. *Whatever color they are.*"

The lawyer sighs deeply. *Oh, she's a stubborn one,* he concludes as he sees he is making absolutely no headway at all with the girl. Elsie seems to have made up her mind. *Well, even so, I'll not encourage her,* he determines.

So he states the ultimatum. "Elsie, as long as you're still fifteen years old, you're under my care. When you turn sixteen, well then, you'll be free to do whatever it is that you please. But until that time comes, I forbid that man to come here! And that's all there is to it!"

The lawyer is hoping that Elsie soon will dismiss the too old (by his estimation), too black (by his standards) colored man from her mind. *If only there were some young colored men nearby,* he thinks. But he knows of none.

Then his wife adds, "And the housekeeper'll feed the chickens from now on, Elsie. You just stay in the kitchen and get the breakfast going."

Still attired in her "Sunday-go-to-meeting" finery, with her black hair pinned up like a grown woman's, Elsie sees her future with Mr. Pacient disintegrating in the flames of her employers' disapproval. However, she is not going to burst into tears. No, she is not going to break down like a blubbering child. Anyway, in her position she has never had that luxury. Hardly ever in her life has Elsie shed a tear. It would not have done her any good, anyway. *Well, I'm not gonna give up,* she determines. No, she is not going to lose this one opportunity. *I gotta make a plan.*

So she asks respectfully, "Sir, ma'am, then can I tell Mr. Pacient in the morning that he can't come calling on me no more?"

"Yes, Elsie, you can, but the housekeeper'll stand there in the doorway until you come back to the house."

Only when the girl retires to her attic bedroom does she allow herself to shed the pent-up tears of disappointment. Not wanting Dollie to hear her, Elsie sobs softly into her feather pillow.

After a restless night of fitful dreams, when Elsie rises much before daybreak she finds the housekeeper already bustling in the kitchen. She greets the girl sympathetically as Elsie begins filling her basket of chicken feed. As usual, she goes outside to feed the hungry hens and rooster and to collect her eggs. Not as usual, though, the housekeeper is at the kitchen door, standing watch as Elsie waits at the edge of the narrow lane. A whistling Crowder, after a peaceful night of happy dreams about a small woman with silky black hair flowing loosely around her face, jauntily comes swinging up the narrow lane.

Now he sees her up ahead, standing by the fence, waiting there for him! *'Magine that! She's waitin' jest fer me. Hard tuh believe.* Waving to her then, he hastens his steps. Drawing nearer he soon can see that her face is all dejected and tear stained. Alarmed now he asks, "Miss Elsie? What's the matter? Somethin's happened?" His heart sinks at the thought that perhaps she has changed her mind about him. "Yuh changed yore mind 'bout me comin' tuh call on yuh again?"

"No, no, no! Not that." She is looking at him with eyes overflowing with tears. "Oh, Mr. Pacient, I can hardly tell you."

"Well, take a deep breath now. And then jest *tell* me." He pulls a clean handkerchief from his coveralls and hands it to her. After dabbing her teary eyes, she pockets the white square with intentions of laundering it, even though she does not know just when she will be able to return it to him, the way things stand now.

"The Mr. and Mrs. say...," stumbling on her words. With head bent downward Elsie tries to continue. Now Crowder is really having difficulty understanding what she is saying since she speaks so softly as it is. "They say...." She gulps. "They say you're not suitable for me."

"That so? Give yuh a reason then, did they?"

She raises her rear-stained countenance to look directly at him while attemptimg to explain. "Well, first off, they think you're too *old*. I told them that you're *only* twenty-seven."

"Well now, Ah can understand that, Miss Elsie. Twenty-seven's a lot older than fifteen. But that's given me the chance tuh have enough money tuh provide fer yuh. Ah can promise that yuh won't never have tuh work fer nobody no more."

"Yes, I know that." She uses the handkerchief again to dry her eyes and to blow her nose before attempting to continue. "But that's not the *only* reason, though."

"Oh, no? What's the other reason?"

"They say...." She is finding it difficult to speak the words. "They say..." She heaves a deep sigh before continuing. "They say that you're too...." She simply cannot finish. She does not want to cause him the pain she is certain her words are going to inflict.

"Too...*what*, Miss Elsie? Jest say it! Please!"

Before she can form the words she has to swallow hard to keep from crying again. "Too *black*. That's what they say. They say that you're too black!" She finally is able to get the words out.

"Oh. *That's* it? Yes, Ah can believe that they would think so." Crowder is not in the least bit surprised that those two white people would be of such an opinion. Elsie, however, is quite surprised by his calm response.

Crowder had been well aware of color differences when he was a slave. He had observed that the more privileged house slaves were usually lighter in color than the field hands. Slaves such as the ones the shade of the light complexioned, green eyed Cassie were often given certain advantages. They were the ones picked as personal maids to the ladies, valets to the gentlemen, butlers, servers in the dining room, gardeners, and coachmen. And after the war ended the lighter ones seemed to get the better paying jobs.

Besides that, the lightest Negroes could "pass for white," thereby escaping the degradation of slavery. They could go north or west or even cross the Atlantic Ocean to Europe to easily be assimilated into the population there. And prior to the Civil War each year hundreds of people designated as "mulatto" had done exactly that. Without a trace they had completely disappeared into the white world, simply by changing their names and their locale.

Now a kind of caste system, a "colored aristocracy," has developed based upon skin tone. Light skinned colored folk aim to marry only other light skinned colored folk so their children can "get up in the world." In such colored circles a man such as Crowder Pacient, uneducated and dark complexioned, never would be considered a desirable husband for a light skinned daughter such as Elsie Vedan. Recalling his slavery days he knows that slave girls from the "big house' seldom "stooped" to choose men from the fields.

So *he* is not surprised at all, but *Elsie is!* Her isolated existence in a small town in Pennsylvania has not afforded her the opportunity to see many colored people. She knows nothing at all about them. She knows nothing about certain light complexioned mulattos deliberately erasing all signs of their negritude, mistakenly presuming if they act *white*, they will be accepted by the majority population. She is unaware that certain mulattos maintain such codes as the "brown paper bag" test. If darker than the bag a person would not be welcomed in certain "colored" circles, especially in Washington, D.C. Or the "Blue Vein Society" of Nashville, Tennessee or the "brown church door" where requests for membership are decided by comparing the applicants' skin shade to that of the door. In some places exceptions to these codes might be made, perhaps if the darker skinned person were highly educated or extremely accomplished.

All Elsie knows is that she has been told she is colored which guarantees no future for her in this Pennsylvania farming community composed mainly of persons of Scotch-Irish and German ancestry. She also knows that Crowder Pacient is a colored man assuring her that he can and will provide for her. So no, she does not see his brown skin being an impediment at all. She sees only his generous spirit and the intent of his heart. And these are sufficient enough for her.

Crowder needs to ask now, "Miss Elsie, what do *yuh* think? That Ah'm too black?"

Truthfully she answers him. "No, Mr. Pacient. I don't." And for further reassurance she adds, "I'll be sixteen on August 1st and I can do what I please, the Mr. says. I'll marry you then." She takes a deep breath before adding, "That is, if you still want me to," as she looks bravely into the eyes of a man she knows so little about, but already has come to trust.

Crowder nods to the affirmative. "All right then. Miss Elsie, Ah'm gonna hold yuh tuh that promise." Then he asks, "And when Ah pass by in the mornin's we can speak some. Fer tuh make some plans'n all?"

"Oh, no! I can't do that. The housekeeper's been told to feed the chickens from now on. The Mrs. says that I can't go out in the yard no more in the morning."

For a moment Crowder feels dejected by the unfairness of it all. Only for a *brief* moment, though. The unfairness of life has always been as a boulder set squarely in his path, lying in wait for him to dash his foot. But thus far it has not deterred him from fulfilling his dreams. First those of freedom and then of coming to this beautiful state of Pennsylvania. And he is determining now that it is not going to prevent him from having this pretty young girl as his wife.

"Got an idea then. If yuh jest stand by the kitchen door Ah'll see yuh every mornin'. Long as Ah see yuh there wavin' at me, then Ah'll know yuh be keepin' yore promise."

And so it is to go on for three and a half months. Crowder's passing up the narrow lane and Elsie's waving to him from the kitchen door.

Chapter 16

Three and a Half Long Months

Crowder realizes that he has some serious problems to solve if he plans to be married in August. For instance, where will the bride and groom live? Certainly not where *he* is boarding. Concerning him most is his ability to make enough money to support three people when Dollie turns sixteen and comes to live with them as he promised. Elsie has made it clear she will never leave Dollie behind.

Not that he has any objections about providing for Dollie. He had met the younger girl when he had come calling that one time, taking to her right away. *It seems only fittin'*, he thinks, *that Dollie, bein' Elsie's only sister, should live with us 'til she gets married.* Perhaps, he figures, when he finds a permanent place to settle his family a colored husband might be found for her, too.

He realizes that he must earn much more money than he is now. There are many large farms in the Harrisburg area and he was given promises from several men who had served with him in the 103rd Pennsylvania Volunteers that if he were ever looking for work to come by their farms. In Private Crowder Pacien they had recognized an indefatigable worker.

"No more cookin', though," he had responded with a smile.

So on one pleasant Sunday afternoon in May, he dons his newly purchased suit and hitches rides on passing wagons. Crowder's friend, the corporal from the 103rd, Pennsylvania Volunteers, had returned to his father's farm in Cumberland County near Mechanicsburg. Crowder is going there to see if any permanent work might be found. After asking directions he finally is able to locate the place which he quickly assesses to be in great disrepair.

Nine years have passed since Crowder last saw his friend. It was on July 13, 1865 in Harrisburg when they were issued their final pay. As the corporal was heading back to the wife and son he had left in his parents' care four years prior, he took the time to seek out Crowder Pacien for reminding his friend to look him up someday. And now Crowder is doing just that. Many things can happen to a man in nine years and so Crowder knows he really is taking a chance in expecting to find the older veteran still here.

Crowder swings open the wooden gate whose hinges squeal out their need of a good oiling. He treads the gravel-covered path around to the back of the house and then raps loudly on the edge of the screen door. A tall, thin, blue-eyed middle aged woman answers. A crown of thick graying blonde braids adorns her head. Wiping her wet hands on her apron she stands just inside the screen door. "Yes? And what can I do ya fer?"

She is presuming that the colored man is looking for some immediate work in payment for a meal. However, he does not look at all like the other transients, black or white, who drop by from time to time. She is taking notice that his clothing is clean and neat, his shoes blackened, and the hat held in his left hand, lint free. *He certainly has a lovely smile*, she is thinking.

"Afternoon, ma'am. Name's Crowder Pacient. Ah'm lookin' fer a corporal who served with me in the 103rd."

The woman recollects that name, Crowder Pacient, because innumerable times her husband has mentioned his colored friend who had served with him during the war. Luckily paroled from Andersonville after contracting malaria, the corporal eventually arrived at Roanoke Island where his regiment had been reconstituted. There he and Crowder had renewed their acquaintance to became fast friends, the white man from the North and the black man from the South.

Crowder's revelations about his former life on the North Carolina plantation had a profound effect on the corporal. Because of them the reasons for the war became more relevant to the Pennsylvanian. Never having known a colored man before, the corporal heretofore had no real sympathy for the plight of the slaves. They had been too far distant from his father's Cumberland County farm in Pennsylvania. He certainly had not joined the army to *free colored slaves*. Indeed not. He had joined the army *to preserve the Union*. And that was the only reason, but as the issues of the war changed, it had become apparent to him in reality he was fighting for the *freedom of all men*, especially men like Crowder Pacient. *Freedom is well worth the fight*, the corporal had written home in his letters to his wife.

Now the woman is unlatching the screen door to swing it wide open. "Oh my, yes, Mr. Pacient. My husband's mentioned ya many times. How-do? Please, won't ya come on in now?"

"Thank yuh, ma'am. How's the corporal doin' these days? It's been a mighty long time since Ah last seen him. Nine years tuh be exact."

"Well, 'fair ta middlin',' I s'pose. He come back home from the war with 'the shakes,' ya know. Brought them back from that filthy Reb prison they put him in. Andersonville. He had ta bury his cousin there. But I su'pose ya know all that already. My husband still suffers now'n again. When them shakes come he has ta take ta his bed 'til the quinine medicine the doctor give him settles him down. Him'n the boy's been tryin' ta keep things goin' here, but, I can tell ya, it's gettin' harder'n harder fer them all the time."

As she directs Crowder to the cool parlor where the drapes are drawn in order to keep out the heat from the afternoon sun, she is explaining, "My husband's restin' now, ya see. Gets tired real easy nowadays. Usually after church, he jest goes upstairs ta lay down 'til dinnertime. Ya'll take supper with us now, won't ya, Mr. Pacient?"

"Be delighted, ma'am. Thank's fer the invite." Crowder is quite hungry after his long journey today. He has a healthy appetite, something remaining with him all of his life.

The corporal's wife opens the drapes covering the window where the sun's rays no longer can reach. "I'll let in some light fer ya. Now I'll jest go and get ya a cool glass of water. Ya must be thirsty after yer long trip out here. I got a whole bunch of things ta do in the kitchen, but jest make yerself ta home. Take yer hat?" Leaving the parlor she tightly closes the door to keep the coolness in and the heat of the kitchen out.

Crowder chooses the straight-back rush caned chair as he surveys his surroundings. The parlor is a small room, more so than either the sit-in kitchen or the long dining room. In addition to the single wooden chair the room has been furnished comfortably with a forest green velveteen upholstered love seat with the requisite lace doilies adorning its back and arms. A burgundy overstuffed-chair is draped with a beautifully crocheted white throw. A small round marble-topped table holds an unlit kerosene lamp with glass globe decorated with tiny pastel colored flowers. A small pump organ with a swivel stool has been set between the two front windows and a worn Turkish carpet covers the wide polished slats of the floor.

Several daguerreotypes of very serious looking folk hang on fading floral wallpaper. Carefully scrutinizing the photographs Crowder easily identifies the one of the corporal and his wife all bedecked in their wedding finery. Descendants will question in future years, "Why such somber faces? Why didn't anyone ever smile in those old photos?"

Perhaps they had no desire to reveal mouths full of decaying teeth as was quite common. Or perhaps after searching for the distinctive red and white striped pole they were able to locate a tonsorial parlor where a barber had extracted their painful teeth, thereby leaving unsightly gaps in their mouths. Or perhaps it was just that the photographer took so long in setting up his equipment they could not fix smiles on their faces. Regardless of their reasoning, they never smiled.

A neat, comfortable sitting room, it is used strictly for entertaining company as is dictated by the custom of the day. *Ah know Elsie would love tuh live in a house like this*, Crowder is thinking. Unlike him she has lived in comfortable surroundings all of her life. He certainly is aware that the corporal has the advantage of having inherited his parents' homestead. Crowder has no house to offer a wife. All he has to offer Elsie is the "sweat of his brow."

While he sits patiently, just thinking and daydreaming, delectable odors waft into the parlor from the kitchen. Despite the closed door he can detect yeast rolls baking, fresh coffee brewing, and a well seasoned chicken roasting. As his empty stomach growls noisily in anticipation he is grateful no one else is around.

Now he hears the corporal's wife conversing with someone in the kitchen. Soon a young man, looking just like the corporal as Crowder remembers him, swings open the parlor door. Tall and lanky with the sparkling blue eyes he has inherited from his mother, he is attired in his Sunday best. Following church services the custom here is for a young man to escort his betrothed to her home, partaking in a light repast with her family before returning to his own home.

"Afternoon, sir. Ma sent in this glass of water ta cool ya." After introductions he adds, "Ma sez ya served with my Pa in the 103rd. I'm very happy ta meet ya."

Crowder stands to shake the son's hand and to relieve him of the glass of water. "Yes, yore Pa's a mighty fine man. Yessuh. Mighty fine."

"Thank ya, sir. I'm sorry ta say that Pa's not doin' so good nowadays, though. He gets 'the shakes' bad, ya know, and they're comin' more'n more often now, I think. Makes him so weak, they do. Hard fer him ta put in a good day's work. Now he's worryin' about the harvest comin' soon."

"Ah, well. Now that's jest the reason fer me comin' by tuhday. Yore Pa told me many years ago if Ah ever needed work tuh come by his Pa's farm."

The boy replies, "Well now, Grandpa's been dead nigh unto five years. Pa'n me, ya see, we been tryin' ta keep the farm goin', but it's gettin' too hard fer us. Can't get enough hired help fer the plantin.' And then fer them ta stay on fer the harvest if we do get a good crop. Yes, it's jest getting' harder'n harder. Ya lookin' fer work, ya say, Mr. Pacient?"

"Yes, suh. That Ah am. But Ah need steady work, though. Ah'm fixin' tuh take a wife soon. Need year-round work. Not jest at plantin' or pickin' times, ya see."

"That so? Well, Pa'll be down real soon now. Ya can talk to him about it. Ma sez ya'll be suppin' with us. She's a real fine cook, I'm tellin' ya. Then we'll see what Pa has ta say about the work. I know he's gonna be right glad ta see ya, sir."

Just at that moment the parlor door again flings open, revealing Crowder's friend the corporal, looking so much older than when he had left the army nine years prior, bent and gaunt, dark circles around his brown eyes. "Well now! Would ya look at what the cat's dragged in! Can't believe my eyes! Crowder Pacient, as I live and breathe!"

With delight, right hand extended, he greets his former army buddy. "My! My! Ya look great! Jest great. A little snow on the mountain, I see." Laughingly he pats his own sparse pate. "At least *you* got some."

Smiling expansively, the older man offers, "Come on, now! Let's go on out on the back porch and get washed up. Then we'll set down ta one of my woman's good meals. Best cook in the county, I always did say. Now jest ya take off that hot jacket off and make yaself ta home."

After the partaking of the very fine meal certainly living up to both the husband and son's expectations, the three men retire to the front porch for rocking and talking as men do on lazy warm Sunday afternoons. No serious work ever gets done on the Lord's Day--just what has to be done—like feeding the animals, collecting eggs, and milking cows.

The corporal plucks his tobacco tin from his shirt pocket. Filling his clay pipe with pinches of tobacco, he carefully packs it in with his little finger. Retrieving a flint match from the small metal box he carries in his other pocket, he strikes the match across a nail on the sole of his shoe. Then he puffs several times as the tobacco ignites. Crowder joins him by pulling out his own pipe.

After exhaling, the corporal asks, "Sure does taste a lot better than that old corn silk we had ta smoke durin' the war. Remember that, Pacient?"

"Yessuh. Certainly do. That's when Ah first started smokin', ya know. Remember my good friend Richard West? Don't know what happened to him after the war. Well, he's the one who introduced me tuh the pipe in the first place and Ah did enjoy it. That corn silk was jest fine fer me way back then. Well, that's 'til Ah tasted *real* tobacco."

"Umm. That's so. Nothin' like good tastin' tobacco. But ya know that's what helped ta make the South so rich. Yes, sir! Tobacco. Certainly did make all kind of problems, too. The least of which was makin' yer people slaves. Well, we solved that problem, we did. And forever, I say! No more slavery ever again in these United States. Thank the good Lord fer that! Ah, but when I think of the cost!" Shaking his head sadly, he is remembering Andersonville and the cousin he had left buried there.

As his mind snaps back to the present the corporal asks his guest, "So then, what're ya doin' nowadays, Pacient?"

"Well, suh. Been workin' on different farms fer the past nine years. Yuh know, ever since Ah last saw yuh over there in Harrisburg. Nothin' steady, though. Jest enough tuh get by on. Didn't want tuh be too tied down. Wanted tuh do some movin' around. Plenty of new places Ah wanted tuh see. Never had any definite plans before. But now that Ah'm about tuh take a wife? Well, Ah need tuh be lookin' fer *steady* work."

"Ah, that so? See my place?" The corporal waves his pipe from side to side as he surveys his property. "It's fallin' down all around my ears. Can't keep no hired men no more, ya see. They're all headin' east ta work in the coalmines. Work's more reliable there, so they say. Can't blame them, though. They got their families ta feed. Now, I only got this one son and we been doin' the best we can, but it's jest not good enough now. Sure could use a strong back like yers."

"Much obliged, suh." This is exactly what Crowder has come all this way to hear. Now he is relieved. His mission has been accomplished.

He points out to the corporal, "Can see yuh need a lot a work done 'round here. Ah'm thinkin' that yuh need tuh start with them wooden fences 'round the pastures. They're gonna need fixin' real soon. Yuh don't want the horses gettin' loose on yuh. Yuh might be all right fer a little while, but not too much longer. Not through the winter, Ah'm shor. A heavy snow's gonna push yore weaker fences right on down."

As he is listening to the conversation transpiring between the two older men, the son sighs in relief. Perhaps his father will not have to worry so much anymore. Mr. Pacient seems to know just what needs to be done. The corporal's wife certainly will be relieved when she hears the news. Her husband and son will not have to work as hard anymore. And the corporal is relieved, contemplating, *Maybe Pacient is the answer to my prayers*. "Well, this certainly has been a good day, I think. So then, when can ya start?"

"Got some things tuh finish up where Ah am jest now. Fella Ah'm workin' fer now knows Ah'm lookin' fer more work than he's got fer me. Imagine Ah could start about the middle of July. How'd that do?"

"That'd do jest fine. Jest fine. Let's shake on it." He reaches out his right hand to Crowder. The deal is sealed. "Yer gettin' hitched sometime soon, ya say?"

"Yessuh. Certainly hope so. In August."

"Well, ya jest might want ta see the cabin down back. Pa built it fer me'n my bride, way back when. My boy's gettin' hitched soon, too, ya know, but him'n his wife're gonna live right here in the house with us. It's big'n empty, ya see. Soon, maybe, it'll be filled with little ones runnin' all around. We only had the one boy, ya know. And my wife's jest itchin' fer some grandchildren," explains the corporal with an optimistic smile.

Crowder is definitely interested in the corporal's generous offer, although the word "cabin" does conjure up some unpleasant memories, but he assents to see it. "Never look a gift horse in the mouth." He knows all about horses. *Somebody gives yuh a horse, yuh don't look at its teeth tuh see how old it is. Yuh jest say, "Thank yuh, suh."*

So he responds, "Yessuh. Thank yuh. Think Ah would like tuh take a look at that cabin."

"All right then. Come on around the back. Be more than glad ta show it ta ya."

The three men descend the three wooden slats leading from the porch to slowly amble around the side of the weathered old farmhouse, its white paint all mostly scaled off. Past the back porch where each Monday the laundry gets tackled on a corrugated tin scrub board. Past the clothes line with its forked wooden pole for keeping freshly laundered white sheets from sweeping the ground. Past the wooden outhouse, its identifying crescent moon cut into its door.

And then on to the large (at least to Crowder's eyes) sturdily built log cabin. Surprised, he thinks, *Hmm. Don't remind me of Aunt Cassie's in the least bit.* The corporal pushes hard on the squeaking door. *Could use a little oil here, too,* Crowder is thinking. The empty cabin consists of a single large room with a fireplace at one end, a sleeping loft equipped with a ladder at the other end, two glassed windows on each side, a lot of dust and cobwebs, but with great potential, he is sure. *This'll suit me jest fine. Only hope it'll suit Elsie, too.*

"Looks like this's my lucky day, Corporal. A job'n a place tuh live, too."

"Yessir, my friend. Lucky fer both of us, I'd say. Now let's go back'n talk about wages. Ya see what dire straits I'm in, but I'm sure we can work out somethin' agreeable ta both of us."

Crowder is certain that they can, too.

When on Monday morning he strides up the narrow lane, he sees Elsie giving her wave from the kitchen doorway. She has no way of knowing that he has been busy securing their future. She simply is keeping her promise. And he can not even send her a note because neither Crowder, the former slave, nor Elsie, the bound girl, is able to read or write.

The weeks are passing by ever so slowly. There are all of the usual chores to be completed. In addition to these the housekeeper knows that since the sun is very hot by noon now, the perfect time has arrived for renovating bed pillows. So on the first morning Elsie and Dollie awaken to a hard rain shower, they remove the feather pillows from all of the beds. After stripping off their outer cases the girls lay the pillows outside on the grass for drenching. When the sun comes out again the pillows will dry. Then by evening they should smell air-fresh, ready for Elsie and Dollie to fluff up and return to the beds.

Every task seems to take so much more time nowadays. Elsie is the one preparing the breakfasts now. She is the one toasting the white bread and frying the thick slices of ham or bacon. Before frying the eggs in sizzling bacon grease she first cracks each eggshell over a small dish, carefully checking for blood spots or even possibly an embryo. In spite of all of the necessary precautions, sometimes the rooster does manage to get into the hen house.

Every day as she goes about her work Elsie watches for Crowder as he comes swinging up the lane. It is mid June and with the sun's rising earlier each day she, too, must rise earlier if she is to be at the kitchen door when he passes. So even before the rooster stridently crows at the first rays of light, the girl is jumping out of her side of the bed in the attic.

Before she feeds the chickens the housekeeper collects the eggs, taking them into the kitchen for Elsie to fry. Afterwards the woman goes out to the barn to the cow requiring milking early each morning. *The chickens 'll jest have ta wait.* So leaving Elsie and Dollie to prepare breakfast in the kitchen, the older woman heads off, carrying a lit kerosene lantern in one hand and an empty tin milk bucket in the other. She really has no desire to see Elsie's standing there in the kitchen doorway as she waves to the colored man as he passes by the house. It simply pains the woman too much. Having observed him from the kitchen door on that morning when Elsie had given him the disappointing news, the housekeeper is in total agreement with the lawyer and his wife. *That man's much too old and much too black fer our Elsie.*

Elsie and Dollie are never required to milk the cow. They are deathly afraid of the huge bovine. Afraid her swishing tail might lash across their faces. Afraid a heavy hoof might land on their small shoeless feet. Afraid Bossie might kick over the pail of milk, or worse yet, the kerosene lantern. The housekeeper, a tall heavy-boned woman, does not let the animal intimidate *her*. Anyway, there are plenty of other tasks for the girls around the house. Churning, baking, laundering, ironing, dusting, sweeping, scrubbing, bed making, dish washing, mending and on and on, so it goes.

Elsie feels that she should be making some necessary items to take into her new life. She knows she is going to need at least a new petticoat, several sets of drawers, a night shift, as well as some pillowcases, sheets, towels, and washcloths for her new home, wherever that is going to be. *These are the basic essentials,* she is presuming. However, she must verify with the housekeeper. Having lived in the same house these many years, she is closest to a mother that Elsie and Dollie will ever have. Even though Elsie is very much aware of the fact the older woman does not approve of Crowder any more than do the lawyer and his wife, still the girl needs someone's advice.

"Pet," the housekeeper suggests, "why don't ya jest wait 'til ya go off'n get a job? Who knows, ya might meet a man jest like *yourself.*

Elsie knows exactly to what the housekeeper is alluding. A colored man who also looks white. *Am I su'posed to look for a husband just for that reason?* Elsie thinks not.

The older woman does offer some suggestions, though, but of course Elsie has no money with which to purchase any fabric. *I guess I'll just have to wait 'til Mr. Pacient comes to fetch me,"* she decides to herself. *He says he's got money saved up. So I'm sure he'll let me have some,* she concludes, having complete faith in a man she barely knows.

For her wedding Elsie has been daydreaming over a beautiful bustled dress of cool shining white silk she saw illustrated in a *Harper's Bazaar* magazine. The exquisite gown comes with an underslip of rustling white taffeta. In the ad, a sheer Honiton lace veil covers the bride's hair. *And with it,* Elsie dreams, *I could wear a new pair of buttoned-up shoes with heels to make me taller.* As it is she barely reaches Crowder's chest.

Wouldn't white shoes just be so elegant? Then practicality sets in. *What on earth would I ever do with a pair of white shoes afterwards?* But quickly she responds to herself, *Well now, it's only a dream, anyway. So, why not a pair of white shoes with high heels? And, oh, how I'd love a pair of white two-clasp kid gloves and carry a beautiful nosegay of tiny white roses and baby's breath.* Such impossible dreams these are for a bound girl!

No, she will have to be married in her same blue "Sunday-go-to-meeting" dress, her same black high top shoes and the same small round bonnet she wears to church each week. She might be able to change the ribbons, though, in order to freshen up the looks of the hat and she will carry a small bouquet of yellow roses from Dollie's garden.

The lawyer's wife has been watching Elsie carefully as the summer weeks are fleeting by. The woman can see that the girl has no intentions at all of changing her mind about marrying Mr. Pacient. For there she stands, waving from the kitchen door *each and every* morning!

One day without seeking her husband's approval, the lawyer's wife informs Elsie that stored in the attic is some leftover muslin the married daughter had not needed for her trousseau. The lawyer's wife is very fond of Elsie, having watched her grow from the small child too short to reach the sink to become this determined young woman. Certainly, as a wife and mother, the Mrs. is quite aware of just what a girl needs when she is about to be married.

So when the woman offers Elsie a package tied with grocer string, she suggests, "Elsie, now you can use this fabric to make yourself a beautiful petticoat and some nice drawers. I have plenty of lace and ribbon for you to pretty them up with. Then they'll be just perfect." The wife presumes that since

Elsie is such a petite girl she will be able to fashion a number of nice items out of the left over fabric. She will need at least two yards for a pair of drawers, simply two tubes overlapped at the front and tied with a drawstring. A simple elastic gathered petticoat should require at least three yards, probably even less in short Elsie's case. *There should be more than enough fabric here*, the wife has concluded.

The girl is overwhelmed. Tears fill her dark brown eyes. Elsie is certain the lawyer would not approve, while realizing that on her account his wife is going against his wishes.

The wife continues, "And the next time we go over to Mechanicsburg, we'll look for some unbleached muslin for sheets and pillowcases. And we'll need some fabric to make bath towels and tea towels, too." With a twinkle in her eyes she continues,"You know, I've been looking in the linen closet and I just think we need to replace some of the old linens in there. Wouldn't you agree, Elsie?"

"Yes, ma'am, I certainly do," the girl answers gratefully as she follows the woman's gist.

The lawyer's wife simply will not allow Elsie to go into her marriage without some of life's necessities. Elsie will not have a bridal shower as did the daughter of the house with well-wishing friends and relatives presenting her with colorful hand-stitched quilts, delicate cut-glass vases and candy dishes, fragile china bowls, sets of drinking glasses, monogrammed silver salt and pepper shakers, tablecloths of damask with matching napkins. Nor will she be given any dainty silk undergarments, filmy nightgowns for hot summer nights, or heavy woolen robes for chilly winters. No, she will have none of these lovely things. However, she will have *something*, the wife determines. And, if perchance, Elsie does change her mind about marrying Mr. Pacient, well then, she will have sundry articles already stored in her hope chest when her Mr. Right does come along.

Her daughter's own beautiful highly varnished, sweet smelling red cedar hope chest had been imported from the far off island of Bermuda where there is an abundance of cedar trees. The chests may be ordered through Harper's Bazaar magazine. However, other less privileged girls may use sturdy wooden boxes built, painted or highly varnished, and then decorated by their fathers, brothers, uncles, or even perhaps by their intended.

The lawyer's wife knows she certainly cannot ask her husband to build such a one for Elsie and she most definitely cannot ask Mr. Pacient. All of a sudden she is remembering an old trunk hidden away somewhere up in the attic. Clothes from a by-gone day are stored in it, articles of no real value to anyone now. So the wife rummages through the storeroom in the attic until she finds the trunk. She empties it out, thoroughly cleaning it before calling Elsie up to the attic.

"Child, I can see you're not thinking about changing your mind about marrying Mr. Pacient. *A man you scarcely know, I must add!*" She feels duty bound to place emphasis on that fact.

"No, ma'am, I haven't."

"So now, Elsie, whether you marry Mr. Pacient or not, I'm going to give you this trunk. It's to be your hope chest, you see. Every girl should have one is what I think. You should be making some nice things now for when you're married. And I'm still hoping, I want you to know, that it'll be some time from now."

Then she lifts the lid of the small trunk for Elsie to peer inside. "See here now. You can start with this patchwork quilt I made for the church bazaar. The ladies won't be missing it, I'm most rest assured. Look. We'll put it in first." In the bottom of the trunk she neatly places the folded colorful quilt over which she has labored so many hours. She is thinking now that she is glad Elsie is going to be the one possessing it. "Now then, you can add your own personal things on top. We'll just keep it out of sight up here in the attic, I think."

Tears welling in her eyes, Elsie says, "Oh, thank you ma'am. I don't know what to say."

"What I *want* you to say, Elsie, you won't."

"I know."

"I just want you to be happy. I want you to know that. You've grown to be such a fine girl."

"Thank you, ma'am."

"I'm asking you again now. How do you know that Crowder Patient is the man you should be marrying? Really, child, I don't see how you can be so sure. You've never met any one else," the lawyer's wife is stressing.

"I just know, ma'am. "I just know."

Crowder, too, is being kept busy. In his spare time he hitches a ride out to the corporal's farm where he is always greeted warmly. The corporal's wife seems to have an overabundance of "extras," as she calls them and is always asking Crowder if he wants "this or that." Since he has absolutely no idea what Elsie might like, he just responds gratefully with, "Yes, ma'am" to everything.

The once empty cabin now boasts of a wide double bed; an oak bureau; a square table accompanied by four wooden chairs with caned seats; and a tall open shelfed cabinet for dishes and glasses. Since the corporal's wife loves to crochet, she has hung lovely white curtains over the windows. She even has braided colorful rag rugs for covering the wide floor slats. Knowing that a woman must have a mirror for primping, she has nailed an oval one directly over the cater-cornered washstand. On it she has placed a porcelain wash basin and pitcher, white with tiny blue flowers resembling forget-me-nots painted on their surfaces. Two brand-new white bath towels and wash cloths hang on a narrow wooden rod just beneath the mirror. The corporal's wife takes an admiring look around the room, quite satisfied with her handiwork. She thinks that by the time August arrives here will be a home fit for the young bride, *colored, just like Crowder.*

During some years July in York County can be unbearably warm. This year 1874 is one of those years. The attic room is stifling and the open window invites mosquitoes at night to feast on the blood of the human inhabitants sleeping there. Poor Dollie seems exceptionally prone to the female mosquitoes' demand for blood, awakening every morning with new welts, some swelling to the size of nickels. Rubbing them with cut onion is not enough to relieve their annoying itch and the afflicted girl scratches them until they bleed. She can not seem to help it. When one morning Dollie is unable to open her right eye after a mosquito attack during the night, the housekeeper becomes alarmed.

After receiving the report of Dollie's predicament, the lawyer's wife orders, "You girls just might at well move down to the second floor then." She is speculating that perhaps if Elsie feels more comfortable at "home," she may not be as compelled to marry the first man who has shown an interest in her. The lawyer's wife is thinking, *There are young colored men in York and Harrisburg. If Elsie should want to leave Dillsburg to seek employment in those cities she just might meet someone more suitable.* And so the wife is hoping that perhaps the mesh screens on the second floor bedroom windows will keep out the mosquitoes as well as thoughts of the too old (in her opinion), too black (in her estimation) man.

Elsie and Dollie are delighted to be moving downstairs. They now have open windows protected by mesh screens. They now can feel cool breezes blowing in during the night. They now will be able to sleep more comfortably than they ever have before. Even so, thoughts of Crowder Pacient remain with Elsie still. And so there she stands at the kitchen door every morning.

Finally the wife requests her husband to do some serious inquiring about the colored man. "Find out where he's been working," she suggests. "Find out what kind of person he really is. Elsie doesn't know the first thing about him. Find out all that you can. Please! Before it's too late."

It does not take long for the inquiring lawyer to hear about Crowder Pacient's reputation. All he has to do is go to Fohl's harness shop where Dillsburg men gather. Where they can find out what is going on in their "neck of the woods." What he is able to uncover about the colored man is that he has the reputation for being a hard worker, never missing a day, putting in more than the required amount of time if need be, pleasant in demeanor, always polite, never in any kind of trouble. These certainly are attributes one might want in a fellow about to marry one's daughter.

Elsie may not be their daughter, but the lawyer and his wife want the same for her as they had wanted for their own. They want her to be taken care of by a man who will love, respect, and provide for her. And they are quite sure that man is not Crowder Pacient. *He's far too old and he's much much too black for our Elsie,* they both agree.

Each new morning finds Elsie's standing at the kitchen door, waiting to catch a glimpse of her intended as he passes up the lane. She does not expect to see him in heavy rain. Only on two days, though, will that be. On one of those gray dreary mornings Elsie suddenly is awakened by a flash of lightning followed by an *immediate* loud clap of thunder, indicating that the lightning is striking very close by. Elsie is deathly afraid of it.

This had not always been so, but nowadays she swiftly jumps into her bed, yanking the covers over her head. The reason she is so afraid now is because she actually has been struck by lightning. It happened last fall when she had a lot of canning to do.

The tomatoes were already overripe and in danger of rotting if she did not attend to them right away. The fire blazed in the kitchen wood stove where the housekeeper was sterilizing the glass jars in which tomatoes would be "put up" for the winter. The kitchen already was very steamy, hot as a furnace even with all the doors and windows flung wide open. With perspiration trickling down Elsie's face and back, her clothes were sticking to her body. *Some cooling rain certainly would be nice,* she had thought.

With a metal hook, and using both hands she had lifted off one of the heavy iron stove lids, setting it on the back of the wood stove to be out of the way. Then with a long metal fork she lowered each tomato over the flames just close enough for the thin skin to crackle, allowing the peeling to go much easier. So with her bowl of tomatoes all ready to peel, Elsie settled down at the kitchen table.

And while she was all engrossed with skinning the tomatoes, a bolt of lightning hit the house. Conducted by the paring knife she was holding in her hand, the bolt traveled through her body, exiting through the nails on the bottom of her shoes, literally tearing them from her feet! Amazingly, she was just a bit dazed, dizzy for only a short while. Why or how she survived the lightning bolt, she does not know, but once struck, she has become very wary.

But not even bolts of lightning will keep Elsie away from the kitchen door, even though on this particular stormy day Crowder is not to pass by.

Today is Elsie's 16th birthday, August 1, 1874. Although it is a smoldering summer day, the housekeeper has prepared Elsie's favorite meal. Chicken potpie. And as she had done each year before, the housekeeper bakes a yellow pound cake sans icing. All that sugar is much too sickeningly sweet to suit Elsie's taste. *This may be the last birthday cake Elsie'll ever eat in this house,* the older woman sadly contemplates while gathering all the necessary ingredients.

What a long day this has been for Elsie! Now with her usual chores completed, she pauses long enough to enjoy a slice of her birthday cake. The red sun is perched low on the western horizon with nightfall swiftly approaching. In the second floor bedroom she shares with Dollie, Elsie dons her light blue-flowered calico dress, brushes and braids her dark hair, ties a soft blue bow on the top of the plait, pinches her pale cheeks and then sits on the edge of the bed to wait. The hands of the grandfather clock in the downstairs front hall poise to strike seven. *He came around seven before,* Elsie is thinking. *Maybe he will again.*

Dollie already has annoyed her sister by asking for the second time, "Do you think he's really gonna come, Sister?" Elsie does not want Dollie to know that she, too, is anxious, not having spoken a word to Crowder in three and a half long months. But she answers her sister with, "Yes, I do. He promised. Now please don't ask me again."

There is a loud knock at the back door as the clock begins its count to seven. It is a lovely summer evening and a beautiful birthday for Elsie Vedan because Crowder Pacient, hat in hand just like the one time before when he came calling, is waiting on the other side of the door.

The lawyer opens the door. "I've been expecting you, Mr. Pacient."

And he has, even though he has not voiced his thoughts to his wife. He knows that Elsie has been standing at the kitchen door these last three and a half months watching for Crowder Pacient to pass up the lane every morning. In the kitchen by the flickering light of a kerosene lamp the lawyer has observed the girl bent over the rattling treadle sewing machine. There she busily was climbing the creaking stairs to the attic where she and her sister no longer sleep. He correctly surmises that she has secrets hidden up there somewhere. Secrets he would not be surprised that his wife knows all about. Consequently, he has had no doubt at all that Crowder Pacient is going to call on Elsie's sixteenth birthday.

"Come on in, then, Mr. Pacient. I'll just call Elsie."

"Thank yuh, suh."

Descending the stairs Elsie sees her future husband's gazing up at her with that certain look in his eyes and with that wonderful smile on his face. He has come to tell her of his plans for their future.

"Miss Elsie, we'll be married Tuesday evenin'. That is, if it's all right with yuh."

"That certainly will be all right with me, Mr. Pacient."

"Then Ah'll come fer yuh right after supper." After having delivered the words he has come all this distance to say, Crowder takes his leave, respectfully bowing his head to the lawyer and his wife.

On Tuesday evening, August 4, 1874, Crowder with name spelled "Patient" and Elsie Vedan are married by the Rev. Fleck at the parsonage of the Evangelical Lutheran Church, Mechanicsburg, Pennsylvania, a town near the corporal's farm. As Crowder places on Elsie's small left ring finger the gold circlet she will never remove, he means every word of his vows. He promises to love her, to cherish her in sickness and in health, for richer and for poorer, and for better and for worse *until death will part them.*

And for fifty-five years he will keep those sacred vows.

PART B

SECTION IV

CROWDER AND ELSIE'S NEW HOME

MARRIAGE CERTIFICATE.

This is to Certify, That Mr. *Crowder Patient* of *Willsburg, York County, Penn,* and Miss *Elsie Vedau* of *Willsburg York County Penn* were, by me, lawfully joined in HOLY WEDLOCK, on the *Fourth* day of *August* in the year of our Lord one thousand eight hundred and *Seventy Four* at *Mechanicsburg* in the presence of the following witnesses:

May the God of all grace enable you faithfully to fulfil the solemn covenant made in His presence, and after having lived together in a state of holy joy and pious friendship, may you meet in Heaven in perfect happiness never to be terminated.

H. R. Fleck Pastor of the *Ev. Lutheran* Church in *Mechanicsburg Penn*

Marriage Certificate of Crowder and
Elsie Patience, August 4, 1874

Chapter 17

The Beginning

*T*oday is Monday and Mondays are always wash days. The water drawn from the well already has been heated and poured into a large tin tub. While vigorously rubbing soiled laundry on the corrugated tin scrub board Elsie is worrying over her sister Dollie. Elsie thinks, *She must be lonely, sleeping in that big bed all by herself.*

Crowder is aware that it is Elsie who is lonely for her sister, never having been separated from her before. And so for the past year as often as feasible he has borrowed the corporal's creaking wagon to drive Elsie down to Dillsburg where Dollie remains bound to the lawyer and his wife. "Just two more years," Elsie has sighed to her sister. "Then you can come live with us." She sorely misses Dollie even though there certainly is more than enough work to keep Elsie busy with cultivating her little vegetable garden and performing all her wifely chores.

Now that she is expecting her first child, she wants her sister with her more than ever. The last time she had gone for a Sunday visit Elsie told Dollie the good news. "Oh, Sister!" Dollie had exclaimed with delight. "I'm gonna be a aunt!"

The lawyer's wife also felt joy for Elsie. *This is what she wanted, so I'm going to be happy for her,* she conceded to herself. *She'll have a family of her own now.* The lawyer, finally reconciled to the fact that Elsie had married the too old (in his opinion), too black (in his estimation) man, had invited Crowder out to the stable to see the newest foal. Men's talk going on in the stable and women's in the kitchen.

"You say the baby's due in January, Elsie?" asks the wife.

"Yes, ma'am."

The lawyer's wife does not want to say anything to alarm the young mother-to-be or to concern Dollie, but she wonders who will be attending Elsie. She is sure that the girl knows nothing about what is involved with bringing a baby into the world, especially on a remote farm during the month of January with its unpredictable weather. So the Mrs. offers, "If you want to come back here to have your baby, Elsie, you're more than welcome."

Of course with such a suggestion Dollie is elated and Elsie is grateful because she has been a little apprehensive. She knows that she needs to be around other women when her "lying-in" time arrives. She also is well aware that the corporal's wife is overburdened with taking care of her ailing husband. The corporal's daughter-in-law bore twin sons several months ago and she now is overwhelmed with her new responsibilities. And as much as she depends on Crowder, this is one thing Elsie does not want to have to be.

So gratefully she replies, "Thank you, ma'am. Surely I'm much obliged. Yes, I would like to be here when the baby comes." Then with apprehension in her voice she hesitantly asks, "Are you sure the Mr.'s not gonna mind?"

"Oh, yes, Elsie, I'm sure." She chuckles then. "Why, would you believe it? It was his idea in the first place."

So it had been. For not long after Elsie had married Crowder Pacient and left Dillsburg the lawyer had begun worrying about the girl. "What's she going to do when she has her babies? Who's going to take care of her way off in the middle of nowhere?"

"Can't really say. I only hope she can find a good midwife thereabouts," his wife had responded, recognizing the real concern in her husband's words and praying that as head of the household he might act upon it. He had worried about his own daughter when remembering that it had not been easy for his wife to bring their children into the world. And he certainly is aware that many young mothers die from the complications of childbirth. Sadly, for too many women a pregnancy is a death sentence.

So his suggestion was that before Elsie's "lying-in time," she come "home" just as his own daughter had. His wife was in total agreement.

Farmers had been predicting a hard winter for this year and their predictions have come true. For by the middle of December there already had been two heavy snowstorms. Now very early on Christmas morning Crowder bundles Elsie in layers of heavy woolen blankets for the drive over muddy roads to Dillsburg. There she is going to remain for just the holiday week, visiting with her sister and resting in the care of the housekeeper whose plans are to ply the young mother-to-be with mountains of food.

"Remember, now. Yer eatin' fer two," she insists. Glasses of cold buttermilk, applesauce mixed with cottage cheese, fried scrapple, apple pan dowdy, funnel cake, and chicken potpie, all of Elsie's favorites. Then, having to leave in order to care for his work team back on the farm, Crowder bids his very pregnant wife farewell with the expectation of returning for her the very next weekend.

Elise loves being "home." And she will not even be disturbing Dollie with restless sleep because the expectant mother is being "put up" in the daughter's old bedroom. Now for the very first time in her life Elsie has a fleeting feeling of what it must be like to be someone's daughter. Made to feel safe and secure. *This is the way mine will feel,* she vows to herself.

Crowder does not return the next weekend. For a treacherous blizzard sweeps through Pennsylvania, dropping twenty-eight inches of snow, blowing five to six feet drifts to block the roads. People become snowbound for days. Without food and water their trapped animals die in isolated barns. There is absolutely no way for Crowder to get back down to Dillsburg, but he knows that Elsie is safe there. When he finally does get through, he readily agrees with the lawyer and his wife that it would be best for the expectant mother to remain with them until after the baby is born.

Several weeks later in January when Elsie introduces Crowder to his new-born daughter all she can say to her elated husband is, "Isn't she the most beautiful baby you ever seen? And she's ours. *Our own family!*" They name her Florence.

Since recently delivered mothers require a long recuperation period in order to regain their strength, Elsie stays on for several more weeks before Crowder comes to fetch his wife, his new baby, and the baby's nurse, *Aunt Dollie.*

The lawyer's reasons, "Elsie needs you more now."

Dollie is fourteen years old when she comes to live with Elsie and Crowder. As expected she is a big help to her sister, but this is not the only reason Elsie is so elated with her being here. One day Elsie approaches her husband with, "I want Dollie to go to school. I want her to learn to read and write." Crowder nods in agreement.

Hesitantly his wife continues, "Costs some money for schooling, you know."

"Don't yuh worry about that none. Ah got enough money fer Dollie's schoolin'," Crowder assures his anxious wife. Being very thrifty he always manages to have a small horde of coins put away. Even though he never learns to read or write--just his name so he will not have to continue marking an X--he cannot be deceived when it comes to counting his money.

"She's got to have some decent clothes, too," Elsie is continuing. "You know, books and a slate, and...."

Crowder chuckles at his little wife's enthusiasm. *When my Elsie gets her mind set on somethin' it's jest like a dog with a bone,* he is thinking. "Now, yuh jest go ahead'n decide what the girl's gonna be needin'. Then get it." The fortunate Dollie could not have had a better brother-in-law and Elsie knows by now she could not have chosen a better husband, regardless of what the Dillsburg lawyer and his wife had thought.

Later Elsie excitedly tells Dollie the good news. "Pet, guess what? You're gonna go to school! Crowder says that you can!" Dollie is delighted, looking at both her sister and brother-in-law with gratitude. This is something she has longed for, to learn how to read and write. And finally it is going to happen! However, she feels the necessity to reveal something she has kept all to herself these many years.

"Sister, how can I go to school with a name like 'Dollie?'"

Now this is the first time Elsie has heard her sister voice any dissatisfaction with her name. And so she is looking at the younger girl with surprise. "What's this? You mean you're telling us that you don't like your name?"

"No! I hate it!" Dollie states emphatically. "Whoever named me that in the first place, anyway?"

"Well, I su'pose somebody who must'a thought you looked like a pretty little doll baby. But you know I don't know about that any more than I know how I got my name. You never said nothing about it *before*, though, Pet. How come?"

"No reason to before. But I'm saying it now." Dollie pauses, looking dubiously at both her sister and brother-in-law. "Before I go to school you'll let me change my name to something else, won't you?"

Relaxing in his favorite rocker positioned to catch warmth from the fireplace, Crowder has been listening to the conversation. He is remembering when he had not wanted to keep his name, either. So now looking over at his very intense sister-in-law, he asks, "Got a name yuh want tuh be called, then?"

"I want a name that's got some *dignity* to it. Now 'Dollie' just don't." She pauses before answering Crowder's question. "I think I'd like to be called *Mariah*."

With a smile on his face Crowder rises from his comfortable seat. Walks over to where his wife is standing. Takes her right hand in his left as she looks at him quizzically. "Jest come on," he directs, guiding Elsie to Dollie. Then he clasps the two right hands of the sisters as if they were meeting for the very first time. Chuckling he says, "Mrs. Elsie Patient, let me introduce yuh tuh Miss Mariah Veden."

Sometime in the future a sepia colored class photo will reveal several young girls posing with their teacher. Some students sit while others are standing. All are looking prim and proper with the serious facial expressions found in old photographs. Attired in the ruffled navy blue dress Elsie had assisted her sister in stitching and with a large bow pulling back her wavy light brown hair, Mariah Veden stands proudly in the back row.

Young Mariah enjoys going to school. She especially loves to read, and Elsie loves to be read to, especially when she is preparing dinner or doing some of her "sitting down" chores. One afternoon when Baby Florence finally is napping, Elsie takes the opportunity to tend to some mending. Dipping deep into her sewing basket, she pulls out the dried gourd she uses for mending holes in Crowder's socks. Next she breaks off a long piece of thread, rolls the tip between her lips, squints her right eye as she threads the needle, and expertly ties the knot before slipping a sterling-silver thimble onto her left middle finger. Then she begins to darn. "Read something to me, will you please, Pet."

"Be glad to, Sister. Just let me get my book." Walking across the cabin floor to the sturdy wooden bookcase Crowder has built for her, Mariah with a flash of inspiration suddenly turns, saying, "Say, I've got a great idea, Sister! Why don't you let me teach you to read for yourself?"

Elsie looks up with shock at her sister. Such a thing has never occurred to her. "Oh, my! No, Pet! I don't have no time for all of that! I've got way too much *work* to do."

No matter how many times in the future whenever Mariah makes the offer, Elsie always will refuse. She is of the mind that her time for "book learning" has passed, especially now with the new baby on its way. She hopes it is a boy.

Back row, 2nd from right+: **Mariah Veden**
standing with her classmates (circa 1878)

Plenty of backbreaking labor needs doing on the Cumberland County farm where the ailing Civil War veteran and his son are trying their best to keep it going, now with the able assistance of Crowder Patient. One thing he learned early on is that many Pennsylvania farms are extremely rocky. In comparison to the rich dark loamy soil he remembers so well on the North Carolina plantation, the ground here is quite difficult to till. Everywhere rocks of all sizes and shapes lie in wait to crack an unsuspecting plowshare.

The corporal's father was the first one to farm this land after felling trees hundreds of years old and moving huge boulders. Then there were the multitudinous flat sedimentary rocks he was forced to remove, also, before making an attempt at tilling the ground. With those rocks he constructed retaining boundary walls to outline his entire property. Years ago piled on top of each other, the rocks even today are still firmly set in place, held by only the force of gravity, no mortar at all having been used. He had even encircled his well with a waist-high wall of those same kind of flat rocks. His smoke and dairy houses, several other small storage buildings as well as the foundation of his wooden bank barn were constructed entirely of large rocks. All of these, however, he had secured in place with mortar.

Consisting now of four persons, the Patient family is quite content with living here on the corporal's farm. Crowder has plenty of work keeping him busy while Elsie revels in caring for her much wanted family. Florence is toddling around, getting into everything and Mariah is an asset in keeping the child entertained. Having worn herself out, while nestling in her aunt's arms Florence finally drops her head and Mariah carries her niece to her crib.

Taking note of her sister's magic, Elsie perceives that Mariah might make a good teacher. At the nearby one-room-schoolhouse where no one seems concerned about a colored girl's attending she is doing well. *"Maybe some day,"* Elsie dreams.

"Elsie!" Crowder suddenly bursts into the cabin. "Elsie! The corporal's wife wants yuh tuh come up tuh the house right away! He's taken *real* bad this time."

"Mariah! You stay here with the baby now!" Elsie quickly unties her apron, throws a shawl around her shoulders and makes for the door.

The two hurry to the farmhouse where they find the shivering, shuddering corporal lying on his large double bed. His usually florid face now the color of putty is covered with sweat as his frantic wife attempts lowering his body temperature with cool wet cloths. The pungent odor of onion is very strong in the bedroom because the corporal's wife is using an old-fashioned remedy for "drawing" a fever from a person's body. She has wrapped her husband's hot feet in towels holding several baked onions.

The corporal's breathing is laboriously shallow and hard. Hallucinating now, he cries out in terror, "Get back! Get back now! Don't come no closer!" It seems as if he were reliving some terrible time. Possibly Andersonville.

The frantic wife informs Crowder and Elsie, "He's never been this bad before. Give him his medicine like I always do. Had ta send my boy ta fetch the doctor, but he's off deliverin' a baby, his missus sez. Seems the midwife jest had ta give up'n send fer him. Never can tell how long that's gonna take, ya know." She is aware, anyway, that the doctor cannot do much for her suffering husband if the quinine is not working. It always has before. However, this time is going to be different.

Crowder's friend the corporal dies on this day in early spring, just before the azaleas and dogwoods bloom up in the woods. His wife and son bury him at a place very special to the corporal. A lovely spot by a gurgling stream where he used to go just to be to himself. An area shaded by red maples, pin oaks, red pines, spruces, and hemlocks. A hallowed place where he said he felt closest to God. For the corporal, a most fitting permanent resting-place.

Several days later the son approaches Crowder. "I stayed on with my Pa ta help him out, ya know, sir. But we both know *I* can't handle all this without *him*. Anyway, the farm's Ma's now and she's been hankerin' ta move ta town. Think ya best be lookin' fer another job right away 'cause no tellin' jest how long we'll be stayin' here. Soon's we find a buyer we'll be off. Sure hate ta do this ta ya, sir. Ya been such a good friend."

Crowder has no difficulty at all in understanding the predicament of the corporal's son. His problem, however, is how to tell his very young wife who has grown quite comfortable living here in "her" cabin and enjoying the company of the corporal's kindly wife and daughter-in-law, *her first friends ever*.

The corporal's wife was in for quite a surprise after Crowder had fetched his bride. The older woman had been most anxious to finally see the young wife who was going to live in the cabin down back. "Why, Husband, I do believe she's a *white* girl!" she exclaimed while peeking discreetly through the crocheted curtains covering the dining room windows.

Following their wedding in nearby Mechanicsburg the newlyweds were rounding the farmhouse on their way to the cabin the corporal's wife had helped Crowder furnish these last months. He was carrying Elsie's small trunk on his shoulder. The corporal's wife accused her husband with, "Ya didn't tell me he was marryin' a *white* girl. Thought she'd be colored, *jest like him*."

His curiosity piqued, the corporal peeked then, too, while replying, "Hmm. Ya may be right about that. She don't look colored ta me neither. Well, he didn't say nothin' a'tall 'bout what she was. Jest s'posed she'd be colored, *jest like him.* Anyway, she jest might be, ya know. Remember what I wrote ya about the colored folks I seen down South? Some of them's white as us." He looked intently at his wife as he continued, "Don't make no difference ta me no how *what* she is." He pauses before adding, "Hope it don't ta ya, neither."

"No, it don't."

"All right then. We'll jest let it be."

Some weeks later, however, it does come up on a Monday afternoon when the two wives are unpinning clean white sheets from the clothesline. It helps considerably to have the cooperation of two persons to make sure the clean sheets do not wipe the dirty ground. "Don't want ta have ta do the wash all over again," the corporal's wife maintains and on this issue both she and Elsie are in agreement. For they know that each wash day is tedious enough with having to change each bed, with making sure that last week's top sheet becomes this week's bottom one. And with several beds to change the women certainly do want to avoid any extra work.

The corporal's wife, much taller than the petite Elsie, unpins a sparkling clean white sheet from the clothesline, throwing the wooden clothespins into the cloth bag tied around her waist. "Got it?" she questions. Elsie does. Then each woman grabs opposite sides and together they begin the ritual of folding. Being extremely careful to keep a tight grip, they both give their respective end a sharp flap, proceeding then to fold the sheet lengthwise. On this particular afternoon Elsie decides to set straight her situation, perceiving correctly that the corporal and his wife may think of her as being white. She is well aware of their discreet, yet curious assessment of her.

Moving a few steps forward to relieve the corporal's wife of her end of the sheet in order to finish the folding, Elsie inquires," Ma'am, do you know what a *mulatto* is?"

"No, Elsie, don't believe I do." The older woman is engrossed in unpinning the next sheet.

"Well, that's what *I* am. A mulatto. I su'pose you and the corporal think that I'm *white*. Well, I'm not."

"No? Catch this sheet now, Elsie!"

The girl reaches up as the sheet leaves the line. "No. I'm not white. I'm one of those kind. A mulatto. A *half and half* is what I call it."

"A half and half? How's that?" the woman is asking as the two begin the folding process once again.

"Well, they say that one of my parents was colored. Don't know which one 'cause I don't know who my Ma and Pa was. Been told that me'n my sister are orphans from down Washington way."

"Well, that's very interestin', I must say." The corporal's wife pauses before adding, "I guess I'm one, too, then. A mulatto, that is."

In surprise Elsie stops her work to study the corporal's wife. "*You*? No! How could that be?"

"Well, my Ma's German and my Pa's Scotch-Irish. Don't that make me *a half-and half,* too?" She laughs merrily.

Elsie is thinking hard as she makes the last folding. "Hmm. Don't know about that, ma'am. Just know what the Mrs. in Dillsburg told me. Me'n my sister are mulattos." Then gazing intently at the white woman's flaxen hair, pale skin and cobalt blue eyes, Elsie informs her seriously, "No, *you* can't be, though. I'm sure *colored's* got to be in there somewhere."

"Oh well, now, Elsie, we're jest not gonna worry about any names people want ta make up, are we now?" the kindly older woman suggests.

"No, ma'am, we're not."

Elsie had known right from the beginning of her marriage that her husband is searching for just the right place to permanently settle his family. Particularly such a place where there would be a sizable population of colored people. A place where Mariah and later, when the time comes, their daughter Florence might be courted. So Elsie is not surprised at all when her husband informs her, "We gotta be movin' on. This place's 'bout tuh be sold. So Ah'm out of a job. Got tuh see if Ah can find work some place else."

"How soon we gotta be going then?" Elsie's eyes begin to sweep the comfortable cabin she and Crowder have called home for the last year and a half. She focuses first on the double bed with the patchwork quilt the Mrs. gave to Elsie. Then on the pillows she so laboriously had stuffed with goose down. Her eyes drift to the foot of the bed where the old trunk, her hopechest sits. Her eyes take in the colorful rag rugs' covering the wide slatted floor of the cabin and the blue striped gingham tablecloth's covering the table. Finally they land on the oval mirror nailed on the wall over the cater-cornered wash stand's holding a basin and matching pitcher decorated with tiny blue flowers resembling forget-me-nots. Then she turns to look again at her husband, awaiting his answer.

"Soon."

After the war many young men had been content to return to their parents' homesteads, expecting to remain there for the remainder of their lives. One very young private, underage when he had enlisted, with whom Crowder had been mustered out in Harrisburg, was going back home to his father's farm in York County. All throughout the four terrible years of war he had maintained that he was most anxious to get back to the peace and tranquility found in his mountains.

And so, on the next Sunday Crowder informs Elsie that he is off to find the young private who had said to look him up if ever in need of a job. Starting out just before dawn as the roosters are raising a discordant early morning chorus, he leaves his pregnant wife behind in the hands of her competent sister. To Elsie this second pregnancy is quite a surprise because she was of the impression that as long as she was still nursing she could not conceive again. Misconceptions abound during this period of history because women do not discuss intimate matters.

For instance, before Elsie went off to wed Crowder, Mariah had inquired of her sister, "How soon will I have a niece or nephew? I can hardly wait to be a aunt." With naivete Elsie had replied, "Don't rightly know, Pet. Some time after he sees me in my petticoat, I su'pose." She certainly knows now there is more to it than that, but she never discusses it with her sister, even allowing Mariah to enter into her own marriage just as Elsie herself had. In complete ignorance.

With the new baby's not being due for several months Crowder is unafraid leaving his wife. He knows Mariah will look after her sister just as she does each day while he is away working. Also he knows that during their traveling back and forth to the outhouse the corporal's widow and daughter-in-law are in the habit of calling out, "Elsie, how ya doin'?" And her answer is always, "Oh, fair to middling. Just busy taking care of the child." Or "Just cooking." Or "Washing." Or "Cleaning." Or "Trying to crochet."

The corporal's wife always chuckles upon hearing the latter because try as she may, Elsie simply cannot get the knack of crocheting. She wants always to be holding the hook in the wrong hand--her *left* hand. "Ya can't do it that way, Elsie," the corporal's wife softly admonishes the discouraged girl.

"Can't do it neither with the hand *you* use, ma'am," Elsie replies in frustration. Always she uses her left hand instead of her right like other people, feeling more comfortable when holding her fork, or the flat iron when pressing clothes, or a needle when stitching while a shiny metal thimble sits on her tip of her *left* middle finger. So she wonders, *Why is it that I always want to use my wrong hand?*

When she discussed this with the corporal's wife a disturbing story was related to Elsie. "Ya know, some time ago I heard tell about a boy goin' off ta school. It seems like he wanted ta use his wrong hand, too. Know what his teacher did ta him?"

Elsie had no idea. "No, what'd she do to him?"

"Well now. She tied his wrong hand behind his back and made him use his right hand! Would ya believe that? And ya know what else?"

Elsie could not believe there was more to this troubling story. What she heard already had upset her enough. "No. What else?"

"Why, he started ta stutter. That's what! Couldn't talk straight no more, would ya believe?"

"No!" Elsie is shocked. "Mercy honest! Why wouldn't they just let him go on and use his other hand?"

"Can't rightly say. Jest know they wouldn't."

Nothing lasts forever. Of this Elsie is certain by now. They had planned to stay here for at least another year before moving on in search of the Utopia Crowder expects to find. Instead, he must locate another job now as well as another house for his family. And soon she will be saying "Good-bye" once again to people who have been kind to her. But before having to bid Elsie a final farewell, the corporal's widow presses a gift into her friend's hands. "Elsie, I want ya ta have this Bible ta keep."

Gazing in surprise at the small brown book, Elsie responds, "Thank you, ma'am, but you know I can't read any of the words. Neither can Crowder."

"Never ya mind about that, Elsie. Mariah's learning to read now and yer children will go ta school and they will learn ta read, too. And when they do then *they* can read it ta both of *ya*. And, see here." She turns to the center where several pages are set aside for the recording of marriages, births and deaths. "Everybody's got ta have a Bible in their home is what I think. For the dates, ya know."

She continued, "Look! This is where we'll put yer names. See? Here. Let me fill them in fer ya now. So tell me what the dates are." In her best Spencerian script the corporal's widow records the Patient wedding date as well as the birthdays of Crowder, Elsie, and Florence. "And should the good Lord bless ya with more children, Elsie, then Florence can write their names in the Bible fer ya when she's old enough."

And that is how Crowder and Elsie Patient come into possession of a small brown leather covered Bible where with pencil all the names of the children born after Florence will be recorded in childish script.

Crowder, hitching rides on passing wagons, makes his way to the farm of that very young private who also had been in Co. C when the 103rd was reconstituted on Roanoke Island. Traveling along dusty wheel-rutted bumpy roads, Crowder is enjoying the pleasantness of this early spring day, not too cold, but just right. Pondering over what kind of work he is going to be able to find, he realizes he must locate both a job as well as decent living quarters for his family very soon, not knowing just when the corporal's farm might be sold.

Eleven years have passed since Ah last seen my friend, the private. May not even still be livin'. The corporal izzen't. These are the perturbing thoughts running through Crowder's head as he nears the area where he has been told the farm is located.

The wagoner slows the horses and points. "See! Jest up ahead there! Take that road'n go down the hill. And at the bottom ya jest take the very next one. It's there, on the left. No way ya can miss it. Road'll lead ya right up ta the house."

"Much obliged, suh," Crowder calls as he agilely hops off the wagon.

A small herd of black and white Hereford cattle laze among brown boulders large as the rounded bodies of the seated animals themselves. Several horses graze in hilly pasture paddocks enclosed by sturdy white wooden rail. Crowder pauses briefly to ingest the view. *Looks like it's taken care of real good,* he concludes. Continuing his slow amble up the road, he first comes to a large bright red bank barn where the animals are housed downstairs while through the back of the barn hay gets loaded on an incline to the loft above. And like a sentinel on guard, next to the barn a cylindrical silo stands tall.

Upon noticing the colorful circles painted on the barn Crowder knows he is on the farm of "fancy" Pennsylvania Deutsch, descendants of Germans who for religious freedom had migrated here over two hundred years ago. Being called "fancy" is to be contrasted with the Amish and Mennonites, people of "plain dress" who do not "hold" to hex signs. The first time Crowder had seen them was in 1870 when he was working at a farm in Mt. Joy, Lancaster County. His Lutheran employer there seemed to have been partial to the birds because he had painted red and blue "distelfinks" on all of his signs, informing Crowder they were on his barn to bring good luck and happiness.

Up ahead, shaded by an enormous three trunk sycamore with patchy peeling bark and small brown spheres hanging from the branches, a mid-sized farmhouse sits, constructed completely from rocks dug from the surrounding land. A front veranda the width of the house holds several wooden rocking chairs. As Crowder approaches, a dog barks menacingly from inside the house.

Suddenly a window sash is flung up. A man's voice booms out. "Who's that out there now?"

Crowder, wondering if he dare go any nearer with that dog so intent on guarding the house, shouts extra loudly in hopes the man can hear him. "Sir, name's Crowder Patient. Lookin' fer a private from the 103rd."

"All right, then. Wait 'til I get the mutt out of the way." The man returns minutes later, opening the front door to stand on the porch. A short white haired, thickly bearded old man stooped nearly perpendicular, leaning heavily on his cane beckons to Crowder.

"Come on up, then. Can't be too careful nowadays, ya know," he explains. "Duke always lets me know when somebody's comin' up the path."

When Crowder looks around warily, the man reassures him, "Don't worry yaself none about Duke. Put him down in the cellar already. Here, come on inside. It's a little chilly today, I think. My old bones, ya know. We'll set a spell in the kitchen. It's warm over here by the stove." He hobbles along, leaning hard on his cane for support. "Lookin' fer my boy, ya say?"

"Yessuh. Told me some time back, jest after the war, that is, tuh look him up if Ah ever needed work."

"Here now, make yaself right ta home. Jest hang yer coat'n hat over there on a peg. Won't be needin' them now. It's warm enough out here."

After the two men are comfortably seated at the kitchen table, the old man queries again, "So yer lookin' fer my boy, is it?"

"Yessuh."

"Well now. Let me tell ya about him. Come home back in '65, he did. Hung around some. Was too restless, it seems. Jest couldn't stay put. No, he jest couldn't. Don't know why. So he headed off east. Over there somewhere by Wilkes-Barre, it was. Said he wanted ta try his hand at minin' coal. Now why the thunder he want ta do a fool thing like that fer? Boy growed up here in these mountains, breathin' the freshest air the good Lord ever made. Go down under the ground? Whatever fer?"

The old man shakes his head in puzzlement. "Jest can't fathom such foolishness, I can't." He ceases his talking for a while, just sitting and gazing out into space. Crowder politely waits for the father to continue. "Well sir. Got the news one Monday. Back in '69, it was. A cold day fer September, I remember. Felt like snow was in the air already. Mailman knocked on the door. Had a letter from some kind'a mine inspector."

He ceases his speaking once again as he is remembering. Then after emitting a heavy sigh he continues, "Letter said that there was a terrible fire at a mine over there somewheres by Wilkes-Barre. Called by the name of Avondale, it was. Nobody, not nobody got out. Not *my* boy. Not nobody. They *all* jest choked ta death down there. Happened on the 6th of September, it did. Right about nine o'clock in the morning. That's what the letter said."

Crowder is stunned and saddened by the news he is hearing. He had known there was always the chance of the private's not being alive, but hearing of the tragic way in which he had died is indeed overwhelming.

The old man goes on, "Well sir. My two other boys went on over there ta some place called Plymouth. Brought their brother back home, they did." Pointing with his cane he concludes with, "Buried him up yonder, jest over that hill there." Heaving another sorrowful sigh, he laments, "Why couldn't he jest'a stayed home in the first place? Always wantin' to wander off, ya know. Jest like the time he left ta go ta the war. He was too young. Only sixteen, he was. His Ma'n me didn't want him ta go, but he jest went anyways. Was we ever glad when he come back home. But fer some reason he jest couldn't stay put."

Surprised at hearing of yet another town by the name of Plymouth, Crowder has no answer for the bereaved father. Eyes welling, he recalls the young private who had described the lofty mountain ranges surrounding his father's farm. Told how he and his brothers would collect huckleberries and blackberries for their mother's pies. Said he longed to be back fishing and swimming in the clear cold mountain streams. Wanted again to go hunting for opossum and woodchuck in the woods. Quail and grouse, too. Swore he loved his mountains. Seemed mighty anxious to get back to them. Now Crowder is wondering just what happened to change all that.

"Can't tell ya how sorry Ah'm tuh hear that, suh. Yore boy was a fine soldier and a good friend."

"Thanks fer sayin' that, Patient. It's good fer a old man ta hear. Now about that work yer lookin' fer? Like ta be of help ta ya, seein' my boy was yer friend'n all. But my other two boys are runnin' the farm now, ya know. Jest can't speak fer them. One'll be here in a while. Ya welcome ta wait around, if that suits ya."

Crowder has come this far so he figures he might as well wait to talk with the young private's brother. The garrulous old man continues talking, glad for the company. "My boy carries his Ma ta church every Sunday, ya see. I don't get there much any more. Rhumatiz, ya know. My woman always stays fer the eatin' afterwards and she's always bringing a pile of food back. Gives her a day off from the hot stove, it does. I always joke with her about always bringin' enough fer an army. Today that'll be a good thing, I think. Ya'll have some of the good vittles the women make, Patient?"

Crowder replies gratefully, "Thank ya, suh." Now sitting at the kitchen table while they wait, the two men smoke their pipes and begin to share memories of the one person they have in common.

Soon the old man's son arrives. Toting more than enough food to feed several people, he has delivered his mother from church. Following the requisite introductions she dons her apron, sets the table, and plies her husband and his guest with the still warm ham, well seasoned string beans, stuffed cabbage, buttered rolls, German potato salad, and chocolate cake slathered with a thick chocolate icing. The son already had eaten his fill at the church.

"Like some coffee, Mr. Patient, ta wash down yer cake?"

"Yes, that would be jest fine, ma'am. Thank yuh kindly."

"Don't mention it," the woman replies, carrying a full coffeepot from the wood burning kitchen stove to the table.

Detecting his son's surprise the old man explains the purpose of Crowder's being here. Never before has the son seen a colored man sitting in his parents' kitchen, simply because it never has happened before. True, there have been transient colored men passing through from time to time looking for work, but none have ever been invited to sup at the kitchen table.

This son also had served in the Civil War, but there had been no colored *soldiers* in his regiment. There had been the usual contracted contrabands--cooks, laborers, teamsters--but no *bona fide* soldiers. He is aware that his stint in the army had helped free men like this one, but he is not so sure about sitting down to "break bread" with them, especially not at *his* table.

Suspicion in his voice, the son asks the visitor, "So then, ya say that ya served with my brother?"

"Yessuh. That Ah did." Crowder is enjoying a rare treat--chocolate cake with thick chocolate icing. His wife bakes only pound cake and never ices it.

"And jest where *was* that now?"

"Roanoke Island, North Carolina. That's where Ah was born. North Carolina, that is." Crowder picks up the napkin to wipe away any cake crumbs lingering on his lips.

"With what regiment?"

By now Crowder realizes he is under interrogation, but then again nothing much surprises him anymore. "103rd Pennsylvania Infantry." After dipping a spoon into the sugar bowl, pouring from the cream pitcher, and then stirring, he ventures a sip of coffee. *Umm. Good and strong! Almost as strong as Ah used tuh make it myself.*

"And with what company?"

"C. Company C. That's the very one." Carefully Crowder replaces the china cup in its saucer. Then, while waiting for the next question to be fired, he looks unflinchingly into the disapproving eyes of the still standing white man who had not seen fit yet to join his father and the colored man at the table.

Finally the father gives his son a look as if to say, *That's enough now.* Absorbing the silent message in his father's stern countenance, the son gives a slight shrug of compliance before again speaking. "Both my brother'n ya was lucky," he concedes. "Not bein' there at the Battle of Plymouth ta see the elephant, that is."

Only Crowder and the young private's brother know what he means by that. Every veteran knows to be in a battle is "to see the elephant." "Yessuh, yuh certainly are right about that."

"Son, Mr. Patient's lookin' fer work," the old man ventures, more than ready now to change the subject.

The son, finally deciding to pull out a chair in order to sit down at the table, asks, "Ma? Got some more of that good coffee of yers?" Then turning back to Crowder he asks, "So then, Mr. Patient. Jest what kind'a work ya lookin' fer?"

Crowder replies, "Well, Ah work best with horses. Plowin', drivin'. That kind'a work."

"Well now, me'n my brother tend ta most'a that. We already got a couple'a seasonal hired men. Did hear, though, about some man named Green lookin' fer drivers. His business is breedin' horses. Then he needs them delivered ta their new owners, ya see. Maybe ya'd like ta look in ta that."

Yes, Crowder certainly would. And that is how he happens to come into the employ of a certain Mr. Green of York County. This kind of work is exactly what he wants to be doing. Working with horses. His new job is to deliver them from the Green's breeding farm to their new owners. Sometimes he is forced to be absent for several days at a time, but he has no worries about leaving his pregnant wife with her capable sister in the small house he has rented for his increasing family.

Chapter 18

West Pittston, Pennsylvania

The weeks pass by quickly with Crowder's traversing to various areas of western Pennsylvania, passing through places new to him. Places ending with "-ville," "-ton," "-town" or "-burg." He is very much enjoying his travels as well as his job.

In early fall when Crowder leaves with a delivery of horses, he will be heading in a new direction. Heading northeast. Heading to the anthracite coal fields of the Wyoming Valley where his friend, the young private, had been killed in a mine disaster. Heading to a bustling small city called Pittston situated on the eastern bank of the Susquehanna River. "Be back in six days or so," he anticipates optimistically.

However, this trip is going take him longer, driving northeast for the first time on roads paralleling the river and wagon trails winding through the mountains. He cannot make an accurate prediction because there is always the possibility of bad weather slowing him down and then there is the return trip to make. Therefore, he is not certain just when Elsie should expect him back. So with caution he tells her, "Six days," and then adds on the "or so" to keep her from worrying.

On the very first day Crowder's eyes behold the wide valley called Wyoming, he determines it is here in this beautiful verdant place where he is going to establish his permanent home. So before heading back to York County he inquires at several farms about employment. Out in the Back Mountain area in Centremoreland he is able to locate a job driving a team of horses in the fields. This is exactly what he wants to be doing.

"How soon before ya can move here?" the farmer asks.

"Well, suh, jest give me a few weeks tuh get ma affairs settled and move ma family. Got tuh find a place fer them ta stay."

"That so? How many ya got in yer family?"

"Well now, there's ma wife Elsie and my baby daughter Florence. Then Ah can't forget about ma wife's sister. She's sixteen and a real good worker. Maybe yore missus could use her in the house?"

"Never can tell. Have ta ask her about that. Say, tell ya what! Ya can live in the old house down back if that'd suit ya. My Pa built it fer my brother'n his family. That was right before he went off ta the war. Never did come back. His wife got married again, ya know, and the house's been empty ever since. Might take some work, though, 'cause nobody's been living there for all these

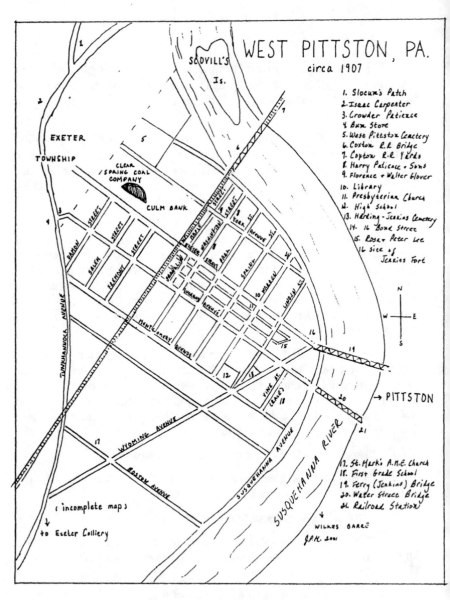

West Pittston, Pennsylvania (drawn by author)

years. But ya can take a look at it, if ya want ta. See if ya might wanna live there. Ya won't have ta pay me nothin' fer it. It's jest sittin' there empty, anyways."

Crowder can see at first glance that before the small house can be fit for human habitation it will need a great deal of cleaning. He is sure, however, that in no time Elsie and Mariah will be able to make the place livable. And the view of the mountains is so spectacular now with deciduous trees painted in their blazing fall colors, *anyone* would be happy living here. At least these are *his* feelings, but he cannot be certain about his wife's!

After returning home he can hardly wait to tell Elsie his good news. But first the horses and wagon must be returned to Mr. Green's stable before Crowder can hurry to the small rented house where his family has been anxiously awaiting his return. He is now three days late. "Elsie! Guess what?" he calls to his wife as he flies through the doorway.

She is very relieved to see that her husband has returned safely, but not being a very demonstrative person, all she remarks is, "Bout time you got back here. We was getting worried."

In answer to his "Guess what?" she responds, "Gonna move again, I su'pose. That's it?" She knows her husband is always on the lookout for just the right place to settle his family permanently. Mariah is already sixteen years old. It is time for her to think about marrying, but there are no colored men around here. In fact their family is so unique they draw attention wherever they go. Curious stares often are the response to the sight of two seemingly white women, an older black man with hair streaked with silver, and a little brown baby.

"Sister?" Mariah had questioned Elsie once. "Why're they always looking at us?"

"Who, Pet?"

"You know, Sister. *People*!"

"Oh? People're looking at us, do you think?

"Yes, I do."

Elsie seriously reflected before she answered, realizing that whatever answer she gave her sister eventually would trickle down when sometime in the future her children might ask the same question. "Hmm. You know, Pet, I do believe it's because they never seen such a pretty girl like you before. Yes, I'm sure that's it."

Mariah let out a hearty laugh, knowing full well that is not the reason. "I don't think that's it at all, Sister."

Elsie concluded with, "Well then. Just let them look and don't you pay no attention to them. That's what I say." Now discerning the excitement in her husband's voice, Elsie easily can figure that they are going to be moving once again.

"Found jest the right place fer us tuh settle, Elsie. Yuh'll love it, Ah'm shor!"

"See, what'd I tell you?" Elsie knowingly looks in the direction of her sister. The two of them had just been commiserating on why Crowder was so late getting back. Elsie had told her sister she was not worrying *yet*. She said he probably had gone exploring, and she was absolutely correct.

"And just where is this wonderful place?" she asks her excited husband.

"Got tuh go north over a couple of mountain ranges. Tall mountains. *Really* tall ones like Ah never seen before. And way farther away than Ah ever been before with the horses. That's why Ah'm so late gettin' back. Hope yuh wasn't too worried."

"Well, couldn't help wondering. Must'a gone 'round Robin Hood's barn getting back is all I can say." She smiles up at him now, very glad he has returned safely, but not willing to let him know just how glad.

"Well yes, Ah'm back now." Crowder is so full of enthusiasm. "Got tuh tell ya what Ah saw! When Ah went over the mountains, why, Ah entered *such* a valley. Cut right through by a mighty river. The Susquehanna, they call it. That's the way Ah went, jest followin' that river north."

"What kind'a name is that? Susquehanna?" Elsie asks.

"Indian, hear tell."

"See any colored folks there?" Mariah queries with interest.

"No, Ah didn't, but Ah heard tell there's some around. Workin' fer rich families. Drivers, cooks, maids, and the like."

"Wonder if they have any children." Mariah is thinking that it would be nice for her niece to have playmates of color like herself.

"Sorry. Didn't think tuh ask 'bout no children. Jest have tuh wait'n see, Ah su'pose."

Elsie thinks, too, that it would be nice for her child to know other colored children so she will not always have to be be the "different one." And perhaps now a nice colored husband might be found for Mariah, too. "Just when you think we'll be going?" Elsie knows that when Crowder makes up his mind about something, it soon will be done.

"Have tuh go before winter sets in," he replies. "Got tuh beat the snow."

This will give her just about three weeks to get ready because at dawn the hoarfrost is already on the ground.

Elsie does not like anything at all about this journey they are making to her husband's "heaven on earth." She is chilled "to the marrow" all of the time, even though encased in her heaviest clothing. Her feet are numb. Her hands are freezing in spite of her woolen gloves. Her body just is not acclimated to the out-of-doors. She has always been *inside*. During the daytime she abhors the bumpy ride she must endure in the wagon drawn by the horses Crowder purchased from Mr. Green with the intent of selling them when he gets to Centermoreland. At night she detests sleeping in the woods even though her husband assures her there is nothing to be afraid of since he had taken this same route before.

The full moon illuminates the area on the riverbank where Crowder has stopped his wagon for the night. The bright reflection smiles up from the surface of the dark deep Susquehanna River. Earlier he had made a fire so he could fry the shad he fished out of the river. Elsie has no experience with cooking over an open fire and so Crowder's army "know-how" comes in handy. Afterwards, he pitches a waterproof canvas tent to shelter the women and child. Fortunately, there are no signs of rain.

Crowder is enjoying this time of sleeping out-of-doors. He enjoys gazing up at familiar stars, especially the "drinking gourd" with its brightest orb's leading him north once again. He is invigorated with inhaling the fresh balsamic odor of the woods. He finds enjoyment in listening to the Susquehanna's steady flowing downstream and to the rustling sounds of the wind's breezing through hemlocks, cedars, spruces, and red pines. His suffering pregnant wife, on the other hand, wants only to go to sleep, even though her body is accustomed to the comfort of a soft mattress—not this hard ground.

In the middle of the night an owl suddenly hoots from a tall spruce. Frightened, Elsie bolts up straight, startled awake from her fitful sleep. "Jest a hoot owl. That's all," Crowder reassures his uneasy wife. He tells her that back on the North Carolina plantation the presence of an owl indicated good luck and so he thinks it to be a good omen. Of course, this means little to Elsie. She has never slept in the out-of-doors before. She knows nothing about hooting owls' bringing good luck. Certainly she never before slept under a tent or on the hard ground. And she determines she is *never* going to sleep anywhere except in a soft bed after she gets to where they are going. This she vows to herself.

Florence is fussy, sleeping fitfully, too. Even Mariah cannot work her magic on the unhappy child, tending to her most of the time now because Elsie is constantly nauseous with this pregnancy. The kind of food she is forced to eat on the trail does not agree with her at all. Simply the *smell* of coffee sends her running for the bushes. "Jest a little while longer," the concerned husband assures his uncomfortable wife.

Finally Crowder is able to settle his small family in the farming area of Centremoreland where during that first summer a baby boy is born. They name him Harry. And during the three years in Centremoreland another baby girl is born, called Rosa. With the Patient family's multiplying so quickly Crowder now must provide for three adults and three children. So he feels he requires a job paying him hard cash, one doing more than just supplementing his very small salary with milk, fruits, vegetables, and free rent.

His employer, although reluctant to see his good worker leave, realizes the little house in the back no longer is large enough for the burgeoning Patient family. He suggests, "Why don't ya make a trip over ta West Pittston. It's not too far from here. Jest over the mountain. Take the wagon. Ya can make it over'n back in a day. I'll give ya my cousin's name. Tell him I sent ya. He's got a business across the river in Pittston. Maybe he'll have somethin' fer ya. Never can tell." Crowder had been in the small city of Pittston once when he delivered the horses for Mr. Green, but at that time he had no reason for crossing the river to the pretty borough on the opposite side.

Originally a part of Exeter Township, the borough of West Pittston, Pennsylvania, situated at the northern entrance of the twenty-three mile long Wyoming Valley, is appropriately dubbed "The Garden Village" due to its distinctive beauty. Unlike many of the hilly settlements in the Valley, due to its flat terrain West Pittston had been laid out very easily on the western side of the Susquehanna. At first this land on the western bank had served the very same purpose as the Valley of the Kings on the western bank of the Nile. Because the ancient Egyptians believed that the sun *dies* each day in the west, they buried their dead on the *western* side of the river, reserving for the living the eastern side where the sun is *born* each day.

Similarly the first occupants of this small section of Exeter Township were also dead. They included the Harding brothers, Benjamin and Stuckley, brutally killed by Senecas and Tories on June 30, 1778. It happened during the period of the Revolutionary War just days before the Battle of Wyoming, better known as the Wyoming Massacre. The British had demanded the surrender of the several forts situated along the Susquehanna River. Instead of surrendering, however, 375 men organized and marched to face their enemies' gunfire. Only

174 were to escape. The gunfire lasted a short thirty minutes, but on July 3, 1778 the savage massacre following the battle that lasted twelve horrific hours.

Buried also in this small West Pittston cemetery is the family of Judge John Jenkins, one of the first settlers. As the town has grown around it until this year 1882, for over one hundred years the small triangular Harding-Jenkins Cemetery has sat at the point where Wyoming Avenue and Linden Street merge.

The earliest settlers here had built a small log house surrounded by a stockade, calling it Jenkins Fort after the family who lived in it while operating a raft-ferry across the Susquehanna River. As recently as thirty years ago in the year 1852 *three* homes only had been built on this western side. But now facing the river are magnificent mansions requiring retinues of servants, a number of them southern colored folk anxious to leave the South and its discriminatory "Black Codes" put firmly into place following the short-lived Reconstruction.

At this time West Pittston is basically residential with few businesses except for anthracite mining and a knitting mill. Added in later years will be a machine shop, iron works, brass works, as well as a lumber, a cut glass, and a biscuit company. Even so, generally West Pittston will always be considered a *residential* community.

In some ways this place very much reminds Crowder of Edenton, North Carolina. Both lovely small towns are situated on waterways. Both with spacious well-kept homes (wooden ones painted white and others built of brick or stone) majestically standing on wide tree-canopied streets and avenues. Both with red brick sidewalks where hitching posts stand at attention waiting to tether horses. Intricate black wrought iron fences protectively enclose many of the properties and gracing the front of these mansions are neatly manicured lawns adorned with perfusions of brightly colored flowerbeds.

Horse stables and carriage houses have been built in the rear, accessible to the narrow unpaved dusty alleyways providing a back entrance onto the large properties. These remind Crowder of Dillsburg where the same type of alley can be found. And oftentimes above the carriage houses are living quarters for coachmen. It is in such a place Crowder is attempting to settle his family. A place Elsie determines to leave, however, as soon as she sees it. And as quickly as possible!

Crowder is so full of enthusiasm for his new found Valley. Dillsburg is situated in a hilly area of Pennsylvania and at the time he was working there, he thought of the town as being surrounded by *high* mountains. Now he knows differently, relishing the majestic sights he is discovering here. Wherever he turns he sees endless ranges of very high rugged Pennsylvania mountains, in the fall painted in their blazing fall colors, the likes of which he had never seen in the lowlands of eastern North Carolina where most foliage turns to various shades of gold and brown. How awed he is here upon observing the magic of summer's green replaced by fall's gold, crimson, orange, and rust.

He enjoys driving his new employer's fancy fringed black surrey pulled by a dappled gray horse. Chuckling, he thinks to himself, *Never did get tuh drive Marse's carriage like he wanted me tuh*. Now in this new job, besides caring for the horse, he might be called on at any hour of the day to drive the old Mrs. somewhere. Perhaps "over town" across the Jenkins Bridge to Pittston to purchase some yarn, thread, ribbon, or other notions, or south to Exeter Borough to the fruit, vegetable, and fish markets, as well as driving the younger family members around on their many jaunts. And sometimes during these quiet moments his mind may begin to wander, but he jerks it right back to the present since he does not relish remembering anything about his painful past.

Crowder has a great deal of work to accomplish downstairs in the carriage house as well as caring for the horse in the stable while his wife has much, *too much*, work to do upstairs. And with Elsie, Crowder, Mariah, Florence, Harry, and little Rosa, the quarters are too cramped.

"We can't live like this!" insists Elsie, standing with arms akimbo, stamping her little foot while protesting to her bewildered husband. "This is worser than at the corporal's when we was living in the cabin. Besides I don't like living upstairs. It's too hard doing the washing. In fact, to tell the truth, I don't like *nothing* about this place. Nothing a'tall!"

Finally Crowder is forced to admit what his wife says is true even though he does not want to face the facts. He had been figuring that since he does not have to pay rent for the coachman's quarters, he can squirrel away even more money for that house of her own he has promised. *Well, at least we're here in the Valley*, he is thinking. *He* certainly is content here. Now he must find ways to make his wife content, also, since she certainly is doing her best to make him most aware that she is not!

Eventually he is forced to make the decision to find some other place for his family to live. When Crowder informs his employer of his plight the man suggests, "Why don't you check with my friends, the Schooleys? They just might need a coachman." So in late 1882 Crowder is in that family's employ, but just for a short while. As a coachman he really is not doing what he wants to do, even though the living quarters being provided for his family are much larger. No, he has decided he wants to be out in the fields, plowing with a team of horses. He is a *farmer*.

Upon making this known, his employer suggests, "Say, Patient, my cousin Mary Schooley's married to Isaac Carpenter. He's got a huge farm up there in Exeter Township. Over past the 'Bum' Colliery. Don't have any idea why it's called that. Anyway, it's really Steven's Colliery. Know where that is?"

Crowder says that he does. Everyone can see the colliery's ugly looming breaker down the back road just past the "Bum Store," the coal-company's store on Tunkhannock Avenue directly across from where Luzerne Avenue ends. He knows little about the coal mining operation, having no knowledge that the mine pit and all of the associated buildings collectively are called a *colliery*. One of these buildings is the tall dingy breaker. He is not aware that here chunks of coal get sorted by very young boys who sit hunched over iron chutes ten hours a day, laboriously picking out useless slate and rock. Crowder Patient really has no interest in coal mining at all, especially because of what had happened at the Avondale Mine to his friend, the young private from York County.

An anthracite coal colliery with looming breaker in background (circa 1898)
Courtesy of the Anthracite Heritage Museum, Scranton, Pa.

The man continues explaining, "Carpenter land, you see, extends to the river in one direction and to the mountains in another. It's big. You just might find some work there."

So Crowder starts out on one warm Sunday afternoon, walking up Tunkhannock Avenue, passing cultivated fields bordered by a profusion of pink wild roses and blue-violet chickory, milkweed plants with orange and black monarch butterflies winging about, yellow centered daisies, delicate white Queen Anne's lace, and orange black-eyed Susans. Choke cherry and red mulberry trees growing wild shade the narrow walking path leading to the area where Exeter Street merges with Tunkhannock Avenue. Crowder easily locates the sprawling property next to a babbling creek. Isaac Carpenter's tall three story mansion stands shaded by a young copper beech, elephant-gray trunked and with leaves shiny as newly struck pennies.

Crowder is able to see on the opposite side another house farther up Exeter Street, originally a dusty old stage road traversing north from Wilkes-Barre to Montrose. This home on the eastern side of the now macadamized road belongs to Isaac Carpenter's cousin, Jesse. Prior to the Civil War it had served as an Underground Railroad station for conductors like William Camp Gildersleeve who, as a boy, had observed the evils of slavery first-hand in Georgia where his father was a pastor. As an adult, because of his outspoken abolitionist views, William had been tormented, even to the point of having his Wilkes-Barre home plundered. Even to being taken to court by an irate slave owner. Even to having been beaten, blackened with ink, and chased out of town. Afterwards he became even more committed while dedicating himself to assisting slaves to reach safe havens such as Montrose, Pennsylvania located not far from the New York border.

Totally unaware of the vital role this abolitionist family had played before the Civil War, Crowder Patient, about to begin a long and fruitful association with the cousins Isaac and Jesse, steps for the first time onto Carpenter property.

Several years later throughout the spring and much of early summer the family watches with excitement as their new house is being raised slowly. It will be so much larger than the cabin in which the last two babies had been born. There are going to be three bedrooms with the parents' at the top of the stairwell, the girls' to the left and the boys' to the right. Downstairs a spacious kitchen will run the width of the house in the back and in the front a dining room and parlor with the front door and a small foyer set between them.

The Patient family which has grown so rapidly, a new arrival just about every two or three years, has outstripped the cabin offered to Crowder when he first had become the employee of Isaac and Jesse Carpenter. Seems to the ex-slave that he could not escape living in cabins. This particular one had been built many years before for one of the Carpenter families long since moved upward and onward. On the eastern side of Tunkhannock Avenue in an area still remaining in Exeter Township rather than being part of the newly formed borough of West Pittston, the cabin had not been fifteen walking minutes from the farm where Crowder was put in charge of the horses. The cabin had been comfortable enough at first when the family was smaller, but not after Lillian and Jessie had put in their appearances.

"Ma," Crowder excitedly had announced one day. He always called his wife that now in the presence of the children. "The Carpenters offered me a great deal tuhday."

The family was just finishing with supper and Mariah had gotten up from the table to serve the dessert. Warm bread pudding dotted with plump raisins, drenched with sweetened cream. There was never a lot of chattering going on while the family ate their meals. The parents may have inquired of the two older children about their day at school. They may have discussed chores and what errands needed to be run, but in general everyone concentrated on their eating. Elsie was quite particular about her children's manners.

She had grown up observing a German household where there had been silver plated eating utensils, a china service as well as the every day pewter dishes, fragile glass ware, white linen tablecloths and matching napkins with individual silver rings. The napkins got changed once a week on Sunday and following each meal a person's napkin was rolled neatly, soiled or not, and put back in its ring for when the table got "readied" for the next meal.

The custom in that well-to-do Pennsylvania Deutch household was to finish eating before conversing. Certainly no one ever talked with a mouthful of food. No one ever noisily slurped soup or chewed loudly. No one ever sat with elbows on the table, or lounged, or reared back in a chair. Even though Elsie does not have all of the necessary accoutrements for gracious living as had the lawyer's wife in Dillsburg, she does maintain the same kind of etiquette in her own household. Crowder by now knows enough to let his determined little wife "run the show." "*My* children will have good table manners," she has determined. "No telling just where they might be invited someday."

In time Elsie will acquire several fragile cut glass candy dishes and vases of her own, a dainty pink rose-budded cocoa set complete with small cups, a cobalt blue tea pot with matching creamer and sugar bowl, as well as silver plated flatware. She will have a set of white china dishes encircled with a fine gold band and Florence will crochet beautiful tablecloths to grace the dining room table, but while living in the Carpenter cabin, Elsie uses inexpensive pewter.

From her seat closest to the fireplace where she might easily ladle seconds from the kettles, Elsie had replied, "And just what is this great deal the Carpenters offered you?" She certainly was hoping they would not be moving again.

She was reasonably certain Crowder was content enough here since besides establishing a satisfying working relationship with Jesse Carpenter, they had become friends. Jesse very much reminded Crowder of his old friend, the corporal. Since Jesse also had served in the Civil War the two veterans often discussed those terrible days.

Rumors about town had it that Crowder upon finding Jesse wounded on a battlefield, saved him, and in gratitude the white man brought the black man north with him to Pennsylvania. Not so. Neither is it true that as a runaway slave Crowder had rushed up to the white man, Jesse, and begged for protection. Nor is it true that Isaac Carpenter had gone South before the Civil War and brought Crowder north via the Underground Railroad. The white "they say" can be just as unreliable as the black "grapevine."

The truth of the matter is that Crowder Patient came north to Harrisburg to be discharged from the 103rd Pennsylvania Volunteers Regiment in which he was a *bona fide* Union soldier. No one brought him to West Pittston except *himself.*

The Carpenters counted Crowder as one of their most valued workers, not missing a day of work in the past five years. So to encourage him to stay on in their employ after noticing his family was growing rapidly and realizing the possibility of Crowder's perhaps wanting to move on to a better paying job, the cousins Isaac and Jesse had a surprise for him. They revealed that they were going to build a sturdy two-story house on the front of the lot where the cabin was located. And they were offering the new house to Crowder to occupy with his family and, amazingly, *for as long as he wanted.*

Looking at both his wife and sister-in-law Crowder exuberantly continued. "Ya'll never believe it! The Carpenters tell me they're gonna build a big house up front. And they're gonna let *us* live in it. A brand new house, would ya believe? And *rent free*, no less!"

"You don't say? Now, why would they want to go and do a thing like that for?" Elsie had asked in astonishment. She could understand their *lending* them the old cabin. It was just sitting there empty, anyway, and Crowder, a driver in the employ of the "well-to-do" Carpenters, needed a place to settle his family. Certainly that she could understand. *But to build a brand new house just for us?* This she could not fathom. Again she asked, "Why would they want to do that for us?"

Crowder also was overwhelmed by such a generous offer. He did not understand it, either. But he knew better than to "look a gift horse in its mouth." At auctions he used to watch Amish men checking teeth to determine the age of each prospective horse. They were looking for that "mark" or dark central depression on the surface of incisors in horses *claimed* to be less than eight years of age. In older ones that mark disappears and the astute farmers could not be fooled into buying any horse whose teeth had flattened with age. So those men had very good reason for looking in a horse's mouth.

Was Crowder's "gift horse" *security for life?* It seemed to him that was exactly what the Carpenters were offering him. Not only a permanent position, but also a rent-free house for him and his family. *And fer as long as Ah want.* Jesse had made that perfectly clear to him. Hard for Crowder to believe.

Still, the pragmatic Crowder wanted to provide for his wife, just in case of his early demise. Always that had been of concern to him, but he had no solution. Many times he had thought, *Su'pose the horses get spooked by a bear when Ah'm takin' the wagon over the mountains tuh Scranton? Su'pose a bridge washes out when me'n the team's crossin'? Su'pose the ferry collapses when Ah'm drivin' the team over tuh Scovill's Island? Su'pose ma heart suddenly fails? What's gonna happen tuh ma family then?* These always have been his concerns.

So he thought, *Got tuh find a way tuh protect Elsie, too, out of the Carpenters' offer. Promised her Ah'd always take care of her. Promised her she'd never have tuh work fer nobody ever again. Got tuh make sure of it.*

So then, hedging a bit, Crowder turned first to Isaac and then to Jesse before replying. "Well now, Ah'm much obliged tuh yuh both fer the offer. It's mighty kindly of yuh and Ah do want tuh take it. Yessuh, Ah do want tuh very much, but...."

"But? But, what?" Isaac had asked in surprise. Certainly neither he nor his cousin Jesse can imagine why the hesitation on Crowder's part. "Is there a problem?"

"Well now, Mr. Carpenter. Yuh know that we don't have no family, me'n Elsie, 'cept fer Mariah'n the children the good Lord blessed us with. Wonder sometimes what's gonna come of them if somethin' bad happens tuh me. Ah don't dwell on it and Ah don't ever talk tuh the wife about it, but it does give me some cause fer worry."

"Yes, Patient. I certainly can understand that," Isaac had responded sympathetically.

"So then, Mr. Carpenter, let's put it this way. Ah'll make a deal with yuh. Promise tuh stay on workin' fer yore family long as Ah'm fit. In exchange fer that Ah ask yuh tuh let ma wife stay in the house, even if it's long after Ah'm gone. After all, Ah'm twelve years older, yuh see."

"Deal!" Isaac did not even hesitate, instantly extending his right hand to Crowder. Jesse was smiling, too, expecting to forge a long association now with this man whom he admired and called "friend." When Crowder relayed all of this conversation to his wife all she could say was, "Why, I never!"

Now the sounds of sawing and hammering are reaching the cabin as Elsie watches "her house" rising. She knows the house is not *hers*, really, and may never be, but as long as she lives here she will act as if it were. Tight-lipped as Elsie is nobody will ever "know her business," *not even her own children.*

"How soon will our new house be finished?" excitedly the children ask her each day, sometimes more than once.

"Soon. Very soon, I should think."

Several rainy April days have prevented the builders from appearing and so the house is rising very slowly. Because the old cabin becomes unbearably warm in the summer, Elsie is looking forward to soon being in her new house where she will be able to fling up window sashes to catch cooling breezes. Besides, Jessie the newest baby, named for their kind benefactor Jesse Carpenter, will be much more comfortable by an open window while lying in her crib. Her older sister Lillian, born three years before in July, had been very cranky and miserable in the heat of that summer.

At last moving day finally is here. Furniture needs to be carried up to the "big house" sitting there right up front on the corner of Luzerne and Tunkhannock Avenues. The shiny brass numerals 828 have been nailed onto the house right of the front door. On it is a small knob for manually ringing the doorbell. Also there is a slot for the mail. Certainly the house is not large in comparison to the one Crowder remembers on the North Carolina plantation, but it is still a big house compared to where they have been living. The irony of moving up to "the big house" from a cabin below is not lost on the ex-slave. *Wish Marse could see me now!*

The family climbs the steep stairs to the back porch after passing the compost heap and the Concord grape arbor. Then past "Miss Jones," the outhouse, surrounded by tall multicolored hollyhocks making a futile attempt at camouflage. Past the narrow gurgling creek where the children hunt for tadpoles in the spring. Past the wooden swing hanging from the apple tree. Finally they enter the spacious kitchen where the vacant walls stand begging to be papered.

Elsie is quite overwhelmed at what she is beholding. The kitchen has been furnished with a large cast iron coal stove, logo *Pittston* emblazoned across its door. With its flour sifter, sugar storage bin, and several drawers, a tall green Hoosier storage cabinet stands against one wall. Wooden chairs with caned seats have been set around a rectangular table long enough to seat eight at a time. Equipped with a modern cold water spigot, not the usual water pump, a stone sink sits in the side pantry where over a wide shelf tall glass door cabinets have been built for storing dishes and glasses. As she assesses everything, Elsie's grateful thoughts are, *It may not be near as grand as the house in Dillsburg, but for us it'll do just fine.*

Then she crosses the kitchen to a screen door on the opposite side of the room. Unhooking the latch she steps out onto a wide porch running the length of the house, facing Tunkhannock Avenue. As she gazes at the beautiful sky now streaked with pink and orange, the sun slowly being hidden by the western horizon, she envisions herself on this porch. Shaded by thick vines of English ivy, protecting her from the heat of the afternoon sun. Sitting here peeling her potatoes, stringing her green beans, shelling peas and lima beans, husking corn, churning butter, piecing patches for the quilts she must make for cold winters, or mending rips, all the while tending to her brood of children running and tumbling on the lawn. Then after a long and tiring day Crowder can sit out here, too, and rock, smoking his pipe as he patiently waits to hear his wife's soft voice inviting from the kitchen, "Come to supper, Pa."

Crowder had promised his young wife a house someday. A house of her very own. This is the closest he will come to keeping that promise. For more than forty years the deal with the magnanimous Carpenter family will be a most satisfactory one for both Crowder Patience and his wife Elsie.

What's that the Bible says?" Elsie ponders. *Something like, 'My cup runneth over.' Think it must mean this.*

One spring day Elsie stops her usual chores long enough to gaze out of the kitchen window to admire the long slender branches of bright yellow blossoms on the forsythia bush she had planted the very first year she was in her new house. Also she takes great pleasure in the sight of the snow-white blossoms on the pear tree, the pink blossoms on the cherry tree, and the fragrant lilacs Crowder had planted for her at the same time. This view to the north delights her.

Later, while washing the dirty breakfast dishes in the pantry sink, she stops for a moment to gaze out of the window there, beholding an entirely different sight altogether. This view to the east depresses her as she thinks, *"Wonder what was over there before? Wonder if a body ever could see clear across to the river from here?"*

She is well aware the Susquehanna River is over in that direction, *somewhere*. However, now all she is able to see is the enormous Clear Spring Coal Company's ugly culm bank of mine debris looming as a black mountain, devoid of any greenery and on which before dusk she can spy little bug-looking things crawling up and down its sides. *Things* which in reality are *people*. Desperate people scavenging to find small usable chunks of coal co-mingled with the unusable refuge brought up each day from the bowels of the mine. Desperate people looking for any sized pieces of coal for warming their homes and for cooking their suppers.

One of those persons climbing the dirty culm bank is a small Italian woman who lives with her several children in a dilapidated shanty nearby. A number of years ago during the middle of the day, the mine whistle had shrieked unexpectedly. Shrieked for *her* because her husband had been killed in an accident underground in the mine. Killed by heavy rocks suddenly pouring down on his unprotected body.

Widowed then, unskilled, and unable to speak English, she had to find ways to provide for her young children. Now her two sons are working as breaker boys at the mine colliery, each dutifully handing over to his mother his daily wage of fifty cents. The three little girls, when they reach twelve years of age, will go to work at the nearby Wyoming Valley Knitting Mill. The children are aware that their earnings do not belong to *them*. No, they belong to the *family*, the accepted way of life for most European immigrants in the Valley.

And so late each afternoon Elsie can spot the small woman attired entirely in black from the shawl covering her dark hair down to the worn high top shoes covering her feet. With an empty brown burlap sack flung over one shoulder, she trudges past 828 on her way to the looming culm bank. Perpetually dressed in black, as her "old-world" culture dictates, she is going to wear her "widow's weeds" for the remainder of her life.

One day Elsie and the woman in black have a confrontation over the dandelions growing so profusely in 828's front yard. Without a bordering fence, there is absolutely nothing for discouraging anyone from walking directly onto the lawn. Elsie's corner lot is especially enticing then to a woman who has need to supplement her children's meals with salads of healthy dark green dandelion leaves.

When she is out "hunting" one of her hands always keeps the burlap sack securely flung over her shoulder. In her other hand she carries a short sharp knife. Upon spying a healthy looking dandelion plant, regardless of whose yard it is in, she deftly digs deep enough to separate it from its long taproot. Then she proceeds to stuff the bunch of serrated leaves deep into her sack.

Elsie does not want those ugly holes dug in *her* grass, enjoying the way it looks in early spring when bright dandelion flowers dot her lawn. She takes delight in their egg-yolk yellow's matching perfectly with her trumpet daffodils and forsythia bushes, even though the sight lasts but a very short while. For very soon afterwards the dandelion flowers go to seed. Then her children have great fun blowing the white fuzz all around the yard.

One day upon spying the woman in black as she approaches 828, Elsie goes to stand at her front door ready to say, politely, of course, not to dig in *this* yard. The woman in black is slowly meandering up Luzerne Avenue, peering intently into each yard she passes. Some properties are protected with fences having latched gates. These she passes by quickly, soon nearing the tall honey locust tree at the edge of 828's unfenced property.

Seemingly, the woman in black is completely oblivious to Elsie's standing there on the stoop of the last house on Luzerne Avenue. It is as if she were invisible. Now Elsie calls out loudly to the woman taking her first step onto the lawn of 828. "No! Stop! Don't come in my yard!"

The woman in black totally ignores Elsie, defiantly bending to dig a choice dandelion plant. She pushes it deep into her brown burlap sack. Flinging it back over her shoulder, she continues on her way, all the time never once acknowledging the seething Elsie.

When Crowder arrives home that night, his incensed wife greets him with her one-sided version of the encounter with the "foreign" woman. This is what Elsie calls any of the new immigrants who have replaced the older families of the neighborhood. The newcomers have come from far away Italy, Czechoslovakia, Poland, Lithuania, Wales, and Ireland to work in the coal mines. The Irish brogue Elsie easily recognizes because she has heard it before, but the other languages are all like babel to her. So to Elsie, anyone who does not speak English she labels a "foreigner."

"Maybe she jest don't understand yuh," Crowder proffers.

"That's the same thing I told her," Mariah adds, entering the kitchen from the dining room where she has been cutting out new school clothes for the children. The farmer's wife for whom she had worked in Centermoreland, upon seeing that the girl had the knack, taught Mariah the art of hand stitching, as well as the skills of crocheting, tatting, knitting, and embroidering.

"Humpt! Fiddlesticks! She understands me all right!"

"So then, Ma, what're yuh goin' tuh do about it?" Crowder questions while taking his place at the head of the table where the children await their father's grace.

"Just gonna wait for her tomorrow. Then I'll shoo her out of my yard with my broom. That's what I'm going to do!"

"Well, good luck then," are Crowder's final words, looking with amusement at his determined little wife.

Heavy rain for two days prevents the woman in black from passing by on her way either to pick coal from the culm bank or to dig dandelions in her neighbors' yards. But on the third day, toting her brown burlap sack accompanied by the short sharp glinting knife, she comes plodding up Luzerne Avenue where Elsie has been on the lookout.

The woman in black slowly approaches 828, quite aware that Elsie is waiting for her. Carefully scrutinizing the grass, all of a sudden her eagle eyes fix on an extremely healthy looking dandelion plant having benefited immensely from the rain. With determination in her footsteps she treads onto Elsie's lawn, bends over and commences with her digging!

Oh, is Elsie ever irate! Now leaving her doorway, she fully intends to admonish the intruder. Broom in hand Elsie descends the three doorsteps onto the grass. The bent over black swathed little figure quickly glances up with piercing eyes. Only for a moment, though. For after a slight brandish of her glinting knife she resumes her digging, doing all of this without making a single utterance. In that instant Elsie realizes the futility of accosting a woman with whom she can not even converse, especially one so adept with a knife and especially one who might possibly be misunderstanding why Elsie has a broom in her hands.

That evening from the pantry where Crowder is washing up for supper, he calls out to his wife, "Seen yore friend tuhday?" Of course Elsie knows very well to what "friend" he is referring as she busily stirs the chicken potpie she prepared for supper. Stalling at first, Elsie finally replies. "Yes, I did see her."

She is filling the children's bowls first so the small squares of cooked dough will cool sufficiently so as not to burn their mouths. Pausing then a moment before continuing, she says, "But, you know, I got to thinking." She now ladles some more squares, piping hot as her husband prefers, into Crowder's bowl as he takes his seat at the head of the table.

"Have to feel sorry for the poor woman, though, I want you to know. Not having a husband and with all those children." With that said she quickly turns back to the stove to avoid having to look directly into her husband's omniscient eyes. Crowder is chuckling to himself because he realizes full well who has won "The Battle of the Dandelions." Without making any further comment he commences with the grace so his hungry children can eat their supper. "Let's all bow our heads now."

The woman in black never digs too many dandelions in Elsie's yard, but she always makes sure she takes one or two of the choicest. And this practice will continue for years until the day Elsie spies the black funeral crepe on the front door of the small shanty up the street.

Chapter 19

One Memorable Winter

As if by magic, heavy wet snow has fallen overnight—the snowball, snow fort, snowman kind. The kind of snow adored by children. As the Patience children excitedly gaze out of their second floor bedroom windows they see their world mantled in white. Across Tunkhannock Avenue it is impossible to discern just where the baseball field begins or ends. All covered over, too, is the narrow wagon road connecting the large backyards of the neighbors who live there at the end of Luzerne Avenue. The children cannot even detect where the front sidewalk lies.

They are enthralled by what they are able to see, though. Tree limbs heavily weighed with the newly fallen snow. Brilliant rays of the sun glistening on encrusted high drifts, reflecting back the lightest of blue tinge. From beneath the eaves prisms of long slender icicles casting a myriad of rainbows onto the world of white. To the children's delighted eyes the yard indeed has the appearance of a magical land.

Scurrying down the stairs and through the chilly dining room into the warm kitchen they find their mother busily stirring a pot of oatmeal. Aunt Mariah is toasting slices of white bread speared on a long metal fork carefully held over an open hole of the blazing coal stove.

Earlier that morning Crowder had tended the fire prior to pulling on his galoshes as he got ready to trudge through the almost impassable snow, making his way up Tunkhannock Avenue to the Carpenter's farm. While attempting to follow the tracks of a sleigh which had gone through earlier, he quickly realized, though, *Gonna take much longer tuhday. Can tell it already.* While struggling in the knee-deep snow, he was determined. *Got tuh make it, no matter how long it takes. Got tuh see after ma horses.*

For he knew that *he* must make it to the farm because no one else is responsible for the animals' feeding, but himself. His horses require feeding at least three times a day and he can not leave any more food behind than they are to eat at one time. He knew that if he should, those greedy animals would keep on eating until they consumed all that there was, which dangerously distends their stomachs. He was aware that sometimes horses die from gluttonous overeating. So feeding the horses on time is *his* job and the Carpenters count on his seeing to it. And so as he was laboriously plowing through snow drifted high across the road, he very soon realized that the usual fifteen-minute walk might take closer to an hour on this morning.

Meanwhile back home at 828 the children are exuberant over the first snowfall of the year. "No school! No school today! Whoopee!" Harry exclaims joyfully.

After hastily completing their breakfast the three eldest children pull on their galoshes, snapping them shut with the little metal toggle fasteners. As they bundle into their heavy over coats and pull on woolen hats, scarves, and gloves, their mother is reminding them, "Now before you go frolicking outside there's chores to be done. You know the steps and paths'll all need sweeping. Florence, you grab that broom now."

So the eldest child quickly heads outside to sweep down the back porch and the steps. The snow must also be removed from all the footpaths leading to and from the house. Harry knows this is *his* job. One path down back to "Miss Jones," the outhouse, one to the chicken coops, and one to the sidewalk on Luzerne Avenue. So he fetches the coal shovel his father had left for him on the back porch. Being the only boy, now taller than his petite mother, he does many of the heavier chores around the house. Too little yet for any serious work, Rosa trails after her big sister Florence while toddler Lillian and baby Jessie remain in the confines of the cozy warm kitchen.

Afterwards the three red-nosed eldest children come stomping up the steps of the back porch. They are ready now for their cups of hot cambric tea—hot water mixed with lots of sugar and canned evaporated milk. "Knock all that wet snow off those galoshes and put them in the box over there in the corner!" Elsie orders, not wanting puddles of water all over the kitchen floor she prides herself in keeping highly varnished.

In an attempt to warm their freezing hands the children huddle around the cast iron stove. "Don't get too close to that stove now!" their mother admonishes, hanging her children's damp coats on the wall pegs for drying. She is remembering how last year little Rosa had tripped over Harry's feet, her left arm striking the side of the hot stove when she toppled forward.

Rosa had screamed in agony. Elsie rushed to her child, grabbing her up to cut back the burned sleeve of her dress. Rosa was sobbing uncontrollably as Florence and Harry stood by helplessly. He was feeling guilty because his feet were the ones his little sister had fallen over.

"Can I help, Ma?" he had asked with great concern.

"Yes, Son. Yes, you certainly can. Go get me a clean sheet. Tear it into strips. Now you can get the butter for me, Florence. She then turned to console her injured child. "Now, now, Pet. Ma's gonna fix your arm for you."

With the little finger of her left hand Elsie deftly smoothed on a thick layer of butter, the common remedy for burns in those days. "This'll soothe it, I'm sure," she explained to her distraught children. Then she wrapped the little arm in a piece of clean white cloth secured in place with the thin strips of cloth Harry had carefully ripped.

Every morning afterwards the diligent mother would change the bandage protecting the seared flesh on her child's arm. With great care Elsie would clean the wound with warm water, then reapply more butter. She had no idea how long it might take for the ugly wound to heal and so she meticulously tended her daughter's arm until finally it scabbed. Yet in spite of her mother's careful ministrations, Rosa is going to bear the scars on her left arm for the remainder of her life.

So Elsie really does not need to remind her children about the hot stove, but she does anyway. "Better to be safe than sorry, is what I always say."

Suddenly Harry says, "Listen! What's that?" The children cease their chattering long enough to hear the peeling of bells—copper sleigh bells. Through the front window of the dining room all eyes are focusing on the approaching Carpenter sleigh pulled by Crowder's team of horses. "Whoa!" they hear as the sleigh pulls in front of 828.

Taking advantage of the ample snowfall, Crowder has come to take his family for a sleigh ride. "Tell everybody to come on out now!" he calls as Harry swings opens the front door. It will take but a few minutes for the excited children to bundle back into their heavy clothing and run down the path Harry had shoveled and thoroughly sprinkled with ashes from the coal stoves. Florence quickly begins to help her mother with the two very excited younger children. Lastly, Mariah and Elsie pull on their own button artics. Now the whole family is piling into the sleigh, wrapping themselves snuggly in the heavy woolen blankets they find stored under the seats. Even Elsie is going along for the ride. The kitchen cleanup will just have to wait today.

"Get along there now!" The sleigh bells merrily peel again as Crowder slaps the reins and the team pulls out onto the empty snow-covered Tunkhannock Avenue.

"How many more days 'til Christmas, Ma?" How many more times a day is Elsie going to be required to hear that question being asked?

At school each of the children had created calendars. So in the Patience kitchen there are three calendars hanging on the kitchen wall. Elsie will send the eldest children to their respective calendars so they can answer the question whenever it is being asked. She is able to count even though she does not read or write so when they ask she is aware of just how many days are left. But she is not going to be constantly answering.

"Nine days 'til Christmas," she hears one of her children announce. "Nine more days before Santa Claus comes."

"I want a pair of skates." "I want a sled." "I want a new doll." "And I want…" After hearing the litany of her children's many requests, the mother allows each to ask for *one* item only. Thus far she has been able to grant each child's wish. However, she tells Crowder with great concern, "Hope nobody asks for something we can't get them this year."

Of course, that day will come with Harry's asking for his very own pony. Florence will want a fancy egret plumed hat she spied in a store window "over town" in Pittston. And Rosa will request an expensive porcelain doll whose blue glass eyes open and close, a beautiful doll dressed in red velvet trimmed with white ermine. But for the time being the children still are small and so are their Christmas wishes.

During the week prior to Christmas the children gather around the dining room table to write their letters to Santa, the older ones reading each one to the parents who need to know just what their children are requesting of the old man from the North Pole. Then the individual letters are sealed in envelopes addressed to Santa Claus. No stamps needed, just the return address on the back flap. Finally, one by one, they are tossed into the dining room's blazing pot-bellied stove to fly up the chimney. Destination? The North Pole, of course. Every child knows that this is how Santa receives the requests from *good little girls and boys.*

Christmas Eve finds Crowder scouring the Carpenter land for just the *perfect* evergreen. He had never seen such a sight as a Christmas tree until 1863 at the Federal army camp in Plymouth, North Carolina. Some Pennsylvania soldiers had chopped down small swamp pines, decorating them with whatever they could find. Red holly berries, pinecones, paper snowflakes and thin strands of Spanish moss as pseudo-icicles. They had not looked at all like the beautiful evergreens Elsie decorates with such care, but the homesick men had done their best to brighten the day. A lavishly decorated Christmas tree with lit candles had its origin in Germany, therefore also being the custom where Elsie had grown up in western Pennsylvania. And since Crowder is married to a girl reared in German ways, the tree now has become a tradition with the Patience family, too.

He has a lot of choices since the woods are thick with pines, spruces, and hemlocks. A perfectly symmetrical spruce is what he is searching for, spruces lasting longer after being cut, he is aware. Elsie wants it to be tall enough to almost reach the ceiling of the dining room, leaving just enough room for the star. So after chopping down the one that suits him best, he heaves the evergreen onto the rear of the horse driven cart.

Now he must conceal the tree from the eagle eyes of his children until tomorrow morning when they will see it set up in front of the dining room window. From there its beauty can be beheld by all, inside the house, as well as passers-by.

On Christmas Eve the sun is setting very early. Darkness quickly descends and so "early to bed" for the children. But not until the requisite plate of sugar cookies and glass of milk have been set out for Santa. The boys insist on leaving out a few apples from the barrel in the cellar, too. "Do reindeers eat apples, Pa?' they question their father.

"Oh, Ah'm pretty sure they do, " he replies with a twinkle in his eyes, not really knowing if they do or not. His horses certainly do. That much he does know.

So until his excited children are ensconced safely under their warm quilts, Crowder will not set up the tree to be decorated by his wife's clever hands. Just like the lawyer's wife in Dillsburg, Elsie adores preparing for the Christmas holidays. A red felt poinsettia in each window, a red-bowed evergreen wreath on the front door, and a beautifully decorated tree in the dining room.

Early the next morning when the enthused children noisily scamper down the stairs they know Santa Claus had paid them a visit. Their eyes round at the sight of the beautiful tree he has left for them. And the cookie plate is empty! The milk glass, too! Even the apples are gone!

"See, Pa, Santa's reindeers do like apples," states little Percy with delight.

"Seems so, Son."

Hanging from the clothes pegs on the kitchen wall for lack of a fireplace mantelpiece like Elsie remembers in the Dillsburg home are the children's stockings filled with small items. The most favorite treat is a juicy sweet orange transported by rail from far-off Florida, Christmas being the only time of the year they can be found in local stores. Walnuts fill the toes of each stocking as well as candies such as horehound, lemon drops, and licorice. Each child receives a new pair of woolen gloves and a neatly hemmed fresh white handkerchief, fancy tatting around the edges of the girls'. Each girl also receives a colorful new ribbon for her hair and each little boy, a fancy marble called an alley. This year Harry is delighted to discover a jackknife in his stocking. Florence finds a crocheting needle and a ball of white yarn because Mariah is planning to teach her young niece the art of crocheting. And peeking out of each child's stocking is a large red and white striped peppermint candy cane.

Under the tree the children have placed a number of packages all tied with saved grocer paper. The children have made small presents for their parents, decorating the outside wrap with colorful crayon drawings. This particular year the very creative Florence has collected samples of schoolwork and drawings from her brother and sisters, compiling a scrapbook covered with red construction paper contributed by her schoolmarm. This is her special Christmas gift to her parents.

Following the very filling Christmas dinner of tender pot roast, thick smooth brown gravy poured over mashed white potatoes, tiny creamed onions, sweet corn pudding, flaky buttermilk biscuits, honey glazed carrots, and creamy coleslaw, and, of course, pie for dessert, the fun time begins. The time has arrived for roasting chestnuts and for the molasses taffy pull! First though, the small brown chestnuts must be pierced. Otherwise, they will explode in the oven with loud "pops," dispersing a multitude of tiny particles to burn in the oven, emitting a most unpleasant scorching odor.

So while the chestnuts are roasting, Elsie stirs together all of the taffy ingredients and then boils the molasses mixture until the "moment of truth." That is, when she tests the consistency by dropping a bit into a glass of cold water to determine its readiness. The drop is going to fall *slowly* to the bottom if it is ready. Too soft, the drop will not firm at all. Too hard? Then it will drop much too fast. So it must be *just right*.

When she determines it finally is ready Elsie carefully pours the hot bubbling mixture onto a greased tin cookie sheet, waiting until the taffy is cool enough not to burn the children's hands, but not too cool so the taffy becomes brittle. Again it has to be *just right*. Slathering their hands with butter, two children at a time pull globs of the taffy into long strands. Now the very last execution is to cut the strands. This is the mother's task. With her big kitchen shears she cuts each strand of the still warm dark brown taffy into little squares.

"Each of you now. Take only two pieces," she instructs as she doles out the super-sweet candy after it has cooled and hardened. "We don't want no teeth going bad." She is very aware of bad teeth because hers tend to decay easily, resulting in her already having lost several. "For each baby, lose a tooth," she has heard. *That's what's happened to me. Must be true then, what "they say,"* she concludes. Even Crowder's tobacco applied to her painful teeth seldom helps nowadays.

By now the hot roasted chestnuts are ready to enjoy, too. In future years there will be little change in this traditional Christmas scene at the Patiences, except for the arrival of a new member every two or three years.

Chapter 20
Elsie's Sister Mariah

"Sister?" Mariah addresses Elsie one afternoon as the two are preparing supper. The younger woman is paring and quartering white potatoes, plopping them into a kettle of cold water to prevent their turning brown. "I was thinking."

The many hours bent over her sewing provides plenty of opportunity for thinking. Recently her thoughts have been returning to Dillsburg. She does not understand why they should because she and her sister seldom speak about those days when they were two poor little bound orphan girls.

By nature not being a garrulous person, Elsie does not talk much anyway and when she does what she utters usually is of some importance. Mainly about the children, or the garden, or chores needing to be completed. Her own experiences have been limited and the life she leads now provides few opportunities for growth. So she does not have much to say and she is not one to chatter about banal topics.

Elsie has been surprised to discover that the older she gets the more layers of resentment she is building concerning her former life of servitude. She sometimes wonders what her life would have been like if during the smallpox epidemic she and her sister had been placed in an orphanage in Washington, D.C. She knows for certain she would not be living here in West Pittston, Pennsylvania, but she wonders if her childhood would have been better by having been in an environment with others like herself. Colored people. Or would it have been far worse than being a lonely bound girl in Dillsburg, not knowing who she was and having no way of ever finding out?

Who was her family? Is Mariah really her sister? They do not look at all alike, short Elsie with straight black hair and dark brown eyes, and the taller Mariah with wavy light brown hair and hazel eyes. Had they just been two little orphaned girls thrown together in the crisis? She has no idea that in Dillsburg's 1870 census nine-year old Dollie had been recorded with having no last name. Not even Vedan, as twelve-year old Elsie was listed. Of course there is no way to answer her questions, but for some reason her mind does seem to fix on them.

She is aware now of how slaves had been made to suffer. Crowder has told her about some things, not too much, however. Just enough, though, to make her realize that life as a bound girl in Pennsylvania certainly was far better than that of a slave girl in the South. Even though she, unlike never had to live in constant fear of being whipped or much worse raped and even though she had enough to eat, slept in a soft bed, she had not been taught to read and write, the necessary tools for success. And she has become resentful of that.

228

By now Elsie also realizes that she and her sister had been deprived of being like other children. Like those living along the pleasant tree-canopied streets of Dillsburg, care free and happy as they played their games. She realizes, too, that she and her sister had never been hugged or kissed or nurtured as the children of the lawyer's daughter were. No one had ever loved Elsie except her sister Dollie and, so, consequently, the two cleaved together like two halves of a walnut. *Inseparable.*

Finally she came to the realization that she and her sister really had *no childhood*. None at all. The lawyer and his wife had been kind to the girls, but they were servants. And like Crowder she simply does not care to dwell on the past. He has relayed to her very little about his life as a slave and she has told him little about her life as a bound girl. And neither have any intentions of ever discussing their painful pasts with their children. It will be as if the parents had simply *materialized* in West Pittston, Pennsylvania out of nowhere, devoid of any prior lives. The *beginning* is with them.

Seldom then does Elsie's mind wander back to Dillsburg except at Christmastime when she cannot help but remember how she had been invited to stay in the daughter's bedroom until Florence was born. Each year as Elsie decorates her Christmas tree, hanging the two delicately painted glass orbs the lawyer's wife had given her, she remembers how much the Pennsylvania-German woman had loved the holiday season. She would decorate each room lavishly with fragrant white pine and red spruce boughs cut from the nearby woods. In each window she would have Elsie hang a large felt poinsettia with bright red bracts and small yellow flowers set prominently in each center.

So especially at this time of the year Elsie always makes a concerted attempt to put away any feelings of resentment, just being thankful for her life as it is now.

"And just what're you thinking about?' Elsie is responding to her sister's remark.

"Well, I was just thinking that it might be nice to send a Christmas greeting to Dillsburg. Just to say we're fine, you know. Just in case anyone ever wondered what's happened to us. And I'm really curious about what's happened to *them*. What do you think, Sister?"

"Curiosity killed the cat, you know, Pet," Elsie replies.

"Oh, you and those sayings of yours, Sister!" Mariah laughs.

Even if they had wondered what had happened to the girls, the lawyer and his wife not having thought it important enough for Elsie and her sister to learn to write, would never have expected to receive any correspondence from either of them. But Mariah has attended school, learning to write in beautiful Spencerian script. For the past several Christmases she has been sending greetings to the women she sews for, thanking them for their patronage, and wishing them happy holidays. *Good for business*, she correctly figures.

This year for some unknown reason Mariah's mind instead of concentrating on her stitches has been digressing to thoughts of the folk back in Dillsburg. *The housekeeper's boy is a grown man by now. Wonder if he went into business for himself. Or maybe he even went on to college. He was always reading. There was nothing to stop him except maybe the lack of money.* Then her thoughts jump to the married daughter and her brood who on every pleasant Sunday would make the trip down from Mechanicsburg, spending the day with the aging parents. *All of those children have to be grown, too, by now*, Mariah muses.

Dollie, as Mariah was called back then, and Elsie were always so exhausted that on each Sunday night they would fall asleep as soon as their little heads touched their goose-down pillows. Sunday was always such a hectic day. The dining room first had to be beautified with the fine china and crystal requiring washing and drying before the table could be set. All the silverware had to be given a polish until it gleamed. And a sumptuous meal had to be prepared and served.

Then following the dinner always served promptly at one o'clock, there were so many soiled dishes, glasses, and silverware to again be washed and dried before being returned to the glass door china closet. The heavy white damask tablecloth with an intricate rose pattern, brushed first of its larger crumbs, was grabbed up at all four corners before being carried out of doors for shaking. Finally with its matching napkins it got deposited into the tall wicker basket containing Monday's laundry.

Afterwards, the table would be cleared and "readied" for the next meal. During the week the lawyer's wife always kept her dining room table fully set with her less valuable pewter, stemware, and cutlery. She never knew just when unexpected company might appear at her door.

Out in the kitchen the dachshund, Missie, was allowed to languish under the table where she caught all kinds of crumbs falling from the table. Some by accident, others deliberate. She would eat anything, except onions, Dollie knew. However, the canine was never allowed in the dining room during mealtimes. *Missie would be really helpful in here*, the girl often had thought since she was the one sweeping the rug where bits of food dropped beneath the children's chairs.

Then there was the light supper always served promptly at six o'clock. Only when the last pot had been scoured, dried, and hung back in its proper place in the pantry would the two bound girls be finished with their tasks for the week. And on Monday morning, bright and early, the new week would begin with Elsie's rising at dawn to feed the chickens in the barnyard.

Her tasks nowadays are not so much different from what they had been back in Dillsburg, except now her labor is for her own family. Still meals to prepare, dishes to wash and dry, aluminum pots to scour, and chickens to feed. So she adheres faithfully to the strict schedule she has set for herself, allowing no deviations. Monday is for washing; Tuesday, ironing; Wednesday, mending; Thursday, shopping; Friday, baking; Saturday, cleaning; and Sunday, preparing the family dinner. Her early training as a house servant certainly has prepared her well for her present life as a farmer's wife.

So Elsie is perfectly content with the life she leads now. A life revolving solely around her family. Therefore, she is a little taken aback when Mariah broaches the idea of sending a Christmas greeting to the folk they left behind in Dillsburg. Reflexively then, Elsie asks, "Remember the address?" knowing that it is impossible for Mariah ever to forget the brass numbers on the front door of the large Georgian russet brick house. One of the younger girl's daily tasks had been to polish the brass doorknocker and knob, as well as the shiny numerals 62.

"Oh, yes, Sister, of course I remember. Don't you?"

Elsie nodded, "Can't never forget."

"Well then. What do you think? Wouldn't you like to know how they all are? I know I would."

"Well, Pet, to be truthful, I don't think much about them at all," Elsie replies. "But I su'pose I wouldn't mind them knowing we're doing just fine. And that my husband takes real good care of us all. And that we have four beautiful children. All brown, not at all like the Mr. said they would be. He said they'd be black. Don't know where he got that fool notion from, anyhow. Well, he certainly was wrong about that!"

She pauses, thinking about what else to relay. "And while you're at it you mize well tell them about your fine dress making business. How successful you are. Tell them how smart you are, going to school and all." She pauses momentarily then, contemplating, "No, I guess you shouldn't say that, after all. Sounds an awful lot like bragging." Her face lights up with a smile as she chuckles, "Well anyway, they can see that for themselves when they get your letter."

"Oh, Sister," Mariah laughs at her sister's sudden burst of enthusiasm. "I only intended to send a short Christmas greeting, not write a lengthy report."

"Well, if you're gonna to do it, do it right, like the Mrs. always said," Elsie responded firmly.

The following letter was delivered over a month later for Miss Mariah Veden, Tunkhannock Avenue, Exeter, Penna. in care of Crowder Patience:

Mechanicsburg, Penna.
January 20, 1884

Dear Mariah,

How delighted I was to read the Christmas letter you sent to my parents. However, I am sorry to be the one answering it. Your letter was forwarded to my home. I know Father and Mother would have been happy to hear from you because they often spoke of you & wondered how you were getting along.

Father died in '77 and then Mother sold the old homestead & came to live with us. Two years ago she caught a bad chill & took to her bed. In January just two weeks after Christmas she went to sleep forever to be with the Lord. You know how she loved the holidays so I feel she was trying to keep up her strength. My parents are buried together in the family plot next to the church at home in Dillsburg.

You might like to know that the housekeeper remarried. You remember the farmer who raised the best corn? His wife passed away & left six children. Our housekeeper accepted his proposal & moved on the farm with him. Her boy is doing very well. He is married & has two little boys of his own. He owns the apothecary shop now. Next time I'm down to Dillsburg I will be sure to tell his mother that I heard from you. I haven't been there since Thanksgiving. It has been too snowy & cold to go anywhere this winter.

Please express to Elsie my congratulations on her four children. I know how busy they must keep her, as did my own five. Also let me say that I like the name you chose for yourself. Mariah has a nice ring to it.

I hope to hear from you again. God bless you all.

By the time Mariah finishes reading, tears have welled in Elsie's eyes. Carefully the letter gets refolded and placed back into its envelope. "I'm glad you did write the letter after all, Pet."

And with finality the door to Elsie's past slams shut.

THE MATRIARCH
Elsie Veden Patience at Harvey's Lake,
Pa. (circa 1899)

Summer Sundays are always very special to the Patience family because many of those sultry afternoons are spent in pleasant out-of-the-way spots where people gather in the hopes of finding some relief from the heat. Picnics are favorite activities, baskets laden with all kinds of foods toted by the strongest persons in each family.

Eleven year-old Harry, the only boy, is the strongest in his family now, simply because his father cannot leave his work long enough to accompany the family on these all day jaunts. Mariah anticipates the outings because she is still looking for her "Mr. Right." Every once in a while a new young colored man might put in an appearance, such as happened last week at Harvey's Lake where the excursion train had carried the family the twelve miles across the mountains from West Pittston.

She had spied the pleasant looking stranger supping with another colored family. There had been no opportunity for inquiring about who he was since the reclusive Elsie always holds her little group tightly together. Anyway, no proper young lady would go wandering off to meet a new person, and especially not if that person were a *male!* Well, anyway, he definitely had caught Mariah's eye. However, she was not aware that she had caught his as well.

Mariah is reticent about sharing any of these feelings with her sister. So Elsie is not cognizant of any of this because already she has chided Mariah with, "Pet, you're just too picky. There's not that many colored men coming by this way. And you know you're not getting any younger." Mariah is well aware of that fact, recently having blown out the twenty-four candles atop her birthday cake, a yellow pound like the Dillsburg housekeeper always baked, except thickly slathered with chocolate icing as Mariah prefers.

She has had several gentlemen callers, but none of them "strike her fancy." One amorous young man came calling on several consecutive Sunday evenings last fall. She was polite to him, but finally he got the point when she always left him on the porch in Crowder's company to rock and converse while smoking their pipes. Recently, another young swain had tried to tie her up in conversation after Sunday School, but she was not in the least bit interested in him, either. And so Mariah has determined not to say *anything* at all to her sister about this particular young man who does happen to "strike her fancy."

All week long, as she goes about her dressmaking business, tirelessly walking to the homes of the rich ladies residing in their capacious Victorian mansions along the Susquehanna River, her mind travels back to the young man she had seen last Sunday. *Wonder if he'll be at the lake next Sunday? Hope it doesn't rain. Hope one of the children doesn't get sick and Sister decides not to go.* All of these thoughts keep replaying over and over again in Mariah's head.

Just who is he? Where does he come from? Why is he here? Is he engaged or committed to one of the girls in that other family? How can I ever find out?

Fortunately, it is not raining on Sunday. The children are all feeling well, eager to take off for the lake. The sun is not too hot and so Mariah is not perspiring profusely as she does sometimes when water just pours from her head, trickling down her forehead and the back of her neck. How she detests that! Today as she lays out the cool white lawn dress she had been working on all last week she is remembering the inquisitive question asked by her niece Rosa. "Why're you working so hard on *that* dress, Aunt Mariah?"

"Just thought I'd like to have it done for Sunday, Rosie," she had replied with a smile, not wanting to reveal that she wanted to look extra special just in case a certain young gentleman might show up at the lake. And it was only last night by the light of the kerosene lamp in the kitchen she had finished hand stitching the hem.

Prior to donning her lovely new dress, Mariah talcum powders herself well, hoping to stay as dry as possible. At the West Pittston station while the family waits for the excursion train to pick them up, she thinks, *Thankfully the day is mild.* Even so, after the long breezy train-ride over the mountain to the lake she is not looking quite as fresh as she would wish. Tendrils of golden brown hair have escaped from beneath her wide brim straw hat and since there has been no rain recently her black high top shoes are dusty already.

After arriving at the lake they find several other families already having claimed the choicest shady spots under the spreading Norway maples. On blankets or quilts people lounge while chatting, eating, drinking, and fanning in an attempt at keeping as cool as possible on this humid midsummer's afternoon. Scanning the crowd for the young man she had observed last week, Mariah discovers him to be nowhere in sight.

Maybe he's just been delayed, she reasons to herself with optimism. *Or, then again, maybe he's not planning to come at all,* she concludes with disappointment. *Oh, well. Anyway, I don't know how I'd get to meet him even if he does show up. He's with another family. I don't know any of them, so I can't just go over to say hello.* Now after a long week filled with anticipation she is feeling a bit deflated.

"Something wrong, Pet?" Elsie inquires after taking note of Mariah's sudden changing mood.

"Oh, no, Sister. Everything's just fine. Guess I'm just a mite hungry."

"Well now. If you'll just play with the children for a little, I'll get everything together. How's that?"

It is perfectly fine with Mariah. She adores her four nieces and one nephew and they in turn adore her. Their big playmate, she is willing to throw balls to them, jump rope in the summer and ice skate in the winter. Elsie is much too busy running her household and Crowder is always working. So, naturally, Mariah is happy to play with the children. As she unpins her hat, her hair falls from its bun. She tries to poke it back, but to no avail. *So, who cares? I'll just braid it up*, she decides as she tugs at her wavy hair to form two plaits, making herself look nearly as young as her nieces. *There! That'll keep it under control.*

Now leaving her hat behind on the ground, she calls to the children, "Come on now! Let's all get in a big circle and throw the ball to each other." She has created this game so all of the children can play.

When it is Harry's turn he throws the ball high, much too high for his short aunt to catch. And so it goes sailing over her head. As Mariah turns to retrieve the ball her hazel eyes immediately fix on the young man from last Sunday. Thin, not very tall, a light-complexioned man with wavy black hair and dark brown eyes. If she had not seen him with that family last week she would never have thought him to be colored. He is walking all by himself, carrying his round straw hat in one hand, slowly making his way in the direction of Elsie's little group. Now the ball is rolling directly toward him! Stooping to scoop it up with his free hand while smiling up at Mariah he asks, "This yours, Miss?"

"Why yes, it is. Thank you, sir," she replies, a little short of breath. Deeply flushing, she is very much aware of her unkempt appearance. One hand automatically reaches up to touch a braid already coming undone.

"Name's Isaac Gould." As he hands her the ball, he takes notice that there is no ring adorning her left hand. Encouraged by the sight he continues with his introduction. "I recently moved to Pittston."

"How-do, Mr. Gould? Glad to make your acquaintance. I'm Mariah Veden and that's my family over there." She nods her head in the direction of Elsie and the others.

By now the children are scampering toward them, inquisitive about the stranger who is conversing with their aunt. Impatiently they tug on her while pleading, "Come on, Aunt Mariah! Please come on back to the game!"

"Mind if I join you?" Isaac Gould asks the children.

No, the children do not mind at all and *neither does Mariah.* So Isaac removes his suit coat, turning it inside out before folding and laying it neatly on the ground. Then he places his round straw hat on top. Soon he is laughing, too, just having a grand old time. Elsie is closely scrutinizing the young man engaged in playing ball with her sister and children and so when she calls her family to the repast she has spread, she invites Mr. Gould to join them.

"Yes! Yes, Mr. Gould. Please! Come'n eat with us!" The children exuberantly add their voices to the invitation.

Last week after Isaac Gould had spotted Mariah he knew he wanted to meet her. However, being the guest of another family with an unmarried daughter, he certainly could not ask about some other girl. It simply would not be fitting. *I'll just have to wait until next Sunday,* he had figured. And so all throughout the week his mind had been conjuring up the face of the pretty young woman he had spied at the lake. He hoped she would show up on the next Sunday. He hoped it would not rain. He hoped nothing would prevent him from seeing her again. One problem he has, though, is that he has no idea how he is going to secure an introduction. A gentleman would never approach any young lady without a proper introduction!

How easily his problem has been solved. *By a ball, no less,* he laughs to himself. *A ball introduces us!* By now the children all have warmed up to Mr. Isaac Gould. Elsie is enjoying his company while Mariah simply glows from his attentiveness.

Elsie as head of the little group, taking notice of an eligible bachelor interested in her sister asks, "Mr. Gould, would you like to come by the house for Sunday dinner some time?" Mariah, afraid that he may refuse, uncontrollably blushes.

"Why, thank you. I'd like that very much." Quickly glancing over at Mariah to discern her thoughts, he sees that her face is flushed. He sees, also, that she is smiling, the sight of which further encourages the now quite smitten Mr. Isaac Gould.

After that first dinner invitation, the young man can be seen often visiting at 828 Luzerne Avenue. He might be sitting on the vine-shaded porch, rocking and talking with Crowder while the women are inside fixing Sunday dinner. He might be strolling with Mariah in her garden while she inspects her flowers, especially her favorites--the pansies. He might be on the side lawn playing catch with the children.

Finally comes the important day. The day on which the ardent suitor seeks Crowder's permission to ask Mariah for her hand in marriage. Isaac assures that as an inside foreman in Coal Mine No. 9 he amply will be able to support a wife.

"Well then. Ah think that'll be jest fine, Mr. Gould. Jest fine," Crowder responds as head of the household, contented that Mariah at last has found a husband. And a reasonably well off one at that.

The very next month Mariah Veden and Isaac Gould exchange their vows in the front parlor of 828 Luzerne Avenue. The bride and groom move into a house in Pittston, just about an hour's walking distance away. Although the sisters will not see each other every day, they will be together on weekends because every Sunday Elsie expects them to be at 828 for dinner, a tradition she will keep through three generations, even to her great-grandchildren.

Several years pass and Mariah is disappointed because she has not been able to present her husband with a child. Finally, after accepting the dismaying fact there may never be any Gould children, she reestablishes her dressmaking business.

Specializing in creating fancy shirtwaists of chiffon, net, lace and silk, she builds a lucrative business for herself, sewing for wealthy ladies in the community. Mariah is in great demand to create one-of-a-kind outfits fashioned out of Canova canvas, crepe, damaise mohair and worset checks, all special fabrics directly ordered from England by her ladies. Florence and Jessie both have shown an interest in their aunt's work and so she creates tasks for them to do. Jessie especially loves searching Mariah's button box, fascinated by the variety of colors and designs she discovers there.

To her great surprise at the age of twenty-eight Mariah becomes pregnant. Both she and Isaac are overjoyed. Elsie also, because now she, too, will be an aunt and the Patience children at last will have a cousin. The months pass by quickly as Mariah prepares for the arrival of her long-awaited baby. So much needs to be accomplished. The nursery has to be painted and outfitted. So talented with the needle, Mariah is enjoying hand stitching tiny white baby clothes trimmed with dainty lace. With the clicking of her knitting needles she creates little woolen outfits for chilly days. Mariah Vedan Gould is radiant in her pregnancy.

Elsie is right there with her sister when the mid-wife delivers the dark-haired baby girl with hazel eyes. "Beautiful, just like your mother," the ebullient Isaac exclaims as he admires his newborn daughter. The midwife carefully places the baby girl in her father's waiting arms.

"Both doin' fine Mr. Gould." While exiting the home the midwife is assuring Isaac with these words. Climbing onto her horse-drawn cart, she concludes to herself, *Not a hard birthin' at all. In labor jest through the afternoon. Didn't scream once, she didn't. Jest moaned some. A very easy birth, it was. Wish all my deliveries was this easy.*

The next day the baby still seems to be doing fine. However, the new mother is quite feverish. Her brow is wet from perspiration, her bed clothing soaked. "Mariah, are you all right?" Elsie anxiously questions her sister after noticing that Mariah is very weak, even weaker than she had been yesterday. Weaker even than a newly delivered mother rightfully ought to be.

"I'm just so tired, Sister," was Mariah's wan response before she slipped back to sleep. That was several hours ago. Now the baby is crying incessantly. Elsie goes to the bedroom door to knock.

"Isaac?" she calls in concern. She needs to know why the baby is so unsettled. She is wondering, *Isn't Mariah feeding the child enough?*

"Come on in, Elsie," Isaac softly answers. When Elsie opens the bedroom door she can see her distraught brother-in-law sitting on the bed, cradling his wife while trying to get her to swallow some cool water. However, Mariah is barely able to lift her head. And the poor baby is screaming in her cradle.

Elsie first attempts to comfort the baby before she takes a good look at her sister. After feeling Mariah's feverish brow, Elsie becomes frantic. "She's burning up! Isaac, you gotta go for the doctor. Go! Quick!" Isaac is hesitating. "Don't worry. I'll be right here beside her. Go now! Hurry!" She remains by her sister's bedside, wringing out cool wet cloths, attempting to lower Mariah's body temperature. The new mother is delusional. She does not even know who Elsie is.

On October 8, 1888 just two days after the birth of her beautiful healthy daughter, Mariah Veden Gould succumbs to that dreaded disease for which there is no cure at this time in history. Puerperal fever, commonly known as "child bed fever." The rapidly spreading infection had snuffed out the life of the new mother.

Watching her sister breathing her last, Elsie sobs uncontrollably. "No! No, God! Please don't take Mariah! Please don't take my sister!" Many years later Lillian is to say this was the first time she saw her perpetually stoic mother lose control. She has lost her beloved sister. She has lost the only link to her past.

Herself still nursing, Elsie now gives to her sister one last gift. With her own body she determines to keep Mariah's child alive. Isaac names his daughter Hazel as a reminder of of his wife's beautiful eyes. And so Hazel Gould is to live as a member of her aunt's household until her father remarries.

Isaac Gould with his wavy black hair and just slightly tanned skin easily could have passed into the white world, but he does not choose to even after marrying his second wife, a Caucasian who does not wish to associate with the colored Patience family. However, until his death, Isaac Gould continues to be part of Elsie's family and for many years remains a trustee of St. Mark's AME Church in West Pittston.

Tintype circa 1904
Front row: C.E. Cuff, Lillian, Chester,
Jessie
Back row: Elsie, Isaac Gould, Rosa

Chapter 21

Some Northern Brands of Discrimination

*T*he small borough of West Pittston, Pennsylvania is hundreds of miles from the small town of Edenton, North Carolina. The free man Crowder Patient is light years from the slave boy Toby who had but one name. And freedom to do as one chooses is in direct opposition to being enslaved. Still, *total* equality eludes the Patient family as it does all blacks, even those living in the North.

Fortunately, Crowder Patient has been able to find a place to work and to live in contentment. A place where he is rearing his children in peace, where they attend school while learning to read, write, and cipher. Some might say that this should be enough for an ex-slave. But no, it cannot be enough for any black as long as overt segregation is rampant in the South where lynchings are reported in newspapers and where the 1914 Jim Crow laws will be set firmly in place to keep blacks "in their place." Not as long as white supremacy is being espoused by the likes of the Ku Klux Klan. And not as long as *covert* discrimination exists in the North.

To Crowder and Elsie Patient, however, the last house on Luzerne Avenue does seem to provide the perfect safe haven for them and their family. However, they know that cruelty oftentimes lurks just outside their doors. Elsie would like to think that by closing her doors tightly enough she is keeping out the world. This works for only so long. It works only until her innocent children must go through those doorways and out into the world. Many times to face extremely painful experiences.

The old Carpenter cabin long ago had been torn down and the yard at 828 with its large vegetable garden now extends to the narrow road where horses pull their wagons. The closest neighbors to the Patient family are those living on their left as well as those directly across from them on Luzerne Avenue.

When Elsie and Crowder move into the new house on the front of the lot there is no welcoming for them. Never are they to be on friendly terms with any of those neighbors. In fact this question has circulated throughout the neighborhood: "Why the Sam Hill did the Carpenters build a *brand new house* for that colored man and his white wife?" Followed by such unkind statements as, "Disgraceful how that old colored man's married to that young white girl, ain't it. And havin' all those children!" Folk tsk-tsk at the very thought.

Elsie has no idea what the white "grapevine" is relaying. It would not matter to her in the least bit, anyway. Content with being in her new house, she is kept very busy caring for her increasing brood of children. Conversing with her neighbors is something she is too shy to do, anyway. On Mondays as the laundry is being pinned in the morning and unpinned in the afternoon, upon seeing her next-door neighbor she might exchange a "How-do." But that is all. No neighborly "small-talk" ever is exchanged over the wooden fence separating the properties of 826 and 828.

Crowder's life is so filled with work on the Carpenter farms that he has no opportunity for cultivating friendships, even with any of the other colored men in town. Anyway, their line of work is not the same as his, being coachmen and butlers while he is a farmer plowing and planting the Carpenter farms. He might have something more in common with gardeners and hostlers (horse groomers), though, but there is little time in his life for socializing. And so during the years before the children have to attend school, Crowder and Elsie's family live in complete isolation.

As the years pass, even though the children make friends at school and have playmates in the neighborhood, these never are invited to 828 and the Patients never go to anyone else's home. The wall of race is set firmly in place with little interaction with neighbors until many years later. Only after friendly Italian families move into the houses next door and across the street.

Recently arrived from Naples the ambitious men in these families erect large glass enclosed steamy greenhouses, opening lucrative businesses for the propagation and sale of vegetables. Tomatoes, green peppers (for some unexplained reason incorrectly called *mangoes* in Wyoming Valley), egg plants, cucumbers, onions, garlic, lettuce, romaine, escarole, arugula as well the Italian herbs basil, broad leafed parsley, and oregano.

As they grow older the Patient children and their neighbors are able to break down some of the barriers of language and cultural differences. For instance, even though they never go running in and out of each other's homes as *close* friends might, Jessie and the young Italian woman next door converse over the fence separating their back yards. Jessie will offer from the trees in her parents' yard apples, pears, and sour red cherries for pies in exchange for her neighbor's superb tasting vine ripened tomatoes and plump bright green "mangoes."

One day Jessie is in for a surprise. Over the fence the neighbor is offering a plateful of steaming food. "*Mangia!* Eat!" the neighbor insists. And after taking her first bite of the delicious spaghetti Jessie gets hooked on Italian food. So with great enthusiasm, she learns how to concoct the garlicy red sauce (called gravy by some) requiring slow simmering for hours on the coal stove. She learns how to shape the requisite meatballs. To sprinkle a finished plateful of pasta with finely grated Parmesan cheese, even adding red pepper seeds for zest. To dunk hard biscotti cookies into her coffee. To slather butter on chunks of Italian bread, always crusty on the outside and soft in the middle. And now just a mixture of olive oil and vinegar punctuated with Italian herbs is all Jessie ever is going to put on her leafy salads.

And so Jessie is the one introducing the spicy Italian cuisine to a family with palates used to their Ma's bland food. Elsie, of course, will not deem even to *taste* this "foreign" food. She especially hates the unfamiliar odor of cooking garlic permeating the air in *her* house, pointedly going around flinging up all of the windows when Jessie is preparing *her* spaghetti sauce. Never having been very flexible anyway, the older Elsie grows the more rigid she becomes. Especially when new ideas invade her space. Elsie Veden Patience very much is afraid of *change*.

Florence always is going to remember exactly when she first heard that derogatory word "nigger." It was on her very first day at school after the family had moved to West Pittston. As she was being enrolled there her last name was recorded with the spelling of *Patience*. In Centremoreland it had been *Patient* and probably would have remained so had the family not moved.

Elsie returned home after having escorted her eldest child to the second grade classroom. All of the other parents had left, too, and the schoolmarm was attempting to settle the class. Some children already had taken seats. Shy Florence sat down beside another girl who promptly got up and moved over to the next row. Nobody wanted to sit next to the brown girl. Not in front of or behind her. So there she was, sitting all by herself until the teacher got around to seating the students in alphabetical order.

It was then she heard the boy seated behind her hiss, "Nigger!" At first she did not "pay him any mind" because her attention was on the teacher. She never would have paid any attention to him at all had he not pushed his sharpened pencil up underneath the seat to poke her. "Oh!" she exclaimed in surprise and pain, immediately turning around to gaze into a surly face.

Then he hissed it again. "Nigger!" Florence had no idea what that word meant, but by the expression on his face she knew it had to be something most awful! *But why is he saying it to me? Well, I guess I'll just have to wait 'til school is over and I can ask Ma.*

The children had a short first day. Promptly at noon Elsie was standing at the corner anxiously watching for her eldest child. She had brought along an apple for Florence to munch on since she should be hungry by now and a long walk lay ahead of them before they would arrive home for their midday meal. Crowder had promised his daughter that he would be there waiting to hear about her first day at the new school.

Distancing herself from the other mothers, Elsie had with her five-year old Harry and the almost three-year old Rosa who vehemently was objecting to being pushed in a perambulator. Baby Lillian had been left home at the cabin with Mariah who was busy at her sewing machine. With two small children in tow trekking the nine long blocks down Luzerne Avenue to the school on Warren Street was a struggle for Elsie, but she had to make sure her Florence got home safely on this her first day.

As she ran down the steep school steps, upon spying her mother, the little brown girl proudly waved the drawing she had created that morning. "Pretty as a picture" she was in a creation of her Aunt Mariah's. A long sleeved, light blue-flowered dress covered by a ruffled white pinafore with a big bow tied in the back. Her curly dark brown hair was tightly braided, secured with bright blue ribbons. She was full of excitement as she greeted the little group waiting for her there on the corner. With curiosity on their countenances, the white mothers glanced in the direction of the brown children and their "white" mother.

"So what happened today in school?" Elsie was all questions. She was very excited. Here was her first child fulfilling the parents' dream of their children going to school, learning how to read, write, and cipher.

As the mother and her children were beginning their long trek home, Florence was overflowing with enthusiasm. "Oh, guess what, Ma? My teacher read us a story. All about a silly girl who went to a bear's house!"

"A bear's house? Now why in the world would she want to do a fool thing like that for?" Elsie asked, most puzzled.

Little Harry was all wide-eyed. His father had told him about the bears living in the woods near the Carpenters' farm. Crowder warned that they were very dangerous and could eat a little boy. So Harry also was puzzled. He was wondering if they would not eat a little girl, too, especially if she went to their house.

Florence continued, "Don't know why exactly. I think she was hungry. I know she was sleepy. 'Cause she went upstairs and took a nap in the bear's bed."

Now the mother was thoroughly confused. She thought this was a very strange story indeed. *Bears have beds?* Their having a house is odd enough to her way of thinking. She thought Florence must have been talking about their den. *But beds? What kind of fool things are the teachers telling the children?*

"And when she was upstairs sleeping? Guess what happened then, Ma?" Florence continued.

"What happened, Florence?" asked inquisitive Harry, all ears.

"The bears came back!"

"*Bears!*" Elsie exclaimed. "I thought you was talking about just *one* bear."

"Oh, no, Ma. My teacher said there was *three* bears! A daddy bear, a mommy bear, and a *baby bear.*

"I'd be real scared!" Harry piped up.

"Oh, she was, all right. She was *real* scared. When she saw those three bears staring at her? Well, she just jumped right out of that bed! It was the baby bear's bed she was sleeping in. She jumped out of the window and ran fast. Very fast. All the way home!"

Elsie shook her head in bewilderment as she pondered, *"Now that's a strange thing for the teachers to be telling the children, I think. But what do I know? But bears with beds?"* She was sure that part could not be true.

The little party was almost home. Just one more block to go, up the hill. Elsie already was short of breath. She was not used to walking so far. Rosa was protesting about being pushed in the carriage. "Be still now, Pet. We're almost home. Let Ma stop here now. Just for a spell."

Florence was still talking. "And you know what else happened today, Ma?"

Elsie has caught her breath, ready now to continue on home. "And what else happened today, Pet?"

"The boy behind me kept saying "nigger," so I could hear it. What's that mean, Ma? Why'd that boy say that to me?"

The mother sighed deeply. *This was bound to happen sometime*, she was thinking. However, she had not prepared her child for the eventuality since she really had no idea how. No one had ever levied that epithet at her. Never had she experienced any of the blatant prejudice directed against colored people because she had not been identifiable as such herself. Therefore, she knew nothing at all about arming her unaware children against the cruel barbs of discrimination. She only knew that she was going to have to take this up with their father.

So just what would the ex-slave tell his brown children? A man who all of *his* life very much had been aware of the kind of hatred the color of his skin could and did generate among certain people. A man who knew the necessity of arming his children well since prejudice and discrimination were "facts of life," even in this small northern borough.

"Want tuh know why that boy called yuh that, do yuh now, Florence? Well now, come on over here by me an' Ah'll tell yuh." Then the father beckoned to his son, also. "Harry, yuh come on over here, too, an' hear this 'cause yore gonna be goin' tuh school soon, jest like yore sister." Setting one child on each knee he instructed them, "Now yuh listen real good, Son, 'cause Ah s'pose somebody's gonna call *yuh* that, too. 'Nigger.' That's the mean name some white folks wants tuh call us colored folks. Yuh see, some white folks plumb don't like us, mind yuh. An' its *only* 'cause we're brown."

The ex-slave had no idea of how the word had come into being. He had no idea that it started as a mispronunciation of the Spanish word "negro" (properly pronounced nay-gro) which simply means "black." He had no idea that southern whites evolved the word first to "neger" (nay-gah) and finally into the offensive ephithet "nigger" (nig-gah).

Florence was confused. "But why, Pa? Why don't they like us 'cause we're brown? I just don't understand." Young as she was, she really wanted to know the answer because already she has been made to feel different. At school that day nobody wanted to sit by her.

"Can't rightly tell yuh that, Daughter. Ah jest don't know. The good Lord made us all and He loves us all. And that's whut Ah do know. Florence, Harry, now Ah want yuh tuh be sure and remember this. There's *always* gonna be people yuh run into who jest plain won't like yuh. They won't want tuh get tuh know yuh at all. They'll never get tuh know what a good friend yuh'd be. An' that's a pity, it is. But, Ah'm tellin'yuh now, there's nothin' yuh can do about it. All ya can do is jest stay outta the way of those kind'a folks."

"But, Pa? What about that mean boy? He sits right behind me. And he poked me with a sharp pencil, too."

"Well now, Daughter, if he bothers yuh tuhmorrow, yuh jest gotta march yuhself right up tuh yore teacher an' tell her what he did."

The next day during the silent reading time the very same thing happened. "Nigger," she heard being hissed from behind her. So Florence very carefully slid her chair back just far enough to be able to stand up. She tiptoed to the teacher's desk and whispered, "Miss T?"

The young teacher lifted her eyes from the spelling papers she was correcting. "Yes, Florence. Do you need something?"

"Yes, ma'am. My Pa says I should tell you that the boy behind me is calling me a bad name."

There was no need for Miss T to ask Florence what the bad name was, already surmising because the day before as soon as she had seen the little brown girl walking into her classroom she was afraid such a thing was bound to happen. "All right, Florence." Miss T put down her pen and closed the top of her bottle of black ink. Drying the ink carefully on the desk ink blotter she directed, "You just go back to your seat and finish your reading now. I'll take care of this."

Once Florence had returned to her seat, Miss T summoned the boy to her desk. She ordered, "You go to the cloak room! Now!" Even though she was speaking softly the whole class could overhear four of the most dreaded words in a teacher's vocabulary. *Go to the cloakroom!* Simultaneously, then, every face lifted and every eye focused on the teacher and the boy.

The cloak room! No one wanted to be sent *there*. That was where the teachers kept their wooden paddles. And Miss T was no exception. Soon the sound of a whack, followed by an explosive "Ow!" emanated from the inner sanctum where the children's coats and hats hang. With a great deal of curiosity while having absolutely no idea just what the boy was guilty of, the students were closely watching as their teacher marched the boy back into the classroom.

"Now then, young man, just get your books out of your desk and take the *last* seat in the *last* row!" The *last seat* was in isolation, way in the back of the room, even behind the students whose last name began with "Z."

With the fast approach of February 14th, eight-year old Florence is beginning to get a sick feeling in the pit of her stomach. This is because she is dreading Valentine's Day, a day when she would like to be excused from going to school. However, unless she is throwing up or running an elevated temperature, Florence will be trekking down Luzerne Avenue as usual, crossing the railroad tracks and on to school.

Each year on Valentine's Day customarily the school children exchange their homemade cards. In Florence's class last year one especially popular girl whose long auburn curls were always neatly drawn back by a large colorful bow, had received the most. The boys even as well as each of the girls in the class had given her a pretty card. She collected so many she did not know where to put them all until the teacher provided a brown paper sack for her to carry them home.

Even though she made one for each person in the class, as her teacher had suggested, Florence herself had received only a single card in return. It was from the one girl who would play with her at recess. The one who would ask, "Florence? Want to go on the teeter-totter with me?" The one walking up Luzerne Avenue with Florence at lunchtime. "Bye, see you later," she would promise as the two girls parted at Maple Street. The one who always waited at the corner after lunch as Florence sped down Luzerne Avenue in hopes of crossing the railroad tracks before the watchful guard in the tower lowered the black and white striped gates.

It is not that Florence does not enjoy going to school. She usually does. She loves to read and to write and especially to draw. Her penmanship is beautiful and many times her teacher has complimented her. The little girl especially enjoys learning about countries far away like Egypt with its ancient pyramids, China with its Great Wall, and Italy with its Leaning Tower of Pisa.

What she does not like about school, however, is the way the other girls gather together in their little cliques, never ever including her. Whenever her one and only friend sometimes may be taken in, then Florence keeps to herself. At recess whenever the whole class is instructed to form a circle to play "Little Sally Water Sitting in a Saucer," she is never chosen to be Sally. Whenever they play "The Farmer in the Dell," she is never picked, not even to be the cheese. And whenever they play "A Tisket, A Tasket," she is never given the chance to run. It seems that to her classmates Florence is invisible.

However, whenever there is a class spelling bee her classmates recognize her ability. This is the one time she is *not* excluded. The captain having the first pick will call out, "Florence." Happily she will take her place on the team, very visible now.

Florence's younger sister Rosa has her first taste of real discrimination in the third grade. By this time she is quite aware of derogatory names she might hear levied against her. Her older siblings Harry and Florence have so educated her. Already she has been called "chocolate drop." So by now she is fairly immune to name-calling.

Very familiar with the ditty about sticks and stones hurting you, but *names* not, Rosa knows that they *can* and *do*. She is well aware that she will not be chosen during the recess games, even as the farmer in the dell's cheese, so she does not expect to be. Her sister Florence has forewarned her about Valentine's Day, so she does not ever expect a bag brimming with cards. So it is not either of those situations hurting her. No, it is *someone's birthday party*.

One of the girls in Rosa's class is going to celebrate her ninth birthday by having a party right after school at her home close by, and everyone is invited. That is, everyone except Rosa. She is not even aware of the party because her classmates do not include her in their conversations. In fact, they barely speak to her at all.

So just before school gets dismissed the teacher instructs, "Class, line up now! We're going to walk together to the party, two by two. Everybody grab the hand of a partner! Quickly now!"

Rosa, surprised, asks her teacher, "Ma'am, where are we going?"

"Why, we're going to the birthday party, Rosie. The whole class is invited, you know. You're not coming, Rosie?"

"No, ma'am. I don't know nothing about it."

Immediately, the teacher realizes what has happened. Rosa was not given an invitation because she is not welcome. *Well, we'll just see about that,* the teacher thinks. "I guess she must have lost your invitation, Rosie, because *everyone* is invited. That I'm sure of. We'll just let your sister Florence know and then we'll go to the party together, you and I. How's that? Here, you hold my hand. You can be *my* partner."

Positive that the girl had not lost the invitation, but wanting to go to the party anyway, Rosa will do exactly what her teacher suggests. And never having been to a birthday party before, she would really like to see what one is like. Bravely, yet with trepidation, little Rosa clasps her schoolmarm's hand tightly.

The procession of children, two by two, walks the several blocks to the girl's home where the beaming parents with their two younger children are standing on the top step of the front porch, waiting there to greet their daughter's classmates. Holding tightly to little Rosa's hand and looking directly into the mother's eyes the teacher announces, "Well, here we *all* are!"

And the mother looking back into the teacher's eyes replies without hesitation, "Welcome, *everyone!*"

Just as Elsie had years before, Italian mothers newly arrived to West Pittston at the beginning of the twentieth century, attempt to insulate their children from the alien world lurking just outside their doors. Being extremely clannish they continue to converse in their regional dialects, adhere to the strict mores of their culture, stick to their Mediterranean cuisine, and keep their Roman Catholic faith. However, this insulation works only until the law forces them to enroll their children in the public schools.

Newly arrived from Italy, a six-year old girl unable to speak English gets placed in the first grade. Her apprehensive young mother is forced to leave her daughter amid an incomprehensible babel of children's excited voices. She would much rather be keeping her child in the safe confines of home, but the law must be obeyed.

Day after day pass with the little Italian girl having no understanding of any of the teacher's directions, given, of course, in English. However, what she does do is to follow her parents' explicit orders to be well behaved and obedient, sitting at her desk quietly with eyes and ears open at all times. Perhaps, they hope, as if by magic, their daughter soon will be speaking English fluently.

However, one morning when the little girl does not follow a directive she does not understand she is sent to the cloakroom as a punishment. Not comprehending the reason for her being in here, after the door closes behind her she takes an inquisitive look around the dim room, observing her classmates' hats all thrown haphazardly on the shelves.

Oh, what fun! Mistakenly she believes she has been given the *privilege* of straightening the cloakroom. So she begins by arranging the hats neatly on the shelves. Then fascinated by all the varieties she decides to try on each one. And when the teacher finally gets around to opening the cloakroom door she is astounded to see not a penitent little girl anxious to return to her seat, but a smiling little girl with a classmate's hat jauntily perched on her head.

Less amusing, however, is the discriminatory treatment accorded the newcomers, being bombarded with such derogatory taunts as "ginny wops," "garlic eaters," and "spaghetti eaters." These Italian children learn quickly, just as the Patience learned two decades prior, that names *can and do hurt*.

At this time of history in West Pittston anyone living west of the railroad tracks is considered by some as "no good." This is the section of town where the Catholic immigrants (Irish, Italian, Slovak, Lithuanian, and Polish) are settling as former Protestant residents abandon the area. Even in the year 2001 an Italian-American woman in her eighties will remember well when her schoolmarms would invite children from their classes to take nature hikes on Saturday mornings. Including, however, only those who lived *east* of the tracks, those children residing on the "good side of town." How hurt the girl had been when observing those particular classmates, *the chosen ones*, gathering in front of the Bum Store at the edge of town, insultingly directly across the street from where she lived.

Soon most immigrant parents come to the conclusion that the best way for their children to succeed in America is for them to speak English exclusively. The older children, perhaps, may continue to converse in the regional dialect of their parents, but usually not the younger ones. And, sadly, in the future no attempt will be made to teach the successive generations the language of their ancestors.

Chapter 22

The Building of a Church

*F*or some years now a small number of colored people have been worshipping together on Sunday afternoons in the Old Band Room located "over town" in Pittston at the corner of Lagrange and East Railroad Streets. It is where members of the Thistle Band (after the national flower of Scotland) meet to play their instruments, the name in later years changed to the Leek Band (after the national symbol of Wales).

Walking the distance to the Old Band Room is long, especially for the Patience family who for precisely that reason does not attend the services. The majority of the colored folk live in West Pittston and so they come to the conclusion that they are in need of a more convenient place for worship. Graciously the members of the large First Presbyterian Church of West Pittston open their Sunday School rooms to the colored people who desire eventually to establish their own church. And until that future time they are welcome to hold their Sunday afternoon services at the large stone edifice on Exeter Street.

One summer morning when Crowder is driving some Carpenter workers over to Scovill's Island in the Susquehanna River just north of West Pittston, the man sitting up front next to him asks, "Say, by the way, Patience. Yer family go ta any church?

Crowder replies, "Well, no. Can't say that we do."

The man continues on then, "Didya know that a bunch of colored folks meet at my church on Sunday afternoons? That's the big church way down on Exeter Street. Corner of Warren. Presbyterian, it is."

"Hmm. That so?" Crowder responds with some interest.

"Yeah. Say now, why don't ya bring yer family down next Sunday? See if ya like it. They hold both Sunday School and church services. Starts around about two o'clock."

"Thank yuh. Much obliged fer the invite. Got tuh speak ta my wife about it first, though." He is unsure about Elsie's wanting to go, as shy as she is.

So after dinner Crowder waits until his wife finishes "picking up the kitchen" and "readying" the table for the next morning. Finally Elsie eases into her rocking chair and in preparation for mending some holey socks, reaches down into her sewing basket. Crowder casually mentions then, "Elsie, something happened tuhday. A fella on the wagon asked me if we go tuh any church."

"Humpt. You don't say! That's being a bit nosy now, don't you think?"

"Never yuh mind about that now. The man means well. Told him, No, we don't go tuh no church. But it got me tuh thinkin'. The oldest children can read now. They should be learnin' what's in the Bible, Ah think." Crowder is of the mind that his colored children should know exactly whatever white children knew about the Bible because he is remembering when the only words he had known were what Marse was fond of misquoting. "Servants, obey your masters."

"He says that some colored folks meet in the afternoons tuh have church. Got me tuh thinkin' now. So, Elsie, Ah want us all ta go next Sunday. It's that big church way down on Exeter Street."

Elsie's less than enthusiastic response is, "Well now. That's all fine and dandy, but just what are the children su'posed to wear to church? Can't expect them to wear their school clothes now. They're not anywhere good enough for church." She is remembering some of the ruffled dresses Dillsburg girls customarily wore to church. "They're gonna need some nicer clothes. But I can't get them all ready by *this* Sunday," Elsie informs her still enthusiastic husband.

Several weeks are to pass before Elsie feels that her children are ready to attend church services. Although she is not nearly as accomplished a seamstress as her deceased sister had been, still she is able to stitch a pretty dress and matching bonnet for each of the girls. *Thank goodness it's summer,* she thinks. *Don't have to worry about no coats. They'll have to wear their same school shoes, though. Just have to blacken them up. Then they'll do just fine.*

Attiring Harry proves more difficult, though, since his parents have no desire to spend their precious money on a suit for a boy who will rapidly outgrow it. And so Crowder consults with his employer and good friend Jesse Carpenter. "Don't worry about it, Patience. Our nephew has outgrown all of his clothes. Seems like he just stretched up overnight. I'll just ask his mother to pack some things up for Harry. For sure he'll need a jacket and knickers with braces, a white shirt and a string tie. Must have a hat somewhere he can wear, too. That all right with you?"

Yes, it was fine for a man who makes it a habit never to "look a gift horse in the mouth." "Much obliged, Jesse."

Finally the Sunday arrived when the Patiences are going to go to church, Crowder sporting his black "burial suit," so called because every man necessarily must have a suit in readiness in the event of his sudden demise. Elsie is attired in the simple lawn white dress Mariah had stitched up for her years ago for some "just in case" situation like this. As Elsie knows, every lady always is expected to wear clean white gloves as well as a hat to church. High on a closet shelf she still has those she had worn years ago for her wedding. After giving them a good brushing and changing the ribbon on the hat, she concludes, *Looks good as new.*

Traipsing down Luzerne Avenue to Warren Street, first crossing it and then turning left (the opposite of the direction to school), the girls are happily chattering away. However, Harry is walking far ahead of the group, not wanting to be seen anywhere near his silly sisters.

In the future the family will not attend the church services every week, sometimes due to inclement weather, or because Crowder has an emergency on the farm, or one or more of the children is ill. But as often as possible the oldest children attend Sunday School at the First Presbyterian Church on Exeter Street. However, Elsie is never comfortable, even just with the walking there from 828. Always she is aware of inquisitive glances directed at them--the old dark colored man with graying hair, his young white (so they are presuming) wife with straight coal black hair, and their brown children. And so, she desires nothing more than to remain in the privacy of her home.

Finally she informs her husband who does not seem at all to be perturbed because he probably has not noticed the glances. "You know, I just can't go to church with you any more. I feel too uncomfortable. All those people looking me up and down all the time."

"That so?" Crowder looks at his wife with humor. "Now, Elsie, if Ah do remember it right, yuh told Mariah once that the people were lookin' at her 'cause she was so pretty. Ever stop tuh think maybe that's why they're lookin' at *you.*"

"Fiddlesticks! That's a horse of different color! You know full well why I told Mariah that. This is not the same thing at all!" Elsie exclaims indignantly, stamping her little foot, arms akimbo.

"All right. All right now, if that's how yore feelin'. But, Ah'm tellin' yuh, Ah want the children tuh keep on goin' tuh church."

Crowder tries being empathetic to his wife's feelings, but he really can not be since he had no problem at all accepting who *he* is. And at first glance anybody can decide to accept or to reject him on the spot. However, that is not so in Elsie's case. People, both blacks and whites, are always curious about her. And she does not like it one bit.

So Crowder informs Elsie that he will attend the church services whenever he is able and then relay to her whatever the preacher says. And so with this new arrangement she is satisfied. When the man who had invited the family to the church remarks to Crowder, "Haven't seen your Missus lately. Hope she's not feelin' poorly."

Offering no explanation Crowder simply tells the man, "No, she's fine. Thanks fer askin'." He does not further explain that his wife is in the "family way" again, an acceptable excuse for her absence—her "confinement." However, such delicate matters are not verbalized during this prudish Victorian period in history.

One Sunday a very charismatic colored man appears at the afternoon worship services. He can really pray. He can really sing. And can he ever preach! Just like down home and the people rejoice. He informs them that he is a preacher and is quite confident that he will be able lead them in the building of their own church right here in West Pittston where the majority of the area's colored people are living.

Enthusiasm is high. These colored folk have been "hungering and thirsting after righteousness" because most of them have not been in what they think of as *real* church since they have left the South where church-going is what people do on Sundays. Where church-going takes up most of the day what with getting there early for Sunday School, then attending the worship service, and staying later for the communal dinner prepared by women who *really* know how to cook. Who always load tables with overflowing platters of crispy brown pieces of chicken and fish rolled first in corn meal and then deep-fried in lard. Who heap bowls full of white potato salad, baked macaroni and cheese, well seasoned greens of some sort—collards, kale, mustard, or turnip when in season and when not, green string beans "put up" last summer. Who make yeast rolls tasty as any dessert, concoct creamy banana pudding, and bake deep dish peach cobbler and sweet potato pie, as well as assorted cakes.

So these displaced southern colored people are very excited about the project. They quickly get busy selling sumptuous chicken and waffle dinners, planning ice cream socials, and conducting Friday night fish fries. At bazaars well supported by both whites and blacks in the community the women sell such items as homemade yeast rolls, apple and sweet potato pies, molasses cookies and glass jars of jellies and jams, corn relish, piccalilli, watermelon rind preserves and peaches spiced with whole cloves.

Crowder is delighted once again to see the sweet potato pies since he has not tasted one since he left Roanoke Island after the war. It is one kind of pie his wife has no idea know how to bake. Once when he had asked her if she knew how to make one she told him that she did not know even what a sweet potato was. She knew white potatoes, of course, but the other kind does not grow in Dillsburg, Pennsylvania. And so since she had no idea what a sweet potato pie is supposed to taste like, she will not take the chance at failing to please her husband. Like many women of her time Elsie bakes by sight, taste and feel, simply because she is not able to read a receipt (recipe).

To sell at the bazaars Florence crochets dainty doilies, necessities in every well appointed home. Jessie stitches pretty ruffled aprons with matching quilted hot pads. Charles Moore, a budding entrepreneur, bags his specialty, roasted peanuts to sell along with sticky caramelized popcorn balls and crystallized grapefruit skins. In later years he will be known as the "Peanut Man" when his Model T Ford chugs up and down the streets of West Pittston every Saturday as he peddles his wares.

By utilizing doors removed from their hinges coupled with saw horses, the men erect long tables on which the women spread their best white table cloths for displaying the goods for sale. These occasions provide a great time for socializing as well as for raising the requisite cash for building their *very own church*. The majority of these colored people, migrants recently from the South, just do not feel comfortable worshipping in any church where never is shouted a fervent "Amen." In their black churches back home they are accustomed to hearing "Amens" being lifted to encourage the preaching. They are well aware the more "Amens," the livelier the preaching, and visa versa. Just one more remnant of the African "call and response."

So in time a sizeable amount of revenue gets raised and subsequently turned over to the "preacher." However, by the time the people find out he is *not* at all what he said he was, it is much much too late. The charlatan has absconded with all of their hard-earned money! Needless to say, they are devastated at being so duped, and by one of their *own* kind, at that!

Crowder is so disappointed, disgusted, and disillusioned that he withdraws his support for any future plans for building a church. He tells his family that he will continue attending the Presbyterian Church when he is able, even though in the future his own son Harry would be instrumental in the building of a "colored" church in West Pittston.

Today, the 11th of December in the year 1907, is a beautiful crisp, cloudless cold winter day. Only to support their son Harry have Crowder and Elsie consented to attend the dedication of the newly erected St. Mark's AME Church at 207 Boston Avenue. Crowder and Elsie realize that Harry, as well as former brother-in-law Isaac Gould, son-in-law Walter Glover, and Rosa's suitor S. Peter Lee, have worked long and hard for this day. First they had to persuade the Pittsburgh Conference of the African American Episcopal Church to establish a church in this town with as few blacks as are living in West Pittston, Pennsylvania, that number hovering somewhere around seventy-five and with not all being interested in supporting a church.

Many questions had been posed. "How can so few people maintain a church?" "How can they afford a pastor's salary?" "How can they provide a place for him and his family to reside?" These are extremely *pertinent* questions because a pastor of the AME Church receives his appointment from the bishop of the conference. He would not, knowingly, send one of his ministers into a situation of poverty.

Truthfully, some weeks may pass when the pastors receive little cash. Even so, they are never devoid of a warm place to sleep or invitations to supper. Also true is that oftentimes frigid temperatures might greet parishioners on a particular Sunday morning because during the past week nothing had been sent down the chutes into the coal bin located in the church cellar. Perhaps payment for the last month's supply of coal still is owed the coal-man and he is not going deliver any more until that past-due bill is paid in full. Oftentimes special offerings are collected in advance for the "coal fund" so toes and fingers will not freeze during the next week's worship services.

By 1904 there were already two AME churches in the area, one each in Wilkes-Barre and Scranton. However, both cities are too far away for folk having no means of transportation, even though the Laurel Line, that dependable electrically powered train passing through patches of mountain laurel, conveniently connects Pittston to both cities. For these hard working people whose only day off is Sunday, getting to and from those cities would take much too long. Since West Pittston has the only other sizable population of colored people in Wyoming Valley, it seems feasible to build a church here. The hope is that most of the colored people in the Greater Pittston area, regardless of their prior church affiliations, will support this Methodist denomination's effort. Most will because black churches always serve not only for places of worship, but for social gatherings, as well.

The African Methodist Episcopal denomination was begun in Philadelphia by a former slave able to purchase his own freedom. A bricklayer by trade, his name was Richard Allen. In 1794 colored people were being denied the opportunity to worship on an equal basis with whites at the St. George's Methodist Episcopal Church. First of all, in that "city of brotherly love" colored people were being segregated to the balcony and secondly, during the sacrament of communion they were not allowed to drink from the same chalice as the white congregants.

So in righteous indignation Richard Allen set about organizing his own church—the *African* Methodist Episcopal, becoming its first bishop. Afterwards the denomination grew so rapidly that in many places with a sizable number of colored people there could be found an AME Church. Many extremely small, just like the one in West Pittston.

Yes, it will be true that there never will be an overabundance of funds for maintaining the small colored church in West Pittston. And over the years the members eventually will dwindle due to their exiting the Valley in search of better opportunities or their becoming aged and dying. The last minister being

Rev. Christine Giles, St. Mark's AME Church is going to continue functioning until the year 1954 when it will be sold to the congregation of the Apostolic Church. When asked to fill the pulpits from time to time at local churches Rev. Giles will be considered indeed unique. Not because she is *colored*, though, but because during this period of history few persons will have heard an ordained *woman* deliver a sermon from a pulpit.

Like the one in Wilkes-Barre some black congregations might purchase their church from an established white congregation, one perhaps moving into a newer or larger edifice. However, the West Pittston church was built from "scratch" on the Boston Avenue lot purchased for the sum of $700 with the small, narrow white clapboard edifice costing the astronomical construction figure of $2,900.

And now with Crowder right behind her, Elsie is pulling the steep set of seven steps before reaching the heavy double doors opening into a small narthax. Inside the small sanctuary the center aisle has ten plain wooden pews on each side. No carpeting covers the wide slatted floor and the windows are frosted simply because no member has any money to donate toward expensive ornate stained glass. St. Mark's AME is a church possessing only the bare necessities.

On a platform in the front of the sanctuary stands a pulpit on which a very large Bible has been placed. For visiting dignitaries two straight-backed chairs with burgundy velveteen cushioned seats flank the minister's larger one, all resting against the wall. Also set on the platform is the upright piano on which Florence often plays her husband's favorite hymn, "*Oh, for a Thousand Tongues to Sing.*" And on the floor in front of the platform is a wooden railing where congregants kneel to receive the sacrament from the table on which are found the carved words, "*Do this in remembrance of me.*"

Communion or "the partaking of bread and wine" customarily is celebrated in an AME church on the first Sunday of each month. Ministers distribute to each communicant first a small chunk of unleavened cracker, followed by an individual tiny glass of grape juice. Never wine in this Protestant denomination foreswearing alcoholic beverages. By rows the communicants solemnly kneel at the railing while the congregation softly hums "*Let us break bread together on our knees,*" as well as other appropriate hymns as the pastor recites the familiar words of Jesus at His last Passover supper with His disciples.

Elsie is here today only because she had promised her son, but she is not at all comfortable. She is never comfortable around colored people, having made friends with one only, a much older woman employed as a "live-in" at one of the mansions facing the river. On Thursdays, the maids' only day off, she treks the mile up Luzerne Avenue to Elsie's for lunch. But most of the other colored women regard Elsie as "stand-offish." She may appear so simply because she always is uncomfortable in their presence.

Elsie had been reared in the ways of a Pennsylvania German. Yet she has been told that she is a mulatto, really meaning absolutely *nothing* to her. She knows nothing about mulattos or other colored people, for that matter. She had never lived with them. She does not understand their ways, their southern speech, their mannerisms, their food preferences, and now their animated way of worshipping. The way someone "raises" a hymn with everyone else's joining in then. The way they clap and sway while singing. The way they raise fervent amens during the preaching. Nothing at all like the formal Evangelical Lutheran Church services she was used to in Dillsburg.

Crowder, on the other hand, has always enjoyed the religious services of colored people. He especially enjoys their harmonious singing. He has found the staid worship in the North light years away from what he remembers in North Carolina. So he thinks that maybe at the new colored church he may hear once again some of the old songs Aunt Cassie had loved. That is, until he discovers that the ritualistic AME Church is not at all like the impromptu "bush church" he remembers in the piney woods of North Carolina.

So now only to please her oldest son, Harry, Elsie holds onto the banister to pull up the steep stairs. He is standing at the top, holding the double doors open for his parents. Attractively attired in one of Jessie's latest creations made especially for this occasion, Elsie enters the church. Now as she approaches the front pew where her son had reserved spots for his parents, looks of envy are darted in her direction. The colored women in West Pittston are mostly domestics (maids, laundresses, and cooks), and many just recently up from the South. Their clothes may be clean and neat, but not *stylish* like Elsie's whose daughter is the sought after seamstress for several rich white ladies.

And besides, they figure as they gaze at her finery, *she thinks she's better'n us 'cause she owns* (they mistakenly presume) *that big house up there at the end of Luzerne Avenue.* They are forced to live uncomfortably in small stuffy attic rooms, over smelly barns or stables if their husbands are coachmen, or in tiny rented houses set in dusty unpaved alleys behind the big houses.

Never mistaking her as white because in the South they have seen plenty of Elsie's kind many times before, they prejudge her as being "uppity," disliking her immediately simply because she is light in complexion. Misinterpreting her shyness as arrogance, they refuse to greet her graciously as church members should. After several Sundays of this kind of treatment, Elsie vows *never* to set foot in "that colored church" again. She instructs her family not even to *bury* her from there, even though she knows most people are usually "laid out" in their own front parlor. However, she will be required to set foot in "that colored church" at least one more time when she has to bury one of her children so well known and respected in the community that an at-home parlor funeral overflowing with people and flowers will not suffice.

Through the years Elsie's reputation among the colored population certainly will not improve as she becomes more and more reclusive, seldom venturing from the confines of 828, but always holding "court" each Sunday afternoon for her children and their children. "Going to Grandma's" becomes the thing to do.

Strange thing," she muses. *"I was too colored to be white in Dillsburg. Now I'm too white to be colored in West Pittston.*

St. Mark's AME Church (circa 1920)
207 Boston Avenue, West Pittston, Pa.
Photo from West Pittston Centennial 1887-1957
Courtesy of Mayor William Goldsworthy

SECTION V

CROWDER AND ELSIE'S FAMILY

PATIENCE CLAN

GENERATIONS

1st	2nd	3rd
Crowder Patience m. *Elsie Veden*	Florence m. Walter Kirk Glover, Sr.	Rosa May (Jackson) Elsie Veden (Andrews) Walter Kirk, Jr. Harry Brazier Jessie Pearl Edward Niles Robert Florence (Smith)
	Harry Brazier m. Elsie Miller	Robert Jesse Kenneth Veden Wilmer Miller Charles Edgar Harry Bruce Harold Lee
	Rosa Veden m. Simon Peter Lee	0
	Lillian Mariah m. Charles Edward Cuff	0
	Jessie Pearl m. Nathaniel Garrett	0
	Percy m. Mary Adams	Ruth (Norman) Dorothy (Watson) Leroy Thomas Lillian May Charles
	Chester m. Edna Lucas	Chester Douglas. Bernice Lee
	Nyles m. Edna ??	0

Chapter 23

Florence the First Child

Elsie is determined to provide her children with opportunities she herself never had. For instance, Florence, the oldest child, takes piano lessons from the organist at the Presbyterian Church and becomes quite proficient at the keyboard. Sometime in the future when Lillian is asked the reason for her not playing the piano so she might accompany her beautiful singing voice, she will respond, "By the time I was ready to learn there were so many children in the family. I don't suppose there was enough money for lessons for all of us." Perhaps that is so, but for the *first* child there had been.

When hearing that a certain Mrs. M teaches dressmaking skills to young West Pittston girls, Elsie approaches her husband with, "Now this is exactly what I want for Florence. Dressmaking is a respectable profession for a woman. That's what the Mrs. back in Dillsburg told me. And good seamstresses are in great demand, you know. Most of the time those store bought dresses just don't fit right. After all, Mariah had a lot of ladies to sew for and Florence really enjoyed working with her."

Following his wife's untimely death, Isaac Gould had given Elsie her sister's expensive Singer treadle-sewing machine. When he had presented it to his wife it had been quite a surprise. She was at the home of one of her customers, there executing a fitting when Isaac had set the machine in the kitchen near a window where on bright days the sun might illuminate Mariah's work. Anxiously awaiting her return he had pulled out one of the kitchen chairs from the table, there to sit reading the Pittston Gazette. Finally he heard the sound of the front door opening, followed by his wife's "Isaac, I'm home!"

"In the kitchen, Dear."

In the kitchen? Mariah was wondering why her husband was back there, when after work he usually was puttering around in his tomato patch or reading his newspaper as he rocked on the back porch. And anyway, it was not anywhere near suppertime yet. Upon entering the kitchen she found him seated at the table where he had been eagerly watching the doorway for her appearance.

Concerned now Mariah asked, "Anything wrong, Isaac?"

"No, not a thing."

"Then why are you sitting out here in the kitchen like this? Are you that hungry?" She was unpinning her hat and hanging her coat on a wall peg. "If you just give me a little while I'll have your supper ready in a...." She suddenly stopped speaking as her eyes focused on something *new* sitting over in the corner by the window. Something covered with one of her blue and white checkered kitchen tablecloths. Something sitting next to her old New Home sewing machine.

"Why, Isaac, what on earth is this?" she was asking as she quickly went over to it.

Isaac had a wide grin on his face as he stepped close behind her. "Well, Mariah, why don't you just pull the tablecloth off and see for yourself?"

Whisking off the tablecloth, she discovered a highly polished oak table. Looking underneath it, she sighted the wrought iron treadle. "Oh, Isaac, is this what I think it is?" she was asking as she carefully lifted the lid.

"Ooh! Ooh! Why, yes, it is!" she answered herself with delight as she viewed the brand new sewing machine's lying in its recessed compartment. All she seemed to be able to exclaim was, "Ooh! Ooh!" as she made her inspection. She always had wanted an efficient modern Singer sewing machine, but never dreamed of being able to own one. *And today is not Christmas or my birthday even!*

"This must have cost a pretty penny, Isaac," Mariah marveled as she lifted the machine to its upright position. After gently rubbing her hands across the coolness of the black metal, the name of Singer emblazoned across it, she slowly rotated the wheel back and forth, watching the needle raise and lower. She was thinking of how easy it will be now to stitch a new shirt for Isaac and for herself a pretty calico dress. Hand stitching a shirt takes about fourteen hours and a dress at least another six. With her old sewing machine she had been able to complete the same jobs in half that amount of time. Now with this new Singer in her possession she should be able to stitch up the same shirt in just an hour and a quarter and the dress in less than an hour's time. Mariah was in rapture!

Isaac answered his wife's query concerning the price. "Yes, it did cost a fair amount. Got it for all of $80.00." Then observing the shocked expression on his wife's face, he quickly added, "But that's not too much. Not as long as I know you like it." He was relieved that there seemed to be no doubt at all as Mariah demonstrated her gratitude by rewarding him with a sound kiss.

One summer morning while leaving her youngest children in the care of the three older girls Elsie calls on Mrs. M to inquire about dressmaking lessons for Florence. Attired in her "Sunday go-to meeting" clothes in order to make a good first impression, Elsie steps up onto the porch to rotate the small knob of the doorbell at Mrs. M's residence.

The bell's shrill ring is answered by Mrs. M herself, dressed stylishly in a straight long black woolen skirt and a starched white high collared shirtwaist, an heirloom cameo pinned at the neck. "May I help you?" she inquires, peering over her *pince-nez* at the unfamiliar small woman standing at the door.

"Good afternoon, ma'am. I've come to talk to you about my daughter. She wants to learn dressmaking and I hear that you give lessons to young girls."

"Why yes, I do. Won't you come right in now?" Mrs. M then escorts Elsie into the cool recesses of the parlor where drapes have been pulled to keep out the heat of the sun. "Now let me just light a lamp first." While she is striking a match she asks, "And just how old is your daughter, may I inquire?" She blows out the match and then sets the chimney and globe back onto the glowing kerosene lamp.

"She's just thirteen, ma'am, but she always helped my sister who was a dressmaker herself. She recently passed away. So you see, my daughter already knows how to sew a fine stitch."

"First, let me say how sorry I am for the loss of your sister." Mrs. M respectfully extends her condolences before going on to explain, "Now, let me tell you about the lessons. Each will last for two hours at a time and the cost will be twenty-five cents. I'm going to take just five girls. I'll be most happy to have the privilege of working with your daughter, especially now that I know she's had some experience. First, though, I'll get my list so I can add her name to the others. Will you excuse me, please?" Turning to graciously smile at her guest, Mrs. M exits the parlor.

Now left alone Elsie views with a discerning eye the well appointed room as she patiently waits for Mrs. M to return. *Not as elaborate as the parlor of the Dillsburg lawyer,* she is thinking, *but very comfortable.* She observes standing in one corner an upright piano whose round stool has a swivel seat capable of being lowered or raised. *I must find some way to get our own piano so Florence can practice at home. Then she'll be able to teach the others, too.*

Mrs. M returns with a small notebook. Flipping it open she turns to Elsie, "Now then. Let me get some information. Your daughter's first name, please?"

"Florence."

Mrs. M already is adding the name to her list of girls. "Umm. Florence, you say? My, what a pretty name! That's the name of a very old and beautiful city in Italy, you know," she imparts, again peering over her *pince-nez* at her visitor.

"Yes, ma'am," Elsie replies as if she really does know. She has never heard of Florence, Italy before this day, but she certainly is not going to let on. *Never tell a body more than she needs to know,* is her motto.

"And now then. Florence's last name, please?"

"It's Patience."

"Patience?" Mrs. M asks, quite surprised. Now she removes her *pince-nez* in order to get a better look at Elsie. No longer a smile is adorning Mrs. M's face. Instead a frown furrows her brows. "You are, then...*Mrs. Patience?*"

"Yes, ma'am."

Everyone in town knows about the old colored man with the gray hair who is married to the young woman thought of as being white. Everyone in town knows they live in the last house on Luzerne Avenue. Everyone, including Mrs. M, have seen the brown Patience children walking to and from school. But this is the first time Mrs. M has seen the Patience *woman*.

"Oh, I'm so sorry, Mrs. Patience, but I can't take *your* daughter. I can't have a *colored* girl here." Observing the stunned look on her visitor's face, Mrs. M further explains, "Now, it's not that *I* have any objections, of course, but you know how *some* parents are. They just wouldn't want their daughters here with yours. I really am sorry, Mrs. Patience. It's just that if I accept her....well, you have to understand. It would hurt my business." And with that said she abruptly stands, ready to escort Elsie out the door.

Again she reiterates how really sorry she is, but to Elsie's keen perception it is this woman *herself* who does not want to teach a colored girl to become a successful seamstress. *Well, there's more than one way to skin a cat,* Elsie determines. *Just have to find another way.*

And so she does. Although Florence will not be in a class with four other girls, she does become an accomplished seamstress under the tutelage of another white woman in town. One who has no objections at all to teaching a girl as apt as Florence, regardless of the color of her skin. Elsie's major goal for her daughters in life is that they will never have to work as maids or cooks or washerwomen in the homes of wealthy white families. Crowder had promised his wife she never would have to labor in anyone else's kitchen other than her own. And she has determined to do *the same* for her girls.

Elsie is surprised when on one blustery December afternoon she is hearing the unexpected ring of the front door bell. Unexpected because the mailman has already made his daily double rounds. The life insurance man already has been by collecting his weekly five cents per person. The iceman never comes to the front door. He and the butcher's boy always go around to the back porch. Since Crowder has already had enough fuel delivered to last until spring it can not be the coal man. So Elsie is not expecting anyone. Quickly wiping her hands on a towel and removing her ever-present apron, Elsie leaves the kitchen to open the front door. And who should be standing there, but Mrs. M?

Elsie's first thoughts are, *What in heaven's name is this woman doing here? Oh, I know. She's coming to tell me that she has changed her mind. She'll teach Florence, after all. Well, it's too late, Mrs M. Florence is doing just fine.* And the mother is all prepared to tell the woman just this. "Won't you please come in out of the cold, Mrs. M?" Elsie politely invites.

Imperiously sweeping into 828 Mrs. M observes the orderliness and cleanliness of the house. The wide slats of the floor are highly polished. The wooden furniture gleams. Delicate Nottingham lace curtains cover the windows. *Mrs. Patience certainly knows how to keep a nice home.*

Elsie invites her unexpected guest to seat herself in the dining room kept comfortably warm by a blazing fire in the pot-bellied stove. Here in this room the children gather around the table to do their homework immediately after arriving from school. Elsie herself may not be willing to take the necessary time for learning to read and write, but she certainly knows how to supervise.

"Won't you please take a seat, Mrs. M?"

"Thank you, Mrs. Patience." Before stating her purpose for being here, Mrs. M seats herself straight as a ramrod on the front edge of one of the dining room chairs. She is now eye-level with the shorter Elsie who remains standing. Mrs. M smiles expansively as she begins, "I've come to see you today, Mrs. Patience, with a proposal I'm sure you'll like."

Too late, Elsie is thinking. Prepared at least to politely listen to what the woman has to say, she pulls out a chair and seats herself at the dining room table directly across from Mrs. M.

"My husband's fiftieth birthday is next week." Mrs. M is still smiling expansively at Elsie. "So, you see, I'm going to throw him a surprise party. Lots of friends and family, you know. My sister and her family are even coming up from Philadelphia. That's quite a distance. From Philadelphia."

Elsie is not in the least bit interested in Mrs. M's husband's birthday party or the sister from Philadelphia, either, as she responds, "That so?"

Mrs. M continues, "Now what I was wondering is, Mrs. Patience, will you consider allowing your daughter Florence to help with the serving?"

This is not at all what the mother was expecting to hear! When Mrs. M's words finally register Elsie is taken aback. *She wants my Florence to help with the serving?* For a moment Elsie is speechless, too shocked for her lips to form any words. Looking aghast at Mrs. M, Elsie quickly takes to her feet while replying indignantly, "My Florence is not good enough for you to teach dressmaking to, Mrs. M? You think she's only good enough to be your *servant?*"

Now it is Mrs. M's turn to be surprised. She does not understand Elsie's vehement reaction to the request, having no idea that Elsie is experiencing a flashback of herself as a thirteen-year old bound girl. Mrs. M had presumed the colored family would be overjoyed with having the opportunity to make some extra money, speculating, *After all, everyone can use more money. And besides there are all those children.* Now while observing Elsie even more closely she is thinking, *And I do believe that the woman looks like she may have another on the way. Disgusting! Just like rabbits!*

"Mrs. Patience, please! Why, I only thought that you might like Florence to earn some extra money."

"What I want is for Florence to be prepared to earn money *after* she finishes her schooling! And not one day before! And she will finish! I'll make sure of that. Right now her father takes care of her just fine, Mrs. M."

Now it is Mrs. M's turn to be taken aback. She is just trying to be helpful, but obviously for some reason, unbeknownst to her, Mrs. Patience has taken offense. *And here I am extending Christian charity just like the Good Book says.* Rising, she retrieves her pocketbook from the dining room table while stating, "I'm certainly sorry if I have offended you, Mrs. Patience, but if you change your mind...."

Mrs. Patience is not going to change her mind. Elsie is assuring Mrs. M of this fact, now that it is her turn to be escorted *out.* And the mother has no intentions at all of telling her eldest child about this unexpected visit. No, because the girl just might get it into *her* mind that she would like to earn some money.

__Glovers__ on Easter, April 25, 1943
Florence; Walter, Jr.; Niles; Walter, Sr.
326 Chase Street, West Pittston, Pa.
Courtesty of Rita Glover

Chapter 24

Harry the Coal Carver

On January 15, 1896 just fifteen days prior to his eighteenth birthday, Harry Brazier Patience, employed as a laborer at the Exeter breaker, is reported by the mining inspector as "having had an arm painfully squeezed after being caught in a conveyor." Just several weeks before, Harry had come home with an unsettling story.

In the pantry behind the curtain pulled for privacy he had been squatting, knees to chin, in a round galvanized tin laundry tub now much too small for his tall lanky frame. There he patiently was waiting for his mother to pour a bucketful of warm rinse water over his soapy back. Rinsing well is necessary to keep his skin from itching. However, Elsie was preoccupied with taking care of her son's filthy work clothes she insists must be "aired out" on the back porch.

"Ma, you'll never guess what! A miracle happened at the mine today!" He was calling out to her with much excitement in his voice. "At least that's what the men say it is, a miracle."

"Why? What happened?" his mother asked with interest as she very carefully hoisted the coal-dust laden shirt and trousers with her broom handle, flinging them on top of the dirty coveralls already lying in a pile on the back porch. Harry had two pairs of those outer pants, wearing the same pair all week until it got washed on Mondays. Always worn for two days in a row, his same shirt and trousers, though, have to be put on again the following morning, the reason why Elsie airs them on the back porch railing.

Harry continued. "A fellow went back in the mine. Wasn't supposed to do that. *Never* go back after the dynamite's set! That's the rule. But he did anyway. Guess he just wanted to check on the blast he'd set. Didn't go off when it was supposed to, so he thought it'd failed. Well, it went off all right! Just as soon as he went back in there! How he got out alive, nobody knows. Just got his hair all singed off and his face cut some. That's all! Nobody could believe it! And *that's* why they're calling it a miracle."

There were so many stories circulating. Of fires and explosions, major and minor injuries, near deaths and deaths. "Son, don't yuh see now? That's jest the reason why we never wanted yuh workin' in the mines," reiterated his father after overhearing the conversation transpiring between his wife and son. Finally getting around to pouring a bucket of warm water over her son's back, the alarmed mother was in total agreement with her husband.

At dawn for years from her pantry window Elsie has been observing breaker boys, some as young as seven years, passing up the narrow wagon road behind 828. Following behind their fathers and older brothers, traipsing off towards the looming breaker and the gaping black mouth of the mine pit. Even from the distance after the five o'clock whistle blew she could detect the fatigue in the already bent little figures trudging back to their homes to be eagerly embraced by their relieved mothers. How thankful Elsie had been that she was not one of *them*. Her boy was attending school!

Crowder had heard about how many young boys died from "consumption," literally coughing to death. And he knew that many fatal accidents occurred like that one at the Avondale mine where the young private had lost his life. No, that kind of work was not at all what Crowder and Elsie wanted for *their* boy.

The concerned mother wondered, *But what else is there for Harry to do around these parts when he's a man?* Crowder used to take his son up to the Carpenter farms when the boy was much younger. "Son, here yuh can breathe clean fresh air. Yuh don't need tuh be goin' down in no mines," the father had kept emphasizing. Certainly there were always jobs on the farms to keep a *young boy* busy, especially during the summer months when he was not in school, but that type of work was not at all what *this Patience boy* desired for his future.

Elsie and Crowder Patience long ago had determined that each of their children would attend school in order to learn how to read, write, and cipher. So each evening the occupants of 828 would be found busily preparing for the next school day, the children studying and the mother supervising.

"Harry, spell Mississippi," instructed Florence, who as the oldest child always got to "play" teacher.

"Mississippi. M, I, double S, I, double S, I, double P, I."

"That's correct. Now, Rosie, you spell Tennessee."

"Tennessee. T, E, double N, E, double S, double E."

Her children's appearance was very important to Elsie. So near the hot coal stove in the kitchen she kept a short clothesline for hanging the children's underwear, laundered daily by her and the older girls. The girls' wide ribbons got washed, too, and then dried with a very hot flatiron on the blanket and pressing cloth Elsie threw over the kitchen table. And the rhythmical slap-slap of a rag buffed the pairs of high-topped shoes after their fresh blackening.

In the mornings the "stair-step" Patience children paraded down the Luzerne Avenue hill on their way to school. With hair neatly combed and brushed, clothes clean and pressed, shoes shined, books and slates held by straps, they were fulfilling their parents' dreams. Standing in the doorway of 828 Elsie admired her brood of handsome brown children whom she loved just as she had told the Dillsburg lawyer she would.

Soon after Harry's tenth birthday he had approached his stunned parents with, "Ma. Pa. I want'a stop goin' ta school 'cause I want'a go ta work. Ta be a breaker boy, ya know. Lots of the other boys who used ta be in my class are workin' already."

Crowder gave him the vehement answer of, "No! Yuh not goin' tuh be no breaker boy!" Harry could not understand his father's adamant attitude. He could not possibly have known that his father was recalling his boyhood in North Carolina. Even as a slave he had not been expected to work in the fields until he was twelve. And now here was his freeborn son wanting to go to work at the age of *ten*!

No, Ah won't have it, Crowder determined, but he had no intentions of explaining why to his son. At that time in his life Harry knew nothing about his father's past. Children did not question their parents about anything. That was the period in history when "Children should be seen and not heard." Again Crowder insisted, "No, Son, yuh not goin' tuh work! Now yuh can put that idea right outta yore head."

Respectfully, the boy then turned to each parent as he pleaded, "Ma. Pa. Beggin' your pardon, but why not? Some of the boys are makin' upwards ta *fifty* cents a day!" That certainly sounded like good money to a boy who had *none* jingling in *his* pockets.

Crowder went to work each and every day of the week. He felt he was receiving from the Carpenters a salary sufficient enough for the basic needs of his family. He brought home from the farm an ample supply of milk. In her large garden Elsie grew cucumbers, string beans, beets, peas, and tomatoes which she "put up" for the winter. She cultivated patches of cabbages for sauerkraut and potatoes to be stored in the root cellar. Apple, pear, quince, and sweet cherry trees produced fruits for preserving. A wooden arbor supported heavy vines of Concord grapes for juice, jelly, and jam. A coop of chickens provided eggs and meat. The family never went hungry. They wore clothes made by their aunt and Crowder even could cobble respectable looking shoes for his children. So what more did they need? Certainly not fifty cents a day at the expense of their son's life!

"Son, yuh goin' tuh school! Yuh got tuh learn tuh read'n write'n do numbers!" Crowder was insisting.

"Sir, beggin' your pardon, I already can do *that*."

"Well then, maybe not good enough!" his father forcefully retorted, having no idea what "good enough" might entail.

Harry was satisfied with what he *could* do already. He had a beautiful "hand," so his teachers had told him. He knew he could read well, taking turns with his sisters when they read the Bible and newspapers to their parents. Without any hesitation at all he was able to pronounce words containing more than three syllables. Not only was he able to add, subtract, multiply, and divide, if some square or cube roots were thrown in, he could do those, too.

"Pa, don't know what else I need ta learn," Harry said in his *most* respectful tone because by then he knew he was making absolutely no headway with his parents.

"Whatever it is that they teach yuh until yuh get through tuh the end. That's what!" his father insisted. At that time the *end* in West Pittston was the 8th grade. Some more fortunate children were able to go on to high school, girls mainly because boys would enter the work force as soon as they were able to find employment.

"Yes, sir." Harry knew he had to comply with his parents' ultimatum. And he did, for a while. That is, 'til he heard about boys' attending school during the day and then laboring in the mines on a later shift. *This could be an option,* he had thought.

It was not going to be an option, though, especially when his older sister Florence revealed that boys in *her* class were falling asleep at their desks. At that disclosure Harry darted her one of those meaningful looks that only a younger brother can give to a meddling older sister.

"Enough said about goin' tuh work! No more now!" When their father said that, the children knew the discussion was over and had better not be begun again.

So Harry did not go to work at the Exeter Colliery until he reached fourteen years of age, hired to be a breaker boy. However, he was growing much too tall to be cramped over the narrow chutes, yet he was not old enough to be trained as a laborer. Subsequently, he became a slate picker and later at 17 years hired as a laborer working for experienced miners. Those were the men whose specific job was to set the dangerous dynamite blasts, many having learned their exacting trade in far-off places like Wales. And this was Harry's aspiration, to become a certified miner.

Coal mining, a most dangerous occupation due to its cave-ins, explosions, and noxious gases, demands highly skilled men. It is not for the faint of heart to descend 1200 feet or more into the bowels of the earth where deadly gases can snuff out a man's life in minutes. Every so often, the mine whistle unexpectedly pierces the air with its foreboding shriek. Always set for running, women in an instant fly out of their houses. That dreaded sound means only one thing. There has been another accident at the mine!

As they fling shawls over their shoulders or quickly tie babushkas under their chins the women are praying, "Please, God, don't let it be my Evan (or my Guiseppe or my Stanislaus or my Mike). Please, God, don't let it be. Please, God, don't let the 'Black Maria' stop by my door," referring to that dreaded wagon painted in mournful black. The "Black Maria" which transports dead men from the mine. Back home to their grief stricken women who then must prepare the bodies for burial.

During the mid-1700's coal was first discovered to be a usable source of fuel. After that, life in Wyoming Valley, the home of the hardest of all coal, was never again to be the same. The "black gold" anthracite, paving the way to untold riches for a handful and leading to untold despair for thousands of others, placed Wyoming Valley firmly on that road called "progress."

Eons ago during the Carboniferous Age coal had been produced from prehistoric extinct plants, becoming buried deep in the earth. Later squeezed to the surface and exposed in shiny black outcrops, with use of just a pick and a shovel it easily could be stripped. Subsequently, during the Revolutionary War several small businesses sprang up for the express purpose of sending much needed fuel to forges manufacturing ammunition.

Around that same time a blacksmith, Obadiah Gore, made a startling discovery. With his brother he had been discussing their quandary. "Daniel, we need ta find a way ta keep these fires burnin' longer."

With their business steadily on the increase Obadiah Gore was becoming frustrated with having to waste so much valuable time each day going out to chop large supplies of firewood. And due to recent migration of newcomers to the Valley the supply was steadily decreasing. For instance, just the week before a whole stand of oaks had suddenly disappeared to make room for a new farm.

Several smithies already had set up shop in the Valley, developing keen competition for fashioning and repairing farm implements, shoeing horses, making wagon wheels, and working with wrought iron, some designs very intricate. Therefore, being able to have a continuous supply of firewood was becoming a serious problem.

"A good farrier's certainly worth his weight in gold," one farmer had acknowledged while stating his great satisfaction with Obadiah's excellent work. One of the farmer's mares had a mind of her own and she abhorred going to the blacksmith's. *Detested* the loud clashing noise when the hammer shaping her new shoes hit the anvil. *Detested* the hissing sound when a red-hot shoe hit the cold water in a wooden barrel. *Detested* having to stand three legged as brand new iron shoes got nailed to each of her four hooves. And if a bit were not kept in her mouth she well might have *demonstrated* that displeasure.

She especially detested having her teeth floated (filed). How was she to know the importance of having her molars filed evenly? She was just a horse. How was she to know that her teeth will continue growing throughout her lifetime and if not filed correctly they would develop sharp spurs to painfully irritate and cut her cheeks? How was she to know that if the molars on her top jaw are not meeting the bottom ones correctly her oats would not be ground, causing the unchanged grain to pass into her stomach and then down her intestines to be defecated as manure? How was she to know that it was possible then for her to starve to death on a full stomach? Well, her owner certainly knew and that was why a good farrier like Obadiah Gore was deemed so valuable.

He was quite capable of handling temperamental horses and that was one of the reasons his excellent reputation was spreading and his business growing. Therefore, he was being faced with a dilemma requiring an immediate solution. "Now, look here at this, Daniel!" While addressing his brother, Obadiah was rolling around a small lump of coal in his palm. "Now I know this black stone'll burn, but it takes much too long ta get started. Needs more air, I should think. So I'm gonna try usin' bellows ta bring more air in. Maybe that way I can keep the fire burnin' longer." So that is exactly what he did and that is exactly what happened.

Because of this initial experiment, blacksmiths found that the hard stone coal known as anthracite could provide a longer lasting and less smoky source of fuel than wood. But a pair of bellows must be used.

Never would anyone have considered the fuel found so abundantly right here in the Valley to be of any use in homes. The overall opinion was that the black stone was much too hard to ignite. Homeowners were finding the softer bituminous coal from the western part of the state easy to burn, albeit quite smoky. Not until almost half a century following the Revolutionary War did the burning of anthracite coal in homes become feasible. All due to an innkeeper by the name of Judge Jesse Fell, a Quaker import to Luzerne County from Bucks County. Because in 1806 he had been the first burgess of the borough of Wilkes-Barre he was a very well known personage in the community.

Situated on the northeast corner of Washington and Northampton Streets in Wilkes-Barre, Jesse Fell's inn was a popular "watering hole" for men to gather, discovering what was happening in their "neck of the woods." The judge was an amiable innkeeper, but he had a major dilemma. His place was just too drafty for comfort. On one chilly evening as a regular customer was preparing to leave earlier than usual he remarked, "Jest can't keep warm enough in here, Judge. Even if I stand right in front of the fire, the back'a me would still be cold. Too bad ya can't keep this place warmer."

Yes, too bad I can't, Judge Fell thinks. *But there's no feasible way to put any wood burning stoves in here. And the fireplace simply isn't giving off enough heat. That I know. I've just got to think of something else.*

Jesse Fell began to mull over the possibility of using the slow burning anthracite coal with which he as a blacksmith was quite familiar. He knew that kind of coal would need a continuous air supply, though, in order to stay ignited. In the past when he was smithing he would hire young boys to pump a pair of bellows to provide the necessary steady flow of air.

I certainly do like the way that stone coal burns, though. But how to keep such a fire going inside the tavern? Bellows won't work in here. Nobody can stand all day coaxing a fire to burn. No. I've just got to find some other way to burn that anthracite coal without using any bellows. Ingeniously, by using his smithing skills he was able to contrive a grate allowing the anthracite to burn longer, hotter, and less smoky than wood or the softer bituminous coal.

Unbeknownst to him, when Judge Jesse Fell bent for the first time to ignite the fire in his newly invented grate he was also igniting a whole new industry. That seemingly innocuous event taking place on February 11, 1808 at the Fell Tavern, Wilkes-Barre, Pennsylvania, was an event equaling the opening of Pandora's box. Out flew *anthracite coal mining!* For by the year 1899 more than 54,000,000 tons of coal would be mined annually during an era marked by oppression and hardship. Only by the blood and tears of immigrants and others will the pockets of the ambitious coal barons become caches of gold.

Crowder had never wanted any son of his in the mines. He remembered well the old man's story of what had happened to his boy, the young private who was Crowder's friend in the 103rd Pennsylvania Volunteers. The one who could no longer be happy on his father's farm. On that fateful September morning he had been with the 110 men and boys returning to work for the first time following a strike. Glad finally to be back to work, with his carbide lamp lit, each man "pegged in" as a record that he had gone down into the mine pit. However, not one would ever "peg out."

Three whole days were to pass before the bodies could be found. Located in a place too terrible for words. Where bodies of fathers were found protectively clutching their sons. Where bodies were found with mouths permanently gaping from desperately gasping for air. Where bodies were found kneeling with hands clasped in final desperate supplications.

Of all the things Crowder was not aware, one was that each week on an average ten miners lost their lives, due most often to rocks falling on their unprotected heads and bodies. Even so, all that he did know about the mines was enough to alarm him. Of course, he never relayed any of this information to his wife. In fact it was his habit to burden her with as little as possible about the unpleasantness of life. As he had promised, he was providing for her financially and since her marriage Elsie never has had to work for anyone except her husband and children. But he also created for her a very insulated life. *No need tuh worry herself none,* he felt. He wanted always to be her protector. So he made it a habit always to withhold any unsettling information from her.

So obediently complying with his parents' wishes then, Harry had continued attending school. He completed the 8th grade with knowing how to speak correctly. With having the ability to memorize and recite long passages, to solve basic geometry, and to be familiar with geography, history and other topics he would have missed had he become a breaker boy at the age of ten. And so when the fourteen-year old Harry informed his parents it was time for him to look for work at the Exeter Colliery, Crowder had to respect the tenacity he observed in his oldest son. He was recognizing that same quality which many years before had induced a slave boy named Toby to dream and then prodded him until those dreams were brought to fruition.

"All right, Son. If that's what yuh really want tuh do." Crowder reluctantly had given his permission.

After that Harry was the first rising in the mornings. Much before dawn he would light the kerosene lamps in the kitchen and then check the state of the fire he had left in the coal stove the night before. Prior to retiring to his bed he first had closed the draft to the chimney and slightly tilted the iron lids of the stove, intending to leave enough hot coals to be still "live" in the morning.

Because if they were not, then he would have to build the fire again and from "scratch." Having to shake down all the cold ashes. Clear out all the dead coals. Ball up some newspaper to top with small sticks of wood and stuff it all in the cold stove. Then ignite the newspaper in order to get the wood burning. Finally throw on a shovel of coal from the tin coal pail. Because for Harry to be able to "wash up" in the morning he had to heat the frigid water pouring from the single spigot in the pantry sink. Such modern conveniences 828 was equipped with, that of running water and a faucet, when the majority of houses still had manually operated water pumps.

Hopefully then, much before dawn when Harry arose from his bed he would find the coals in the kitchen stove still "live." If so, then the water in the teakettle would be boiling away before his Ma came down to fix his breakfast.

"Got to have a hot breakfast before you start off." This Elsie always would insist.

As Harry was consuming his mother's buckwheat pancakes, the batter having risen over night in a heavy brown crock, Elsie would be packing a hearty lunch for her son. She would stuff his tin lunch box with whatever meat she had left over from dinner the evening before, accompanied always by two thick slabs of buttered white bread, adding perhaps a hard-boiled egg, several sugar cookies (still Crowder's favorite) and an apple from the barrel in the cellar. She has heard it said, "An apple a day keeps the doctor away." Elsie will do anything to keep him away from *her* door.

Therefore, each spring she customarily plies all of her children with a sulfur and molasses tonic as well as hot sassafras tea. She doses herself and Crowder with senna leaves for keeping their systems functioning properly. And in the winter the Patience children all wear small sacs of stinking asafetida around their necks, an herb supposedly guaranteed to keep sicknesses away. And due to its most disagreeable odor it certainly is successful in keeping *people* away. Possibly, inadvertently it is also keeping sicknesses away because the Patience children all are quite healthy.

Sometimes after they had eaten their lunches, Harry and other young slate pickers would pull out their jackknives to whittle little figurines out of coal. Dogs, cats and birds were among their favorites. Harry had learned his whittling skills from watching his father creating wooden toys such as little people whose movements depend upon the maneuvering of strings. Crowder also enjoyed carving whistles as well as small boats for his children to float in the gullies by the side of Tunkhannock Avenue after heavy rainstorms.

Although they never had seen the characters in a "Punch and Judy" show, his children loved the little figures their father would carve them for making up their own plays. One Christmas he had even surprised his girls with a simply constructed doll house, including some miniature furniture. Florence especially loved it, quickly setting about to make tiny crocheted curtains and bedspreads.

One year when Valentine's Day was approaching, Harry thought he might like to make something unusual for his mother. *Perhaps a small piece of coal could be carved into something really special,* he speculated. He had shown her many of the objects he had carved before, but now he wanted to make something very different.

He finally decided, *I think I'll try making her a heart since it's for Valentine's Day.* After several unsuccessful attempts, he finally saw in his mind's eye exactly the heart he wanted to create. First thing, he figured he would have to chip away at an irregular chunk of coal to make it flat. However, he had no success on the first try. The piece of coal disappointingly shattered in his hand. He was not successful even after several tries. *Just can't get a smooth flat piece*, he had thought in frustration.

Finally success! He was able to chip away at a piece of coal without shattering it. On it with a pencil he outlined the shape of a heart. Then with the point of his knife he chipped and scraped until finally he had a small heart lying intact in the palm of his hand. *This is it!* He was very pleased with himself. After sanding it smooth he then took a soft clean cloth to polish the small heart until it gleamed.

As Harry was admiring the beauty of the anthracite he saw in its blackness a certain indescribable glow. Surprisingly, he found the stone coal not at all hard to carve. And after being washed to remove any loose dust, anthracite, the hardest of all coal, was a perfect medium for the gifted whittler, Harry Patience.

His mother was delighted with Harry's Valentine present and so were his sisters. Jessie suggested, "Why don't you put a string around it? Ma can wear it around her neck then."

"That's a good idea," her brother agreed. "But how am I going to do that?

His young sister optimistically had responded, "*I* don't know. But I'm sure *you'll* find a way."

He was able to come up with an idea finally. Around the edges of the next heart he carved he dug a groove deep enough for holding a piece of string. After tying the string so the heart could dangle he had shown it to Jessie who was delighted, demanding that he make one for her, too. "After all, it was *my* idea in the first place," she reminded him with a laugh.

When Crowder saw around his wife's neck a piece of grocer string with the dangling shiny black heart he suggested that Harry should go to Clousen's hardware store "over town" in Pittston. Perhaps there he might find a fine wire much more durable and certainly more attractive than grocer string. Yes, there he did find a thin wire perfect for wrapping around the edge of the heart. Then he twisted a loop to hold a small jump ring through which a thin chain might pass. The owner of the hardware store then connected Harry with a jeweler's supply store where he could purchase inexpensive gold chains for the gleaming black hearts.

Harry Patience was finding out that whenever people saw his unique handiwork he would be asked to carve a heart for their mother or sister or sweetheart. And surprisingly to him, they were willing to pay whatever he asked. The boys in the mines had been quick to recognize Harry's unique gift and soon he was getting more orders than he could fill.

One day a young laborer requested a small cross to be worn as a necklace, just like the heart. Up for the challenge, Harry tried unsuccessfully several times. *Patience* is what it takes. Well, that was his name and that was what he needed. Finally he was rewarded with success. Then two items were in great demand. Later he was asked to carve other items such as watch fobs, hat and stickpins, and small charms.

Believing that the crystalline sulfur stone or "Pennsylvania diamond" found also in the coal mines, might add an interesting touch to his creations he began placing a small circle of that sparkling material in the center of his hearts. And sometimes for added decoration he might carve two little leaves on both sides of the sulfur stone circle.

Soon Harry was carrying home small chunks of coal so he might work in the evenings, relying only upon the glow of a kerosene lantern for light. In warmer weather he would work outside on the back porch where the wind could blow away the fine coal dust. Even though a neckerchief covered his mouth, oftentimes he caught himself hacking and expectorating black flecked sputum. He was aware those working in the mines, including the young breaker boys, chewed tobacco, constantly spitting out black coal dust with the brown tobacco juice. Because Harry did not like the taste of the tobacco he had not gotten into that habit. He had also heard of another method miners used for getting rid of the coal dust inside their body. At least, so they thought. They would dose themselves with castor oil, hoping to protectively "coat their entrails," not realizing what was really happening. Coal dust penetrated their lungs, not their digestive tract.

Without resorting to either of those methods, Harry, nevertheless, had reached the conclusion that as much as possible he needed to avoid inhaling the irritating dust which just might be causing him harm. He had no idea of the large number of miners suffering from the fatal lung disease *anthracosclerosis*, the result of years of inhaling fine particles of coal dust. He just felt that perhaps a neckerchief over his nose and mouth might possibly serve as protection.

Although it had not occurred to *Harry* that maybe he could start a small business of his own with his coal carving, it had occurred to his parents. Seventeen year-old Harry Patience's only aspiration up to that time was to become an experienced miner with official papers, something neither of his parents really wanted for him. So in the meantime, they kept encouraging him in his hobby. Soon he had more orders than he could possibly fill, having to enlist the help of his younger brothers Percy and Chester. There were many tasks they could perform to make the work go faster.

✦

Four years have passed since Harry began working at the colliery. And on this fateful day, January 15, 1896, when he arrives home in the middle of the day, his left arm swollen and lacerated, his distressed mother insists, "No more, Harry! I don't want you going back there! You don't need to!"

The son hears what his mother is saying, but he knows there are no other jobs available to him except perhaps on the Carpenter farm with his father. There is no money in that line of work, he had figured early on. However, he knows there is money to be made as a miner. And so respectfully he responds to his concerned mother, "You know I've got to work, Ma. I'm a man now."

"Yes. Yes, you certainly are a man, Son. Don't I know it? Be eighteen in just a few weeks. But say now, ever think of starting a business of your own? You know, with your coal things." When she sees a flicker of interest in her son's eyes she promises, "The family'll help you."

And so the coal carving business of Harry B. Patience is born, successful for years because Harry's unique work will be in great demand. Known not only for the beautiful hearts and crosses he first had carved with his jackknife, he develops special machinery in his shop, allowing him to create much larger pieces. Requested constantly by enthusiastic customers are his ashtrays, paperweights, pincushion and toothpick holders, vases, shaving mugs, candlestick holders, and many other objects. An especially popular item for men is a ring with a setting of sparkling sulphur stone, commonly called Pennsylvania diamond. Harry purchases the rings from Aaron Hastie, a machinist in town who molds them out of Monel metal, perfect for the sulphur stone settings since the shiny nickel-copper alloy is incapable of rusting or tarnishing.

After wedding Elsie Miller from Milton, Pennsylvania, a small town south on the Susquehanna River, Harry sets up his first shop at their home at 16 Bond Street, West Pittston, Pennsylvania. As the years pass, his dreams come true. Well known by both blacks and whites, a respected member of the community, he becomes a successful entrepreneur in Wyoming Valley.

Throughout the years he will teach the art of coal carving to his six sons, his business called Harry B. Patience & Sons. Only two, however, are to make it their life long occupation. His youngest son Harold and his fourth son Edgar who will take coal carving to even a higher art form. That of sculpturing. In the year 1972 Charles Edgar Patience will be listed in "Who's Who in America" and in the year 2001 several of his sculptures will be on permanent display at the Anthracite Heritage Museum in Scranton, Pennsylvania.

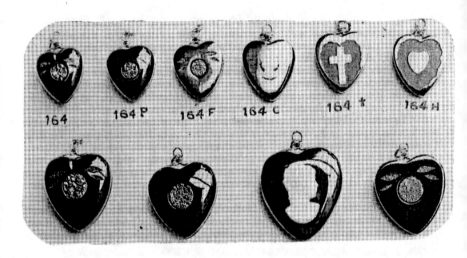

164   164 P   164 F   164 C   164 †   164 H

■ ■ COAL ART ■ ■

HARRY B. PATIENCE'S SONS

From catalog of Harry B. Patience & Sons (circa 1920)

__Harry Brazier Patience__, coal carver (circa 1920)

Harry B. Patience & Sons (circa 1916)
Front row: Edgar, Robert, Harry B.
Back row: brother Percy, Kenneth,
Wilmer, Bruce

34 Washington Street
West Pittston, Pa.
Harry B. Patience & Sons
(circa 1920)

283

__Harold Lee Patience__, youngest son of
Harry B Patience
On side of 34 Washington Street
West Pittston, Pa, (circa 1920)

__Charles Edgar Patience__,
4th son of Harry Patience,
reknowned coal sculptor
(circa 1933)

"Next week a roving photographer's going to be here in West Pittston," Jessie excitedly informs her brother Harry and sister in-law Elsie. "He'll come right here to the house, you know," she explains, extremely anxious to have a picture taken of her young nephews, Bob and Kenny, whom she adores. No longer are tintypes popular. A new and improved kind of photograph is now in vogue called a daguerreotype. And best of all is the fact that the roving photographer will carry all of his heavy equipment directly to the home!

"We *must* have their pictures taken. That's all there is to it!" Jessie is insisting. Elsie's youngest daughter is just like her mother when she gets her mind set on something. "And we'll tell Florence, too. She can bring all of her children down here." Harry and his wife are living near Wyoming Avenue while Florence and her family are within walking distance away on York Avenue near where the railroad-bridge crosses the Susquehanna over to the Coxton railroad yards on the east side of the river.

Florence is married to the tall handsome blue-eyed Walter Glover, a mulatto born in Harper's Ferry, West Virginia, site of John Brown's famous failed insurrection. Induced by an ad he had read in a Washington, D.C. newspaper, Glover had come to West Pittston to be a coachman for a wealthy family in town. Other eligible young colored women had been eyeing this charming gentleman from the South, but Florence was the one who had caught *his* eye. And so the requisite introductions had been made.

"She's so *old*," was the whisper circulating among the envious younger women who thought Florence's advanced age of twenty four made her have "one foot in the grave." "Do yuh see all that gray hair she's got?" Florence's thick dark brown hair already was prematurely streaked with silver just as her father's had been.

It was not that she had no desire to be married before that time. There just were no eligible young colored men around, even though, unbeknownst to her, this was one of the main reasons her parents originally had settled in Wyoming Valley. They were hoping that when it came time for Florence to be courted, a suitor would be found here, but that had not been the case. So she was spending her days concentrating on her growing dressmaking business, expecting, perhaps, never to marry. But one Sunday afternoon Glover had made his appearance at the West Pittston Presbyterian Church where he met the Patiences, subsequently being invited to supper. Within months he and Florence were married.

At the time of the traveling-photographer's visit to West Pittston both Florence and Harry have several children between them. Rosa Mae; Walter

Kirk, Jr.; Elsie Veden and Harry Brazier are the Glovers while Robert Jesse and Kenneth Veden are the Patiences. Each family's picture is going to be shot separately, the children positioned from the eldest to the youngest. All are in beautiful frilly attire, the Glovers' especially lovely because of their mother's creativity. Each white dress has delicate lace trimming and each child is wearing a pair of long black stockings. Curly hair is adorned with ribbons.

The photographer is not able to distinguish the girls from the boys because at this time in history little boys get clothed just like girls, all bedecked in dresses and even with ribbons tied in their hair. Custom of the day dictates that when boys reach school age, mothers then and only then will allow their little boys to look like males. How some of the mothers carry on as they watch the barber cutting off their sons' long locks!

__Glover Children:__
Rosa May, Elsie, Walter, Harry
(circa 1906)

Patience Children:
Kenneth, sitting: Robert, standing
(circa 1906)

    If in the future more photos were to have been taken, the Glovers would have the largest group because altogether fifteen children will be born to Florence and Walter, although not all will live even into childhood. Seven Patience boys will be born to Harry and Elsie, Bruce's twin dying right after his birth.

Chapter 25

Lillian Mariah the Third Daughter

When the 20th century arrives it brings a number of major changes to the Patience family. Florence now is living on York Avenue with her husband, Walter Glover, and their new baby girl, Rosa May. Harry has opened a coal carving business at his home on Bond Street. He, too, has married and his wife is expecting a baby. And a young gray-eyed blade hailing from Lewisburg, West Virginia has begun to pay court to pretty Rosa Veden. But Lillian Mariah, the third daughter, has yet to have a gentleman caller.

Short, tending toward plumpness, she is not petite like her mother had been, or pert like Rosa, or willowy like Florence and Jessie, causing her to be quite self-conscious about her appearance. Her legs, for instance, are thick compared to the thin and shapely ones of her sisters who used to tease her because when she ran her chubby legs would flash from beneath her dress. Children in school ridiculed her "fat" legs. With her high top shoes laced tightly around her wide ankles she was always very uncomfortable. And nowadays peering into her hand mirror she detests the very noticeable gap separating her two top front teeth. She puzzles, *Nobody else in the family looks like this. So why do I?* No, Lillian is not satisfied with her looks at all.

In addition, she is not at all talented like her big sister Florence whom everyone admires. Lillian does not play the piano. She does not sew with any appreciable skill. She cannot seem to be able to develop the technique of knitting or crocheting, even though she is not left-handed like her mother. She has neither the knack nor the desire to be digging in the garden like Rosa. The youngest sister Jessie, more like Florence in both looks and disposition, already can stitch up a fashionable dress in no time and to top it all, she likes to putter around in the garden. Elsie, in attempting to encourage her third daughter, reminds her how everybody so admires her beautiful lustrous dark brown hair and clear unblemished skin.

So Elsie keeps Lillian busy in the kitchen where they both enjoy baking. On Fridays the delectable odors emanating from the kitchen are of baking yeast bread and fruit pies, regardless of the season. These might be apple, huckleberry, sour cherry, peach, rhubarb, blackberry, or Hubbard squash (according to Elsie, far superior to pumpkin). Elsie always "puts up" sufficient jars of fruit so that each week several varieties of pies can be set out to cool on the back porch. The children have grown to expect them at the Sunday dinners and each has a favorite.

So while her sisters busily are going about their more creative enterprises, Lillian learns how to cook. Even though her mother would never be considered a "great" cook if she were being rated, Elsie's meals are substantial and filling. Her husband never complains, only too glad that he does not have to prepare the meals himself. And her children are used to their mother's bland, but filling fare. She certainly can bake a delicious pie, though.

Lillian develops a serious interest in food preparation, enrolling in Cooking School classes held "over town" in Pittston. She becomes a superb cook, a reputation she will retain for the remainder of her life, all 102 and a half years of it. And besides loving to cook, the girl seems also to be developing a love for reading. "Lillie, outen that lamp and come up to bed!" It seems her Ma has to call down from upstairs every night. Even the youngest sister Jessie is beginning to stay up later to read now. "You'll ruin your eyes!" Elsie admonishes.

In an attempt to keep warm even after the embers in the kitchen stove have lost their glow, the two girls huddle under the same blanket, reading as they sit at the kitchen table. After recognizing the ability of the Patience girls to learn quickly, their schoolmarms have lent them books. Never quite ready to blow out the kerosene lamp and retire, they must, however, obey their Ma's orders.

In the fall of 1903, Lillian meets Charles Edward Cuff, initially observing him at a religious revival where a large canvas tent is pitched on the local fairgrounds. People have traveled from all around the area with the high expectations of hearing some very fervent preaching. They always look forward to these tent meetings. Not only is it a time for repenting and "getting right with the Lord," it is also a social time, especially providing an opportunity for single young men and women to appraise one another.

Several members of the Patience family are in attendance, including Crowder who always looks forward to these religious revivals. *Not like Ah remember with Aunt Cassie*, he thinks, *but close enough*. As the small group is locating seats where they can get a good view of the speakers, the audience already is singing a lively hymn led by an enthusiastic song leader. Revival songs are always lively and peppy with everyone's standing as they clap and sing with gusto.

As the speakers file onto the stage to take their respective places, the several ministers from local Protestant churches are recognizable to the Patiences. One man, however, is not. He is a short, slightly portly, very brown young colored man wearing round wire rimmed spectacles. A surprise to the Patiences since they have never seen him before. A surprise especially to Harry who thinks he knows all of the colored people around town. *I wonder just who he is. Guess he must have come just for the revival.*

Upon being announced, Mr. Charles Edward Cuff, YMCA delegate from Mercersburg, Pennsylvania, rises from his seat to read the Scriptures. He briskly walks to the lectern on which he places his open Bible. He begins the familiar passage. *"Make a joyful noise unto the Lord, all ye lands."* His voice is pleasant sounding, resonant and melodious, carrying well to the members of the audience who are holding onto his every word. He concludes the 100th Psalm with the words, *"and His truth endureth to all generations."* In unison the people raise a loud and affirming "Amen." For some reason people always seem to be more expressive at revivals than they are in their own churches.

Lillian is quite impressed by Mr. Cuff's reading. *Just who is he?* She is wondering, but will not have a chance on this particular evening to find out. Her younger brothers have grown restless and cranky. Ahead of them yet is the half-hour's walk up the hill to 828 with Crowder's most likely having to carry little Nyles before continuing on to Carpenters' to see about his horses.

Not for several months will Lillian hear anything again about the young colored man she had seen at the revival. Not until she happens to see in the window of a business "over town" in Pittston a flyer announcing that Charles Edward Cuff is organizing a Bible study group for young men. Sponsored by the YMCA it is being called the "Overcomers' Club." Recognizing his name, she wonders again just *who* Mr. Cuff is and how does he happen to have stayed *here* in the Pittston area where opportunities are so few for colored men.

Simon Peter Lee, Rosa's suitor, a very devout man, has a burning desire to be able to read his Bible with ease. Not having had the opportunity to attend school where he had grown up in West Virginia, he does not read well and this bothers him. Rosa, on the other hand, reads very well, very well indeed. She completed her 8th grade schooling, but in Peter Lee's "neck of the woods" there had been no schools for colored children.

Lillian mentions to Rosa about the flyer she had seen concerning Mr. Cuff. Then as Rosa is relaying the information to Peter Lee an idea suddenly occurs to him. *Maybe my readin' could get better if I go tuh those Bible classes, too.* Peter Lee is of the mindset that he may not be as intimidated by another *colored* man's teaching him. So with this goal in mind, he treks across the Jenkins Bridge to Pittston to join the Overcomers' Club. After discreetly inquiring and then discovering that Mr. Cuff is a single man without any family living nearby, Peter Lee seizes the opportunity to invite him to stop by 828 where the Patience family gathers *en masse* every Sunday afternoon.

"They won't mind. Don't worry yerself none. People are always jest stoppin' by. I know yuh'll be welcome, too." Mr. Cuff graciously thanks him for the invitation while adding that he will do just that one of these days.

Sometime in the future on a balmy Sunday afternoon, residents cooling themselves in the shadowy recesses of shaded front porches observe a young colored man strolling towards the house on the corner of Luzerne and Tunkhannock Avenues. "Going up to the Patiences," they knowingly remark. He is attired neatly in a summer weight beige poplin suit, immaculate white shirt with high collar stiffly starched, black bow tie, and perched on his head a round flat straw hat sporting a wide black grosgrain band.

Peter Lee and the other men are on the side porch, rocking and talking, eagerly waiting for the food they can smell being prepared by the Patience women in the kitchen. Elsie had just poked her head out to tell them dinner was about ready. Upon spying Charles Edward Cuff's making his way up Tunkhannock Avenue, Peter Lee moves from the porch to the edge of the lawn.

"Mr. Cuff. How-do? Good tuh see yuh, sir! Come on up and get acquainted." The other men all rise to shake hands with the newcomer. Now upon hearing an unfamiliar voice outside on the porch Elsie swings the screen door open once again. This time to investigate.

"Mrs. Patience, want yuh tuh meet Mr. Charles Edward Cuff. Knew yuh wouldn't mind if I invited him tuh come up tuh the house. He's finally decided tuh put in an appearance." Peter Lee smiles as he welcomes the visitor.

"How-do, Mr. Cuff? Glad to have you. Now you just make yourself right to home. Hope you're good'n hungry. Dinner'll be ready soon."

"Thank you so very much, Mrs. Patience. I am most delighted to make your acquaintance," Edward replies as he reaches out to enfold her small hand in his.

My, my! Don't he talk nice, though, thinks Elsie who tends to get her verbs mixed up at times.

At the dinner table the conversation flows easily as Lillian is being impressed with the well-spoken Mr. Charles Edward Cuff. In the course of the afternoon, he reveals that his long-term intention is to study for the ministry. "I really have hopes of becoming an evangelist." He then goes on to explain."You see, in Binghamton, New York there is a good Bible school. It is my desire to enroll there some day. That is to say, when I can save sufficient funds." Everyone at the table is *quite* impressed. A minister, no less! In colored communities ministers always are regarded highly.

Later after rocking a bit with the men on the porch and before total darkness descends, Mr. Cuff excuses himself to take his leave. Directly addressing Elsie, he says with an engaging smile, "Mrs. Patience, I am much obliged for your wonderful hospitality. Thank you so very much. This has indeed been a most pleasant afternoon."

Elsie responds with the invitation, "Well then, please come again, Mr. Cuff. Any time you please."

"Thank you, ma'am. I will plan to do just that."

"Well, what do you think, Lillie?" Florence and Rosa can barely wait to pry their younger sister. *They* certainly are impressed with Mr. Cuff. He *is* an eligible bachelor. After all, there are no other ones around. And Lillian is quickly nearing twenty-one.

She definitely is impressed with Mr. Cuff's intelligence and self-assurance, but Lillian certainly is not going to reveal any of this to her "busy body" sisters. Anyway, he did not appear to be at all interested in her. He had not once looked in her direction. At least that is what *she* thought.

Charles Edward Cuff's main interests at this time of his life are in squirreling away enough money to go to school, in conducting his Bible study intended to help young men turn their lives around, and in studying The Word in order to increase his own personal knowledge. His interest has not been in any particular young woman, even though at the dinner table he was quite aware of a head of luxurious brown hair and a ready smile with a charming gap between the top two front teeth.

Jessie notices that now before Ma tells them to "outen" the lamp, Lillian has taken to reading Pa's small brown leather Bible, something she had not done heretofore.

Charles Edward Cuff has been able to secure a position as a coachman, too, just like Walter Glover and S. Peter Lee. *But for me this is only temporary,* he determines, for he has dreams. *Big dreams.* Dreams of being the pastor of his *own* church.

He frequents the AME churches in Wilkes-Barre and Scranton as well as the colored Baptist churches in those cities. Members of his family belong to the latter denomination, the one with which he is most familiar and in which he feels most comfortable. His desire is to become an evangelist; one who fervently makes the appeal for people to surrender their life to God and Baptists seem to be more open to his kind of preaching. Determined, however, to hone his style to have more of a *universal* appeal, Cuff accepts invitations to speak at churches of different denominations, both white and black, in and out of the immediate area.

His *style* of preaching is what draws the people. He refrains from pitching his voice any higher than he usually speaks. He performs no theatrics, for his goal is not to entertain, but to inform. He is a *teacher* of the Bible. From the Methodist Episcopal Church of Richfield Springs a pamphlet extols his preaching as "...clear, plain, forceful, Biblical, without loophole or controversy."

So because of his busy schedule he does not visit 828 again until December when Peter Lee extends an invitation from Elsie to join the Patience family for Christmas dinner. Edward misses his mother, two brothers and sister in Mercersburg, especially now during the holiday season. Therefore, he accepts the invitation with gratitude.

On Christmas day as he approaches 828 he immediately takes notice of the large red poinsettias adorning each window while gracing the front door is an evergreen wreath bedecked with a wide red bow. Then as he mounts the steps he can see the tall beautifully decorated spruce filling the front window of the dining room. Set in polished brass holders the small beeswax candles already have been lit. By Crowder only, though, who has heard of houses' burning to the ground due to carelessness associated with lit Christmas candles. Encircling the branches are strings of popcorn and garlands of red and green paper circles cut and pasted in school by the younger children. Hanging from the branches are wooden reindeer whittled by Crowder as well as crocheted snowflakes stiffened with starch, Florence's handiwork.

Elsie very carefully has hung the precious fragile glass decorations given to her long ago by the lawyer's wife in Dillsburg. When she had presented Elsie with two beautiful delicate glass orbs the Mrs. had said, "I want you to have these, Child. They are for you to remember me by." And so every Christmas season Elsie does. Remembering not only her, but Mariah as well.

On Sundays, Elsie usually prepares roast chicken for her family dinners. Chickens from her very own coop. Chickens whose heads she decapitates with her sharp hatchet after which the fowl get plunged into a large pot of boiling water so the feathers can be plucked easily. The tiniest, however, always require a singeing over the hot fire in the kitchen stove. Next the entrails get pulled out, of course always reserving the gizzard, liver and heart for giblet gravy. Elsie is just doing the things every farmer's wife knows how to do.

And always accompanying her roasted chickens are fluffy mashed white potatoes and the thick brown giblet gravy, light buttermilk biscuits, and vegetables freshly picked from the garden in summer or in winter retrieved from the cellar stock. And of course always there are the obligatory fruit pies for dessert. Her children know that this is their Ma's standard fare and this is what they always can expect, week after week. Seldom is there any deviation from this menu.

However, with today's being Christmas, Elsie is serving a standing rib roast she purchased from the butcher. It is accompanied by fluffy mashed white potatoes and smooth brown gravy, tiny creamed onions, carrots glazed with honey, coleslaw, and the string beans she had "put up" last fall. For dessert, besides her famous pies, she has baked her favorite pound cake, sans icing, of course. She had to warn her two youngest boys not to run, or jump or make any loud noises in the kitchen while the cake was rising in the oven. Everyone knows that even the slightest jar can make the cake "fall," causing it to cave in the middle.

Crowder has set an extra leaf in the dining room table. Elsie covers it with a beautiful tablecloth crocheted by Florence amazingly out of ordinary grocer string. Everybody in the family saves theirs for Glover to roll into balls for the magic touch of his wife's nimble fingers. Now as she is setting the table, Elsie is reserving a place directly across from Lillian for their guest Mr. Cuff. *After all, she's not getting any younger*, the mother schemes.

At the Patience table no meal ever is eaten without the grace being offered first. This is one tradition Crowder and Elsie have in common from their childhood. The Dillsburg lawyer always blessed the table and Crowder, having been the oldest boy in Aunt Cassie's cabin before he ran away, had been the one to do so there. Traditionally in most families, it has become a male role, so in Crowder's absence Elsie will require her boys to take turns.

Today, however, is going to be different. Aunt Cassie had reasoned that men must have more clout with God and perhaps Crowder may have this idea, too. But seated at his table is one, he feels, having even more clout than he has. So Crowder extends the invitation to Mr. Charles Edward Cuff to offer the blessing, something he will always be asked to do whenever he dines at the Patience table.

As is customary following dinner, the gentlemen retire to the parlor where they mull over whatever men are interested in—farming, weather, politics and religion, as well as the latest injustices they have heard levied against colored people. After the ladies complete the "clean up" they join the men to sing Christmas carols, accompanied by Florence at the upright piano Elsie had managed to acquire many years before. Lillian having been blessed with a strong alto voice enjoys harmonizing. She and Jessie sometimes sing some of the popular "tear jerker" ballads of the day. However, it is in Edward's tenor everyone recognizes a real talent, prompting Peter Lee to request, "Mr. Cuff, please. Would yuh favor us with a solo?"

"Why, yes, I would be most delighted to." Edward moves closer to the piano then. "Mrs. Glover, 'The First Noel,' if you please."

Florence plays a few introductory notes and then Edward proceeds to sing the words while the others hum along. Crowder knows that he must leave soon to tend to his horses up on the Carpenter farm. Tears well in his eyes as Edward's pure tenor notes soar. Music always has had a way of touching his very soul. As the last words are being sung, reluctantly he goes into the kitchen to pull on his heavy clothing and galoshes.

Lillian's strong harmonizing alto gives Jessie an idea. Enthusiastically then she suggests, "How about singing something with Mr. Cuff, Lillie? I think you two will sound just great together!" The reticent Lillian now flustered and embarrassed darts a look at her youngest sister, meaning, *Now why'd you do that for?* Jessie pays her "no mind" as Mr. Cuff politely asks, "And what is *your* favorite carol, Miss Lillian?"

Blushing, she replies hesitantly, "Well, I'm partial to 'Silent Night.'"

"An excellent choice! Please, Mrs. Glover?"

The voices of the two young people blend in such perfect harmony that everyone is held spellbound. The piano ceases, allowing Edward and Lillian to sing the next verse *a cappella*. He is quite enthralled by their joint sound. So much so that he suggests, "Miss Lillian, perhaps you'd like to sing with me at some of the churches I visit from time to time?"

Lillian has always been very shy. Such a thought would never have entered her mind! Sing in front of a large audience of people? "Oh, no! I couldn't do that!" she quickly responds.

"Yes, you could, Lillie!" pipes up Jessie.

"I just don't know. I'll have to think about it," Lillian murmurs as she cuts her indignant eyes over at her younger sister. *I'm sure Mr. Cuff's going to put all of those crazy ideas clean out of his head the very minute he leaves here,* she predicts to herself.

The next Sunday afternoon, however, who puts in an unexpected appearance and just in time for dinner, too? Mr. Charles Edward Cuff. Although Lillian has not given him an answer to the possibility of her singing with him at churches, she does agree to practice some hymns. He is hoping she will be as enthusiastic as he is since he has been invited to speak the very next week at The Chapel in Slocum's Patch, a small settlement just north of the Carpenter farms. He really does want her to go along with him so he suggests their singing the hymn "Alone," one whose harmony he knows is perfectly suited to their two voices.

"It was alone my Savior prayed in dark Gethsemene."

Lillian, thrilled, too, with their perfect harmony, feels led to say, "Yes. I think I will go along with you to sing next week." And so Jessie is volunteered by Crowder and Elsie to traipse along with the duo because Lillian is not going anywhere alone with a young man, even as fine a gentleman as Mr. Charles Edward Cuff.

As they find themselves being asked to sing more and more often, through their music a romantic bond slowly is developing between the two young people. Edward is discovering certain qualities in Lillian to make him think she just might be able to survive the demanding role of a pastor's wife, even though he is not yet a minister.

On a lovely Sunday afternoon in the fall of 1905 Edward asks Crowder if he may speak to him alone. So together the two men exit the side porch to slowly amble around the back of 828 to the footpath leading past the Concord grape arbor and then on to the vegetable garden. Crowder, lit pipe in his mouth, is waiting patiently to hear what the young man has to say, suspecting that he knows already.

Edward, with hands clasped behind his back, is praying for the right words, but without having said much of anything and nothing at all of real importance the two men reach the narrow road at the end of the yard. Now as the two men prepare turning back to the house, Edward Cuff finally musters up enough courage to ask Crowder for his permission to pay court to Lillian.

Certainly Crowder harbors no negative feelings towards this young man, except for the reality that Edward is in no position to provide for a wife. Taking a pull on his pipe before removing it from his mouth and then looking directly into Edward's eyes the father gives his answer. "See here now, Mr. Cuff, my Lillie's had a real easy life, yuh know. All my girls have. Never had tuh work fer nobody exceptin' their Ma. No sir, my Lillie's not used tuh no hardship. And that's all Ah can see yer offerin' her."

Edward knows what Crowder is saying is true. His coachman's job pays next to nothing, providing him with room and board, but very little cash. He earns a few extra dollars when collections are taken up for him after his speaking engagements. Lillian's father is well aware that this young man is saving all his hard-earned money for attending the Practical Bible Training School in Binghamton, New York.

"Sorry tuh have tuh say this, Mr. Cuff, but until yore situation improves, yuh can't ask fer my Lillie's hand." Crowder has made Rosa wait these many years for Peter Lee. Lillian will just have to wait, too. He is not going to have his girls suffering by living in poverty. Not if he has any say about it!

From the kitchen window Lillian has been watching as her father and Edward walk together down back. Her father is always showing off his abundant garden to someone. This is nothing at all out of the ordinary. *They're coming back so soon, though*, she thinks, observing them as they return to the house. In one hand Crowder is carrying a large ripe tomato he had spied along the way, begging to be picked. Neither man is saying anything at all now.

Lillian has no idea they have been in conversation concerning *her* future, even though she has been hoping that one of these days Edward will ask for her hand in marriage. Custom, however, dictates he should approach her father first. She is wondering, *Is today the day?* Soon, though, she hears the creaking of rockers on the porch rather than the men's coming inside to talk with her. *Oh well, I guess not,* she concedes with a sigh.

It does not help matters any when younger sister Jessie signifies, "I can tell that he *likes* you, Lillie. Then why doesn't he ask you to *marry* him?" Lillian feels that he likes her, too, but she guesses *not enough to marry her*.

On the 4th of July in the year 1906 the annual Sunday School picnic is being held at Harvey's Lake. Florence and Walter Glover are in attendance with their several children. Harry is there, too, accompanied by his three boys, his wife being confined to the house since the next baby (a girl, she is praying) is due at the end of August. Mr. C. E. Cuff is escorting Lillian and Mr. S. P. Lee is Rosa's escort and just as her Aunt Mariah had done many years before, unattached Jessie rounds up all of her nieces and nephews for games.

Picnic baskets loaded with crisp fried chicken, creamy potato salad, buttered yeast rolls, apple pies, pickled red beets and water melon rind, hard boiled eggs, pound cake, and other kinds of delectable foods are depleted quickly. Then the children run around playing all sorts of games, parents laze on blankets while watching over their broods, young people flirt, and courting couples "take a turn" around the park.

Sometime during the past year both Lillian and Edward came to the realization that they were desirous of spending the rest of their lives together, but no actual words had been spoken between them. Lillian's thoughts, *Why doesn't Edward ask me to marry him?* Edward's thoughts, *Is Lillie wondering why I don't ask her to marry me?* Finally he felt the time had come to reveal that last fall he had asked her father for permission to pay court and as an answer he had received a definitive "No!"

"What?" Oh, was she ever furious! "My father said that you couldn't ask me to marry you? He *really* said that?"

"Yes, Lillie, he did. That is exactly what he said."

"My! Well, he said nary a word to *me*. And just what *reason* did he give?"

"I guess he is concerned about your welfare, Lillie. He knows that I do not have any money to speak of and everybody knows that I am planning to be a preacher. And preachers certainly do not make much money. You and I both know that. I suppose he just feels that I do not have the means to take care of you properly."

Lillian was incensed. She was certain she could not approach Crowder on this matter. *It just wouldn't be fitting. He is my father.* Anyway, as she knew, when he makes up his mind about something, it's final. No changing his mind. *But this is my life, after all*, she was thinking. "Humpt! Fiddle-sticks! Anyway, Edward, I'm almost twenty-three years old. *I* certainly think I'm old enough to know what *I* want."

"Well, that is all well and good, Lillie, but the biggest problem is that I do not have any place for us to live. You could not live with me in that small room over the carriage house. That simply would not do." He was reflecting on Crowder's words about Lillian's never having had any hardships. "No, if we marry, you see, we would have to live with your parents."

Lillian knew this was not at all feasible. Percy, Chester and Nyles were occupying the boys' bedroom and she shared the girls' room with Rosa and Jessie. And, besides, her father had made it most clear that he was not going to grant Mr. Charles Edward Cuff permission to marry her.

"Then we'll just elope and tell them about it *later*," she declared with much aplomb.

"Later? What do you mean by 'later?'"

"Oh, I don't know. When the right time comes, I guess. We'll know when that is," she replied optimistically as any young woman in love might.

And so on Independence Day in the year 1906 Lillian declares *her* independence by surreptitiously slipping away with Charles Edward Cuff. The usually shy Lillian boldly goes to Binghamton, New York, a short train-ride from West Pittston, recites her marriage vows, returning to the picnic in the late afternoon. No one seems to have missed them except Jessie whose eagle eyes were focused on her sister's curious activities.

"Where've you been?" she hisses.

"Oh, just *here and there*," Lillian replies nonchalantly.

"Better not let Pa catch you *here or there*."

"Remember, Jessie, I'm going to be twenty-three on the 12th."

"Think that matters to Pa? You'd just better be careful. That's all I can say," is Jessie's parting warning.

Life for the Patience family continues much the same as ever. Working hard all week and on Sundays gathering at 828 for the communal dinner. The family is growing rapidly for in late August Harry's wife gives birth to yet another son--Charles Edgar.

Edward and Lillian live at their respective abodes while continuing to sing at various religious gatherings, oftentimes now not accompanied by Jessie or one of the younger brothers. And so "busy-body" comments begin to be relayed along the "grapevine." "Are they engaged?" *"Don't rightly know."* "Are they courtin'?" *"Haven't heard such."* "Well, do they have an understandin'?" *"Not to my knowledge."* "And Mr. and Mrs. Patience approve of such goin's on?" *"Can't really say."*

After Florence and Rosa feel obliged to alert their mother to the fact that people are beginning to talk, Elsie approaches her third daughter with, "Lillie, it just don't seem fitting for you going all over the place with Mr. Cuff like that." Lillian does not relish deceiving her mother, exactly what she has been doing this past year. And anyway, she is getting tired of having to go "here and there" in order to spend time with her own husband.

"Ma, I've got to tell you something." Preparing to steep a pot of tea, her mother is standing at the kitchen stove where she is reaching for the heavy teakettle.

"Here, Ma. Let me do that for you. You just rest your feet a spell." So while waiting to hear what her third daughter has to say, Elsie settles herself at the kitchen table. "Ma," Lillian begins. "I know you're going to get mad and I know Pa's *really* going to be mad. But I need you to help me." Lillian knows her mother always abides by her husband's decisions. But maybe just this once. Maybe just in this case?

Very curious now, her mother answers, "Why of course, Lillie. You know I'll help you if I can."

Around her neck Lillian is wearing a long thin chain hidden completely from view. Pulling it up and out of the neck of her shirtwaist she shows her mother a shiny gold ring. "I'm married."

"What? Married? You're married?" Reflexively she asks, *"Who to?"* when already she knows *"who* to." Good thing Elsie is sitting. Then she answers her own question. "Mr. Cuff, of course. And just when did all these goings-on happen?" She quickly adds, "Jessie know?"

"Last 4th of July. We went up to Binghamton on the train. And, no, Ma, Jessie doesn't know anything about it. Nobody in the family does."

Elsie had not been able to attend that particular picnic because Nyles had come down with the chicken pox. All of her other children had their turn and then it had been her last child's. Now over a year later, she is looking askance at her fourth child. Never would she in a million years have imagined that the usually reticent Lillian would have run off like that. And then kept it a secret all this time with the family's never suspecting a thing. "Why, I never! Well, you're right about one thing, Lillie. Your Pa's not gonna like this one bit!"

"Yes, I know, Ma. That's why I need you to be here when I tell him. Will you be? Please?" Lillian begs.

"I'll be sitting right here at the table," her mother promises, "but you know what your Pa *says,* goes."

Lillian knows this to be true as she nervously awaits her father's arrival for his dinner. She knows that before she can dare approach him she must wait until his meal has been completed. Until he swallows the last bite of the sour cherry pie she baked especially for him. Until he stirs cream and sugar into his strong black coffee and until finally he sets the empty cup in its saucer.

"Good pie, Lillie." He always has a compliment for her baking. "Gettin' better all the time. Perfect crust."

She uses lard for the shortening like everyone else, but in addition she has a *secret* ingredient, so she says. Something she will not divulge to anyone. Something she learned in Cooking School. She will not tell anyone that she uses *very cold water* and before rolling out the dough she chills it by wrapping it first in wax paper and sitting it on top of the chunk of ice in the icebox. Makes a perfect flaky pie crust every time.

"Thanks, Pa. Glad you liked it. But now before you get up, though, I need to talk to you about something, please."

Crowder has detected something decidedly amiss because Elsie is usually up by now "readying" the table for the next meal, but this evening she has remained seated, slowly sipping a cup of tea. And Lillian has been fidgeting for some reason. Crowder figured he would just patiently "wait'n see."

"Ah'm waitin', Daughter." He cannot possibly imagine what she is going to tell him.

I might as well just say it. No use "beating around the bush." "Pa, me and Mr. Cuff got married."

Now Crowder bolts straight up in his chair. "Married? When? Where? Ah didn't give him no permission tuh ask yuh!" Lillian takes notice that her father appears rather downcast and disappointed rather than angry as she certainly had expected.

"Last Fourth of July. We went up to Binghamton on the train and got married there by Rev. Phillips. He's a real good friend of Edward's."

"Humpt," Crowder mutters. "Well, guess what's done's done." Getting up from the table he nods to his wife and retires to the side porch to smoke his pipe in peace, leaving mother and daughter alone again in the kitchen.

Lillian is quite surprised by her father's reaction. She certainly had expected at the very least a long stern lecture. Although he is not one to lose his temper and go into a tirade, he certainly knows how to deliver a reprimand which can go on and on and on. Not until Elsie shares how she and Crowder themselves would have eloped if things had not worked out for them does Lillian understand why her father took the news so calmly.

The rest of the family needs to be told now. Jessie will be the first one when she arrives home from a dressmaking fitting and she is most "put out" that Lillian had been so successful in slipping past Jessie's eagle eyes. Always having been her sister's confidant, at least so she thought, Jessie had absolutely no inkling of what Lillian had been up to last 4th of July. And now feeling betrayed she is determined to "say her piece." So without even giving her sister a glance, Jessie suggests rather snippily, "Ma, you'd better let *me* take a look at the marriage certificate before you let that man move in here."

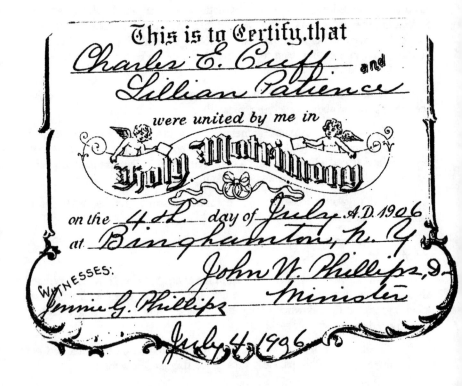

Marriage Certificate of C.E. Cuff and
Lillian Patience, July 4, 1906

Chapter 26

Grave Disappointments

*T*he secret out now, living arrangements must be made at 828 for the young Cuffs. So the large bedroom which had always been the girls' room is divided into two smaller rooms. One for the young couple, the other for Rosa and Jessie. Lillian is certain a Cuff baby will arrive soon now that she and Edward are living under the same roof. However, when year after year pass and still they are not blessed with children, she is very disappointed.

She finally confides in her mother who makes an attempt to advise and console. "You gotta be patient, Lillie. Some women are married for years before a baby comes, you know." She pauses before continuing. "Your Aunt Mariah was like that." But in remembering her beloved sister, Elsie prays that none of her daughters are going to meet that same tragic fate.

Meanwhile Lillian continues being supportive of her husband's goals as he saves his money and studies hard in preparation for fulfilling his life-long dream of becoming a minister. The popular couple still is in great demand, each week traveling somewhere. But still no pregnancy. Finally the time comes when Lillian decides she must consult with a doctor concerning her barrenness. After being examined she is told that nothing appears to be the wrong with *her*.

"Perhaps the problem lies with your *husband*," the doctor suggests. "Has he ever had the mumps? I don't know if you are aware of this or not, but a case of the mumps can make a man sterile."

And that is how Lillian discovers the reason why she will never have any children of her own. Yes, Edward had the mumps when he was a small boy. How distraught he is to realize it is because of him there will be no Cuff children. So in future years whenever Lillian wants her nieces or nephews to visit, he welcomes them, becoming especially fond of the last Glover child, Little Florence, who even in the year 2001 will remember spending wonderful summer vacations with her Aunt Lillie and Uncle Edward.

After a seven-year courtship Rosa Veden, the petite second Patience daughter, finally has her father's blessing to marry her handsome suitor, Simon Peter Lee. On June 10, 1910 the wedding takes place in the parlor of 828. He is coachman to a prosperous physician residing in a large house on Wyoming Avenue and over the years Peter Lee has been able to accumulate enough money to satisfy Crowder's expectations for his daughter.

On their wedding day, the happy couple poses for individual photographs, Rosa radiant in her long sleeved white dress trimmed at the neck with lace. A strand of pearls, a gift from her groom, encircles the high collar. She displays with pride her recently acquired wide gold wedding band.

Rosa Veden Patience Lee on her wedding day,
July 10, 1910

    S. Peter Lee cuts a dashing figure in his new "Sunday-go-to-meeting" suit, white handkerchief peeking from his left pocket and black bow tie around a high stiff collar. He has waited these many years to marry Rosa. There is no doubt in his mind that he can provide for her now and for the children God will send them. This couple has been the epitome of practicality and frugality, traits to follow them throughout their lives.

Simon Peter Lee on his wedding day,
July 10, 1910

The Lees have good reason for jubilation during the first year of their marriage. Soon there will be a Lee to join the Patience and Glover grandchildren. The father-to-be wants a boy. Rosa is just happy to be pregnant. After all, she soon will be thirty-one years old and wants to have her children quickly after having waited so long to be married.

Florence promises her some of the tiny clothes she so carefully stitched by hand for her own children. Peter builds a cradle to sit on Rosa's side of the bed so she can just lean her arm out to rock the baby. During the last few months of "confinement" when ladies "in waiting" do not go out in public, Rosa spends most of her time preparing for and dreaming of her child. Thinking of names. Of course, if it is a boy, it will be named after his father. He will be Simon Peter Lee, Junior. She is so certain it is a boy she has not thought about girls' names at all.

The baby is due in September. Fortunately, this summer of 1911 has not been unusually warm. Rosa has taken care not to overexert herself in her mother's garden. Pete helps her with her chores around the house as much as he can when he is not out driving the doctor on his rounds. The doctor has promised to deliver Rosa's baby. Everything is going extremely well for the S. Peter Lees.

A midwife had delivered all of Elsie's babies. However, this new generation is using the services of doctors. Elsie wonders if her last child in 1898, a stillborn boy, might have lived had he been delivered by a doctor. "*No use even thinking like that*," she chides herself.

On an August day which ordinarily would have been a beautiful one with the sun shining brightly, with not too much humidity to make an expectant mother uncomfortable, and with only one month to go before Rosie's "lying-in time," tragedy suddenly strikes. The baby boy is born too soon. Dead, even though delivered by a doctor. And Rosa is given even more devastating news. Because of "complications" she will never be able to have any more babies.

Rosa and Pete both are heart-broken. There will never be a Lee child. This fact is just too overwhelming for Rosa to bear. She had waited so long to be a wife and mother. For weeks she will not leave her bed except to take care of her personal needs. The doctor sends a visiting nurse to the carriage house apartment to bind Rosa's painful milk-filled breasts, but she will see no one else. "She jest don't want no company," Pete tries to explain to her worried family when they come knocking at the door. And, besides, Rosa simply can not bear thinking about going up to her Ma's on Sundays with all those Patience and Glover children frolicking all over the lawn, chasing butterflies in the afternoon and fireflies at dusk.

And so Rosa withdraws from the world. Most of the time she just lies on her bed, rising only to prepare her husband's meals. Finally the day arrives

And so Rosa withdraws from the world. Most of the time she just lies on her bed, rising only to prepare her husband's meals. Finally the day arrives when the healing process begins. On that morning when she first awakens, her eyes immediately focus on the soiled laundry Pete has piled in the corner of the bedroom. She certainly can not expect her husband to wash the dirty clothing. Anyway, she knows that as a man he would not even know how to begin. In fact, since it is a must for him always to look neat and fresh on his job he had to take his percale dress shirts to his mother-in-law for laundering. At that time Elsie insisted upon his bringing all the laundry up to her at 828, which is what he has been doing these last months.

Now as Rosa enters the kitchen her eyes begin to gravitate around the room, first fixing on the cast iron stove much in need of a good blackening. Then she sees that the linoleum certainly could do with a thorough scrubbing. The lamps need to be polished, refilled with kerosene, wicks trimmed, chimneys and globes washed. *There's a lot of work needing done,* she concludes. And so Rosa, always the meticulous housekeeper, begins tackling her housework.

Very soon afterward, spring's arrival induces Rosa to leave the confines of her house. From her flower beds at 828 the perennial crocuses, daffodils, tulips, and hyacinths planted with her Aunt Mariah so many years ago seem to be beckoning to her. She knows that it is time for their blooming and she is sure by now her mother will have gracing the dining room table a vase filled with long branches of bright yellow forsythia and fuzzy gray pussy-willow catkins. On the morning she informs Pete that she is going to walk up to 828 to check on her flowers, he breathes a great sigh of relief. He has confidence that now his disappointed wife is ready to rejoin the world.

Harry's mother is Elsie and his wife also is Elsie. However, there has never been any confusion between the two because his mother is never called by her given name. "Ma" she is to all of her children, "Grandma" to her growing number of grandchildren, and Mrs. Patience to all others, except her husband, of course. To further lessen the confusion her daughter-in-law always is referred to as Elsie-Harry.

Jessie, in 1913 the only unmarried Patience daughter, residing still as custom dictates with her parents at 828, treks daily down to her brother's home on Bond Street. This takes but half an hour when the weather is pleasant. Her little nephews are adorable, but indeed quite a handful. Running rather than walking, chattering noisily, always hungry, just being typical boys.

After having given birth to seven boys within a thirteen year span, Elsie-Harry in her fourth month of pregnancy is quite weary. She prays that this baby is a girl, feeling like she will just die if it is another boy. It is not that she does not love her boys. On the contrary. It is just that she has enough male children. She wants a girl. *Please, Lord, won't You let it be a girl this time?* She already has a name in mind, one she will not share with anyone, not even her husband. It is bad luck to name a baby before it is born, her mother-in-law has told her. So the name of her baby girl is Elsie-Harry's own special secret.

Seems as though her work nowadays is never completed. Three meals to prepare each and every day. The older boys come home from school to eat a hot lunch with their father who carves coal novelties in his small shop at the back edge of the yard. Then there are the requisite daily trips she must make to the grocery store because she has no way of storing perishables like meat and milk. That icebox sitting on the back porch is not intended to keep food fresh for any considerable length of time. Especially not in summer months when the large chunk of ice delivered by the iceman melts much too quickly even though Elsie-Harry wraps it in newspaper. She has been told this is the proper method to keep ice from melting too quickly, but she is not that certain. She just does it because everyone else does. What she does not realize, however, is that by doing this she prevents her icebox from becoming as cold as it might get otherwise.

Mondays always come much too quickly for the weary mother when she once again has to face a week's worth of piled up dirty laundry. Her little boys' clothing, her husband's coal dust-laden coveralls, her own personal items, the soiled towels, as well as white sheets, tablecloths and napkins, all which require the additional steps of bluing and starching.

Shortly after Monday's sunrise the tedious job commences. First step, the dirtiest of the clothing must be boiled with Fels Naptha soap in the washing boiler, a large oval tin container holding six to eight bucketsful of water, each having to be toted from the pantry sink to the blazing coal stove. Second, she has to lug the heavy wet articles from the top of the stove to the wash tub where she laboriously bends to scrub each piece up and down the corrugated tin board. Third, every individual article is rinsed in yet another tub of warm water. Fourth, each piece must be wrung as dry as possible by hand before being flung into the large round laundry basket.

Fifth, she has to drag the heavy latticed basket out into the back yard where she must stretch up on her tiptoes in order to clothespin each article to the clothesline. Lastly, with a wooden pole slotted on one end she props up the heavy line so no laundry flapping in the breezes can sweep the ground. Eight hours it may take from beginning to end with meals to prepare in between and with five little boys and a baby to tend. Exhausting! And she is not finished yet! The dry laundry must be unpinned, brought into the house and folded in preparation for Tuesday's exhausting job of ironing.

When he is around Harry will help his wife, but often he must be away delivering his wares and procuring new orders. He does make a concerted effort to be home on washday. He is curious, though, why she always insists on laundering only on Mondays. He knows his mother always does her wash on

Mondays, too, but he cannot figure out why these women have to be so rigid. "Elsie, why can't you wash clothes on another day? A day when you know I'm gonna be here."

His wife sighs deeply as she patiently explains to her husband as if to a child, "I *have* to wash on Mondays, Harry. *Everybody* does. Don't you see everybody's clotheslines full every Monday?" Observing the blank look on her husband's face she can see that he has never taken notice. He does not realize that to the housewife the day following Sunday is almost a *sacred* day. Monday is always *wash day*!

Continuing, the wife is laying it out clearly for her husband. "Now you see, Harry, if I hang my clothes out on the line *any other day of the week*, they might get full of smoke." Full of smoke because the only way people have to dispose of their garbage and debris is by burning it out in their backyards. So this unwritten neighborly agreement has passed down from generation to generation. No one ever burns on Mondays. For on this day of the week *every* woman expects to be able to hang her laundry outside to flap in *sweet* smelling breezes.

Please don't let it rain today, Elsie-Harry silently prays each and every Monday as she struggles with the heavy sheets. For if rain begins to fall before the laundry is dry, she will have the daunting task of unpinning and toting it into the warm kitchen for hanging once again, this time on ropes strung across the warm kitchen temporarily for this purpose.

She has no idea of the surprise her husband is planning for her. The house already is wired for electricity and any day now a brand new electric washing machine is going to be delivered to 16 Bond Street. Harry can hardly wait to see the amazed expression on his wife's face when she gets a look at its special feature, a wringer. Her Monday's laundering certainly will be so much easier.

Elsie-Harry is a very petite woman, even more so than her mother-in-law had been. Now "bone tired" every day she welcomes and appreciates her sister-in-law Jessie's help. Elsie-Harry had known Jessie even before being introduced to the tall handsome brother with his wide infectious smile so like his father's. And their first boy, Robert Jesse, is named in honor of the special bond of friendship between the two women. Robert, after Elsie's brother and Jesse, after Harry's sister.

In the winter of 1913, Elsie-Harry catches a "chill" while unpinning the laundry from the clothesline out back. Jessie is right there beside her sister-in-law, lending a helping hand. Frigid winds blow on the mother already fatigued from all of her daily chores, but the laundry must be taken into the house before she no longer can see what she is doing. Nowadays it is dark by five o'clock. Then with dinner completed, the dishes washed and dried, she tells her husband that she needs to lie down. "Just for a little while," she wearily informs him as slowly she pulls herself up the stairs leading to the master bedroom.

Jessie is happy to put the two littlest boys to bed, Harry Bruce and Harold Lee. They beg her to sing a few of their favorite songs and by the time she is finished with a mere two, the little boys have fallen sound asleep. Their father easily can supervise the middle two, Wilmer Miller and Charles Edgar and the two eldest, Robert Jesse and Kenneth Veden, are perfectly capable of getting ready for bed all by themselves. After washing faces and hands, brushing teeth with pig-bristle toothbrushes dipped in a mixture of salt and baking soda, pulling on sleeping gowns, and kneeling by their bed to say their prayers, the boys hug their father and Aunt Jessie "Good night."

When at last she finds the opportunity for peeking in on Elsie-Harry, Jessie sees that the exhausted mother is sleeping soundly. *"Plumb worn out. Too many babies,"* Jessie is thinking.

The next morning when the older boys rise for school, their mother is not bustling around in the kitchen like she always is. Aunt Jessie is there, but that is nothing at all unusual. She often stays overnight. But their Ma is always there, too, perhaps stirring oatmeal bubbling on the hot coal stove, or frying eggs and bacon, or setting the table for breakfast, or tending to one of the boys.

"Aunt Jessie, where's our Ma?" Bob, the oldest, questions. The only time he remembers his mother's not being in the kitchen was when, mysteriously, another baby boy would be in her arms while she remained in bed. He is thinking that maybe there is another new baby in his parents' bedroom. However, he does not hear any crying like babies are always doing. This he knows from prior experiences.

"Where's she? Where's our Ma, Aunt Jessie?" Kenny echoes.

Jessie patiently explains, "You remember last night? Your Ma wasn't feeling so good? Well, she needs her rest. Go on off to school now, boys. And mind what your teachers tell you. Your Ma'll probably be up and around by the time you get home for lunch."

But sadly their mother is not ever to be up and around again. Four months pregnant, Elsie Miller Patience, aged thirty-five years, succumbs from pneumonia just three days after catching a chill while unpinning laundry from the clothesline in her backyard.

"How can she be gone?" Harry laments over his wife's still body clothed in a lovely new pink peignoir. She has been laid out in the parlor of 16 Bond Street. Harry has lost his beloved Elsie, his six sons have lost their precious Ma, and his sister has lost her dearest friend.

__Elsie Miller Patience__, Harry's wife (circa 1913)

Chapter 27

The Evangelists

After fourteen years of marriage, most of the while residing at 828, Charles Edward Cuff finally is able to begin fulfilling his dream of becoming a minister. By 1920 he has saved enough money to take Lillian along with him to the Practical Bible Training School in Binghamton, New York where they both enroll, graduating together in 1924.

Although always willing to sing, the shy Lillian does not care to speak in front of crowds. "He does all the speaking," is her pat answer whenever asked to address any group. She does enjoy writing, though, having learned much in the area of composition at the school. Her sisters receive lengthy detailed letters describing everything from what she is cooking for dinner to who is wearing what.

Edward's desire is to pastor his own church. In the Baptist denomination pastors are apt to remain at one church literally for a lifetime. Therefore, it may be difficult for an ambitious young minister like him to find a permanent pulpit. In light of this Edward gravitates towards the denomination of African Methodist Episcopal which built a church in West Pittston the very year he and Lillian had married. He feels that perhaps as a Methodist he may have a better chance of pastoring his own church.

Unfamiliar with that denomination's formal rituals and tenets he discovers that he will need further study before he can be ordained. For one thing, he will have to learn the Decalogue, recited each and every Sunday morning. It is a recitation of the Ten Commandments with the congregation's singing responses and hymns. The minister is expected not just to *read* the Decalogue; he is expected to *recite* it and with *feeling*.

Meanwhile the Cuffs move to Pittsburgh where temporarily Edward becomes an instructor at the Whiteside Memorial Bible School. However, teaching is not what he really wants to do. No, he really wants to be a pastor of his own church. After completing all the necessary studies, finally he is ready for ordination. And so the Rev. Charles Edward Cuff becomes a member of the Pittsburgh Annual Conference, assigned on November 6, 1927 to his very own church, St. John AME located in Sewickley, Pennsylvania. The tradition of Methodists is that the bishop presiding over the Conference can and sometimes will move a minister each and every year. And this is the reason why during his career the Rev. C. E. Cuff is going to pastor several churches in western Pennsylvania.

**The Evangelist**
Rev. Charles Edward Cuff
(circa 1925)

Although well received wherever he is assigned, Rev. Cuff really would like to stay in one place for a while. And Lillian is not particular either about moving from parsonage to parsonage, never knowing when they go to Conference each summer whether they will be returning or not. But Edward chose to become a Methodist minister and part of the package is the possibility of having to move wherever his bishop deems him most needed.

In these black churches there is the following tradition. The minister's wife is expected to take a permanent seat in a pew right down front to lend her husband support, so it is said. No one else dares sit in that spot. It belongs exclusively to the pastor's wife, as everyone knows. And so each Sunday then the Mrs. Rev. C. E. Cuff does what is expected of her. However, when she strolls up the aisle to take her designated seat she becomes the topic of speculation among the women of the church. The eyes of every woman in the congregation fix on the pastor's wife attired in a fashionable ensemble created by either sister Florence or Jessie, stylish chapeau perched on her head, gloves encasing her hands, and pocketbook neatly tucked under her arm.

"We know just how much we pay him." (Or perhaps they really should say *how little*.) "How can she afford ta dress like that?" are the covetous comments made at the Ladies' Aid Society meetings and Circle gatherings. Well, Lillian is not obligated to explain where her clothing comes from and she does not. The other women can only continue to speculate and, of course, talk.

From their menial labors the church members have very little ready cash for contributing to the collection baskets. Some pastors even make jokes about offerings' making noise. They prefer the quiet kind, they hint. However, not much money ever finds its way into the baskets. Neither noisy coins nor quiet bills. Therefore, for his salary the minister often receives little cash.

What does fall into the basket on any given Sunday could depend on such unforeseen factors as the weather. Rev. Cuff, living conveniently in the parsonage next door, could open the church doors on a *too* snowy, or *too* rainy, or *too* windy, or *too* cold, or *too* hot Sunday to find in attendance only himself, his wife, and perhaps one or two of the faithful. The "fair-weather" church members have stayed at home and this means that the basket will collect next to nothing that particular week.

On the other hand, the pastor and his family are always provided with a rent-free parsonage, coal, water, and electricity as well as Sunday dinner invitations at the homes of his parishioners. Lillian never has to prepare a Sunday dinner in all of the eleven years Edward pastors. A number of hostesses, however, are not very friendly to the minister's wife. They like *him*, but they perceive *her* as being uppity. "Stand-offish. That's what our pastor's wife is," they spread among themselves.

Like her mother, Lillian has lived a very insular life. Understandably then, her shyness may be perceived as "stand-offish," having had little contact with colored people. All of her schoolmates had been white. She had attended the white Presbyterian Church until St. Mark's had been built. And there the majority of the members of that small colored church were members of her own family. Later when she had attended the Bible School in Binghamton she, Edward, and a friend from Brooklyn, New York were the only people of color except for one Native American.

Therefore, Lillian has difficulty in relating to the hardworking, mostly uneducated colored ladies of the churches where her husband pastors, many of the older ones being former slaves and others perhaps just one generation removed. A number are illiterate, requiring the "lining" of the hymns so they, too, might be able to sing the verses, in contrast to the pastor's wife who has been educated and can sing the words directly from the song books. Not only that, she can read the music as well.

And so the pastor's wife does not frequent the meetings of the Ladies' Aid Society where the "grapevine" is always busy. Her noticeable absence further widens the chasm between herself and the ladies of the church, making her become one of the informal topics discussed at the meetings. "And what does she gotta do with herself all the live long day? She don't have no children ta tend ta like the rest of us. She's jest uppity, that's all."

Lillian Mariah Patience Cuff on her 23rd Wedding Anniversery, Elizabeth, Pa. July 4, 1929)

However, at Copeland AME Church in Bradford, Pennsylvania she is fortunate to make several lifelong friends who are supportive of her in 1935 when their fifty-six year old preacher enters the hospital for elective surgery. *Supportive* when unexpectedly he dies from an embolism exactly a week to the day following a successful operation. *Supportive* when their beloved pastor is buried in Oak Hill Cemetery. *Supportive* when the preacher's wife, still in a state of shock, has to be out of the parsonage in two weeks' time before the arrival of the new preacher and his family. And *supportive* when bidding a final farewell as two of Lillian's nephews move their grief-stricken aunt back to her mother's home in West Pittston. Where, they have no doubt, she is going to remain for the rest of her life, contentedly baking pies with perfect crusts for Grandma's Sunday dinners.

Several years later a friend from Bradford who had relocated to Buffalo, New York invites Lillian there for a visit. After observing how much her guest is enjoying herself, the friend offers a suggestion. "Mrs. Cuff, why don't you come back here and stay for a time? You can bake some of your specialties." A widow, also, Pearl Allen has plans to start her own business. A teahouse. Now Lillian has never worked for anyone before. She is not so sure she will like to, but of one thing she is positive, she is not going to vegetate for the rest of *her* life in her mother's house. Not after having seen the big city by the Niagara Falls!

I'm only 52 and I got a lot of living to do yet, she determines. And she has, considering this is 1935 and she is going to live until the year 1986. Upon her return to West Pittston following that enlightening trip to Buffalo, Lillian informs her surprised family, "You'll never guess what I'm going to do! I've decided that I'm going back to room with Mrs. Allen. She's asked me to help her with her new business."

When the family hears this unexpected news they are flabbergasted, her nephews especially. "What? Aunt Lillie's going off by herself like that? Can't believe it. She's always had somebody taking care of her before! First Grandpa, and then Uncle Edward. Why, there's no way in the world she can take care of herself!"

Many years later they will be surprised again by their Aunt Lillie when she takes a westward journey across high, seemingly endless Pennsylvania mountain ranges to Pittsburgh, and long before the advent of superhighways. And in an automobile operated by a *very* newly licensed driver. All because Rev. Christine Giles, pastor of St. Mark's AME Church, must report to the annual Pittsburgh Conference.

Even though the membership of the little church in West Pittston has dwindled, Rev. Christine Giles still is reassigned. Therefore, as a member of the Conference she is required to attend the annual meetings held in Pittsburgh. Since she is responsible for arranging her own transportation, heretofore her husband has driven her. Unfortunately, last year he had been taken ill. So throughout all the winter, Rev. Giles tries her best not to worry. However, she is wondering, *How am I ever going to get to Pittsburgh this summer for Conference?*

In early spring she solves her dilemma. She trades in her husband's old car for a newer second-hand model while determining to learn to drive it herself in time to go to Conference. Rev. Giles, now in her mid 60's, is driving an automobile for the very *first* time ever in her life. As did most women of that period, she always had left the driving to her husband.

In addition to the pastor's presence, each church is expected to send at least one delegate to Conference. Lillian Cuff, recently having celebrated her 70th birthday, decides to accompany her pastor as that delegate, again shocking her concerned nephews. After invoking the protection of their God, the two very determined women take off on their mission, traveling the winding bumpy two-lane highways over the steep Appalachian Mountains to that city by the three rivers. And finally to the worried family's relief they return home unscathed, exalted, and empowered.

Crowder, if he were alive, might look at his third daughter with pride, smiling as he recognizes in her the same tenacity she without a doubt had inherited from him.

Chapter 28

Jessie Pearl the Seamstress

*O*ftentimes, particularly in a large family there may be one child never leaving the old homestead. Jessie Pearl is the one never traveling very far from West Pittston, except for just one time.

Her father's Civil War pension granted in 1912 records Jessie as being a "child" residing at home, even though she is already twenty-five years old. Everyone else has gone from 828, leaving her behind to carry on the dressmaking business she had acquired from Florence when she married Glover. Throughout the years Jessie's reputation as a talented seamstress has spread.

Toting her bag of needles, pins, tape measure, and chalk she walks to the homes of her customers, usually the more wealthy ones residing in their capacious Victorians. Other women, like those "going to business," or neighbors desirous of wearing to a special occasion one of Jessie's original creations will make the trek up the hill to 828. There they usually can find her laboring at a dressmaker's bust, fitting and tacking. Or pumping her Aunt Mariah's treadle-sewing machine. Or down on her knees, mouth full of straight pins, measuring with a yardstick and marking a customer's hem with white chalk.

Due west across Tunkhannock Avenue, on the other side of the large field where men play baseball on Sunday afternoons, is the impressive Fox Hill Country Club. The lush emerald golf links cut short and watered daily entice many persons to take a leisurely after-supper Sunday stroll, of course being very careful where placing their feet. Never ever on the fragile greens. Later this practice is to be disallowed, but at this time a walk along the heartier fringe is an extraordinarily pleasant experience because of the solitude, silence, and serenity found there. At dusk an unforgettable odor of freshness permeates the air and amazingly sounds travel farther than at any other time of the day. Across the expanse of those verdant links all the senses are invigorated.

A young, handsome, medium-brown skinned man, a recent migrant from Washington, D.C., recently has been employed at the country club. Upon seeing the need for capable waiters there, he thinks he might inquire within the colored community. A trip to church might be the most obvious start.

Jessie does not regularly attend St. Mark's. After listening to her brother and brothers-in-law haggle she had become aware of the politics involved with running a church and so she had lost interest. Now on Sundays she remains at home with her Ma, preparing the family dinner usually served around two o'clock, soon after the hour and a half long church service has concluded. She is not at all surprised to see the appearance of a young man several years her junior who has been invited to dinner by Rosa and Peter Lee. They often bring strangers up to the house, especially eligible young men now that Jessie is the only unmarried sister.

"Pa, like you to meet Mr. Nathaniel Garrett. We invited him to dinner." Rosa makes the introduction to her father who is relaxing in his favorite rocker on the porch.

"How-do? Glad tuh meet yuh, Mr. Garrett," Crowder responds in greeting, standing to shake the hand of the newcomer. "Jest pull up a chair and set a spell. Dinner'll be ready soon. Hope you're good'n hungry."

The men settle themselves behind the thick veil of English ivy vines shading the porch. Crowder asks the newcomer, "Jest where yuh hail from, Mr. Garrett?"

"Washington, D.C., sir."

"That so? How yuh happen tuh be up here in our neck of the woods?" Crowder inquires with interest, being quite aware that colored people come and *go* from this area, very few staying for any length of time since there are so few opportunities for them to find work other than menial labor.

"Well, some time ago I met a white gentleman at the establishment where I was workin' in D.C. Real nice man. From up around these parts. Told me about his club here in Pennsylvania. Said that he'd see to it that I'd get a job bar-tendin', if I came on up. So I did. I needed to get away from all that stuff down there in Washington. It sure is different up here, I have ta say that much."

Crowder nods. He certainly knows all about "that stuff" down South. Then he inquires, "Bar-tendin'? Jest what kind'a job is that?"

"I make all kinds of fancy drinks for the members, sir."

Crowder raises a single eyebrow. "Liquor in them drinks?"

"Why, yes, sir."

Crowder does not allow any liquor in his house. He has told his boys so. "Don't cotton tuh drinkin' no liquor," he is now informing his guest. "Seen too many good men plum lose their heads. Get tuh fightin' and cussin' and all kinds'a crazy goin's on. Why, a man from jest up the street gets all liquored up every payday. Gets his money at the mines, he does. But he jest won't go straight on home and hand it tuh his Missus. Oh, no! He's got tuh stop by them beer gardens down the street. And then, would yuh know, tuh top it all off, when he finally does get home he takes his razor strap tuh his missus and then tuh all his children, too. Gives every last one of them a beatin'. For nothin', mind yuh. Yuh can hear them hollerin' clear up here. Jest can't understand a thing like that! No, sir! Ah jest can't."

Crowder remembers well the sting of the lash. It is something one never forgets. For a serious infraction his children might be switched with a stripped forsythia branch, but never had any of them ever received what would be termed a *beating*. And he would rather cut off his hands than ever lay them on Elsie in anger. He just can not understand that neighbor.

Nathaniel Garrett, a guest in the house of this old man, certainly is not going to get into an argument about the pros and cons of drinking alcoholic beverages. Therefore, he simply replies, "Yes, sir."

The next time the young man from Washington appears at the front door of 828, it is to ask Jessie if she might be interested in taking a job at the Fox Hill Country Club. "They're needin' a woman ta work in the ladies' locker room over there."

"And just what is it I'd have to do?" she asks.

"It's like this. After the ladies get finished with their golf game, they want ta fix up. They need somebody ta keep their locker room in order."

"Oh, I certainly should be able to do that," Jessie supposes as she figures that not only would she have her dressmaking business, here now is an opportunity for earning extra money. Perhaps finally she will be able to save enough for a long-wished-for trip to New York City.

Florence is residing now with her husband on a farm in Mt. Zion, several miles north of West Pittston. Rosa is living in the apartment over the garage where her husband chauffeurs after having had to learn how to drive an automobile. Lillian is dwelling in Sewickley with her minister husband. The youngest daughter, Jessie, has been left at home with the aging parents. She knows that Florence's Rosa May or Elsie, as well as Percy's Ruth or Dorothy would be glad to stay a short while with their grandparents. So, indeed, she is just itching to take an exciting trip.

Unfortunately, Elsie develops a "tetch" of arthritis, finding it difficult at bedtime to maneuver up the stairs and so Crowder, ever the whittler, carves a sturdy cane for his wife. Once downstairs she remains in the kitchen for the day, seldom venturing from the house except to hobble down the yard to pay "Miss Jones" a visit.

Neighbors catch a glimpse of the small woman's struggle down the footpath, trusty cane in left hand and the family's communal red and black plaid woolen cape flung across her shoulders. She had pulled it down from the peg in the kitchen where it hangs for everybody's use. Slowly she makes her way to "Miss Jones" where Jessie's thin tissue paper dress patterns get recycled.

Cold weather is not even a deterrent to her making her trek to the outhouse. Not being one to tell "her business," no one guesses why she still insists on struggling outside. No one surmises that she prefers the higher seat of the privy since she is having difficulty now squatting over the chamber pot she keeps concealed discreetly under her bed. And as private a person as Elsie is, she would never ask anyone for any assistance.

Now earning extra cash, Jessie purchases a rather expensive piece of new furniture, a highly varnished cherry mahogany commode. She has her brother Percy set it in a corner of their parents' bedroom anticipating that now her mother will be able to stay inside. "Just look what I bought for you, Ma."

Already wary of a chair with a *lid* for a seat Elsie asks suspiciously, "And what's this for, Jessie?"

"It's for you, Ma." Then Jessie lifts the hinged lid, revealing the spanking new white porcelain lined chamber pot. "Look, Ma! Now you won't have to go way down to "Miss Jones" anymore."

"Humpt! Whoever heard of such a notion? I don't need it! Jessie, you just wasted your good hard earned money on *that thing-a-ma-gig!*" Elsie is shaking her head to indicate her displeasure at having her independence so threatened.

"No, Jessie. I'm going outside just like I always do. Any time I please. And that's all there is to it!" Arthritis now prevents the stomping of her left foot, something she always had been accustomed to doing when she was being adamant.

"Yes, of course you can, Ma, but just in case. You know, like when it's raining you won't have to get all wet. Now when you decide to use it, just be sure to let me know when it has to be emptied. Is that all right with you then?" Jessie is doing her best at trying to keep her mother from becoming any more negative about the commode than she already is.

"Humpt," Elsie's responds noncommittally. At times she makes use of the commode, but generally she does not. So what if it takes her longer now to make the trek down to visit "Miss Jones?" Well, she really does not care. She is doing what *she* wants.

The dapper Mr. Nathaniel Garrett seems to be coming by 828 quite often nowadays. The more inquisitive family members are wondering if he is courting Jessie. They do realize he is a few years younger than she is. Four to be exact. And having come here from a large city, they fear he is much worldlier than their Jessie who has never been any farther away from 828 than Scranton. But he seems to enjoy the company of the Patience family and they seem to like him.

Indeed, yes, he *is* courting Jessie and after receiving Crowder's blessing because of his steady job at the country club, Nathaniel proposes marriage.

Nathaniel and Jessie Garrett *relaxing on the bank of the Susquehanna River, West Pittston, Pa., (circa 1924)*

Jessie soon becomes a well-respected employee at the country club. Not only does she efficiently manage the ladies' locker room, she also checks coats at special weekend dinners and dances. And she has encouraged several of the Patience grandsons to wait tables there.

After the wedding Nat moves to 828, into the little room that had been the Cuffs'. Unfortunately, Jessie is to know the same disappointment as sisters Rosa and Lillian. She, too, had hoped to have a family of her own, but there are to be no babies born to the Garretts. Her only "child" will be the eight-month old infant girl a nephew brings to his grandmother's care in 1933.

"Just temporarily," he promises. "Just until I can resolve the problems I'm having with my wife." But that is never to happen. Instead there is a divorce. Rather than his grandmother, his *Aunt Jessie* becomes the child's legal guardian because, after all, Elsie is already seventy-six years old.

Unfortunately for Jessie, Nat, handsome and younger than she, enjoys going down to Wilkes-Barre where a lot of socializing occurs among some of the colored people living there. Jessie is shy, not enjoying the partying, although she does make several life-long friends. For instance, hailing from the Caribbean island of St. John, Evelyn, the wife of George Johnson, is one. A Spanish American War veteran having served in both the Philippines and China, he faithfully travels each year to West Pittston, proudly marching in the same Declaration Day parade as Crowder.

There will come a time in Jessie's life when she will feel very ugly. It will be in 1938 when she has to have an operation for removing her left eye after an uncontrollable infection destroys it. Her ophthalmologist insists that it be totally removed to prevent the infection's spreading throughout her entire body.

For certain a death sentence because antibiotics are not yet in use. Devastated that she must wear an ugly black patch over the empty socket where her eye once had been and feeling very self-conscious, she becomes weary of explaining to the curious and tactless why she must wear something so unbecoming.

Now with her husband's staying away from 828 more and more, her left eye gone, her former good looks lost, Jessie becomes depressed, resulting in her becoming almost as reclusive as her mother. Nat finally delivers the fatal blow. Early one morning in the year 1939 he informs his wife that he is leaving. Giving up his job at Fox Hill Country Club and moving to Wilkes-Barre to live with another woman. Jessie is completely devastated, never fully recovering from the wake of his desertion. Fortunately, though, she has her job at the country club, allowing her to care for her aged mother, rear her young grandniece, and maintain her dressmaking business. And although she has little savings and receives no financial help whatsoever from Nat, she manages to make enough money to keep food on the table and coal in the bin.

Her household expenses are minimal. Fortunately, there is no mortgage or rent payment due each month. Jessie presumes the house has been paid for. Once when she tries to engage her mother in conversation about it, Elsie just tells her, "Don't worry yourself none, Jessie. Your father took care of all that ages ago."

Several years later as she is straightening the locker room at the Country Club, Jessie unexpectedly is offered a solution to the dilemma of having to wear a black patch. A certain doctor's wife always has been quite friendly, inquiring to Jessie's health and that of her family. She always had some encouragement for Jessie's young grand niece when she came to the country club after school hours before her aunt was off work. Now the doctor's wife is being solicitous after Jessie shares the concerns she has about her changed looks.

"Say, Jessie, why don't you go down to Philadelphia's Wills Eye Hospital and have a *glass* eye fitted? My husband has several friends on staff there. I'm sure he'll be glad to help you with all of the particulars."

This is a completely new idea to Jessie who by now is willing to do almost anything to get rid of the disfiguring black patch. So in April 1945, during the same week President Franklin Delano Roosevelt dies suddenly during his fourth term, Jessie accompanied by her sister Lillian boards a train in Pittston, heading south for Philadelphia.

While visiting with nephew Bob Patience Jessie receives treatment on an outpatient basis with daily bus trips to Wills Eye Hospital, with fitting and refitting, with discomfort, but finally with success. An eye of glass, the exact shade of brown as her own healthy one, is put into place. And when Jessie examines her reflection in a mirror she exclaims with delight, "Why, I'm me again!"

"Well, how do I look?" is the first thing she asks Rosa and Pete anxiously when they meet her at the train station in Pittston.

"Just the same, Jessie. Just the same. Beautiful, just as you've always looked."

This will be Jessie's longest trip, the one to Philadelphia. More important, though, it will be the trip back to her feelings of self worth.

*Jessie Pearl Patience Garrett in one of
her creations (circa 1920)*

Chapter 29

Problems of Hair Care

Crowder always keeps his boys' hair closely cropped just as he does his own. The time arrives, however, when eighteen-year old Harry, emboldened by the sound of coins jingling in his pockets, decides that he wants a haircut from a *professional* barber. Now that he is working seriously at his coal carving, he is desirous of looking like a well-groomed businessman.

So, one Saturday morning, unbeknownst to his parents, he treks down Luzerne Avenue to the barbershop, the tonsorial parlor so easily identified by its red and white candy-striped pole. Through the large glass front window on which the name of the shop is emblazoned in colorful script, Harry observes a customer being shaved as he leans back in a swivel chair. The sight induces Harry to check the little bit of rubble on his young face. *Might as well get a shave, too, while I'm at it*, he figures.

Waiting their turns, several seated men are engaged in reading, smoking, and conversing as Harry swings open the front door. The sound of the tinkling bell alerts the barber. Staring over his spectacles at Harry he asks, "Want somethin'?" as he continues with the shaving.

"Yes, sir. I'd like a hair cut and a shave."

As these words register the barber ceases his work. In the swivel chair the customer with face half shaved, abruptly bolts up. The waiting customers immediately stop their reading, smoking, and conversing. All are looking askance at this colored boy who has the audacity to come into "their" barbershop to ask for a cut and shave.

"Oh, no! No! I can't do that! I don't cut no *colored* hair." First of all, the barber would not know how to even begin. He knows only how to cut straight or wavy hair. *White* men's, so he is thinking. Secondly, he knows without a doubt that his customers would never allow it.

His waiting customers really have perked up now, listening intently to the barber's answer. They know he had better not cut that colored boy's hair. He had better not even think about using the same equipment on his hair as he does on theirs. So they are listening very carefully to the barber's choice of words. *And if he don't say the right thing? Well, there's more than one barber in this town.*

Harry has digested those pointed words, "*Don't cut no colored hair.*" He supposes now that if he had conferred first with his sage father he would have been saved from making this embarrassing *faux pas*. But there comes a time when any man has to make his *own* judgments. Well, now he has. However, because he is a *colored* man he is getting "slapped down." Put in his place!

Now just about everyone in town knows about the colored Patience family living up there at the top of Luzerne Avenue. The barber personally harbors no ill feelings towards the boy, reasoning, *Old man works for the Carpenters. Don't give nobody no trouble. But this here's business.*

The bell over the barber shop door tinkles once again as the dejected colored boy exits, as the waiting customers return to their reading, smoking, and conversing, as the man in the swivel chair leans back once again, and as the barber carries on with the shaving.

A colored family living on Chase Street not far from St. Mark's Church has a son several years older than Harry. He is instrumental in Harry's locating a white barber willing to cut "colored" hair. The two boys had met in earlier years when both had been employed at the Exeter Colliery. After Harry had left there they would see each other occasionally at Sunday School.

Harry asks the young man one Sunday." "Say, your hair really looks great. How do you get it to lay down like that?"

The other fellow laughs. "Why, with my stockin' cap, of course!"

"Your what?" Harry asks.

"My stockin' cap. I sleep in it. It makes my hair lay down right smart."

"Hmm. That so? So you mean if I put on one of those things—a stocking cap, you call it—then my hair'll look just like yours?"

The other fellow is being very careful how he answers that question as he casts his eyes on Harry's noticeably uneven haircut. "Don't mean no offense now, Patience, but I don't reckon so. Your Pa's still cuttin' your hair?"

"Yep. Can't seem to find nobody else.

"Well, that's 'cause you're lookin' in the wrong places. Me'n my Pa'n my brothers? Well, we all go ta the barber 'round on Wyoming Avenue."

"He'll cut your hair?"

"Yes, sir. That he does. Well, not when nobody can see him, though. We go there at night. He can't let his customers see us. So we go ta his back door after dark. He lives right behind his shop, ya see. We can go right in through his kitchen."

"That so? Think he'll take *me*?"

"Sure. Don't see why not. But don't forget it's the stockin' cap that does the trick. Why don't ya stop by my house and I'll show ya how ta make one?"

That evening at dinner Harry casually comments to his parents, "You know, today I found a barber who'll cut colored hair. He's down on Wyoming Avenue."

"Now why you want to waste your hard-earned money like that for? Your Pa always cuts your hair," his ever practical mother responds in surprise as she serves the table, pork and sauerkaraut accompanied with warm apple sauce.

"I'm in business now, Ma. I've got to make a good appearance. Now, Pa, don't get all upset 'cause I said that." Harry looks toward his father at the head of the table.

Crowder chuckles as he replies, "Son, Ah cut my *boys'* hair. You're not a boy no more. You're a man in business now. Look as good as yuh can. That's all Ah'm gonna say."

"Thanks, Pa." Harry now asks Elsie who has taken her place at the other end of the table. "Ma, got any old stockings around here?"

"Stockings? Why I su'pose I do. Should have some in my ragbag." She always saves her stockings too torn to mend for polishing her wooden furniture and blackening the cast iron stoves, as well as the family's shoes. "Now what on earth do you want my old stockings for?"

"Can't explain, Ma. I'll just have to show you," Harry responds with a laugh.

Elsie scrounges through her ragbag, finally pulling out a stocking. "Found one. Here! This do?"

Harry accepts it from his mother's outstretched arm to examine. "Let's see now. Yes, I think so. Thanks, Ma." With his mother's sharp scissors he cuts the stocking as his friend had demonstrated. Cutting it off about eight inches from the wide part he allows the foot section to drop to the floor. And after tying a tight knot at the cut end he stretches his creation to snuggly fit on his head. "Look, Ma! This is what I wanted your old stocking for. To make a stocking cap!

His mother cannot help but laugh. "Why, I never! And why do you want to put that on top of your head for? You do look right silly, I must say! Hope you're not planning to go outside with that thingamajig on!" All the younger children are laughing now at the amusing sight of their eldest brother with a strange looking something covering his head.

"You'll see, Ma," Harry is laughing now, too, as he removes the object of amusement from his head. "You'll all just have to *wait 'n see*."

The very next evening soon after dusk Harry hesitantly knocks at the back door of the barbershop located on Wyoming Avenue. The young man is a bit leery, remembering that disastrous episode with the other barber. When a man opens the door Harry warily asks, "Sir, are you the barber?"

"Yep. That's me."

"A friend of mine told me that you'd cut my hair."

"That I will. Come on in, then." He directs Harry through the kitchen into the shop where shades are tightly drawn. As the barber lights a single kerosene lamp he instructs, "Take a seat right over here now." As Harry sits down in the barber's swivel chair he is about to get his first professional haircut.

When he arrives home his younger brothers all are quite impressed with Harry's new look. "Pa, can we go, too? Can we?" they plead. Their father replies with amusement, "Why, sure yuh can. When yuh earn *your* own money, jest like Harry." Even though they will not have the money for a professional haircut, the younger boys beg their mother anyway for her old stockings so they can mimic their oldest brother.

Soon around 828 there are *four* boys sporting stocking caps.

Years later in 1910, on one of his jaunts to Wilkes-Barre Chester brings home the *Recorder*, a black newspaper published in Indianapolis, Indiana. The Pullman porters on the trains oftentimes bring colored papers with them. Rosa is perusing the newspaper as she waits for the flat iron to heat. Today is Tuesday and with Jessie and her mother she is preparing to tackle the weekly ironing. To one side of the kitchen table Nyles has already strapped the extra leaf Elsie has dubbed her "ironing board."

Rosa is staring intently at a drawing of a colored man and a woman all bedecked in their finery, engaged in an energetic dance. "Hmmm? Interesting! Say, ever hear of a Cakewalk, Jessie?"

"A Cakewalk? What's that?"

"Here! Look! See for yourself." She hands the newspaper over to her sister, pointing to the article catching her interest. "It's talking about two people who won a Cakewalk contest. And this picture shows a man and a woman doing that kind of a dance, whatever it is. Doesn't look like anything I've ever seen."

These two young colored women born in northeastern Pennsylvania know nothing about the dance contests held many years ago on southern plantations. In fact this generation does not want to know anything about plantation life at all. The very word "plantation" stimulates in them feelings of bitterness and shame, conjuring up images of endless cotton and tobacco fields, cabins and "big houses," masters and overseers, whippings, lynchings, and rapes. This generation of blacks would like to forget altogether their slave heritage. They would like to think it never happened. To hear some tell it, their ancestors all had been free, had never been enslaved. The festering sore of slavery is still far too raw for the first freeborn generation. Therefore, they deal with it *by not dealing with it at all.*

Rosa and Jessie are not aware that the Cakewalk itself is a kind of dance contest, the best dancers always being awarded a piece of cake. They have no idea that the lively dance steps had originated in Mother Africa with later movements added, steps from the Irish jigs and reels slaves had observed their white folk dancing. Living in West Pittston, Pennsylvania, in total isolation from anything involving black culture, Rosa and Jessie are not cognizant that the Cakewalk has become an institution among colored people, danced at social events along with Ragtime and Dixieland. And never are they to hear such lively music until Harry purchases a Victrola for playing heavy 78-inch phonograph records.

Unable to solve the Cakewalk mystery, Rosa continues to peruse the newspaper. "Jessie! Mercy honest! Now will you just look at this!" Handing the newspaper over again to her younger sister, Rosa points out, "Read this right here, will you? It says that a colored woman named Madam C. J. Walker has become a millionaire. The first colored woman millionaire, at that. And you'll never guess how she did it!"

"How?"

"Why, would you believe from inventing special hair products just for colored women? It goes on to say here that the very first product she invented she called 'Wonderful Hair Grower.' And it says right here that it's guaranteed."

The Patience women do not need any such product to make their hair grow. If anything, they have too much of a bounty of thick curly hair as it is. Their problem is how to manage it so it is always neatly groomed.

"Now what's got you girls all in a dither about?" their mother inquires from the pantry where she is busily sprinkling and rolling starched white cottons, preparing them for the tedious task of ironing.

Jessie answers her mother. "Ma, this newspaper is saying that a colored woman makes some stuff that'll make colored women's hair grow. It's all got to do with keeping a healthy scalp, so she says. It says right here that in Indianapolis, Illinois…that's where she lives, you know, she's got a factory, a beauty salon and a training school, and all." As Jessie continues to read about

Madam C.J. Walker, she sighs wistfully, "What I wish, though, is that she'd make something that'd make my hair straight!"

"Well, does she?" Elsie asks. Even though she never has had such a concern because her hair already is straight, she understands what is behind her daughter's remark.

Jessie reads on. "No, she doesn't. But it does say that our hair can be straightened by the use of hot metal combs. They're being used in Madam C. J. Walker's salons, so it seems."

"Metal combs?" Rosa inquires. "What kind of combs are they? I've never heard of such a thing before."

"Have no idea," Jessie responds. Isolated as they are in northeastern Pennsylvania, these young women have no inkling of what is occurring in black communities, other than what they read in the colored newspapers. And so after she finishes reading the article concerning the wonderful Madam C. J. Walker, millionairess, Jessie refolds the newspaper, resigning herself to the fact that her thick curly locks will never be straight.

Ever since Florence's birth Elsie has been confronted with the problem of what to do with thick curly locks. The child had suffered so each time her hair had to be groomed. Then came three more tender-headed little girls with similar textured hair. Elsie knew how to plait so she parted each girl's thick mop down the middle and then across the top from side to side. She formed two front braids, subsequently plaited into the two back braids. Finally she would pin them together so they would not loosen while the girls were in school. And always a large colorful bow got added as a crowning touch.

Hair grooming at 828 took place on Saturday afternoons as had been Elsie's custom all of her life. Washing, drying, oiling, combing, and brushing those four heads was a real chore. Elsie had done her best by keeping the girls' hair neatly braided and beribboned and she insisted that Crowder cut their boys' hair in a short style, long before the white neighbor boys of the same ages had theirs cut. She just could not handle long hair on her boys, too, regardless of what custom dictated.

In the late 1800's and early 1900's photographs of colored women reveal very curly unbobbed hair neatly coiffured, often in a pompadour style with the aid of wire rolls called "rats." Some of those women with Native American or Caucasian heritage may have more manageable hair, not having the same problems of hair care as many of their "sisters."

Straight hair is associated with *white* women. Therefore, during this period of history, colored women perceive straight hair as being *good to have*. Hence the term "good hair" becomes part of colored terminology. And so straight hair is what many colored women crave.

Heretofore, colored women would apply some kind of grease to their hair in the attempt at achieving a degree of control over their thick curly hair. Early on it had been lard, in later years petroleum jelly or lanoline. After neatly knotting, rolling or braiding their hair, they often wore colorful head cloths during the week as they were going about their tasks. But on Sunday mornings they attired themselves in their "Sunday-go-to-meeting" clothes, strutting off to church, sporting the widest feathered or largest bowed hat they could afford.

This tradition is a carry-over from slavery days when the women worked for their white master during the week. They belonged to him and they did not care at all about their appearance while serving him. However, Sundays belonged to God. When they served that Master they dressed in their very best, so as to show the world their respect and love for Him.

Colored women in Wilkes-Barre and Scranton would "do" their own hair at home and as the years pass, some more enterprising women even set up businesses in their kitchens, catering there to family and friends. In the evenings after supper, these kitchens become lively spots for the camaraderie of women not welcome anywhere else. In these "home beauty parlors" products manufactured by Madam C. J. Walker find an enthusiastic market.

Living in Wilkes-Barre is a young colored girl, the hired companion of a semi-invalid white woman needing someone to push her around in a wheelchair. Another of the girl's duties is to wash and style her employer's hair. One day as she holds up a hand-mirror, so pleased with the end results, the woman asks the girl, "Say, have you ever considered becoming a hairdresser? You have such a knack."

"No, ma'am."

"Well, you should, I think. Why, you could start your own business right here in this neighborhood. I'll bet ladies would just love to come to a place where they can walk to, rather than having to go all the way up town, you know."

The girl indeed is interested and so relays this intriguing message to her parents. Her father replies, "Sounds like a fine idea, I'm sure, Child. But where do ya su'pose a colored girl like youz gonna get the trainin'?" He knows for certain that no white beauty parlor in Wilkes-Barre is going to apprentice *his* daughter. "And, besides, where ya think ya gonna get the money ta start a business with afterwards? Got any idea what's involved? And in a lily-white neighborhood like that? Uh, uh," her father concludes as he wags his head from side to side. "Ain't no way possible!"

The father justifiably is dubious knowing that colored people better not even be caught walking in that particular neighborhood unless they specifically were going to work for someone there in residence. And besides that, the father is certain he cannot help his daughter financially. His is a large family and he barely ekes out a living as it is as a gardener and handyman. And, besides, there are his younger children to clothe and feed.

Again the girl relays a message. This time back to her employer who agrees readily with the father. "Well, yes. I do have to say that he's right about one thing. I'm sure we won't find a beauty parlor here in Wilkes-Barre willing to train you." Undaunted by that revelation she continues trying to encourage the girl. "So what do you think about going to New York City? They say there's lots of colored people living there in an area of the city called Harlem. Surely, there must be somebody there who can teach you all you'll need to know about hairdressing."

"Maybe so, ma'am. I do have a sister who lives in New York, ya know. I'll ask her ta find out for me. She don't live in Harlem, though. She lives in Brooklyn. Maybe I could stay with her and go ta school," the girl responds with some degree of enthusiasm. But then she adds, "Even so, ma'am, there's no way for me ta start a business. My father don't have no money for nothin' like that."

"Well, tell you what. You just go get the training and I'll be glad to help you to get started. You can pay me back later when you start to earn some money." With apparent delight in her voice the woman adds, "I think this is a great idea, don't you?"

"You mean it fer real?"

"Of course I do. You have great potential. I can see that."

So the young colored girl travels by rail from Wilkes-Barre to New York City, the ticket being paid for by her benefactor. Going off to live temporarily with her sister and brother-in-law in Brooklyn. She lands her first job at the beauty parlor her sister frequents, there becoming the lowest person on a cosmetology parlor's totem pole. A shampoo girl. Tips from complimentary customers drop into her deep apron pockets. Positive comments abound. "That girl's got the greatest fingers. She really knows how to massage my scalp. She's the best."

When she finally is able to accumulate enough money to pay for her tuition, the girl from Wilkes-Barre begins her study of cosmetology to learn how to groom all types of hair. For instance, she is introduced to Madame C. J. Walker's products for colored women. Amazed by the astronomical amount of new information she must learn about the proper care of hair, nails, and skin, the young girl studies diligently. In time she earns the necessary diploma for displaying on the wall of that potential beauty shop. Returning home she takes back much valuable knowledge, as well as a newly acquired husband who is more than happy to leave the big noisy city in which he was born.

The girl's former employer has not forgotten the deal she made with her former employee. Encouraged by the frequent letters from New York, the woman is getting ready for the new beautician to set up her business. The woman insists she has not had a decent coiffure since her protégé had left town and so she is looking forward to once again surrendering herself to the girl's capable hands.

An empty storeroom suitable for a beauty shop has been located with an apartment upstairs as well. Upon presenting herself to her former employer the new hairdresser is directed, "Now you go on straight over there and look at it. Then come back and tell me what you think."

And that is how a young colored woman becomes a sought after beautician by white women living in Wilkes-Barre, Pennsylvania.

The business takes off like a rocket. There do not seem to be enough hours in the day. The young woman works alone, except for one of her young sisters she sometimes hires as a shampoo girl. Working by appointment only, she opens the doors of her shop in the morning at 9:00, generally closing the Venetian blinds by 7:00 in the evening. Then she and her husband sit down to the supper he so capably prepares.

A close friend is Jessie Patience from West Pittston. They were at a park with other friends one Sunday afternoon when Jessie, sick of tackling her own hair and of never ever being really satisfied with the results, asks her friend if she would "do" her hair in the Wilkes-Barre shop. The beautician hesitates a moment before replying, "You know I'd like to. But, Jessie, I can't have any colored customers. My white ones wouldn't come no more. You know how that is. I only have my business as it is because of them. And the lady who helped me in the first place? Well, I don't think she'd like it. In fact, I'm sure she wouldn't."

Jessie, although disappointed, certainly understands her friend's position. "Well, I guess I'll just have to keep on doing my own hair," she concludes with a shrug. She knows she can never get it to look as well styled as that of the women she has seen adorning the pages of the black newspaper.

However, the next day the beautician's mind is troubled. While she shampoos, rinses, hennas, towels, curls, and waves the hair of her white customers she thinks of the women in her own family and of friends like Jessie Patience. After a lengthy discussion with her husband, who has been supportive of his wife in every way from being electrician, plumber, carpenter, and accountant for the business, she develops a strategy. On Mondays she is going to close the shop earlier, six o'clock instead of seven. The sign "Closed" will go up in the front window. The Venetian blinds will be closed tightly and lights in the reception area extinguished. To all outside appearances the shop is closed for the night.

However, it is going to reopen again at seven o'clock when family and friends can knock surreptitiously on the door of the beauty parlor's back entrance. Traveling from Pittston by Laurel Line to the Northampton Street station in Wilkes-Barre, Jessie is met there by the beautician's husband. When his Model T Ford deposits her in front of the beauty parlor she climbs the steep side stairs to the top of the hill where the back entrance to the building is located. Opening the door, she sees one set of steps ascending to the apartment and another descending to the beauty parlor. The husband directs, "Go on down now, Jessie. She's waiting for you."

The beautician is busily tidying her shop. Washing brushes and combs, collecting towels and long capes to throw in the laundry, as well as miscellaneous other tasks. "Come on in, Jessie. Good to see you. Take a seat. Be with you in just one minute."

Retrieving a heavy ring of keys from her apron pocket, the beautician finds the one she needs to open a certain cabinet. In there she has stashed all of her "colored" necessities, keeping the cabinet locked at all times just in case one of her more inquisitive customers might happen to open it and ask, "What's all *this* stuff in here for?" Among other things hidden away from curious eyes, are Madame C. J. Walker's miraculous hair products. The very ones making her the first colored female millionaire.

And so now will commence the tedious ordeal of "doing" hair. For the colored woman who craves straight hair, it is much more than just shampooing and drying. No, for the colored woman who craves straight hair it will be an ordeal perhaps lasting up to perhaps *four or five hours*.

"Here, Jessie, now just take a seat at the sink and we'll get started." The beautician whisks a waterproof coverall around Jessie, fastening it at the neck "Now just lean back to the sink." Jessie gladly gives herself over to the soothing hands of her friend. "Be sure to tell me if I'm too rough now. Some of my customers are very tender headed, you know."

With her hair squeaky clean and wrapped in a large white towel, Jessie is guided away from the sink to a swivel chair. Thorough towel drying becomes the next step, taking a long time because Jessie's hair has never been cut. The beautician complains, "You got a lot of hair here, you know, Jessie. Sorry to say, but this is gonna take a while to dry." Naturally a garrulous person, as she rubs and rubs Jessie's thick hair briskly with a towel in order to eliminate all of the moisture, she and Jessie are "gabbing." This is what happens in beauty parlors, black or white. The "grapevine" is at it again.

When she is sure the hair is completely dry, the beautician is ready to begin the time consuming task of straightening. First she asks, though, "Jessie, how about you just let me cut a little of this hair off first?"

Jessie is hesitant. Not one of the girls in her family have even so much as *trimmed* her hair. Then again, none of them have been in the hands of a real beautician, either, is her reasoning before she answers, "All right. But not *too* much now, you hear!"

"Oh, never you fear, Jessie. I won't take off *too* much. Just enough. I promise you."

Jessie tries to relax. However, the sound of the sharp scissors clicking away induces her to look down. Masses of dark brown curly hair begin to cover the linoleum. Gazing at it in horror she wonders just what she has done, exclaiming, "Oh, no! But you said not *too* much!"

"That's right. That's exactly what I said. And I'm not going to cut off *too* much." The beautician chuckles as she attempts to reassure her friend. "I promised, didn't I? You just go on and relax now, Jessie Patience."

Jessie sighs deeply, attempting to relax, but she is worrying, *Wonder what Ma's gonna say?* She is thinking about how "bobbing" one's hair was the sign of a "modern woman," a term with negative connotation at this time in history. It went along with flappers' short skirts, stockings rolled at the knee, and the racy Charleston. It did not go along with Elsie's view of how her proper girls should look, no matter their age.

With the trimming completed the beautician is ready now to begin the tedious task of straightening Jessie's thick mop. First, though, she must rub an oily product into the hair. The steel straightening comb heating on the small electric hot plate should be ready by now. It cannot be too cool or the hair will not straighten. It cannot be too hot or the hair will singe.

While holding the straightening comb in one hand, with the other the beautician rubs a damp cloth across the comb. Sizzzz! An experienced beautician will know just how loud that sizzzz should be because the heat must be just right. An inexperienced beautician may burn not only the customer's *hair*, but her *skin* as well. Very meticulously the beautician separates strands of hair and with utmost care runs the hot comb through them. After pinning the straightened locks away from the rest, she repeats this over and over again until the whole head of hair has been straightened. The next step in this tedious process is the styling.

Curling irons had been used in Europe for centuries. White women in the United States with a desire for curly tendrils have been using curling irons for years. However, colored women with very tightly curled hair heretofore have had no use for the curling iron until now. Jessie's straightened hair has to be styled, so forming small curls all over her head is the next step.

After that there will be just one more task left before the beautician covers her finished creation with the almost invisible net essential for keeping the hair in place. With a waffled iron she creates neat rows of perfectly marcelled waves. When handing the mirror to Jessie for her approval, the beautician notices that the time is almost eleven o'clock. Four hours have passed.

The preening Jessie admires herself in the mirror, first from the front and then from the back as the smiling beautician holds up a second mirror. Jessie wants to believe that she looks just as glamorous as the photographs of the women she so admires in the black newspapers. Thinking of the long trip back home to West Pittston, she scrutinizes her friend's handiwork, deciding that it has been well worth all of the time it has taken.

By now it has become uncomfortably warm in the beauty parlor. With the front door and windows by necessity closed there is very little ventilation. The beautician has become overheated, mopping the perspiration streaming down her face. Jessie is very warm, too, but there is no recourse. There can be no evidence that a colored woman has been a customer in this all white bastion.

So suffer they must from the heat and the fumes of styling hair, a combination smell of the products used and of the heated hair itself. And so by keeping the door to her upstairs apartment open the beautician allows the high concentration of odors to diffuse in *that* particular direction and not out into the street where an observant neighbor just might be passing by.

By morning all evidence of the colored customer will have disappeared. However, just for certainty, on her electric hot plate the beautician boils a pot of water containing a strong mixture of the spices cinnamon, cloves, and nutmeg. Tuesday morning when the first customer swings opens the front door she sniffs, inquiring, "My, have we been baking *already* this morning?"

The smiling beautician pleasantly responds, "Good mornin', ma'am. And how are you this fine day? Been waiting for you. Come right along now," as she holds a protective waterproof cape ready to be fastened at the back of the customer's neck.

Chapter 30

Percy's Bully

*T*he sixth child of Elsie and Crowder Patience is a slight little fellow at six years of age. To the delight of his parents after a succession of three girls, another boy finally arrived. When Percy's turn comes for attending school he has his older sisters for company, not like Florence who had walked alone.

One afternoon, his arithmetic lesson not complete, Miss T tells him to remain after school in order to finish it. He is upset, knowing that his sisters will go on ahead of him if he is not out on time. Also he is upset because never before has he walked all the way home by himself. So after rushing to complete his "plus and take-away" problems he walks swiftly (No running in the halls!) to the outside wooden door much too heavy for such a small person to push open easily. Then he runs down the steep school steps. Rounding the corner he is able to spy his three sisters not too far ahead of him, moseying down Warren Street, heading toward Luzerne Avenue. They are chattering away, not mindful of *him* at all. Finally, when they reach the corner they pause long enough to turn around to make sure he is somewhere behind them.

The little boy is trudging as fast as his knickered short legs can carry him, but there is no way he can catch up with his sisters. They turn around once or twice more to check on him. Satisfied that he is not *too* far behind, they wave at him to hurry up. "Slow as molasses in January," they all agree. They watch him as he crosses the railroad tracks, being assured that the guard in the tower has not suddenly lowered the gates because a fast moving train with its vast number of coal cars is approaching. Then after that, the girls totally ignore him.

As Percy passes a property surrounded by tall privet hedges, a boy taller and heavier suddenly pops out, blocking the way. Percy knows him from their first-grade class. The boy is repeating the grade, not having been promoted last June. With solely Italian spoken at his home the boy is having difficulty learning English, making it impossible for him to keep up with his classmates. Out of frustration he forever is bullying the smaller children on the playground, especially those who can read well. Even though Percy is one of these, thus far he has been able to stay out of the bigger boy's "line of fire."

But not today. Walking alone, carrying his books by a strap and being totally ignored by his sisters, the smaller Percy is a likely target for the bigger bully. 'Well, ain'-a da little nigger. Walkin' all-a by hisself." He stretches his arms out wide to prevent Percy from passing. "Where-a you sisters, sissy?" The bully knows exactly where they are. He had seen them when they passed by a few minutes ago.

"Go-a cross-a da street! We don'-a want no niggers ova here on this side!" Snatching Percy's books right out of his hand the bully heaves them into the middle of Luzerne Avenue. Little Percy is in a state of fright. He knows he is much too small to fight the bully. Besides, he has never had to fight anyone before, even though his older brother Harry has warned him about some white people who will dislike him for no other reason than because he has brown skin. *That's what Pa says, too.* Percy cannot understand that. There is nobody he dislikes simply because his skin *is not* brown. At least there had not been until *today.*

Retrieving his books from the road, Percy cautiously crosses to the safety of the other side. Crossing to that side of Luzerne Avenue on which he lives, but where he is not supposed to be when he is coming home from school. The children have no reason to until they reach their own home, crossing then directly in front of where Elsie watches and waits by the front door. This is one of their mother's cardinal rules, set as if in stone. Her reasoning being, "Never know when a horse's gonna get spooked. Better to be safe than sorry. That's what I always say."

As the altercation between Percy and the bully is taking place, the sash of an upstairs window is flung up noisily. A white-haired woman leans her head out. "What's-a goin' on down there?" she yells. "Hey! You! Let-a that colored boy alone! Quit-a botherin' him or I'm-a gonna tell yer Mama!" she warns in her broken English. Then she continues her threat in rapid Italian. If the bully were planning any further trouble, the woman's intimidating words should be enough of a deterrent because he knows of her reputation for doing just what she says.

Percy's sisters have reached Damon Street, a block away from home, before they realize their brother is not right behind them. He should have caught up with them by now, they figure. With a worried tone Rosa tells Lillian and Jessie, "We better find out where he is!" Then after quickly retracing their steps the three girls soon are able to spy the forlorn little figure.

"There he is!" Rosa points at her little brother dejectedly walking on the *other* side of Luzerne Avenue. "What's he doing over there?" The girls all start running back down the hill towards him, the eldest sister Rosa in the lead.

After crossing Luzerne Avenue the three girls reach little Percy now standing perfectly still, tears sliding down his cheeks. "Why didn't you wait for me?" he plaintively asks.

The girls are feeling very guilty when Percy tells them what happened. They had not foreseen any trouble. Nobody had ever bothered them before. They had not heard of any trouble happening to the two oldest children in the family, Florence and Harry. How could they have known that today Percy was going to meet up with a bully?

"We're sorry, Percy. We're gonna be in trouble with Ma! We should'a waited for you. We gotta tell her what happened, you know," Rosa warns.

"No! No! Please don't tell her," the little boy pleads. "She'll think I'm a baby."

"You know we gotta tell her 'cause if she ever finds out somehow, we'll all be in *big* trouble. Ma always finds out about *everything*."

The girls know what being in *big trouble* with their mother entails. Elsie is well aware of which chore each of them detests the most and that will be the very one she will assign for punishment. For instance, not one of them wants to have to turn the compost pile with its rotting vegetable and fruit peelings, stinking eggshells, seeds and pulp decaying amid coffee grounds and tea leaves. Not one of them wants to have to empty all of the morning chamber pots or lime "Miss Jones," the outhouse. Not one of them wants to pluck the wet feathers or pull the bloody entrails out of the chickens decapitated for Sunday's dinner. All of these jobs are messy and/or smelly and no one wants to have to do them when they are not their assigned chore for the week. So, no, they do not want to be in trouble with their mother. Best be "up front" with their Ma.

Wondering why little Percy is so disheveled when he arrives home and disturbed as to why her children have disobeyed her by being on the wrong side of Luzerne Avenue, Elsie listens intently to what each of her four children have to say. Then dark brown eyes flashing with indignation, she throws her navy blue woolen cape around her shoulders and slaps a hat on her head "Girls, you stay here with Chester! Me'n Percy are just gonna see about this!"

Percy is certain *he* does not want to see about it, but his mother pulls him by his arm, the two of them retracing his recent trek up Luzerne Avenue. Down the hill to Fremont Street, they go into the corner butcher shop. Elsie is a familiar figure in that shop with its sawdust covered floor and sticky flypaper spiraling from the ceiling. Where hanging from hooks on the wall "dressed" chickens wait to be fetched by customers who had put in an order for them. Where on the floor stand barrels of green olives bobbing in their brine. Where ropes of garlic bulbs and dried hot red peppers hang.

Where for sale are long thick logs of provolone cheese, pepperoni, Genoa and hard salami, cappacola, bologna, mortadella, and olive loaves. Where glass cases hold highly seasoned Italian sausages, prosciutto for slicing paper-thin, mozzarella balls sitting in bowls of water and Romano and Parmesan cheeses waiting to be grated. Where freshly baked biscotti are displayed in a lidded glass container. And where a large walk-in icebox is filled with fresh meat awaiting the butcher's expertise. This is where Elsie usually purchases her meats such as beef and pork. However, she totally ignores all of the delicious smelling spicy Italian foods there, about which she knows nothing and has no desire to learn.

"Ah. Hallo, Mrs. Patience. And how-a you today?" greets the butcher speaking with a decided Italian accent. "And what-a I can get-a for you? A nice roast, maybe?" He regards her as one of his best customers, always transacting with hard cash, never putting anything on a running tab. Elsie does not believe in "credit."

"Thank you, but I'll just have to come back later. Right now I'm looking for a boy who's in my son's class at school." She is holding Percy tightly by the arm while conversing with the butcher. "This here's my boy, Percy." The man in his white apron and butcher's cap gives a friendly nod to the small boy who apparently is not in a happy frame of mind.

"You tell him that bully's name now, Percy!" Elsie prods. Percy reluctantly states the boy's name, but so softly the butcher has to ask him to repeat it. Yes, he knows where that particular family lives. Just down the street from his shop, in fact. Second house past the alley.

Still dragging her reluctant son along, Elsie hurries south towards Montgomery Avenue on Fremont Street. After crossing the alley they soon locate the small weathered gray clapboard house where the butcher said the boy lives. Treading up the three wooden slats serving as steps and onto the creaking porch Elsie rotates the manual doorbell. Answering the ring is a pretty dark-haired much younger woman with a head of lustrous hair even darker than Elsie's was before the silver streaks had appeared. In Italy some years before, an arranged marriage had taken place when the girl was but thirteen, her first child born the next year. The young mother is just about the same height as Elsie, but more slender, Elsie having become rounder with each successive pregnancy.

Surprised to find on her porch a stranger tightly holding the hand of a small brown boy, the woman turns to summon someone inside the house. Immediately emerging from the dim hallway is a pretty young girl very much resembling the woman. "Mama no speak-a da English," the girl tells Elsie. "I learn-a in school. Mama say, What-a you want, Lady?"

Elsie answers, "I'm Mrs. Patience and this is my son, Percy." She nods her head toward the small boy who is trying his best not to be seen. "Do you have a brother in the first grade?"

Now the girl is realizing that these two are here because of something her brother has done *again*. "Yes, Lady. My brother's in-a da first grade."

So Elsie slowly reiterates what had happened to Percy on his way home from school. All the while the young mother has been waiting patiently for her daughter to inform her as to why these two strangers have come to her door. Suddenly her dark eyes flash as her daughter interprets Elsie's angry words into Italian.

"Viene! Viene!" She motions them into the house. No longer smiling, now she, too, is angry.

The daughter escorts the strangers into the sparsely furnished parlor while her fuming mother goes hurriedly down the dim hall to the kitchen at the rear of the house. Elsie soon hears the creaking of a screen door followed by the sound of the mother's bellowing out her son's name. Elsie is very surprised that a woman so small can yell so loudly because she is not able to herself. Instead of summoning her children by her voice, she rings a small brass cowbell. When Crowder first had heard it his mind swiftly catapulted back to that large brass bell which regulated his work on the North Carolina plantation. The sound made him reflect, *That's one piece of metal Marse didn't give up durin' the war. No, Sir!* When Crowder, as Toby, had made his escape in 1863 from the sweet potato fields the large bell was still clanging as it hung from its post.

Two voices can now be heard conversing rapidly in Italian. Yanking her reluctant son by his ear the short mother enters the parlor. Still speaking forcefully, with her free hand she points to little Percy so frightened he is practically on top of Elsie who is sitting at the end of the couch. With the bully's head lowered a fallen flag of straight hair black as his mother's conceals his eyes as he is being interrogated. Then still speaking rapidly and forcefully his mother swats him out of the room.

Even though Elsie has no idea what actually has been said, she gets the gist. "What did your mother say?" she asks the boy's sister.

"Oh, Mama say, 'Ya jest wait-a yer Papa gets home.' That means my brother's gonna get-a da strap." Turning to Percy the girl assures him, "Don-na ya worry, little boy. My brother's not-a gonna bother ya no more."

"Good!" is Elsie's relieved response. When she and Percy arrive home she tells his three sisters not to worry because she is sure Percy is big enough to walk from school now by himself if need be.

Chapter 31

Three Patience Boys at a Minstrel Show

*T*en-year old Percy and eight-year old Chester are the two Patience brothers closest in age and so they are together most of the time. When Chester started to school Percy was the one walking him up the hill.

A classmate of Chester's is a member of a local church. The Patience children had been to Christmas and Easter activities held there, so when his friend invites Chester to another program he thinks he might like to attend.

"Pa, can I go to a program at my friend's church? It's this Saturday."

"Ma?" Crowder always checks with his wife before making a decision concerning the children, even though he expects always to be the *first* one approached.

"Did you ask Percy to go with you?" Elsie asks.

"No, ma'am. Not yet, but I will," Chester replies eagerly.

"No reason why you can't go. You can take Nyles along with you, too, then. Cost any money?"

"No, ma'am. My friend said that all I have ta do is put somethin' in the collection plate. As much as I want."

"Oh," said Elsie. "Well then. That's good." She reaches for a china sugar bowl set on a shelf low enough to be within her short arms' reach. Carefully removing its small top she fingers the contents. "Let's see now. Yes! Here's three pennies. One for each of you boys. That'll do it, I should think."

Early Saturday evening the three colored boys and their white friend enter the church's large fellowship hall where the stage is concealed by a burgundy velvet curtain fringed with gold tassels. Chester's friend asks his guests, "Where ya wanna sit?" The boys scrutinize the rows in order to determine where they might be able to get the best view.

Percy suggests, "Let's go down front so some big people don't get in front of us."

Already settled on the floor in the front are several children whom the boys recognize from school. *This is gonna be a fun night*! Chester is eagerly anticipating as he, too, takes a place on the floor next to little Nyles.

Soon the gaslights along the walls are dimming while behind the stage curtain a band is being struck up. The three colored boys have never heard any music such as this before. It is so lively and so *very* loud! Now the burgundy curtain slowly opens to reveal the source of the boisterous music.

The eyes of Percy, Chester, and Nyles widen in surprise as they behold a band composed entirely of "colored" men strumming guitars and banjos, even making musical sounds on washboards. Attired in loud red suits, enormous white bow ties, and round straw hats they are "colored men" with faces all the same shade. Jet black. Since they are wearing white gloves the boys are not able to determine the color of their hands.

Little Nyles jabs his brother on the arm and whispers, "Ain't they *strange* looking, Chester?" Chester whispers back, "Don't say 'ain't.' Ya know better than that. Yes, they sure are strange looking."

At that very instant from back stage a man with a face the very same shade as the others exuberantly bounces out. Opening his enormous white lips he shouts in his loudest voice, "Welcome! Welcome, ever'body! Ain't we glad tuh see yuh'all heah tuh night! Is we got's a show fuh yuh! So jes sit back an' enjoy da Uncle Tom Minstrels!" The gleeful audience laughs and claps in anticipation of the entertainment about to come. Chester's friend joins in, too. However, the three little colored boys are sitting in a state of utter bewilderment.

And they remain bewildered as act after act unfolds and as joke after joke is told with the receptive audience's laughing and clapping. It is quite enjoying the very loud singing and lively dancing by the "colored" men prancing up and down the stage, waving their round hats in the air. Chester, Percy and Nyles have no idea just who "Mr. Bones" is supposed to be when jokes are told about him. The boys really cannot understand what the men are even saying. *They* certainly have never heard any colored men talking or singing or acting like these.

Following the finale the curtain is closed. As the gaslights are being raised again, Chester's friend enthusiastically turns to ask his friends, "Well, how'd ya like it?"

"It was okay, I guess," Chester answers, not really knowing what to say. "But I'll tell ya this, though, I didn't understand what was so funny." Turning to his brothers he asks, "Did *you*?"

They reply in unison, "No!"

Chester's friend suggests then, "Say, why don't we go backstage? We'll ask my uncle. He's one of the actors, ya know."

"He is? Which one? I didn't see any white man up there," Chester replies in real surprise.

The boy laughs. "Why, they're all white, Silly."

"They are?"

"Sure. They jest *paint* their faces ta look like darkies."

Darkies? Percy thinks. *Chester's friend calls colored people "darkies?"*

"What's 'darkies'?" the younger Chester asks because this word is entirely new to him.

"Well, colored people, I su'pose."

"Ya mean like *us*?"

"No!" The boy is taken aback. "Of course not like *you!*

"Well, *we're* colored," replies Percy with indignation.

The young white boy is quite confused now. Not knowing exactly how to respond, he looks first at Percy and Nyles. Then over at Chester, his friend. He certainly is aware that their skin is darker than his is, but he has never related *them* to the black-faced caricatures he finds so hilarious on the stage. His thoughts are, *Why, Chester, Percy and Nyles can't be "darkies." They're my friends.*

So he continues to insist, "Come on now! Let's jest go back stage and ya can ask my uncle anything ya want ta know."

Percy insists to his younger brother, "No, Chester. We're goin' home now. We don't need ta ask his uncle nothin'. He was up there just makin' fun of us."

"No, he wasn't," protests Chester's friend attempting to explain. "That's jest how minstrel shows are!"

Chester argues, "Why're they puttin' that black stuff on their faces then? All they're doin' is jest makin' fun of colored people."

"No, they're *not*," his friend insists adamantly. "They're only tryin' ta be funny."

"That so? Well then. Why can't they be funny with their *own* faces?" Percy stubbornly asks.

"I don't know why. It's a minstrel show. That's the way they *always* do it." The little boy is about to be in tears now.

"Well, *I'm* never goin' ta go ta a *minstrel show* ever again. Not as long as I live!" Percy vows. Chester and Nyles concur.

When they arrive at 828 their mother is in the kitchen where she is darning holey socks by the light of a kerosene lamp. Crowder, supposedly keeping her company, is snoring loudly as he dozes in his favorite rocker. Since this is Saturday, bath night, the water is heating. Elsie is waiting for her three boys' return home. As soon as they open the kitchen door Elsie puts aside her mending, inquiring, "Have a good time, boys? How was the program?"

"It was okay," Chester answers, having no idea whatsoever how to explain to his mother what he and his brothers had just experienced. And he also has no intentions of explaining why they each still have a penny deep in their pockets.

Tintype (circa 1904)
Percy, Chester,
Lillian and Rosa

Chapter 32

Percy and the Breaker Boys

"Okay, boys. Let's get crackin'!" The foreman loudly hails all of the young breaker boys scattered around after completing their noon meal. "Come on over here, youz. We gonna get our picture taken." Then the professional photographer further adds his instructions, "Men in the back then, please. That's it. All right now. Next I'm gonna want all the littlest fellas right down front!"

The fidgety smaller eight and nine year olds having scrambled to secure their places in the front of the group gaze up expectedly into the camera. They compose a mosaic of small agile boys. Sicilians, Welsh, Irish, Czechs, Lithuanians, Polish, Slovaks, and Huns. Representing more diversity than any other place in the world, speaking perhaps twenty-five or more dialects, and at the end of the 19th century one out of every four workers in the Pennsylvania coal mines is a boy just like these.

Percy recently celebrated his fourteenth birthday when he had exchanged his boyhood knickers for manly long pants, certainly the correct attire for one whose school days are finished, and who now is a worker. He perches himself on a wooden railing, sitting just to the right of boys much younger, many never having seen inside a schoolroom. Several older men, unlit carbide lamps perched on the front of their hats, pose on either side and in the rear. One father proudly drapes his arm over the shoulder of his young son.

"Hold still then!" the photographer instructs as he sets up his equipment. "Gotta get this right now." His head suddenly disappears beneath the black cloth concealing a camera securely perched upon a tripod. Adjusting his equipment always requires time and patience. The normally active little boys are finding it very hard to remain still.

Flash! The photograph finally has been taken. The photographer pokes his smiling face from beneath the black cloth and dismisses the group with, "Very good. That's it! All finished." Almost in unison the boys heave sighs of relief.

The somber looking grimy faces of those young breaker boys being exploited in the name of King Coal have been permanently fixed in time. Looking at the photograph, future generations will ponder over what life must have been like for these immigrant children who were put to work long before the passage of child labor laws. Even afterwards, these laws flagrantly will be ignored by many since the mine owners are in need of their workers, and parents desperately are in need of the daily wages from their sons, some even as young as six and seven.

*<u>Percy Patience</u> sitting on rail left of younger
breaker boys (circa 1901)*

As had those unfeeling plantation owners of the South, mine owners of the North demand continuous supplies of cheap labor. The large immigrant families from Europe seem to have little difficulty in sending son after son to the breakers where they labor six days a week, ten hours each day. And just as the plantation overseer had been, the mine foreman is not reticent about using his rod for keeping up productivity. Most of the boys in the photograph are illiterate and doomed to remain so for the remainder of their lives, not like the more fortunate Percy who is able to read and write. Their niche in the scheme of things is to put their wages into their mothers' hands, that money so desperately needed to supplement the family's income.

However, their duration in the breaker may not be long because abject poverty shortens many a young life. Subsisting in company owned communities called "patches" built in the shadow of mine collieries, crowded into dilapidated shanties having few amenities, often forced to share communal water supplies and privies, these boys are bound sooner or later to catch one of the fatal communicable diseases so prevalent at the time. Smallpox, diphtheria, influenza, pneumonia, or tuberculosis.

Abounding also in this young malnourished population, rickets stunts growth and bows legs while scurvy bleeds gums and loosens teeth. However, with proper nutrition these are preventable vitamin-deficiency diseases. In gardens protected by locked fences constructed from tall unevenly cut wooden planks, mothers attempt growing fresh vegetables, especially potatoes and cabbage, converted to sauerkraut for keeping the family from starving over the winter. Much of the land, however, is not very arable, just being a very thin layer of topsoil filled with jagged rocks. And the weather in the Valley is quite fickle with its flooding one year and drought the next two or three.

Each of the more than 300 company "patches" in the Valley generally is composed of people of the same ethnic group who share a common history, language, culture, and religion. Greater Pittston, for instance, has several such patches. Some have outlandish appellations like Hamtown, Frogtown, and Mudtown. while others are more conservatively named: Stark, Brown, Oregon, and Port Griffith.

Often in these patch towns are Catholic churches are built where Masses are celebrated in the European language of the parishioners, vital to their survival in this strange new world. Unfortunately, though, due to those same language and cultural differences, serious animosities have been known to develop between the various ethnics with some never quite disappearing from the Valley even after all share a common language.

For instance, in later years a Polish girl from Pittston is going to fall in love with an Italian boy from Exeter. Both college educated. Both having high aspirations for the future. Both accepted by each other's parents. Both Catholic. An ideal relationship, it seems, until the girl asks her parish priest to officiate her marriage.

"Of course! Of course! I'd be delighted! He's from our parish then, your young man?"

"No, Father. He's not."

"He's *Catholic*, of course?"

"Oh, yes, Father. Of course he's Catholic. But, no, you don't know him. He's from Exeter."

"Oh! All right then. Now do you have a date in mind?"

"Yes, Father. In June."

"Fine. Fine. Now let me just put your names in my book." He jots down the name of the girl whom he knows. "And now, what's your young man's name?"

When the priest hears the Italian name his face turns bright red as if he were suffering from apoplexy. "You're not planning to marry an *Italian*?" he exclaimed with derision in his voice.

She is taken aback. "Why, yes, Father. He's Italian. What difference does that make? He's Catholic. Isn't that what's most important?"

The priest answers adamantly, "I won't marry you to any *Italian*! No, I'm afraid you can't be married in *this* church. Why, this is a *Polish* church!"

Fortunately, the priest of the fiance's parish in Exeter has no qualms about marrying a couple with different ethnic backgrounds. "This is America," *he* says as he blesses the marriage.

In the Valley generation after generation will continue to identify themselves by the country of their ancestors, perpetuating separatism rather than embracing their commonality as Americans. Even in 2001 descendants of the Europeain immigrants who came to work in the coal mines still call themselves Irish, or Italian, or Welsh, or Lithuanian, or Polish.

One early fall afternoon Crowder is sent to a particular company patch to deliver a wagonload of surplus food donated from the Carpenter farms. A supply of leftover tomatoes and lettuce from what he had delivered to Scranton restaurants the day before. The route north over the mountains to that city, the third largest in Pennsylvania, has become so familiar to him and his horses that after a long wearying day he will take a snooze on the floor of his wagon, allowing his trusted team to safely take him home. And not until they arrive safely back at the Carpenter barn will he awaken.

The instructions given to him on this day are, "Drop the food at the church then. Somebody there'll know what ta do with it." As he drives for the very first time into this particular patch, Crowder is musing to himself, *Now if this don't put me in remembrance of the cabins!* His mind suddenly shifts, catapulting him back to the two rows of dilapidated weathered cabins on the North Carolina plantation.

Got two rows here, too, facing each other. Only thing, these houses are doubles with two doors instead of one like Aunt Cassie's cabin had.. Got a downstairs and a upstairs, though. Seems like there's some red paint left on some of them. Must'a been painted the same red once jest like the Carpenter barns, he is noticing, as his team pulls the wagon along the bumpy road. *These houses got porches, though. Even got windows with glass,* he further observes. *No glass coverin' Aunt Cassie's windows.* Suddenly his eyes shift up ahead to a formidable house painted white with dark green shutters. It sits at the very end of the road, a short distance from his destination, the church. *Sure does remind me of the "big house." Now Ah wonder who lives there? Probably some kind'a boss, is what Ah'm figurin'.*

From an open doorway a weary looking young woman watches an unusual sight. That of a dark brown man slowly guiding his team of horses in the direction of the church. Even with yapping dogs running wild, Crowder has no difficulty controlling his team up the dusty road. Hailing from Europe most of the inhabitants of the patches have never seen a colored man before. Perhaps a brief glimpse on the docks of New York where their ship had disembarked, but not up close. A thin small child clings protectivly to his mother's long skirt and a hungry looking "babe in arms," thumb in mouth, stares out of round eyes. The woman's own eyes are filled with curiosity. Crowder's are filled with pity, as politely he tips his hat "good day."

Crowder's observations are quite correct. Some patches indeed do resemble the old slave quarters he so vividly remembers. Some memories just never go away. However, no one else would discern the comparison except someone like Crowder who has seen both. He is seeing the same dingy weather beaten buildings. The same two rows facing each other across an unpaved dusty road. The same wooden slats serving as front steps. The same crowded quarters with sometimes as many as twenty persons vying for their own space, including boarding unmarried men not allowed to rent a house for themselves. The same necessity for sleeping on floors. And finally, the same kind of a "big house" overlooking it all, the fine abode of the mine boss or supervisor.

Far from their native lands, these European immigrants who had come here seeking a Utopia instead have been enslaved by a system of paternalism. *Their* master? The coal company! For many miners are compelled to live in *company* houses in *company* patches. Then coerced into purchasing all their necessities from the *company* store, including powder and fuses always sold at inflated prices, of course. Required to pay a fee for medical care from the *company* doctor (whether they ever have use of his services or not) and for spiritual care from the *company* approved priest or pastor (whether they ever go to church or not). Even after all the debts they have incurred since the last payday get deducted from their wages, the miners find that *still* they are owing. They never have enough money. They never have enough of anything, *except debt and hopelessness.*

There is no escaping, for most cannot speak the English language and even for those who can, their accents easily identify their place of origin. When they do make an attempt at escape they are confronted with signs stating, "No Irish Need Apply." Like on southern plantations where the rules were made by the masters, here the coal barons make them. As in the South where those rules got enforced by overseers; here they get enforced by the Coal and Iron Police, generally brawny German Protestants from the Pennsylvania Dutch communities. And just as the overseers in the South had felt for the slaves, these police, too, have great disdain for the "foreigners," using any excuse just to exert their authority, even to forcing themselves into the workers' homes.

In Exeter Township on the outskirts of the borough of West Pittston north toward the country area called Harding is a different kind of patch. Not a company patch. It is not connected to any coal colliery, simply a cluster of houses on either side of a road paralleling the highway, just a short distance west of it. This patch is dominated by the presence of the large Slocum mansion whose residents are related to Frances Slocum who at the age of five had been abducted by a Delaware tribe. Not until sixty years later would her brothers be able to locate her. They had made a promise to their mother that they would never give up the search for their sister, and they had not. When finally discovered in Indiana Frances was the widow of a Miami chief, having no desire to leave the family she had established in the West. Eventually, though, her two families were able to meet, developing a lasting relationship.

In addition to the mansion there are other houses in the patch, many having been built and sold by the Slocum family. Here several ethnic groups are managing to live together in relative peace because everyone minds his or her own business. Something much easier to do here than in the enclaves where families may be closely related. Where the reasoning is that everything happening is everybody else's business.

Along the river and close to the patch is one of the Carpenters' farms with its large steamy glass enclosed greenhouses. Here Jesse and Isaac grow vegetables for selling to restaurants. One of Crowder's many jobs is tending to the boilers providing the controlled supply of warmth and moisture for developing plants. Each day as his team pulls the wagon onto the road leading to the barn where the furnaces are located, he expects to see a small boy, a neighbor of the Carpenter's, waiting on the side of the road. Waiting to hear the rumbling of the wagon. Waiting to spy the horses noisily clopping up the bumpy dirt road. Waiting for his daily ride. Waiting for the anticipated invitation, "Hop on, young fella." And that same boy even in the year 2001 will still remember the kindly white haired driver, Crowder Patience.

In this particular patch a small white clapboard chapel has been erected so Protestant families might have a place nearby for worship services, rather than having to walk the long distance to the West Pittston churches. These people share their common beliefs at Slocum's Chapel where oftentimes can be heard the voices of people from Wales who have a long tradition of vocalizing and harmonizing. However, they have no preacher and they have no money to "call" one. Happily, a solution is found when a dedicated member of the First Presbyterian Church of West Pittston agrees to conduct Sunday School at the Chapel on the Sabbath afternoons.

Slocum's Patch is much different from the company patches where abject poverty is central. Rather it is a place where young boys are not forced into the mines to become breaker boys. Instead they walk the six miles south each day to and from their schools in Exeter Borough. Slocum's Patch is a place where fathers are not necessarily miners, many employed in other less dangerous occupations such as railroad workers. It is a place where families are able to thrive.

Before the future building of a dam at Harrisburg prevents the migration of fish, boys from Slocum's Patch on lazy summer days can be found on the Susquehanna River bank. From there they fish for shad near the ferry crossing where the eel racks are placed. Or after crossing the Coxton Bridge to the railroad yards on the eastern side of the Susquehanna, they often climb the steep mountain to Campbell's Ledge, a spot named for Thomas Campbell, the poet who had penned "Gertrude of Wyoming." From the pinnacle of that mountain guarding the Susquehanna River's northern entrance into the Valley, the patch boys can look directly down on the heart-shaped Scovill's Island where Crowder drives his wagon onto the raft-ferry carrying Carpenter workers over to cultivate the land there. Or on hot summer days carefree young boys may be found swimming the Susquehanna as they shout warnings to each other. "Watch out for the deeps!"

It seems that just about every year one of them loses his life in that area of treacherous deep whirling water including Crowder's twelve-year old grandson, Harry Brazier Glover. He drowns there while from the bank his older brother Walter helplessly watches in horror.

Just like the plantation's clanging bell, the colliery's high pitched shrieking whistle signals each workday's beginning and end. Very early in the morning at its insistence males of all ages, carrying their tin lunch pails, pour out through shanty doorways. The older men, unlit carbide lanterns attached to their hats, are clothed in denim coveralls, never to be really clean again no matter how hard the wives scrub. Young boys traipse along behind their fathers and older brothers. Trudging heavy footed into another day of staying alive hundreds of feet below ground, husbands are leaving behind their wives, each knowing there is the possibility of the whistle's emitting three continuous shrieks unexpectedly during that day, meaning only one thing. An accident at the mines! Perhaps changing one of those wives into a widow.

Young Percy trudges along, too, in his hob-nailed shoes, making his way to the Exeter breaker, that ugly monstrosity of a skyscraper, its towering silhouette disrupting the beauty of the once spectacular Pennsylvania landscape. The breakers are man-made specters intent on raping the land of its thick stands of stately oaks and tall pines to propagate huge ugly black mountains of culm (debris from the mine).

Now dotting the horizons throughout the Valley, etched in black against the sky, stand many dingy looming breakers. Risen like phoenixes as if overnight, prompting an out-spoken guest to remark to her wealthy hostess, "My Dear, the Valley certainly has changed since last I visited here, and, I must add, not for the better, either. All of those *ugly* mine buildings are seen *everywhere* now. And those terrible black mountains of dirt all over the place!" She gives a little shivery shrug of her expensively draped shoulders, concluding with, "Ugh!"

Piqued by her visitor's honest observations, the coal baron's wife as she carefully pours cold lemonade into her best Waterford crystal stemware retorts, "I guess that is just the price we have to pay for all of *this*." She gestures haughtily at her most recently acquired possession--the capacious new home her husband has built on "Coal Baron's Row" in Wilkes-Barre.

On this sultry August afternoon the two matrons while hoping to catch some cool breezes are relaxing in the recessed shade of the wide front porch facing the Susquehanna River. Designed by a New York architect, the mansion is an ornate High Victorian Gothic, a blue-gray tinted brownstone built from rocks mined in a place called Nanticoke, just south of Wilkes-Barre, rocks called Wyoming Bluestone. And this house is only one of the very ostentatious homes being erected in the city by the *nouveau riche,* each trying his best to outdo the other.

Until blasted by dynamite the shiny anthracite coal lies in underground veins, some as thick as twenty-six feet. Each day (except Sunday) large chunks get blasted from the bowels of the earth. In darkness lit only by the feeble light from his carbide lamp set on his cap, the experienced miner drills holes in the seams, strategically sets his sticks of dynamite before loudly warning, "Fire in the hole!" as he swiftly abandons the site.

In earlier times the miners would return carrying a caged canary. Its little lungs immediately could detect the deadly odorless methane gas oftentimes unlocked from the coal seams. If the bird kept on with its chirping, the men would continue to the hole. But if the canary fell dead, the men immediately turned back. Now in these more modern times upon returning to the hole the miner carries a Davey lamp from England for detecting noxious gases called "damps," perhaps derived from the German word *dampft* meaning vapor or smoke. Since methane gas is so highly flammable, if present the lamp's flame will burn high. In contrast if carbon dioxide is present rather than oxygen, the flame will become very low or even extinguished.

Young Percy Patience is far from content in his job, that of breaker-boy. By now he has come to the conclusion that all aspects of coal mining are very dangerous. However, he feels that this is the only work available to him. For a long time now he has known he does not want to work on a farm like his father. He has no intentions of becoming a chauffeur like his brothers-in-law, Glover and Lee. Other colored men in town are gardeners and handymen. Therefore, as his brother Harry had done before him, Percy has come to work at the colliery where the pay is good compared to any other jobs available to him.

Very quickly, however, he has come to the realization this is not where he wants to spend the rest of *his* life. It is not as though his parents have encouraged his working at the colliery. Quite to the contrary. And although he knows Harry wants him to work in the shop on Bond Street, Percy believes himself old enough now to make his own decisions. Anyway, he does not want to rely on his older brother. However, he is beginning to wonder if he has done the right thing.

As a breaker boy, the lowest rung of anthracite employment, Percy's job is to hutch precariously for ten hours at a time over a narrow steam controlled iron chute propelling fast-moving chunks of coal downward. They had been carried up to the towering breaker where young boys sit in wait. Using his feet to dam the coal temporarily into a storage pocket, Percy's job, as well as that of all other breaker boys, is to separate the unburnable rock and dull black slate from the burnable shiny black anthracite. Lying in wait at the bottom of the slanted iron chutes are dangerous grinding teeth for grading the coal into the desired sizes. For instance, pea coal is the size generally used in homes. There are other sizes as well, *barley* the smallest and egg the largest.

No machine is capable of performing the breaker boys' exacting work. Not allowed ever to wear gloves, with finger tips bleeding until they callous over, Percy like all of the boys must sit painfully cramped in a box-like compartment, each astride his own individual chute. He was in for quite a surprise on his first day of work. "Hey, Percy Patience, that-a you? It's-a me!" he had heard being shouted. "Ya workin' here now, too?"

The voice behind the neckerchief protecting his nose and mouth from the clouds of coal dust belonged to Percy's old nemesis--the bully of first grade. Percy had not laid eyes on the Italian boy since he had been forced to drop out of school years before when his thirty-three-year old father permanently was disabled by falling rock, no longer able then to trudge off to the mines. With apparent delight the boy welcomed his former classmate Percy, all past animosities long ago forgotten.

"Come-a ova here. Sit-a by me," he shouted in his "broken" English as he bade Percy to the empty seat at the chute right next to his. Percy was having great difficulty hearing the boy over the din. The grumbling machinery was so loud many boys plugged their ears with bits of clay or string rolled into small balls.

"Dose-a udder guys? Don-a speak-a da Englese so good. Not-a like me. See dat guy ova dere? He's Welsh. He can-a if he want-a, but da others? Nah! Now listen-a here, *paesano*! Ya gotta watch. All-a da time ya gotta watch! Know what-a I mean? *Capisce*?" This was the experienced boy's advice being given to the "greenhorn."

Yes, Percy was listening intently, knowing exactly what the boy meant. He was thinking about his brother Harry whose arm had been caught in a conveyor sending up iron chutes large chunks to be deposited in waiting coal cars. To the slightly built young Percy all the monstrous noisy machinery looked hazardous indeed.

The other boy continued his shouting. "Jest keep-a ya eyes open all-a da time! Don'-a get sleepy! Da guy where yer sittin' now? Close-a his eyes! Fell! Way down-a dere!" He pointed downward. Down to where the giant teeth crush the coal, and anything else coming their way. "Dat-a guy? He get-a hurt real bad. He no come-a back here no more."

Fatal and near fatal accidents abound among these little boys. Perhaps due to lack of sleep in their noisy crowded shanties. Perhaps from seldom having enough to eat resulting in the ravages of anemia and beri-beri, weakening both bodies and minds. Or perhaps the tragic little figures simply peter out.

Percy could see how he would need to be extra careful. He could see how easy it would be for small boys to lose their balance, pitching forward into the steam powered mechanical chutes. He had no idea, though, what happens to the mangled little dead bodies. He did not know they got toted home in burlap sacks. Then dumped unceremoniously on the front porches. Left for their screaming mothers to find.

"Aw-right already! Get ta work now!" The foreman pointedly slapped his stick in his palm as he passed by the new boy.

Breaker Boys sitting over iron chutes (circa 1899)
Courtesy of the Anthracite Heritage Museum.
Scranton, Pa.

By the middle of the 19th century the coal lands are completely monopolized by a handful of powerful companies whose tight fists of greed breed lawlessness, even unto murder. Intolerable mine conditions spawn the uprising of militants such as the "Molly Maguires," calling themselves after a woman militant back in Ireland. In Schuylkill County south of West Pittston violence (assaults, robberies, murders) heighten. And all this blamed on the Mollies. Finally, in 1887 on the 21st of June four men proclaiming their innocence right up to the end are hanged in Mauch Chunk (Jim Thorpe, Pennsylvania) for crimes attributed to that organization of Irishmen. That infamous "Black Thursday" will go down in history forever as "Pennsylvania's Day of the Rope."

So finally after determining violence is not going to be the answer to their problems, Irish workers in desperation turn to the struggling labor unions which heretofore they had ignored. *Maybe this might be the answer then,* they are hoping.

The political climate around the mines has never been a healthy one. Controversies always have existed between Democrats and Whigs, exploiting employers and exploited employees, Catholics and Protestants. And especially between the diverse ethnic groups who absolutely have no desire to understand each other, Welsh and Irish being two of them, harboring strong feelings of animosity. Foremost is the experience that the miners from Wales have over the farmers from Ireland, the latter often the "last hired and the first fired." The Welsh usually are allocated the better positions, from boss to miner, thereby allowing them to live in far superior conditions than the Irish. Also the Welsh are "teetotalers," highly intolerant of those with opposite views about alcohol. And most are very anti-Catholic.

However, now in order to be able to solve their mutual problems the mineworkers must learn that they all have to be of one accord. Their petty differences will have to set aside. "United we stand," will have to become their way of thinking. Certainly not an easy task here in the anthracite coalfields of northeastern Pennsylvania.

Working for and being paid by skilled miners, laborers earn their money neither by the hour nor by the day, but rather by the *weight of coal in their cars.* The men are aware that sometimes they are cheated by the company inspectors' weighing. However, they have no way of proving it. Years before when Percy's older brother Harry was working as a laborer at the Exeter Colliery, he had overheard bitter gripes being vented by two Welshmen. They had stopped midday to eat their lunches from their tin pails.

One man was complaining bitterly, "Lots a things ain't fair 'round here, that's fer sure. Here we are slavin' ten hours a day and the bosses jest sittin' in those big houses'a theirs gettin' fatter'n richer by the day, they are. Ain't fair. Jest ain't fair, I say."

With hands streaked with blue scars of coal dust set permanently under his pale skin seldom seen by the sun, he was opening his tin lunch pail to assess what his wife had put in there that day. "Cheese again! Ugh! That's all we can afford nowadays. Cheese! No meat all week!"

He took big bites of his sandwich with the intent of saving the last chunk for the large beady-eyed rats scurrying around waiting for the bits deliberately left by the miners. The men did not mind sharing their lunch with the animals. In fact some had even become rather tame, being given pet names by the miners. In their symbiotic relationship the men have little fear of the rats and visa versa. As indicators of danger they are very important to the men. The rats' acute hearing and keen sense of smell cause them instinctively to abandon an area long before humans can detect any of the dangerous rumblings or noxious "damps" capable of killing a man in mere seconds.

The other miner responded, "And it's the God's honest truth, I'm telling ya. Last pay I give the wife was shorter than the time before. Can't prove nothin', though. But I know I got cheated."

"Yeah. Yeah. I believe ya. Same thing happened ta me, it did. The wife sez ta me, 'And where's the rest then?' Thinks I stopped by the beer garden first. Wouldn't believe me when I told her that's all I got."

"And another thing," the first miner continued, "my brother.... Ya know him. The one that works over at the other shaft. Well, anyway, he wanted ta compare my pay with his 'cause he can't understand why one week he gets one amount. And then another week he's short, he sez. Wanted ta know if the same thing was happenin' ta me. Every day him'n me come ta work at the same time and leave at the same time. Same amount'a work, he does. But ya know what? Sometimes his pay's more than mine. Sometimes mine's more than his. Tis the God's honest truth. And ya know why, don't ya?"

Harry, intently listening to the conversation between the two miners, was certainly interested in knowing why, since he had no one at all with whom to compare wages. His pay varied from payday to payday, too, sometimes considerably. Once when he had asked about it he sharply was dismissed with, "Ya oughta be glad fer what ya got." He had not been, but he had no one to discuss it with because the men in knowing that a lot of unfairness abounded all were very "close-mouthed" about their wages. No man was willing to be the one to "rock the boat." So Harry waited patiently to hear the Welshman's answer.

"Yeah, I know why. Too much junk comin' up. Not enough *good* coal, the inspector sez. Well, I think he's lyin'. He's jest dockin' us ta put more money in the boss's pockets, the crook. And I'll be willin' ta bet some of it goes in his, too. That's what I'm thinkin'."

"That's the God's honest truth now. Hit the nail right on the head, ya did. Well, I don't think that should matter, how much we bring up. We all work hard every day. Same hours'n all, *everybody*. So we should be gettin' the *same* pay then. And besides that, we should have *our* own men doin' the weighin'."

"I'm with ya on that. But what are *we* gonna do about it then?"

"Don't know, but we gotta do somethin' about it soon. Now that's what I'm thinkin'. And very soon." With these words, the miner prepared to return to his work, but not until he threw the last of his lunch to the waiting beady-eyed rat sitting at the miner's feet. "Here ya are, Lucky!" And Lucky went scurrying away happily to eat his lunch in peace.

It is a fact that the quality of coal varies from shaft to shaft and due to the amount of unusable debris of slate and rocks, one laborer may fill half the number of cars, each holding from five to six tons, as another man working just as hard. And during the same grueling time period. Now with the docking on the *increase* and the pay on the *decrease*, the men finally agree that it is time to do something about it. So on September 10, 1897 the spark igniting the acceptance of the here-to-fore unpopular organization of unions flares up in a small town called Lattimer. Near Hazelton high in the mountains south of Wilkes-Barre. Here in an effort to gain better wages as well as improved working conditions dissatisfied workers make an attempt to close the local mine.

They feel that the coal barons are not in the least bit concerned with the frequent mine car accidents or dynamite explosions causing roofs to cave in, raining down life-threatening rocks on the workers. Rightly so, they feel the coal barons are not in the least bit concerned with the frequent fires caused by flammable methane or with the undetectable body numbing "black damp," that insidious gas capable of making a young man *old* long before his time.

And so a bitter confrontation takes place between approximately 300 workers and a posse of eighty-seven armed men loyal to the coal barons. Tragically, its ending is a massacre with thirty-two killed and many others wounded. And to "add insult to injury," even though the members of the posse are tried in a court of law, *all are acquitted* on the grounds that no one knows who actually fired the *first* shot! Now outraged by the injustice of it all, large numbers of mine workers flock to the United Mine Workers Union.

Steadily tensions accelerate during the next five years until nearly 150,000 mine workers finally are united enough *to declare a strike*. United in agreeing not to go to the pits, or to the breakers, or to the collieries. United in agreeing to put aside ethnic animosities for the good of them all. United in agreeing to abide by the Coal Miners Union. And so the Great Strike of 1902 begins.

A list of demands is presented to the stubborn owners. The mineworkers want a 20% wage increase, bi-weekly pay instead of monthly and an eight-hour day instead of ten. They want also a minimum weighing scale using the *legal* ton of 2000 pounds instead of what the owners have been calling a *ton* (changed whenever they please). Most importantly, they want their *own* inspectors to judge the amount of impurities deducted from their loads. It is purely guess work, anyway. And so they feel it is far better having their own men doing the guessing then.

The incensed coal barons retaliate as is expected. "Starve, then, fools. You, *and* your families," is their uncompromising response to the demands of their workers. "And don't think you're going to steal coal from our culm banks, either." So at those ugly black hummocks of mine slag armed guards are posted, forcing weary miners' wives and their starving children to leave as they came, with burlap bags still empty. Forcing them desperately and dangerously to run along railroad tracks as overloaded coal cars rumble past, praying that some precious chunks will drop to the ground. Forcing them to lie down at night both cold and hungry.

As further proof of their omnipotence the company owners begin evicting workers and their families from their homes, dilapidated *company* shacks in crowded *company* patches. Sometimes at the supper hour just when the striking men have sat down for whatever meager food their anxious wives have been able to scrounge. Sometimes in the middle of the night when with the butts of their rifles the sheriff accompanied by the Coal and Iron Police pound on doors. Or sometimes early in the morning even before the crowing of the roosters, pitching all of the family's possessions into the street and then nailing all the doors and windows shut. And always as a warning to the others, "You jest might be next!"

Attempting to offer encouragement to their stalwart husbands, the women, even while tearfully gazing into the pinched-faces of their hungry little children, say, "Youz gotta fight. God'll see us through. Don't youz go back now. Somehow we gonna get by." Daily Masses are filled with the shawl and babushka bowed heads of women on their knees, fervently praying as they finger their Rosary beads.

Finally the adamant coal barons are forced to listen to the loud voice of the Union. For in 1902 Theodore Roosevelt, president of the United States, arranges a meeting with the feisty young John Mitchell, president of the United Mineworkers and the stubborn owners of the coalmines. For the first time in United States history the Federal Government intervenes in a labor dispute. And in the end the two opposing sides agree to abide by the findings of the Anthracite Commission.

Also the workers are returning to work with a 10% pay raise increase, only half as much as they had actually requested, but satisfactory because it had not been over *wages* they were striking. It had been over their *working conditions* and so they are pleased to return to the mines with an eight-hour workday, a sliding wage scale, a legal ton, and their own inspectors.

Now climbing up the ladder of opportunity in the coal mining industry are breaker boys who have reached seventeen years of age, aspiring to work inside the pits as mule boys. Former mule boys are old enough to be elevated to laborers and former laborers to be trained as miners. However, none of these jobs are the aspirations of young Percy Patience.

At the beginning of the 1902 strike he had gone down to Harry's shop on Bond Street, remaining there for several years before traveling south along the Susquehanna to look for employment in Milton. From there he brings back to West Pittston his wife, Mary Adams, to rear their family

Percy's first child, __Ruth__ (circa 1910)

<u>Percy Patience</u>, 6th child of Crowder and
Elsie
(circa 1910)

Decades later in another state, the grandson of a man who had labored as a breaker boy engages in a discussion with one of Crowder's descendants. Both have emigrated from small Pennsylvania coal towns. Both have obtained college educations and now both have ended up being employed at the same place.

The man boasts proudly, "My family pulled themselves up by their bootstraps. Just take a look at all of the European immigrants who passed penniless through Ellis Island. They couldn't speak a word of English and look what *they've* done for themselves. I just can't understand why the colored people can't do the same thing."

In an entirely different conversation and on another day he will relate how after he received his college degree he had determined the need to change his long European name to a shorter anglicized version. Having been rejected by several potential employers, he suspected it might be because of his name. Although no one had said so, he knew "the score." His very first teaching position, therefore, was at a place where he readily was accepted with his fair complexion, blonde hair, blue eyes, and *new name*.

No amount of discussion ever will make him understand that unlike those Europeans who passed the welcoming Statue of Liberty on their way to Ellis Island, the human products of slavery have no "boots" to *put* on, let alone "bootstraps" for *pulling up*. He can not be made to understand that his "boots" are his Caucasian features, most notably his white skin. Yes, *he* pulled *himself* up by *his* "bootstraps" simply by *changing his name and moving to a new locale*.

Crowder's descendant will not have the requisite "boots" in 1958 when after college graduation she is refused a position on Long Island because, according to the school board, "the town is just not ready for a colored teacher."

Chapter 33

Chester the Student

Lillian and Jessie always have been the readers in the family. That is, until their younger brother Chester outdistances them. He, too, is an avid reader, seldom found without a book in his hand.

"Where's Chester?" Elsie may call.

"Out back. Under the pear tree, reading." This is the standard answer given by one or another of his siblings.

"Well, he needs finishing up his chores first!" His mother will then declare.

Just what does Chester read? Taking turns with his sisters, he enjoys reading to his parents various passages from the Bible, as well as news from the *Pittston Gazette* as he scours through the pages in order to learn about local and world events. When he frequents Wilkes-Barre or Scranton he may obtain a colored publication brought into the area by Pullman porters working on the railroad. Perhaps the *Pittsburgh Courier* or the *Indianapolis Recorder*.

In one of those newspapers he has discovered a column especially interesting to him. Entitled "Did You Know?" it always presents an interesting colored personage. From it Chester has learned about such men as Elijah McCoy with his lubricating cap invention and Benjamin Banneker, a surveyor who had helped lay out Washington, D.C. He read about Dr. Daniel Hale Williams who performed the first successful heart operation in 1893. He learned of Lewis Howard Latimer, a pioneer in electricity, and Granville T. Woods credited for inventing the electric traffic light and railway telegraph system.

Crowder's interest was piqued once when Chester read about George F. Munroe, a stagecoach driver capable of controlling six horses at a time. In 1879 he had been chosen to drive Gen. Ulysses Grant on a twenty-six mile perilous serpentine California mountain-road. Then years later he drove two other presidents, James A. Garfield and Rutherford B. Hayes, up into Yosemite.

"Say, Pa," Chester offers one day as he is engrossed in the paper. "Here's something you'll really be interested in. It's about the Civil War." Chester knows that his father is always interested in anything having to do with the war in which he had served.

So Crowder is "all ears" as his son begins to read about a black man from Pottsville, a town sixty-seven miles south of West Pittston. "The newspaper says, Pa, that a colored man from Pennsylvania was the first person to shed his blood during the Civil War."

"Hmm. That so? And jest whereabouts was that?

"Let's see now." Chester begins to read about the colored man, Nicholas Biddle, who had settled in Pottsville prior to the Civil War. As a means of earning a living he vended oysters during the winter and ice cream during the summer. A runaway slave, he happened to bear the same name as a wealthy Delaware financier who may or may not have been his owner. No one could say for sure, because no one knew anything about the colored man at all.

Chester thinks, *Sounds just like Pa, too. We can't get anything out of him, either. He just says, "Son, that's all done and forgotten now."* Chester reads on to discover that Biddle had become an orderly to Captain James Wren of the Washington Artillerists. At the age of sixty-five Biddle accompanied the captain as he left Pottsville on the way to protect Washington, D.C. from Rebel threat when the Civil War had erupted. After all, the capitol was in the South, originally having been parceled from both the loyal Maryland and the seceded Virginia. Dangerously, they were only a mere river's crossing from each other.

First the artillerists from Pottsville traveled to Harrisburg, joining with additional Pennsylvania militia. Then on to Baltimore, Maryland, arriving there on April 18, 1861. Although not allowed to be a *bona fide* soldier, Biddle, proudly clad in a blue uniform, strode along behind the regiment on the streets of Baltimore, Maryland. Since there were no trains directly connecting the North with Washington at that time, the 530 Pennsylvanians had been forced to go on foot from one Baltimore railroad depot to another in order to board a train heading south.

Perhaps just the sight of the blue-clad Union soldiers smartly marching through their city was despicable enough to trigger the ire of angry pro-secessionists along the route. Or perhaps what did it was what to them the *most* despicable sight of all, a colored man wearing the blue uniform of the North. Whatever it was caused bricks to be hurled, one hitting Nicolas Biddle squarely on the forehead, thereby, earning him the distinction of being the first person to shed blood during the Civil War.

When Chester reached that point of the article, his father seemed quite surprised. "That happened after the Rebs fired on Fort Sumter down there in South Carolina," he mused. "Would'a thought somebody's blood must'a got spilled *there*."

"Don't know, Pa," Chester replied, not of the realization that no one had been injured at Fort Sumter. "I only know what this newspaper says."

"Umm. So then, does it say what happened tuh the man after the war?"

"Yes, it does say here that he died in 1876. A poor man without any family. According to this, it seems that generous townspeople raised enough money to bury him in the colored cemetery next to the Bethel AME Church in Pottsville so he wouldn't end up in a "potter's field." That's where paupers get buried, Pa, you know."

"Paupers?" his father asks. "What's paupers, Son?"

"Well, that's what folks are called who don't have any money or any family to see to giving them a decent funeral."

Crowder replies sympathetically, "Ah! That's too bad he didn't have no family." Then he thinks about his own wife and children. *Ah 'm sure a lucky man compared tuh that poor fella Nicolas Biddle.*

Chester also reads in the colored newspapers about the tenacious eloquent orator Frederick Douglass, developing a great admiration for that runaway slave, who, just as Chester's father, had followed his dreams. Likewise, also from those newspapers he has gleaned information about the highly controversial views between the southern educator Booker T. Washington and the northern sociologist William E. B. Du Bois.

He would like to be able to read their books, *Up from Slavery* and *The Souls of Black Folk.* Chester is puzzled over something he has read, about what Booker T. had said when responding to a querying man in North Carolina.

"Professor Washington," the man had asked. "Just what do you propose should be done to allay the present conflict between the races?"

"Colored people should join the Democratic Party," was the professor's prompt answer.

Chester ponders, *Why the Democratic Party? We're Republicans in this house. At least that's what Pa and Harry say we are.* That is, the men of the family are. His mother and his sisters can not vote simply because they are women, the 19th Amendment not having been passed yet. His father maintains that he is a Republican because Abraham Lincoln was. "Didn't he free us?" Like the majority of colored people, Crowder believes that President Abraham Lincoln fought the Civil War with the express purpose of freeing the slaves. And, so, this is the reason for his picture's being displayed prominently on a wall in 828's kitchen.

Seems Booker T. Washington doesn't care at all about which was Abraham Lincoln's party. Well, someday I'm going to find out just why he said that, Chester determines. To Chester another point of interest concerning Booker Taliferro Washington is what he has to say about "entitles." He maintains that being free is an entitlement to possess *two* names, and also a *third*, if one chooses. What amazes Chester the most is that William Edward Burghard Du Bois has four!

Elsie and Crowder had not given any of their children middle names. Perhaps they had never thought to since they themselves had but two with Crowder's having only one when he was the slave boy, Toby. And so the Patience offspring are free to choose their own middle names, if they so wish. Chester has chosen "Douglas" after the orator he so admires.

Not in all of Wyoming Valley can be found a library having on its shelf books dealing with the issues of colored people. So it is impossible for young Chester to read any such material at this time of his life. The only book found on a shelf of the West Pittston Library is Harriet Beecher Stowe's popular novel, *Uncle Tom's Cabin*. Certainly not containing the information he is seeking. So at this time in his life he must depend upon suggestions offered by his white schoolmarms as to what books he might be reading, his favorites being those penned by Charles Dickens.

Once again the newspaper column has featured a colored man from the Civil War period. "Pa, today they're talking about a slave named Robert Smalls. It says here that he stole a ship right from under the Rebels' noses."

Crowder certainly is interested in learning about this particular man. "Yuh don't say now? From right under their noses? Now how'd he get tuh do that?"

"Let's see. Oh, yes. Here it is. It seems that it took place in the Charleston Harbor right near Fort Sumter, Pa."

"Yuh know, Son, that's right where the war started. Down there in South Carolina."

This fact Chester had learned from his history books, but he had never learned about Robert Smalls and his daring escape from slavery. Now he is reading about him in a colored newspaper. What he is learning is that the daring Smalls had escaped by stealing the Confederate *Planter*, formerly a cotton boat. Having worked on boats most of his young life, he knew exactly how to sail one.

Listening intently, Crowder is learning yet about another man who, like himself, had dreamed of freedom. Another man who, like himself, had plotted and planned until he was able to make his dream a reality. And just like Crowder, Robert Smalls had to wait patiently for just the opportune moment. It came one night when the captain of the *Planter* and his two mates decided to sleep on shore instead of on the boat.

Smalls had been waiting for just such an eventuality. Carrying sixteen hidden escaping slaves including Smalls' wife and children, the *Planter* put out to sea. Casually, not hurrying which surely would have attracted attention. Carefully running the gauntlet of Charleston harbor posts. Saluting with the expected toot of the steam whistle. Standing on the deck, the recognizable wide straw hat of the captain pulled down in order to conceal his face, Robert Smalls with folded arms posed as the captain. And the *Planter* successfully passed by the formidable Fort Sumter. Out into the open sea. On to freedom!

As a large white bed sheet was being hoisted, the rejoicing runaways then came pouring out of their hiding places on the boat. Steadily sailing towards the surprised Yankees was a vessel about to change ownership. One moment Confederate, the next Union. Robert Smalls was given a monetary reward, half the value of the *Planter*. Afterwards he became a valuable source of information for the Union navy. And after the war during the short-lived Reconstruction he became one of eight colored representatives to Congress from South Carolina.

After Chester has finished reading about Robert Smalls, Crowder comments, "Well now. That was one special man, Ah must say."

"No more special than you, Pa," responds Chester who has great admiration for his father and for the myriad of men and women who had used whatever means necessary to be free. Crowder had shared little about his life as a slave, but all of his children know that he had been a runaway who had joined the Union Army in order to be free. Every year they wave to their father from the sidelines as he proudly marches with other veterans in the annual West Pittston Declaration Day parade.

All of Crowder and Elsie's girls complete the 8th grade and during this period of time in this region where most people are poor and children have to work, that is a great accomplishment. Thanks to their father's lifelong affiliation with the Carpenter family, the Patience girls never have to help provide for the family. None of them ever will have to "keep house" for white ladies in town; neither will they have to go into the Wyoming Valley Knitting Mills on Delaware Avenue, if indeed they would have been hired due to the color of their skin.

What the girls do after completing the 8th grade is to help their Ma at home, for a woman's lot at the end of the 19th century is to stay at home with her parents. That is, until a suitable husband comes along. And if he never materializes, she forever is destined to live in her parents' home.

There certainly is plenty to accomplish each and every day. Besides doing the usual "women's work" around the house, the youngest daughter Jessie assists Florence with her dress making business. Lillian takes over most of the cooking. Rosa toils in her garden, tending to her vegetables and flowers. And all of them assist Florence and Elsie-Harry with their babies. The Patience girls have no further educational aspirations, simply because they are not familiar with any woman who ever has. That is, except for their schoolmarms, all of whom are white, having no educational advice for colored girls living isolated in northeastern Pennsylvania.

Their brother Harry, too, completed the 8th grade, later making a success of his unique coal carving business, hiring his three younger brothers when he got backed up with orders. For a very short while Percy had been a breaker boy in the colliery, but Chester has no intentions ever of following in those footsteps.

Nyles, the last of the boys, "the handsome one," as his sisters are fond of calling him, does not keep "his nose in the books" like his older brother Chester. No, the more sociable Nyles prefers playing with his friends. Marbles is his game and his leather pouch of alleys has become quite heavy. After school he has to be forced to sit at the dining room table to do his homework. Like his mother he is left-handed. He, too, as the poor boy the corporal's wife had heard about, has been forced to hold his pencil in his right hand. To him the *wrong* hand. Fortunately, though, unlike the tragic boy in the story told to Elsie long ago by the corporal's wife, Nyles does not stutter. Even so, he does not enjoy going to school, except to play marbles during recess.

However, Chester excels in his schoolwork. Now, reading by the light of the kerosene lamp in the kitchen, are three huddled figures attempting to keep warm after the fires have been banked for the night.

Jessie's husband, Nathaniel Garrett, after recognizing Chester's academic abilities is filling the boy's head with dreams of going to college. "Got to finish high school first, though," Nat has told him, "and then you can go down to Howard University in Washington."

Such a dream! No one in this family even has gone on to high school. Eventually, all eight Patience children will complete the 8th grade, though, *the end* for the majority of students in West Pittston. This is the most to which Crowder and Elsie have aspired for their children. But now one of them wants to continue on to high school, and then to go to *college!*

Elsie had been born in Washington, D.C., so said the Dillsburg lawyer and his wife. "It's far away from here," they had told her. And it is also far from the little borough of West Pittston in more than distance, since the nation's capitol now has become an educational center for people of color. Established there is an academic Mecca, uniquely supported by the United States

Government. Initially, Howard University had been instituted in 1867 to educate the fruits of the South's "peculiar institution"—young colored people. Now some forty years later its doors are open to all youths including Native Americans, as well as whites.

As the first member of the Patience family to complete secondary school, Chester graduates in the West Pittston High School class of 1910. A special program honoring the colored graduates in Wyoming Valley is to be held at the Bethel AME Church on South Washington Street in Wilkes-Barre. Orations will be delivered by a number of the area's colored graduates, as well as by several visiting Howard University students.

Chester's family boards the Wilkes-Barre Railway trolley in West Pittston in order to be in attendance when he delivers his oration. Entitled "The Patriotism of the Negro," he includes his father's having served in the 103rd Pennsylvania Volunteers during the Civil War. How proud Elsie and Crowder are of their son who is fulfilling even *more* than the dreams they had for their children, that of simply learning how to read, write, and cipher.

Working for Harry in the coal carving business after school, on weekends, and during the summer months has provided Chester with the necessary funds to begin his freshman year at Howard University. He realizes, however, the necessity of finding a job in Washington, D.C. Going to college requires a sizable amount of money and his father has little to spare.

Brother-in-law Nat Garrett warns the boy that things in D.C. are not at all like they are up here in West Pittston. Chester has read in the colored newspapers about lynchings, burnings, and other injustices being levied on colored folk down South. So certainly he is not naïve.

"Now ya gotta watch yaself all the time down there, I'm tellin' ya," Nat warns him. "Up here ya can sometimes forget you're colored. But down there? Ya better not, *ever!*"

With a fly swatter in one hand Elsie has been chasing round the kitchen. She is trying to keep up with the conversation between her boy and her son-in-law, but since she had served boiled cabbage for supper, when the screen door opened, several uninvited and unwelcome guests had been attracted by the odor. Three large buzzing horseflies. Elsie is trying to pay attention to what the two males are discussing because she is not so sure in the first place about Chester's going away. However, she realizes that by his doing so he can become more than just a farmer, coal miner, waiter, handyman, or chauffeur, the only options open here to a colored boy.

"And just what do you mean by that, Nat?" she queries as she gives one of the flies a fatal swat. The others fly away indignantly, buzzing even the louder. Elsie is watching intently for one to land again.

"I mean, Ma, they got *rules* down there. 'Colored Codes,' is what they call them. Colored folks can't do this. Colored folks can't do that. Always got to watch where ya go and what you do."

"Never heard such nonsense!" Elsie is muttering as she delivers a fatal blow to another of the unlucky intruders.

Nat is talking about what he *knows*. What he himself had experienced growing up in the nation's capitol. "We can't ride on streetcars with the white folks. No, they got streetcars just for us. Goin' the same places, mind ya. Can't drink at their water fountains or use their toilets. Got those just for us, too, when they're workin'. Can't eat in any of their restaurants or stay in their hotels.

"Can't try on clothes in the stores and don't think about puttin' a hat on your head to see if ya like it. 'Cause if ya do, ya gotta buy it then, whether ya want to or not. And why, would ya know, in a shoe store ya gotta go in the back way and then ya gotta sit behind a screen so the white customers up front can't see ya? They'll let ya try on some of the shoes. I imagine they put some aside back there just for us. Lucky if ya can find your right size, though.

"And Chester, another thing, ya wouldn't be allowed to go to school with any of your white friends like ya do up here. They got schools down here just for us. 'Separate, but equal,' so the white folks say. I have my doubts, though."

If he were aware he might continue his litany by informing Chester he could bleed to death following an accident since if the nearest hospital were "For Whites Only" he would not be admitted. Nat is unaware, too, that certain cities like Mobile, Alabama have a curfew for "coloreds." He has no idea that in Birmingham it is against the law for colored and white even to play a game of checkers together. But what he does tell Chester is enough for Elsie to question, "Son, are you sure that's what you want to do? Go down there with all that funny business going on?"

"Yes, I gotta go, Ma. This is my chance. And I promise I'll be careful."

Nat reassures, "Don't worry, Ma. He'll be all right." Then turning to Chester he says, "That is, if he just don't go down there thinkin' he's *white*."

Chester is taken aback. "White? What'd you mean by that, Nat? I know I'm not white. I certainly can see myself in the mirror."

"It's not your *looks* I'm talkin' about, Chester. No, it's your *attitude*. You're gonna have to learn how colored folks survive. We are who we are *with each other*. But we survive in this world by bein' like that little lizard they call a chameleon. Saw one at a carnival sideshow once. It was green at first, but when they put it on somethin' yellow, why would ya believe? That little critter turned yellow! And when they put it on somethin' gray or brown? Turned those colors, too. Just like that!" He snaps his fingers for emphasis.

"Now that's what I mean about us colored folks. We gotta be able to *change*, too, when it's necessary. And we gotta know just when that is."

"Don't worry about me. I'll be all right. I'm sure of it," Chester retorts with confidence.

"Just one last piece of advice. Heed this now, Chester! When ya get off the train at Union Station, be sure to go out the 'colored' door."

"'Colored' door? What color?"

Nat laughs heartily. "See, boy, you're in trouble already. Told ya there are things down there just for us colored folks. Listen here now. You've got to look for the door with a sign sayin' 'Colored.' Then when ya get outside look for a taxi that reads 'Colored.' Just tell the driver....He'll be colored, too, naturally, that ya want to go to Howard University. Now ya got all that?"

Chester nods, "Yes."

"All right then!" Nat continues, "And I su'pose next you'll be wonderin' what color the water will be comin' out of the 'Colored' water faucet."

"Okay! Okay, Nat! Got your point," Chester laughs. His mother, however, does not see the humor in the situation because now she really has cause to worry about her boy's leaving home. And so the final fly gets all the brunt of her concern.

"And, oh, lest I forget," Nat says. "Be sure to bring me a bag of grits when ya come home."

Chester looks puzzled. "Grits? What's that?"

Now Nat is really laughing heartily. He answers Chester's question with, "Oh, don't worry about it. You'll know soon enough."

Following his graduation from Howard University in 1914, Chester returns to West Pittston to reside for a short time, bringing back a wife, the former Edna Lucas, after which time Chester Douglas Jr. and Bernice Lee will be born.

**Chester Douglas Patience, 7th child of
Crowder and Elsie Patience
(circa 1920)**

Sisters-in-law:
***Rosa Lee & Edna
Lucas Patience
(circa 1929)***

Chapter 34

Nyles the Youngest Child

"*A* child's not su'posed to go before his Pa'n Ma! He's just not!" This is Elsie's heartrending lament as she stares down into the open coffin of her youngest child, "handsome Nyles," his sisters fondly call him. Indeed he is handsome, even now laid out in the crisp white uniform of his lodge, the Knights of Phythias.

Being the youngest in the family had not been easy for the boy. Especially when there were four bossy older sisters. *Ma just lets them run "the show,"* he resentfully had felt. Just too many women in his life, telling him what to do all of the time!

"Nyles, stop!" "Nyles, go!" "Nyles, do!" "Nyles, don't."

So as often as possible he would escape to his brother Harry's shop, but young Nyles did not relish getting dirty. Coal carving certainly did require that. And Harry would not let him just sit around doing nothing constructive like simply playing marbles or tossing a ball to his little nephews. No, there was always some task for the youngest brother to do. Nyles readily admitted that Harry's gleaming coal novelties were quite beautiful, but he never wanted to be any part of the process.

"So, Little Brother, what do you want to do with your life?" Harry had asked one day as Nyles was polishing a coal paperweight. He did not mind polishing. It was not a dirty job.

Dreamily, the boy had answered. "Well, for one thing, I want to go some place where there's *more to do.*"

Certainly more to do than working on a farm. More to do than getting covered with coal dust in his brother's shop. More to do than going down in the mines or chauffeuring rich folk. More to do than being a gardener or a handyman. He wants to go to a place where there are more opportunities for an ambitious young colored man like himself. That is what he meant by finding a place with more to do.

"Off to a big city then, huh? That's what you're meaning to do?" Harry queried. He would like to be off to a big city, too. Just to visit, though, because his coal carving business was there in West Pittston. This was the only thing he knew how to do, and he was very good at it.

"Yep. Maybe New York or Philadelphia. Or maybe even down to Washington with Chester."

Harry smiled at that. "Well now. You know Chester's down there studying. That's what you're planning to do, too?" knowing full well that Nyles did not enjoy being "in the books."

Nyles had a difficult time in school. His schoolmarms always complained about his penmanship. "Nyles, now you *know* you can write better than this!" He did not *know* any such thing. They forever were bringing up what beautiful handwriting the *other* Patience children had.

On his very first day of school when he was holding his pencil in his left hand, immediately he had been corrected. "No! No! Nyles Patience, hold your pencil in your *other* hand! We all write with our *right* hands. Our *right* hand is our *right* hand." The teacher smiled at her own levity as she faced the blackboard to draw strings of circles and rows of up and down strokes. "You see, *this* is the way we have to do it." *This* was backwards to Nyles. Never was he going be comfortable writing with his right hand and never would *his* handwriting be called beautiful. In fact it was barely legible. And when in the 3rd grade he was introduced to dipping a pen into an inkpot, his papers were all speckled with black blotches. So, no, school was not a place he liked to be.

He answered his brother's question with, "Don't know just yet where I want to go, but I'll be sure to tell you when I do."

"Fair enough. Just don't be in a hurry, though."

The winter of Nyles' ninth year was one of the coldest ever experienced in the Valley. The Susquehanna was frozen solid due to temperatures low as sixteen degrees below zero. The river had become a solid sheet of ice, extending from the Ferry Bridge (Jenkins Bridge) to the head of the Wintermoot Island in Exeter just south of West Pittston. One Saturday in February, bundled up like everyone else, the two youngest Patience boys took to the ice along with a myriad of muffed ladies and gloved gentlemen. And children of all ages swarmed the ice for a delightful day of skating.

Nyles later exclaimed to his mother, "Ma! There must have been a thousand people out there today!" When he and Chester had reached home, cold and damp, their mother was concerned about their possibly getting a bed confining "chill." So first thing she ordered, "Now you just shuck off those wet clothes and sit yourselves over there by the stove. I'll fix you a nice hot cup of cambric tea to warm your entrails."

Earlier in the day people had been having such a grand time on the ice that they were disappointed to have to go home when the sun set around four-thirty. Especially Nyles commented, "Sure wish they'd find a way to have lights out here. Then we could skate all night long!"

"Ha! Lights out here? That's impossible! What a dreamer, you are, Nyles!" the older Chester had retorted.

Since around 1888 West Pittston had been using electric lights. Nyles had seen them illuminating Wyoming Avenue. He continued wondering then, "So, if they can be used there to light the streets, why can't they be here on the river bank?"

Now if Chester were to be granted a wish about where to put some electric lights, he would want them in his Ma's kitchen so he might read longer in the evenings. Because darkness arrived so early in the wintertime, Elsie expected her children to be in bed by seven o'clock. With electricity in the house she would not have to be calling down every night through the register in the kitchen ceiling, "Outen that lamp now, Chester. You're gonna ruin your eyes." He did not dare verbalize his thoughts about his sister Rosa's having to wear spectacles. *Not because she's up late reading, either.* Of course he kept those disrespectful thoughts to himself. He knew that his mother would not go to sleep until he blew out the kerosene lamp, afraid he might nod off and accidentally knock it over. Not until 1940 will electricity reach 828, long after Chester had left home.

During the frigid winter of Nyles' fifteenth year he learned that a local company was looking for workers to hand saw large chunks of ice to be harvested from the river, packed with peat moss, and then stored in icehouses. Some of those storage sites were simply caves dug out of the sides of mountains, from which during the warm months icemen would procure their supplies for delivery to homes.

Elsie had a wooden zinc lined icebox sitting on her back porch. The top was shallow, intended for very short periods of storage with a bottom roomy enough to accommodate a large chunk of ice. She set the hands on a clock-like card hanging in her front window so the iceman might know just how large a chunk she wanted to have delivered.

Initially enthusiastic Nyles applied for the ice-harvesting job, but very soon he was telling himself, *This work is too hard.* Much harder work than he had ever done before. The navy blue woolen scarf, knitted by his sister Florence, was wrapped protectively around his face, a cap of the same color covering his head and ears. Under his cap his ears were stuffed with wads of cotton as he hoped to avoid the painful earaches he had been prone to since childhood and his mother's home-remedy of blowing in his ears no longer did the trick. Also he wore, not one, but two pairs of thick woolen gloves intended to protect his freezing hands. In spite of all those precautions his hands and feet still developed painful chilblains from the intense cold.

Harry's shop on Bond Street was not nearly as cold as on the river, Nyles soon realized. A cast iron pot bellied stove provided some heat in Harry's "office," as the anteroom was called, but inside the shop proper there was no heat. Nyles had been mighty cold in there, too, but at least he had been sheltered from the wind's frigid breath.

"Go on out and warm yourself by the stove," Harry would tell his younger brother, whose heart, he knew, was not in the coal carving business. But the riverbank provided no such place for getting warm, except by standing near open metal barrels containing fires where shivering men huddled, trying to revive their frozen fingers and toes.

Not only was this job rife with discomfort, it was also a treacherous one. Nyles heard what had happened in 1875 when the thick ice had thawed prematurely, suddenly cracking into gigantic floes pushing up onto the banks, sweeping away anything and everything in their paths--fields, houses, chicken coops, and even large barns. The floes had carried away the two bridges crossing the Susquehanna connecting Pittston with West Pittston, making it impossible for anyone to get across the river except by rowboat, a very dangerous undertaking indeed until the life threatening floes had totally melted.

The sole year Nyles worked as a harvester of ice, people were praying not to have an early spring so such a catastrophe would not repeat itself. Due to the unusual thickness of the ice they were fearful of a devastating premature thaw like that one they so vividly remembered in '75. It seemed that the faithful, although not always reliable harbinger of spring, the groundhog Punxsutawney Phil, had pulled his head out of his Pennsylvania burrow just long enough to be scared by his shadow on February 2nd. He promptly returned to his long winter's nap for yet another six weeks, so "they say." Maybe then all may be well, the more superstitious people were hoping.

Ice chunks needed to be sized uniformly in order to comply with icebox capacity. That year was exceptionally good for the ice harvesting business because the river had frozen so solidly ice could be cut to the desired twelve inches deep before being stored in the icehouses. The river had frozen so solidly the workers were confident it could hold them as well as all of their equipment. There was no doubt in their minds that it would hold the teams of horses pulling the scrapers necessary for clearing the river's surface before the actual harvesting could begin. And since the temperatures were so low they believed there was little danger of that sudden thawing which with no warning could cause the teams and their drivers suddenly to plunge into the freezing water.

Fortunately, there were no catastrophes that winter because the continuous frigid temperatures did keep the river frozen, fingers and toes as well. Nyles right away had come to the realization that kind of work was not for him, either. No, he needed to find something more suited to his *personality*. By now he most definitely knew it was not harvesting ice from the river. And so when he was discussing this dilemma with his oldest brother, Harry remembered that the last time he purchased a supply of wire for his jewelry from Coursen's Hardware "over town" in Pittston, he had noticed a sign in the window announcing, "Help Wanted." "Might be worth looking into," he had suggested to Nyles. "Just tell them that you're my brother.

And so the next day Nyles pedaled his Rambler bicycle "over town" to Pittston to find that the job was his just for the asking. That is, after he said who he was. "Oh, so you're Harry Patience's brother? A fine gentleman, he is. Makes beautiful things out of coal. And so, young man, are you a hard worker like your brother?" *Nyles* considered himself to be a hard worker, even though his brother Harry might not agree. He was certain he would be a *very* hard worker *if* and *when* he found a job he really liked. So he answered, "Yes, sir. That I am."

"So then. Can you start tomorrow morning?"

"Yes, sir."

At the hardware store Nyles became a "Jack-of-all-trades." In other words, he did it all. From waiting on the customers to sweeping up after hours. *Long* hours. Far too long, for far too little pay. So it did not take much for him to realize he did not like this job, either. No, this was not at all what he wanted to be doing and certainly not for the rest of his life.

By that time Nyles was feeling the urge to leave the Valley in order to find work *suited to his personality*. At first his father had found his youngest son's attitude bewildering. "Suited tuh his personality? Now, what do yuh suppose he means by that?" he asked Elsie. "A man does what he has tuh do. These young folk jest expect everything tuh be handed tuh them. Don't understand them at all." After a while he began to think, though, that perhaps he had done exactly the same thing when he had not wanted to be a coachman. He had wanted to be a farmer, one working *just with horses*, no less. *Guess that's what Nyles means*, he had concluded.

A young colored friend of Nyles' hailing from Scranton had migrated to Rochester, New York where he was boarding with relatives. In a letter extolling the merits of *his* job of bell boy at a fashionable hotel there, he wrote, "Come on up here and give it a try. This is a great city to live in."

Nyles knew nothing at all about Rochester, being unaware of its reputation as a liberal minded city. For during the years before the Civil War, this city, conveniently located near the Canadian border, had served as the last stop on the Underground Railroad. Numerous "safe-houses" had been arranged there for fugitive slaves and with generous members of the community donating food and clothing. Even Frederick Douglass's own home near Highland Park had been one such station.

Leaving home was not going to be as easy as Nyles had thought. He never before had been anywhere more distant than Wilkes-Barre or Scranton. Now he was about to emerge from the cocoon of this tightly knit family always gathering at the old homestead for Sunday dinners. Now he was about to leave his Ma who had always favored him because he was her last living child. About to leave his oldest brother Harry, his mentor. About to leave the safety net of his "bossy" sisters.

He was able to get home frequently since Rochester was not so far way. One time he surprised the family by bringing home a wife, a lovely well dressed, well spoken city girl with impeccable manners. Everyone immediately fell in love with Nyles' pretty young wife, Edna.

Edna,
Nyle's wife from
Rochester, N.Y.
(circa 1918)

Nyles enjoyed his job in Rochester. He felt that being a bellboy suited his personality just fine since he enjoyed meeting and greeting people while flashing the expansive Patience smile to his advantage. Quite useful he found for piling up fat tips.

Edna enjoyed cooking and "keeping" the home she was hoping to fill with children. However, there was to be yet another childless couple in the Patience family. Four of Elsie and Crowder's children produced their own families and four did not. Now five years married, Edna had not presented Nyles with a child yet. He tried consoling her by pointing out that they had each other, lots of friends in Rochester, as well as a loving family in Pennsylvania. A life devoid of children would just have to suffice them.

During the spring of his twenty-sixth year, Nyles contracted a cold not wanting to go away. He tried all kinds of remedies. "Maybe I've got the croup," he had told his wife. "Ma always keeps a bowl of sliced onions and brown sugar sitting on the top of the kitchen stove. A teaspoon or two of that syrup is supposed to get rid of 'what ails' you." For Nyles, that "tried and true" cure did not work. As the weeks progressed he was still coughing. The day he coughed spots of bright red blood into his handkerchief was when he finally admitted that he needed to consult a doctor.

"I'm sorry, Mr. Patience," the doctor regretfully informed Nyles. "You have consumption. There is nothing at all that I can do for you."

Nyles knows that hearing the dreaded word "consumption" is hearing a sentence of death. "How much time, Doctor?"

"That depends on you."

"Just give me an approximate time. Please!"

"Before winter sets in, I'm afraid."

Nyles informed his grief-stricken wife that he wanted to go home. Back home to his mother and family.

Outside on the sunny side of her house Elsie was performing one of her most detested tasks. That of stretching her delicate white Nottingham lace curtains which had been manufactured nearby in a Scranton mill. That morning by securing each corner tightly with a nut and screw Crowder had assembled for his wife several rectangular wooden stretching frames.

By early afternoon Elsie had already carefully laundered and starched the curtains and was busily engrossed with pinning them to the frames. Every half an inch or so a short very sharp pin projected from the frame, securing the curtain edges in order to pull the lace very taunt. Then as the curtains dried, their edges would become straight, all ready for hanging again at the windows. Elsie was being very careful not to prick her fingers because any bloodstains would have to be immediately rubbed out with cold water before they had a chance to set permanently into the white lace.

Shouldering his heavy brown leather bag the mailman in his blue uniform was coming by the house for the second time that day. Mail was delivered twice on weekdays—in the morning and then again in the afternoon, but never on Saturday or Sunday. Spying Elsie busy at her curtain stretching he hollered at her from across Tunkhannock Avenue. "Afternoon, Mrs. Patience."

Elsie looked up from her work to give a wave. "Afternoon," she responded.

"Just left ya some mail." Letters at 828 were slipped through a mail slot on the front door where they would fall inside.

"Thank you," she called back. There was no need for her to hurry in to see what had been delivered because she would not have been able to read it, anyway. When she finally did get around to retrieving the letter from the floor of the foyer she was able to recognize her own name written across the front of the envelope, but there was no sense in opening it until Jessie came home. However, she was very curious.

"Jessie? That you?" Elsie called from the kitchen as soon as she heard the squeaking of the front door as someone was opening it. It could have been anybody. Anybody at all, because no one ever locked doors. To do so would have been considered insulting. Friends and family simply walked in, announcing themselves with, "Anybody ta home?"

Jessie answered, "Yes, Ma. It's me."

With the letter in hand Elsie greeted her youngest daughter. "Got this today, Jessie. See who it's from, will you?"

Jessie hung her coat on a wall peg first before taking the letter from her mother's outstretched hand. "Let's see now." She turned the envelope over to read the return address on the back flap. "Why, it's from Edna and Nyles, Ma. I'll just get a knife to open it." As she was excitedly slitting open the envelope she was anticipating, "Maybe there's some pictures in it."

The handsome couple enjoyed having their photographs taken, frequently sending some home to the family. A favorite of Elsie's sat in a frame on top of the piano. Nyles dressed in the white formal uniform of the Knights of Phythias, a secret society of men. Originally begun by white men in Washington, colored men had formed their own organization. How handsome

Nyles is, sitting proudly in a chair, two of his lodge brothers standing behind. His sword lay sheathed in its scabbard across his lap.

Nyles Patience with his Knights of
Phythias Lodge brothers
(circa 1921)

However, Jessie soon realized there were no photographs inside the envelope. Only a single sheet of paper. "Maybe they're coming for a visit," Jessie said optimistically as she began to read.

Dear Ma and family,

It is with much sorrow that I write this letter to you. Today we were told that Nyles has consumption. The doctor says that he can not do anything to help him. Nyles wants to come home to be with his family. We will be leaving here on the first of next month. Please pray for him.

Your loving daughter Edna

"No, no, no," Elsie moaned. It was like losing her sister all over again. Now she was about to lose her youngest son.

What did Elsie know about consumption? Not much. She knew that breaker boys got it. Nyles had never been down in the mines. She knew that consumption was associated with dirt and squalor. Nyles had never lived that way. So she was wondering, *Just how did he get it? And what will keep the rest of the family from getting it?* Then she tried to become optimistic. *Maybe that city doctor don't know what he's talking about, anyways.*

After her initial breakdown, after having to inform her husband that he was going to lose another son, after sharing the tragic news with her other daughters, Elsie got busy making plans to care for her dying boy. *She* had to be strong for *him*. "Jessie, now you walk on down to the library and get some books about consumption. Read them *all* and then tell me about it." For the first time in her life Elsie wished she could read for herself. *Oh, Mariah, you wanted to teach me all those many years ago.*

The small red brick West Pittston Library was located on the corner of Exeter and Warren Streets just a short fifteen-minute walk from 828. With heavy heart, Jessie did her mother's bidding. At the library she was able to locate books informing her that consumption, also known as tuberculosis, was a highly communicable disease, passed easily from person to person. That was the reason why it was so prevalent in large cities where masses of European immigrants lived huddled together in cold tenements. Jessie read how the dreaded disease was passed to other people by thoughtless uncovered coughs, unwashed hands, and by loving kisses.

She also read about how rest, fresh air, and nutritious food were being used in the treatment of consumptive patients. She learned that there were sanatoriums for tuberculars high in the Alps of Switzerland, even in the

Adirondack Mountains of the United States. She read about Edward Trudeau, cured of tuberculosis even after his own physician had delivered the death sentence of three months, if he were lucky. "Do some of the things you've never had time to do before." That was his doctor's only prescription.

A physician himself, Trudeau had been treating tubercular patients living in New York City tenements. However, he had no idea how the disease was contracted. No one did. It might have been from polluted drinking water, or tainted food, or even from the fumes of rotting garbage thrown in gutters, or the slops thrown out of tenement windows. For at that time in history no one was aware of the fact that the highly communicable disease is caused by a germ. A microscopic bacterium passes the disease from one *person to another*. So every time Trudeau was in contact with one of his tubercular patients he was in danger of contracting the disease himself. Eventually he did.

So, following his doctor's advice to do whatever he desired, in 1873 Trudeau retreated to a hotel high in the Adirondack Mountains, his favorite place to get away from the hustle and bustle of New York City. Wrapped warmly in blankets, bathed in bright sunlight, inhaling unpolluted balsam scented mountain air he spent his days resting out-of-doors, waiting to die. Inadvertently, however, by the regimen he had set for himself, instead of dying, he slowly was being cured.

His own physician presumed Trudeau to be dead and buried, although he had not read any obituary attesting to the fact. After all, he had given his patient only three months at the most. Imagine the physician's shock when some time later Edward Trudeau, looking quite fit, sauntered into the office! "I don't believe my eyes! What on earth did you do?" asked the doctor in astonishment.

"Just exactly what you advised me to do."

So that was one of the first successful steps to eradicate tuberculosis in the United States. Using Robert Koch's postulates concerning the theory that *germs* are what cause diseases, Trudeau conducted his own verifying experiments by using rabbits. After having great success with healing two sisters, Dr. Edward Trudeau then dedicated himself to curing consumptive patients at the sanatorium he built in the Adirondack Mountains in the state of New York.

"Ma. Listen to this!" Jessie excitedly was reading to her mother what Dr. Edward Trudeau had done. "It says right here that some people get better just by eating good food, breathing fresh air, and getting plenty of sunshine."

"That's good, Jessie. That's very good. And we'll make sure Nyles gets all of those. We'll fix all his favorite foods and we'll try to fatten him up. He's always been too skinny, you know. And he can sit out there on the porch and just rock all the livelong day. Won't have to do nothing. Nothing a'tall. Just get better," the worried mother says as she awaits her son's return from Rochester.

Peter Lee drove "overtown" to Pittston in the doctor's automobile, one of the few on the roads amongst the horses and wagons. He was going to the brick station located at the eastern end of the Water Street Bridge, there to meet the train bearing home his dying brother-in-law. After carefully parking the automobile he rushed inside the station, hurrying down the steep stairs leading to the tracks paralleling the Susquehanna River. Just in time as the train puffed into the station.

Oh, poor, poor Nyles, Pete thought, watching his deteriorating young brother-in-law and his wife alighting from the train. Reaching up to take the heavy valise from Nyles' hands, he predicted, *Wait'll Ma sees him. It's gonna break her heart!*

Elsie at 828 was anxiously waiting to hear the sounds of the approaching automobile's bearing home her sick son Nyles, the "apple of her eye." She could not keep still so she went out into the front garden to tend the pansies she plants each year in memory of her sister Mariah.

Oh, Mariah, she was mourning. *First you was gone. The last baby boy, too. Now God's gonna take away my Nyles. Why? What did I do wrong? Did I love him more than the others? Is God punishing me for that?*

As the automobile pulled up in front of the house, Elsie quickly ran to it. When she observed the condition her poor son was in, her heart sank, seeing the ravages of the terrible disease all across his drawn face. His usually glowing brown skin had a grayish hue to it. His usually bright dark brown eyes were glazed, the twinkle of humor snuffed out. His usually expansive smile, so like his father's, was wan.

"Well, here I am, Ma." He was so tired. All he wanted to do was to lie down.

Elsie reached out to her son. "No, Ma! You can't touch me! None of you can *touch* me. The doctor says I'm contagious. You all have to be very careful. I've got a whole list of do's and don't's he's given me." And so the broken-hearted mother could not even comfort her son with her embrace.

In the front parlor the green velveteen covered couch could be converted into a double bed. Elsie had wanted it because there always were grandchildren spending the night with Grandma and Grandpa. With heavy heart she made up the bed for her son and his wife where on happy occasions they had slept so many times before. With the two doors closed the parlor provided plenty of privacy for them, one door leading from the foyer and the other from the kitchen.

Edna had been caring for her sick husband these past months, carefully adhering to all of the doctor's orders. Determining not to leave his side. To be near him when the uncontrollable horrific coughing spells attacked him during the nights.

From his downstairs sickroom Nyles had easy access to the side porch where he could sun himself in the afternoons. And from there he would walk laboriously into the kitchen to take his meals at the long table. Between his mother, wife and sisters, he was plied with all of his favorite foods, even though his appetite had virtually disappeared. Even Elsie's chicken potpie, his all-time favorite, could not tempt him. Nothing much interested him anymore. Lethargy had set in. He was sleeping more and more. But as long as he was able, he still would walk down to "Miss Jones," admiring multicolored mounds of Rosa's chrysanthemums along the footpath.

Elsie was optimistic. She had told Edna, "Maybe, here at home with us, he'll get better. Don't you think?" Of course Edna wanted to believe that, but she knew her husband was growing weaker. He was having more frequent coughing spells during the nights, his handkerchiefs stained with bright blood. Becoming short of breath, he had to be helped to his favorite rocking chair on the porch where Edna lovingly tucked a warm blanket around him. There he would sit for hours, sleeping most of the time, gradually having more and more difficulty with inhaling the fresh air, coughing frequently.

The doctor had said *before winter*. Slanting shadows were lengthening earlier in the afternoon. The sun was rising later and setting earlier. Apples and grapes were ready for their picking. Goldenrod and asters were blooming in the fields. Canadian geese honked farewells overhead. Robins and monarch butterflies already had departed for their southern winter abodes. Some deciduous trees already were cloaked in their bright fall colors.

Nyles, sitting on the porch as he watched the setting sun, thought, *Life is just like that sun, coming up for a while and when it's time, going down.* He hummed to himself the dirge he had heard many times sung at funerals, *"Sunset and evening star and one clear call for me. There'll be no mourning at the bar, when I set out to sea."* He knew, however, that would not be so in his case. There would be mourning for him, the youngest in the family, the first to go.

It was far too late for Nyles when he had arrived home. The disease had been much too rampant in his body. No amount of good food, fresh air, or sunshine could prevent his inevitable demise. And so on a late fall Saturday twenty-seven year old Nyles Patience "crossed the bar."

Gathered in the parlor of 828 where Nyles is laid out in his coffin, the somber family clad in their mourning clothes hears Elsie's heartrending lament. "A child's not su'posed to go before his Pa'n Ma. He's just not!" And four years later in 1926, she will be overheard uttering similar words at St. Mark's AME Church when she gazes upon the dead face of another of her children.

*Nyles, youngest child of Crowder
and Elsie
Sitting on front steps at 828 Luzerne
Avenue, West Pittston, Pa
(circa 1919)*

EPILOGUE

August 1929

Creak, creak. Creak, creak. Creak, creak.

On a beautiful late summer afternoon while paring his "apple a day," the peel one long intact piece, Crowder Patience is whiling away the hours, sitting outside on his vine-covered porch reminiscent of the way many people in far-off North Carolina shade their premises. Can't smoke his pipe any more. After a bout with pneumonia two years ago he was forced to forego it. From his favorite wicker rocking chair he periodically addresses his faithful companion, the black and white mutt lying nearby, lazily warming himself in a shaft of bright sunshine.

"No sense dwellin' on not goin' ta work no more," Crowder says aloud. He knows that his work team of horses is gone forever, the old animals' having outlived their usefulness. Shaking his head in bewilderment he reflects to himself, *Sure's hard ta believe. The horses couldn't work no more, so they up'n shot them. Well, seems like I've outlived my usefulness, too,* the old man sighs. *No use thinkin' about that, either, I suppose.*

Crowder never before has had so much time for just thinking. Always he had to be working. First when in bondage, then on the farms where he had been employed, and later when laboring to support his wife and children. Then there were the many hours he had spent tending his own garden. Meticulously brushing destructive iridescent green Japanese beetles off Concord grape leaves, then drowning the pests in a jar of kerosene. Constantly on the lookout for damaging potato beetles and ugly fat tomato horn worms, as well as slippery slimy slugs leaving behind their telltale silvery trails. He always had to labor before, but nowadays he has plenty of time for just *thinking*.

He finds it strange how uninvited thoughts just keep popping up in his head. Thoughts of things he intentionally had put away long ago. For *forever*, he had presumed. Now his mind tends to drift back to the North Carolina plantation and dear Aunt Cassie, the surrogate mother who had loved him, but dared not *too* much. *Wonder what ever happened ta her after the war. Knowin' her big heart she probably jest stayed right there on the plantation lookin' after Marse and Missie.*

When conjuring up the faces of Marse and the several overseers Crowder realizes he does not much care what had happened to *them*. He has heard that many of the spacious plantation houses replete with all of their precious possessions were burned clean to the ground by the Federals. Jesse Carpenter told him that General William Tecumsen Sherman before heading east from Chattanooga, Tennessee totally had destroyed the proud Georgia city

Atlanta, obliterating anything and everything in his path, leaving in his wake nothing but despair.

Crowder has no idea, however, that Sherman had ceased his wide swath of destruction temporarily when he reached the beautifully laid out city of Savannah, Georgia with its numerous squares so reminiscent of London. Because Sherman needed a place to rest, to regroup, and to strategize, he decided to present the beautiful water front city *intact* as an 1864 Christmas present to President Abraham Lincoln. Columbia, the capitol of South Carolina, unfortunately, was not given the same consideration and so went the way of Atlanta.

Wonder what happened ta Marse's "big house" in Chowan County or ta his house in Edenton. No way of ever knowin' about that, though, he thinks. *Well now, guess I should say that I'm sorry ta hear about all that trouble they had down there. Umm. Maybe I should be,* he muses.

However, when recalling the sharp pangs of hunger, bitter winter cold, oppressive summer heat, sting of the lash, permanent separations, and the overall abject hopelessness and misery associated with his enslavement, he really cannot say in truth that he is sorry if Marse suffered any. *Forgive me, Lord, if I jest can't.*

This is the reason he does not want to remember any of those things capable of turning his soul into a veritable vessel of virulence and hatred, but there is no way he can prevent the unwanted bitter memories from resurfacing. He does not want to remember any of those things he has never felt compelled to discuss with anyone. Not his wife, and *certainly* not his children who never have seen their father without a shirt, being totally unaware of the thick crisscrossed stripes keloided on his back. He did have to explain them, though, the first time his shocked young wife had poured fresh rinse water over his back as he was bathing in a large tin laundry tub by the fireplace in the corporal's cabin. But just *how* he came to possess those marks he told her as little as possible.

To get this far he simply had put one foot in front of the other, steadily moving forward, never once pausing to take a backward look. Replacing bitter old memories with new and exciting experiences, figuring the former had been erased when, in reality, they were only masked. And now they just keep popping up as uninvited as that pesky pokeweed in Marse's sweet potato fields. Nowadays in the twilight of his life, he discovers that he is serving a new "marse." An unrelenting master called "time." And "time" bids him to remember!

Now at the sound of *his* master's voice the faithful mutt raises his head in anticipation. After perceiving that Crowder is not about to move from his rocker, the dog just heaves a relieved sigh, promptly going back to his snoozing.

The old man is pondering. *Mercy, how things are changin'! Now take those electric lights, for instance. Folks got ugly wires goin' in and out of their houses. Wires from tall thick wood poles outside. Well, we're still usin' kerosene lamps in this house. Harry had electricity. Had ta have it in his shop down on Washington Street. Needed it for runnin' his machinery there. Poor Harry. Died all of a sudden two years ago last January. Was upstairs shavin' in his bathroom. Jest keeled over dead. The doctor said it was a stroke. He had been taking medicine for high blood pressure. It was such a shock ta all of us and then with young Bruce and Harold still in school and all.* He rocks a bit thinking about his first son, Harry the gifted coal carver.

Then his mind fixes on another subject's puzzling him in this day and age. *So many changes goin' on nowadays. Heard about them inside toilets. Can ya beat that? Puttin' the outhouse in the house? Filthy! What a crazy notion!* He wrinkles his nose in disgust. Everybody knows that a privy has to be placed far enough away from the house so unpleasant odors will not reach the nostrils of the inhabitants and definitely far enough away from the well or creek to prevent contamination of the drinking water. *Now all that mess's gonna be inside? Where do they think it's gonna go, anyway? Well, no toilet! Never in this house!* As far as Crowder is concerned, "Miss Jones," periodically sanitized with her dose of lime, will continue doing her duty here at 828.

Up Tunkhannock Avenue a Model T Ford noisily rattles by, its occupants waving to the old man who as usual is in his rocking chair on the porch. Smiling he waves back, thinking, *Harry's boys got one of those new-fangled contraptions. Offered lots of times ta take me and Ma out fer a ride. They say we can ride in somethin' they call a rumble seat. Looks too dangerous ta me. Anyway they go too fast. Upwards ta thirty miles an hour, hear tell. Much faster than my team could ever go.* The only time Crowder will agree to get into an automobile is each May on Declaration Day when the oldest army veterans are afforded the privilege of riding in the parade as it *slowly* wends its way to the cemetery in order to pay tribute to the war dead.

His son-in-law, Walter Glover, owns a car, also, in which he drives Florence and their youngest children down from the Mt. Zion farm where they had moved after his employer of many decades died. Glover had been under the impression the house in West Pittston where his family had lived for all those many years would be left to him. He said that was what his employer had assured him. However, it seems there was no mention of that "gentleman's agreement" in the will.

So the house had been offered first to Glover to *buy*, but by that time he had amassed enough savings to purchase a farm of his own, something he had always wanted to do ever since he had left West Virginia. On numerous occasions since he had moved his family to the farm Glover has offered to drive his in-laws for a visit, but he is always refused.

Crowder is used to being in control. His horses had obeyed him. Now they are gone. He thinks they would not have liked it at all, having to compete for road space with those horseless carriages driven by seemingly crazy folk's speeding erratically down the middle of the road, honking and scaring the poor creatures half out of their wits, their nervous drivers, too. So Crowder and Elsie never go visiting anymore. Much much too dangerous on the roads nowadays.

He has heard, too, about the telephone. *They're sayin' that someday everybody'll have one of them annoyin' things in their houses. Ringin' all the time, they are, disturbin' the peace. Don't know why a body'd want one anyway. Jest more ugly wires goin' in and out. No tellin' soon the streets'll look like a spider web with wires goin' every which-a-way. It's more than a notion, I say. Anyway what's wrong with walkin' ta a body's house? It's always worked before.* True, one of his numerous grandchildren is always walking in the unlocked kitchen door to bear some sort of a message. *People're jest gettin' plum lazy.* Crowder with great foresight predicts as he rocks, *Pretty soon nobody'll be walkin' no place no more.*

However, he thinks he just might be interested in that box they call a radio. Listening to people's talking out of a box might "catch his fancy," so he imagines. Lillian brought a battery run radio back home from Sewickly where she resides with her minister husband Charles Edward Cuff. That radio is at Rosa and Peter Lee's home. At different times members of the Patience clan will mosey down Luzerne Avenue to visit Aunt Rosie and Uncle Pete just to listen to that magic box they call a radio. *Rosie lives too far fer me ta walk nowadays, anyway, so I guess I'll jest have ta do without that pleasure,* he concludes. He refuses Peter Lee's offer to ride in the doctor's car, as well.

Suddenly he is startled out of his reverie as he hears a loud growl overhead, escalating now into a roar. "Hey, ya two in there! Ya hear that? Come on out'n see!" He calls in through the screen door to the two women inside the house.

Jessie opens the screen door and runs out as she calls, "Ma, come on out! It's an aeroplane!" Quickly Elsie joins her daughter and husband on the steps of the porch where they stand shading their eyes with their hands while gazing in wonder at the giant "bird" soaring noisily overhead.

"Now if that don't beat all!" is all Crowder can say. It would never occur to him that in the not too far future, he, too, could be flying from one end of the country to the other, visiting his scattered descendants.

Back to his rocking and reminiscing. *First Nyles was taken away. Then Harry,* he mourns. *Our youngest boy first and then our oldest. Children're not su'posed ta go before their Pa'n Ma. Elsie's takin' the boys' passin' real hard. Well, I'm gonna have ta be leavin' her soon, too. We been together a mighty long time now, Elsie'n me. Isaac and Jesse Carpenter promised me that she can stay on in the house even after I'm gone. Jessie's here with her husband Nat. He's got a good job over there at Fox Hill. Yes, they'll look after my Elsie jest fine, I know, cause Florence and Rosie got their own houses ta keep and Lillie's off with Cuff. Percy's gone ta Baltimore and Chester's about ta take off fer Richmond. Yes, Jessie'll be here with my Elsie.* These thoughts give him some degree of peace.

Still feelin' fit as a fiddle, got ta say. That is, fer an old man. Plannin' ta ride next year in the Declaration Day Parade ta the cemetery, jest like I always been doin'.

The sun is setting with the western horizon now streaked with mauve, ochre, gold, indigo, and magenta. Dusk is descending with crickets' commencing their chirping and honeysuckle's emitting its strongest odors, inviting flickering lightning bugs to a feast of nectar. Across the baseball field silhouettes of deciduous trees are etched against the darkening sky. The "evening star," the planet Venus, puts in its brilliant appearance. The old man is reminiscing. *This sky reminds me of when I was a boy in North Carolina. So long ago, it was. But I remember it like it was jest yesterday.*

Well now. It makes me want ta thank the good Lord fer this life He give me. There I was. Come in this world a slave. Owned by Marse. Got no Ma. No Pa. Blessed with Aunt Cassie, though. Then lucky I got free. Then lucky again cause I could've been dead at Plymouth. Lucky that Co. C got sent over there ta Roanoke Island. Oh, yes, it was the good Lord what saved me. Mighty grateful ta Him. That I am.

And then the good Lord seen fit ta give me Elsie and the children. My own family. Now He's blessed me with the grandchildren. And it's gonna go on. Our family's gonna go on. Just then the patriarch Crowder Patience is startled out of his reverie as he hears the familiar sound of his wife's soft voice inviting, "Come to supper, Pa."

"Let's go on in now, King. Time fer supper. Ya heard Ma." Followed by his constant companion the old man leaves his rocking chair to swing open the screen door, his walk surprisingly agile for someone almost eighty-three years old.

That winter the blustery wind rattles the windowpanes of the drafty homestead heated solely by coal stoves. Elsie rolls up rags for stuffing at the bottom of the doors and windows. Jessie tacks blankets over the doors leading into the dining room and parlor, attempting to contain the warmth in the kitchen.

Crowder sits for hours wrapped in a thick quilt and rocking in his favorite chair by the kitchen stove. There humming his favorite tunes and paring apples to offer quarters to the numerous Patience and Glover grandchildren who stop by periodically to see how Grandpa's doing, as well as to enjoy a piece of Grandma's pie. On January 25, 1930 he becomes seriously ill for the second time in his life. In the middle of one bitter cold night he begins horrific coughing, awakening his wife. Reaching over to touch his forehead with the backs of her fingers, she finds it to be hot and clammy. Alarmed, she calls out to Jessie who knows this is just how her father was when he had been so sick with pneumonia two years before. And she knows he had been very close to death at that time.

In spite of his doctor's medicine, in spite of his wife's and daughter's loving ministrations, in spite of wanting to stay a little while longer with his Elsie, on January 30, 1930 Crowder Patience succumbs from, according to his death certificate, apoplexy as a side effect of the "grippe" (influenza)." He is recorded as being eighty-three years, one month and five days old. The family lays him to rest on February 3rd in the West Pittston Cemetery where his grave is identified by the GAR Stanchion marker reserved for veterans of the Civil War.

On Declaration Day in the year 1930 the marchers miss the presence of the proud old Civil War veteran, Crowder Patience, who in previous years always had paraded with them.

CODA

The unwritten "gentleman's agreement" between Crowder Patience and the Carpenter family was terminated by Elsie's death in 1940 and the property at 828 Luzerne Avenue subsequently was sold. Unfortunately, the "close mouthed" Elsie who became senile in her later years, had not discussed with her children the terms of the Patience occupancy at 828, indeed if she ever knew. Perhaps Crowder had just told her not to worry, as had been his habit.

Anyway, since neither daughter Jessie nor anyone else in the family seemed to know that the house had not been *given* to Crowder by the Carpenters, and not having the wherewithal to purchase the homestead, she was forced to move. Other members of the family later would say that if they had known about the agreement, they certainly would have joined forces to purchase the house before it was sold to another family. However, that was not to be.

And so in a state of shock, Jessie, then homeless, was taken in by two of her nephews, Edgar and Harold who, at 34 Washington Street, were continuing with the coal carving business of their father, *Harry B. Patience & Sons*. Jessie Patience Garrett remained living there for the next eleven years until her death in February 1951.

All of the children of Crowder and Elsie Patience are buried in the West Pittston Cemetery, except for Chester who is buried in Richmond, Virginia. The longest-lived was the fourth child, Lillian Mariah Patience Cuff, who on February 15, 1986 died in her 103rd year.

SOURCES

Bartoletti, Susan Campbell. *Growing up in Coal Country*. Boston: Houghton
    Mifflin Company, 1996.
Bennett, Lerone. *Before the Mayflower: A History of Black America*.
    Chicago: Johnson Publishing Company, Inc., 1969.
Blockson, Charles, L. *Black Genealogy*. Baltimore: Black Classic Press,
    Maryland, 1977.
_____. *Pennsylvania's Black History*. Philadelphia: Portfolio Associates, Inc.,
    1975.
Boyce, W. Scott. *Economic and Social History of Chowan County, North
    Carolina 1880-1915*. Vol. LXXXVI, No.1, New York: Columbia
    University, 1917.
Breiseth, Christopher N. "Lincoln and Frederick Douglass: Another Debate."
    Journal of The Illinois State Historical Society. Vol. LXVII, No. 1,
    February, 1975, pp. 9-26.
Bundles, A'Lelia. *On Her Own Ground: The Life and Times of Madam C.J.
    Walker*. New York: Scribner, 2001.
Busch, Clarence M. "Reports of the Inspectors of Coal Mines of Pennsylvania,
    1896." State Printer of Pennsylvania, 1897.
Chaitin, Peter M. *The Civil War: The Coastal War*. Alexandria, Virginia: Time-
    Life Books, 1984.
Cornish, Dudley Taylor. *The Sable Arm: Negro Troops in the Union Army,
    1861-1865*. New York: W. W. Norton & Co., Inc., 1966.
Denmy, Robert E. *Civil War Prisons and Escape: A Day by Day Chronicle*.
    New York: Publishing Co., Inc., 1993.
Dickey, Luther S. *History of the 103rd Regiment: Pennsylvania Veteran
    Volunteer Infantry 1861-1865*. Chicago: L. S. Dickey, 1910.
Douglass, Frederick. *My Bondage and My Freedom*. New York: Miller, Morton,
    and Milligan, 1855.
Dyer, Frederick H. *Compendium of the War of the Rebellion*. Dayton, Ohio:
    Morningside, 1979.
Fenn, Elizabeth A. "A Perfect Equality Seemed to Reign: Slave Society and
    Jonkonnu." *The North Carolina Historical Review*. Vol. LXV, No.2,
    April, 1988.
Fogel, Robert William and Stanley L. Engerman. *Time on the Cross: The
    Economics of American Negro Slavery*. Boston: Little, Brown and
    Company, 1974.
Fox-Genovese, Elizabeth. *Within the Plantation Household: Black and White
    Women of the Old South*. Chapel Hill: North Carolina, University of
    North Carolina, 1988.
Franklin, John Hope and Alfred A. Moss, Jr. *From Slavery to Freedom: A
    History of Negro Americans*. 7th Edition. New York: Mc Graw-Hill,

394

Inc., 1994.

Franklin, John Hope & Loren Schweninger. *Runaway Slaves: Rebels on the Plantation.* New York: Oxford University Press, 1999.

Genovese, Eugene D. *Roll Jordan Roll: The World the Slaves Made.* New York: Vintage Books, A Division of Random House, 1973.

Glatthaar, Joseph T. *Forged in Battle: The Civil War Alliance of Black Soldiers and White Officers.* New York: The Free Press, 1990.

Goss, Sergeant Warren Lee. *The Soldier's Story of His Captivity at Andersonville, Belle Isle, and other Rebel Prisons.* Boston: Lee and Shepard Publishers, 1866.

Haskins, Jim. *Black, Blue & Gray: African Americans in the Civil War.* Simon & Schuster Books for Young Readers, 1998.

Hurmence, Belinda. *Before Freedom: When I Just Can Remember.* Winston-Salem, North Carolina: John F. Blair, Publisher, 1989.

_____. *My Folks Don't Want Me to Talk About Slavery: Twenty-one Histories of Former North Carolina Slaves.* Winston- Salem, North Carolina: John F. Blair, Publisher, 1984.

_____. *We Lived in a Little Cabin in the Yard.* Winston- Salem, North Carolina: John F. Blair, 1994.

Jacobs, Harriet A. *Incidents in the Life of a Slave Girl.* Cambridge, Massachusetts: Harvard University Press, 1987.

Johnson, Charles and Patrician Smith and the WGBH Series Research Team. *Africans in America.* New York: Harcourt Brace & Company, 1998.

Lottick, Sally Teller. *Bridging Change: A Wyoming Valley Sketchbook.* Wilkes-Barre, Pennsylvania: Wyoming Historical and Geological Society, 1992.

Keefer, Norman D. *A History of Mechanicsburg.* Mechanicsburg, Pennsylvania.

McPherson, James M. *Battle Cry of Freedom: The Civil War Era.* New York: Balantine Books, 1988.

_____. *The Negro's Civil War: How American Negroes Felt and Acted During the War for the Union.* New York: Pantheon Books, 1965.

Merrill, J.W. *Records of the 24th Independent Battery, N.Y Light Artillery. U.S.V.,* Published for the Ladies' Cemetery Association of Perry, N.Y., 1870.

Mohr, James, editor, Richard E. Winslow, III, assistant editor. *The Cormany Diaries: A Northern Family in the Civil War.* Pittsburgh: University of Pittsburgh Press, 1982.

Mosher, Charles. *Charlie Mosher's Civil War: From Fair Oaks to Andersonville with the Plymouth Pilgrims (85th N.Y. Infantry).* edited by Wayne Mahood, Hightstown, NJ: Longstreet House, 1994.

Moss, Emerson. *African-Americans in the Wyoming Valley.* Wilkes-Barre, Pennsylvania: Wyoming Historical and Geologial Society and the Wilkes University Press, 1992.

Mullane, Deirdre. *Crossing the Danger Water: Three Hundred Years of African-American Writing.* New York: Anchor Books, Doubleday, 1993.

National Park Service. "Freedom Comes to Roanoke Island: A Story of the Civil War." National Park Service, Fort Raleigh National Historic Site, Roanoke Island, North Carolina.

Nevins, Allan. *The War for the Union, Vol. II: War Becomes Revolution.* New York: Charles Scribner and Sons, 1960.

Park History Program, National Park Service. *Exploring A Common Past: Researching and Interpreting the Underground Railroad.* 2nd Edition. Washington, D.C., 1997.

Patience, Alice Patterson. *Bittersweet Memories of Home.* Wilkes-Barre, Pennsylvania; Wilkes University Press, 1998.

Petrillo, F.Charles. "The Bear Creek Ice Company." *The History of Northeastern Pennsylvania: The Last 100 Years.* 8th Annual. Luzerne County Community College, Social Science /History Department, 1996.

Quarles, Benjamin. *The Negro in the Civil War.* New York: A Da Capo Paperback, A Subsidiary of Plenum Publishing Corp., 1953.

Spruill Redford, Dorothy with Michael D'Orso. *Somerset Homecoming: Recovering a Lost Heritage.* Chapel Hill, North Carolina: The University of North Carolina Press, 1988.

Sterling, Dorothy. *We Are Your Sisters: Black Women in the Nineteenth Century.* New York: W. W. Norton & Company, 1984.

Streets, David H. *Slave Genealogy: A Research Guide with Case Studies.* Bowie, Maryland: Heritage Books, Inc., 1986.

The Roster of Union Soldiers 1861-1865. Wilmington, N.C.: Broadfoot Publishing, 1988.

The War of the Rebellion: Official Records of the Union and Confederate Armies. Washington, 1880-1901.

Thomas, Gerald W. *Bertie in Blue: Experience of Bertie County's Union Servicemen During the Civil War.* Plymouth, North Carolina: Bacon Printing, Inc., 1998.

_____. "Massacre at Plymouth: April 20, 1864." *The North Carolina Historical Review.* Vol. LXXII, No. 2, April 1995, pp. 126-197.

Thomas, Velma Maia. *Lest We Forget: The Passage from Africa to Slavery and Emancipation.* New York: Crown Publishers, 1997.

Tobin, Jacqueline L. and Raymond G. Dobard. *Hidden in Plain View: The Secret Story of Quilts and the Underground Railroad.* New York: Doubleday, 1999.

Trudeau, Noah Andre. *Like Men of War:Black Troops in the Civil War 1862-1865.* Boston, Massachussetts: Little, Brown & Co, 1998.

Vlach, John Michael. *Back of the Big House: The Architecture of Plantation Slavery.* Chapel Hill, North Carolina, The University of North Carolina Press, 1993.

Ward, Geoffrey C. *The Civil War:An Illustrated History*. New York: Alfred A. Knopf, 1990.

Wesley, Charles H. *Negro Americans in the Civil War: From Slavery to Citizenship*. New York: Publishers Co., 1967.

Whyte, W. E. *Centennial Chronology of County Luzerne 1886*. Pittston, Pennsylvania: D. R. Hungtingon, Printer, 1886.

Williams, George Washington. *A History of the Negro Troops in the War of the Rebellion 1861-1865*. New York Negro Universities Press, 1889.

Wilson, Joseph T. *The Black Phalanx: African American Soldiers in the War of Independence, the War of 1812 and the Civil War*. New York: Da Capo Press, 1994.

Woodward, C. Vann. *Mary Chestnut's Civil War*. New Haven, Connecticut: Yale University Press, 1981.

NEWSPAPER ARTICLES

Indianapolis Recorder. January 7, 1899-December 30, 1916. Available for purchase on microfilm from Bell and Howell Co. Found in many libraries.

Pocono Today. Stroudsburg, Pa. "Research Needed on Local Underground Railroad." June 21, 1981.

Times-Leader, The Evening News. Wilkes-Barre, Pa. "1857* West Pittston Centennial* 1957." September 6, 1957.

_____. "A Proud Legacy." April 27, 1991.

Washington Afro-American. Graves, Desiree Allen. "Black History Comes Alive in Washington, D.C." July 11, 1998-July 17, 1998, A-10.

OTHER PUBLICATIONS

AAHGS News: The Bi-monthly news letter of the Afro-American Historical & Genealogical Society, Inc. May/June 1994.

"Legacy for All: A Record of Achievements by Black American Scientists." Western Electric.

Schuylkill County Historical Society. Hobbs, Herrwood E. "Nicholas Biddle." Vol. 7, No. 3, 1961.

Songs of Zion (hymn book). Abingdon Press, Nashville, 1981.

The Civil War Times (magazine). "Tribute to Black Veterans." Vol. XXIV, No. 8, September 1998.

_____. Trudeau, Noah Andre. "Like the Lords of the World." May 2000.

The Mining and Preparation of D&H Anthracite. Hudson Coal Company: Scranton, Penna., 1944.

Washington County Genealogical Society Journal. August 1997.

"West Pittston, Pennsylvania Centennial Publication. 1857-1957." *Times*

Leader, The Evening News. Wilkes-Barre, Pa. 1957.

HISTORICAL NOVELS

Forrester, Sandra. *Sound of the Jubilee*. New York: Penguin Books, 1995.
Gourley, Catherine. *The Courtship of Joanna*. St. Paul, Minneapolis, Minnesota:
    Graywolf Press, 1999.
Parisi, Jay. *Patch Boys*. New York:Holt, 1986.
Stern, Philip Van Doren. *The Drums of Morning*. Garden City, New York:
    Doubleday, Doran and Company, Inc., 1942.

INTERNET

Allen Parker Slave Narrative Site-Introduction to the Site. "The Allen
    Parker Slave Narrative." http://core.edu/hist/cecelskid/dcintro.htm
    retrieved on 12:04/01 3:53 P.M.
American Slave Narratives. "American Slave Narratives: An Online
    Anthology." retrieved on 4/28/01 12.42 P. M.
    http://xroads.virginia.edu/~hyper/wpa/wpahome.html
Avondale."Avondale." http://www.cohums.ohio-
    state.edu/history/projects/coal/Avondale/avondale.htm retrieved on
    11/28/98 9:48 P. M.
Bibliography on Researching African-American Genealogy. "Bibliography on
    Researching African-American Genealogy."
    http://www.lib.virginia.edu/~jlc5f/slavegen.html retrieved 9/16/99
    4:01 P. M
Civil War Letters of Edward Nicholas Boots. 101st Pa. Infantry. "Civil War
    Letters of Edward Nicholas Boots."
    http://members.aol.com/qmsgtboots/letters.html
    retrieved on 6/10/98 11:22 A. M.
Civil War Plymouth Pilgrims. "The Civil War 'Plymouth Pilgrims."
    http://home.att.net/~cwppds/homepage.htm
    retrieved on 4/28 9:27 P.M.
Coal Fields Divided Along Ethnic Lines. "Ethnic Lines Divided Coal Fields."
    http://www.leba.net/~jhower/Valley/mollies1.html retrieved on
    11/28/98 6:58 P.M.
Hagerty Family History. "Hagerty."
    http://users.aol.com/EvanSlaug/hagdow.html
    retrieved on 6/13/98 8:36 P.M.
Hazards Coal. "The Hazards of 19th Century Coal Mining."
    http://www.history.ohio-state.edu/projects/coal/Hazards/
    HazardsCoal.htm, retrieved on 11/28/98 9:38 P.M.
Memory of the Molly Maguires Kept Alive. "Memory of the Molly Maguires
    Kept Alive."
    http://www.tnonline.com/coalcracker/mollies.html retrieved on

11/28/98 8:01 P.M.

Military: Civil War: Regimental Roster 103rd Pennsylvania Volunteers: M-Z.
ftp://ftp.rootsweb.com/pub/usgenweb/pa/1pa/military/cwar/103m-z.txt
retrieved on 6/3/98 9:19 A.M.

101st Pennsylvania Veteran Volunteer Infantry: Keystone Infantry. "101st
Pennsylvania Veteran Volunteer Infantry."
http://members.aol.com/qmsgboots/sources.html
retrieved on 6/10/98 0:06 A.M.

103rd Pennsylvania Regiment. "Regimental History: 103rd Pennsylvania
Volunteers." http://users.aol.com/EvanSlaug/103rd.html
retrieved on 6/2/98 8:35 P.M.

"On Strike!" Mayo, Edward. http://www.history.ohio-
state.edu/projects/LaborConflict/OnStrike/onstrike.htm retrieved on
10/25/99 8:54 P.M.

Pennsylvania Dutch Culture. "Bundling."
http://www.horseshoe.cc/pennadutch/culture/
Retrieved on 6/27/01 8:05 P.M.

Recollections of Prison Life at Andersonville, Georgia and Florence, South
Carolina. "Recollections of Prison Life at Andersonville, Georgia and
Florence, South Carolina." edited by C. A. Smith. Excerpts.
http://www.iowa- counties.com/authors/andersonville
retrieved on 4/28/01 10:26 A.M.

Reproduced Molly Article. "The Mollies." Haldeman, Seamus (James).
http://thunder.ocis.temple.edu/~bphilips/mollie.html retrieved on
11/28/98 8:14 P.M.

_____."Organization of Outlaws Born in Ireland-Reborn in Pennsylvania."
http://www.budgettechnologies.com/mollymaguires/mollie/html
retrieved on 4/28/01 9:58 A.M.

Sickle Cell Anemia. "The Case of Sickle Cell Anemia."
http://advlearn.lrdc.pitt.edu/belvedere/materials/Evolution/sickle.htm
retrieved on 8/11/99 10:53 P.M.

Slave Narratives. "Josiah Henson." http://vi.uh.edu/pages/mintz/12.htm, 46
stories (find 1-46 htm) retrieved on 6/13/98 8:06 A.M.

The Ram Albemarle: Civil War: North Carolina.
http://www.albemarle-nc.com/plymouth/history/ram-alb.htm
retrieved on 6/2/98 11:19 A.M.